The
HOLLOW
KING

Other great stories from Warhammer Age of Sigmar

The
HOLLOW KING
A Cado Ezechiar novel

JOHN FRENCH

BLACK LIBRARY

A BLACK LIBRARY PUBLICATION

First published in 2022.
This edition published in Great Britain in 2023 by
Black Library, Games Workshop Ltd., Willow Road,
Nottingham, NG7 2WS, UK.

Represented by: Games Workshop Limited – Irish branch,
Unit 3, Lower Liffey Street, Dublin 1,
D01 K199, Ireland.

10 9 8 7 6 5 4 3 2

Produced by Games Workshop in Nottingham.
Cover illustration by Artur Treffner.

A CIP record for this book is available from the British Library.

ISBN 13: 978-1-78999-637-1

See Black Library on the internet at

blacklibrary.com

Find out more about Games Workshop
and the worlds of Warhammer at

games-workshop.com

Printed and bound by CPI Group (UK) Ltd, Croydon, CR0 4YY

For George Mann.

The Mortal Realms have been despoiled. Ravaged by the followers of the Chaos Gods, they stand on the brink of utter destruction.

The fortress-cities of Sigmar are islands of light in a sea of darkness. Constantly besieged, their walls are assailed by maniacal hordes and monstrous beasts. The bones of good men are littered thick outside the gates. These bulwarks of Order are embattled within as well as without, for the lure of Chaos beguiles the citizens with promises of power.

Still the champions of Order fight on. At the break of dawn, the Crusader's Bell rings and a new expedition departs. Storm-forged knights march shoulder to shoulder with resolute militia, stoic duardin and slender aelves. Bedecked in the splendour of war, the Dawnbringer Crusades venture out to found civilisations anew. These grim pioneers take with them the fires of hope. Yet they go forth into a hellish wasteland.

Out in the wilds, hardy colonists restore order to a crumbling world. Haunted eyes scan the horizon for tyrannical reavers as they build upon the bones of ancient empires, eking out a meagre existence from cursed soil and ice-cold seas. By their valour, the fate of the Mortal Realms will be decided.

The ravening terrors that prey upon these settlers take a thousand forms. Cannibal barbarians and deranged murderers crawl from hidden lairs. Martial hosts clad in black steel march from skull-strewn castles. The savage hordes of Destruction batter the frontier towns until no stone stands atop another. In the dead of night come howling throngs of the undead, hungry to feast upon the living.

Against such foes, courage is the truest defence and the most effective weapon. It is something that Sigmar's chosen do not lack. But they are not always strong enough to prevail, and even in victory, each new battle saps their souls a little more.

This is the time of turmoil. This is the era of war.

This is the Age of Sigmar.

CHAPTER ONE

The girl ran through the wood under the grin of a skull moon. Breath panted from her lungs. The roots tangled the ground under her feet. A branch caught in her hair, and her head snapped back. She pulled at the branch. The thorns tangled deeper. She yanked, panting, tears running through the blood smearing her face.

A howl came from the direction of the road.

'Please...' she cried, the words dissolving into a gasping ball of panic. She wanted her mother, her father, her elder sister. She wanted to be back in the rocking dark of the wagon as it jolted along the road in the twilight. She wanted the world to be a shape she understood, to hear a voice say that everything would be all right. She wanted someone to reach down and pick her up.

The thorns sliced into her fingers. The branches of the trees thrashed. She saw crimson eyes, pinpricks of ember red in the dark, behind her, coming closer.

* * *

Branches whipped Cado as he ran. The moon poured silver down on him. He could smell blood. Could taste it. Death was howling through the forest. The quarry was out there, running, flooded by fear, bleeding. It was fast too. He reached a thicket of trees. His eyes had become red flames in their sockets. The skin of his face pulled back from his teeth. The world was silver and red. It had taken too long to catch the caravan. Too long running along the lich-marked paths, hunger growing inside, as the prey sent a fraying thread pulling him on. Now the wagons of the caravan lay behind him on the road, tipped over, spattered with blood, dying horses thrashing in the harnesses. Now there was just this chase and a world redrawn by hunger.

His senses were singing. The reek of blood was a crimson haze. Magic spiralled through the bare branches. The gasp of breath. Bones rattling. Close. An abyss of hunger open and waiting to swallow him. He reached a rock, bounded onto its top and launched up into the branches of the trees. Birds took flight, cawing, their song splitting the air.

She had been asleep in the wagon, and then there had been shouting. She had come awake blinking, thinking for a second that the shouts were echoes of her dreams.

'Stay here,' her father had said, and she had clutched at the cold-iron hammer amulet and pulled the furs close. The rock and sway of the wagon had slowed, and then the vehicle had kicked, and she had heard voices shouting to ride fast. Her heart jolted. The grave-coins, bone amulets and dried roses hanging from the wagon's roof swung on their cords. She hoped they would keep them safe again. There were things in the forests. For as much as her parents and the other adults tried to hide it, she knew this land wanted them dead.

Two nights ago, she had heard muttering and the click of

cocking crossbows as she lay awake. She had sneaked up and opened the hatch at the back of the wagon. Peeking out she had seen something drifting through the trees. At first it looked like nothing, just a smudge of pale light. It was no more than two hundred paces away. It glowed, fizzed. Dead leaves rattled on tree branches above. The more she looked, the more she thought it had a shape – like an old person bent under a cloak, long arms and thin fingers trailing. She had wanted to duck back into the wagon but stayed, watching as the shape crackled past. Once it turned, and for a held breath she was certain she could see a head, the curve of a hood hiding a face and eyes. It had looked at her while the breath she was holding burned in her lungs. Her fingers had gripped the little iron hammer. She whispered what she could remember of the names her mother had spoken while hanging the charms inside the wagon: Sigmar, Morrda, and others that were just sounds.

Please let all the cruel things of this realm pass… Please protect us… Please let us reach a safe place… Please.

The blurred figure had drifted away through the trees. The guards settled again as she went back inside the wagon and watched the amulets turn on their cords as the wheels rolled on.

Tonight, as she heard the guards shout, she had begun to plead to the names and amulets again. Not whispering. Calling. The wagon had started to shake, wheels bucking over earth and stone. They were going fast, trying to outrun something coming after them. Then the world had tipped over. The wagon rolled and skidded, and the amulets clanged against each other. Toppling bundles of clothes half buried her. She heard the horses cry, and her father shout, and then another sound. A sound that froze her in place. A howl that passed through the wagon's walls like they weren't there. More shouts and then a loud, wet crunching. She had lain still, hardly daring to breathe.

Then she had heard claws on the outside of the wagon. She had looked around at the hatch-door, now on its side and level with the ground. Its bolt had broken, and it lolled on its hinges. The scrape of claws came closer. Her eyes stayed fixed on the hatch, waiting for a shadow to blot out the sliver of moonlight falling between it and the frame. Then there was a shout from somewhere nearby and the scraping of claws paused. She had not waited. She was up and through the hatch and running before her heart beat again.

There had been an instant when she had seen the shadow, looming close, ragged under the moonlight, eyes red. She had run into the trees. She saw a figure ahead of her, running too. She had followed. So had the red eyes of the ragged shadow.

She yanked her hair free from the thorns. Ran, gasping. Small bare feet over dark loam and tangled roots, fear numbing the cuts of sticks and stones. A tall, twisting tree stood in the middle of a clearing ahead. Its bare branches reached up to the rictus face of the moon. Birds crouched upon them. Hundreds of birds. Hunched forms of white and black feathers.

She could see someone running ahead of her. It was one of the caravan guards. Morinar, the kind one with the gut that did not fit under his armour; who always gave her one of the dried fruits from his pack when she asked; who was never scared of the sounds that came from the night, and always smiling.

'Help!' she cried. He turned, armour plates and chainmail jangling. He had a sword in his hand. His face was pale, eyes wide with terror, air gasping from his mouth. 'Help! Please!' she called again. Her foot caught on a root.

She fell. Her knee hit the edge of a stone. Blood… Blood beading her skin, black under the moon's glare. She twisted to look back.

Red. Spots of red in between the trees. And jaws. She froze. A rattling sound of breath through long teeth came from behind her.

The tears had stopped now. The birds shifted on their perches, beaks and feathers rustling. A rattling sound of something that could not breathe growling through a rotten throat. She was shaking. Her eyes clamped shut.

'Mama…' she whimpered, 'Papa…' It was the only thing she could think to say, the prayer of a child in the face of the unimaginable. It was right there, on the other side of her eyelids. She needed to be brave. Be brave and things would be all right. She turned, shaking, and opened her eyes. Glowing eyes looked back at her. Rotting skin and fur hanging from a long, yellow skull. Bits of red and pink hung from its teeth. It cocked its head. The ember light in its eyes flared. Two others padded from its shadow. Death-light and blood drooled from their mouths. Dead muscle tensed under flesh. Jaws hinged wide. She could see strands of hair and bits of cloth caught in the fangs. Be brave…

A sound like a scythe passing through wheat. Black, rotten blood splattering.

The nearest dead wolf twisted. The two halves of its split skull thrashed from side to side. A bubbling howl came from its throat. A shadow landed. It looked human. Almost human. It crouched on the ground between her and the wolves. A tattered cloak covered its back. It had a sword in its hand, bright under the grin of the moon. Two dragons coiled either side of the cross guard. She noticed rings on the thin fingers, black iron on pale skin. The wolves gave a growl. Their heads lowered. The figure in the tattered cloak looked back at her over its shoulder. Red eyes. Skin pulled taut around a mouth of knife-point teeth.

'Run,' it said.

The wolves howled.

The birds in the tree above took flight.

She ran.

* * *

Cado rose, looking at the other wolves. Ghost-light crackled silver in his sight. The fat caravan guard had his back against the tree. The man raised his sword, undecided whether to run, climb or fight.

'This one is not yours,' said Cado. The wolves tensed. Dead muscles bunched. The hunger trapped in their rotting shells would not turn away now – any more than Cado would. He felt the weight of the sword in his hand. The silver runes in its steel breathed cold into the lengthening second.

The wolves pounced. The sword came up. The first wolf's jaws were wide. Cado rammed the tip of the blade through the top of its mouth. Force jolted down his arm. Another wolf landed on him, jaws fastening on his shoulder. Fangs shattered as they met the armour under his cloak. He pivoted, ripping the sword out of the skull of the first wolf and throwing the second onto the ground. It hit with a crack of shattering bone. Pale light fizzed in its mouth and eyes. Cado stamped down. The creature's skull shattered. He whirled. The rest of the pack were already past him. The wolves flowed towards him, blurred shadows, howling. Cado leapt, sword tracing a silver-sickle path through the moonlight. Bones parted. He landed amongst the mess of rotten flesh and guttering magic. The substance of the wolves was already turning to black froth as the sorcery animating them dissolved into the wind.

Cado turned to the fat guard. The hunched birds in the branches were quiet and still.

'They could smell the reek of your god on you,' said Cado, nudging a crumbling wolf skull with his foot. 'You brought them to the caravan. Did you think the innocent could mask you, or were they just a shield to be spent?'

'I don't know what you are talking about,' gasped the guard.

'You almost outran me, but this hunt is over.'

'I… Don't… Please don't. We just wanted to reach safety, please…'

The man had started to move away from the tree, ready to run. Cado levelled his sword.

'You worship lies. You should know when one has run its course.'

He looked up at the fat man's eyes. They were suddenly steady, unblinking. There was no fear there now.

The man opened his mouth, paused, and then smiled.

Cado lunged.

The guard spat a word into the air.

Moonlight shattered into rainbow. The birds exploded from the tree branches. Cawing cries filled the canopy. The guard's shape unravelled. Fat and skin and armour and smile spun into blue fire. The sword in his hand melted. Sculpted muscle unfolded under translucent skin. A grinning mask of bronze now covered his face. He had a knife in his hand. The blade flickered like a flame.

The blow was fast, but Cado's sword turned the blade, and sliced the hand holding it. The man in the bronze mask flinched back. Cado rammed the pommel of his sword into the mask. Its bronze grin crumpled. The man staggered, and Cado was on him before he could recover, hammering blows into the face and chest. The masked man lashed out. Cado grabbed the fist and twisted. Force snapped up the man's arm. Bones shattered from wrist to shoulder. Then Cado slammed him onto the floor. He lay, gurgling, blood and breath forming pink bubbles in the mask's mouth slit.

Cado tied the man's limbs, broken and whole alike, then hooked his fingers under his chin and began to drag him back through the forest towards the caravan. Above him the birds were wheeling.

The caravan was still intact, but there was almost no one left alive. Almost. One guard, gasping last breaths, legs worried to ribbons, lay where he had collapsed, trying to crawl away. He looked too old and thin for the scraps of armour he wore. Most of his blood was now soaking the ground he lay on. Cado paused above him, looking at the worn dagger still clutched in the bloody hand. Others must have survived, he reasoned: travelling chests and bundles had been opened, possessions taken. Two of the five wagons were gone. He could read the hoof and foot marks where someone had harnessed the surviving horses to them. He wondered if the girl had been amongst them. Maybe. None of them had seen the dying guard. Or perhaps they had; perhaps they had heard his gasping pleas for help. Either way, they had not stopped to give succour. He was not surprised; the underworlds were not kind places for the living. Everything dissolved into agony and loss. Only revenge and justice remained true in such an age.

The beliefs of mortals had made the underworlds. Across existence the living had told stories and dreamed of what would follow death, and with time those beliefs had become real. Places of punishment, plenty, reward, reincarnation and eternity – conjured into being with all the variety of imagination, hope and fear that life could create. There had been mountains and forests crossed by rivers, the waters of which carried the souls of the dead; great networks of caves where grey shades moved between stone tables to set them with two cups and talk again to every person they had met in life; orchards that never seemed to end, where the trees always bore fruit and the dead lay in warm shadows under green boughs and winter would touch neither leaf nor air.

That had been the beginning of the Realm of Death: an archipelago of kingdoms made by the beliefs of the living, in which only the dead dwelt. But in time the living had come. Colonies of mortals had made the underworlds their homes. Cultures had grown. The ways of the newcomers had intertwined with those of the dead. It had been the first invasion of the afterlife, and from it the Realm of Death had become a Mortal Realm. Then Chaos had descended. The followers of the Dark Gods had stepped from the shadows. Realms and underworlds had burned. Blood had soaked the ground as daemons feasted on the souls of the dead. The past had become fire and ashes. The lives of mortals became ones of cruelty and suffering. Long ages of pain, with no light of hope or rest from the hunger of the Ruinous Powers.

Finally, a change. There had been a war, a new invasion to add its layer of blood to those that had come before. This one wrapped itself in promises of hope and help. It echoed, to Cado's ears, the hubris of the past, spoken in a new voice. Faith, alliances, light, order and majesty… all of it so crushingly familiar. All of it empty of anything except inevitable failure. The Realm of Death was a broken dream still sliding into darkness. Chaos had breathed its taint into everything, and the unquiet dead took what little kindness remained.

In the great cities of the underworlds, the living clung either to the protection of the servants of the Lightning God of Heavens, or the tyranny of the undead and the shadow of Nagash. Both were a lie. Sigmar, Lightning Born, could not undo the poison poured by the Dark Gods into the Realm of Death. It ran too deep. Nagash and his legions tried to make empires of bone and shuffling corpses, as immune to corruption as they were to time: another bargain, made with a lesser torment.

The people who had led the caravan through the forests had been humans. Either their forebears had survived under the hand of Chaos, or they had come to resettle this land. Regardless, they were fleeing whatever life they had made. They were trying to find safety, Cado guessed: a city guarded by the forces of Sigmar, a way out, other mortals to join up with. All lies told like stories to soothe frightened children. Now all that remained of their credulity and hope was an old man in battered armour gasping his last in shallow, bloody breaths. Cado paused and knelt beside him. The guard did not react. Pain and the nearness of death had stolen his sight. Cado could feel the tug of hunger rise to the reek of the man's blood. Slowly, carefully, he reached out. The guard flinched at the touch of Cado's hand on his neck. Cado flexed his fingers and felt vertebrae crack in the man's neck. Then he stood and picked up his captive again.

He dragged his prisoner to one of the remaining wagons. It had slewed off the road and pitched onto its side when its wheels caught a rut. A tree bore its weight now, branches bunched against its side. The tree was in bloom, Cado noticed. Purple blossom covered its twigs and branches in thick clumps, petals open to the moonlight. He fastened the prisoner to a wheel with an iron chain and pitch-dipped rope. The man's head lolled forward, unconscious. The bronze mask still hid his face, blood dripping from under its edge. Cado watched the thick scarlet droplets slide down the man's chest. The heart inside that chest was still beating… Warm… soft… the rhythm of redness.

He had gone very still. The smell of the drying blood and torn flesh all around him was suddenly a haze threading his senses. Hollowness opened wider inside him, screaming with silent hunger.

He stepped back, closed his eyes. The world was red threaded with black. A high, dry shriek filled his head. The blackness was roaring up from inside.

Hunt now, run through the night and find the living. Rip, tear and feast…

Red warmth. Emptiness filled with crimson. The comfort of iron and copper on the tongue.

He held himself motionless. Slowly the shriek faded to a dry chuckle. He could still hear a remembered echo of that false laugh when he opened his eyes.

The face of the moon was looking down on him from a break in the trees above the road.

He shivered then raised his hands in front of him. Nine rings sat on the fingers. Each was iron. He looked at them for a second, forcing himself to read the names etched on the metal. His eyes closed briefly again. He touched his right thumb to the ring on the index finger.

A cold shiver just behind his shoulder, and then her voice breathing into his skull.

~You are troubled.~ Solia's voice was the same as it had been when she had been his tutor. He opened his eyes. The blurred haze of her shade was just behind him and on the edge of his sight. If he turned and tried to look, her presence would shift too, so that she was always just out of view.

'I am…' He paused. 'Weary.'

~The dead can't become tired, my boy. It's a privilege left to the living.~ He almost smiled at that, but it faded as she spoke again. ~The weight you bear, I can see it is growing heavier.~

Yes, he wanted to say. Heavier by the day and by the year, each one added to the others. Links on a chain dragged behind him through time. Every prey brought down, every new road trodden… heavier with each step.

~It shall end, one day, my prince,~ said Solia.

My prince… She had called him that even when he had become a king. He could still remember her standing on the balcony on the high wing of the palace. Straight-backed, black hair fading to grey where it fell down her blue-and-ivory robes.

'Scholastis Solia,' his father had said, and she had turned and knelt to him.

'Your majesty,' she had replied. His father had said something and then turned and left. Cado had blinked, looked down, and begun wrapping his fingers over each other, then remembered his mother and nurse's scolds about fidgeting. He put his hands behind his back. He wanted to look where his father had gone, but that was not what you did. Solia, still kneeling so that she was on a level with him, had smiled.

'Do you know why I am here?' she had asked.

'To teach me,' he said. 'You are my...' He tried to form the word that his mother had said. 'My tutor.'

She smiled more broadly. There were flecks of amber in the deep blue of her eyes. He smiled back.

'That's right, my prince,' she said.

~You have not fed,~ said Solia's shade.

He shook his head. He had not fed since before he had crossed the boundary into this underworld. Even then it had only been the congealing remains of a single vial. Warm blood, rich with fading life, and the beat of a panicked heart... he had not tasted that since he had left the City of Rivers. The rictus face of the moon had twisted through darkness and crescent once since then.

'I have the prey we were tracking,' he said and nodded at where the man in the bronze mask lay against the wagon wheel.

~So you have,~ she said, and he could imagine her frowning, eyes taking in details as she listed them. ~It *is* one of the Hidden Ones, an acolyte of Change. No marks of the higher mysteries. Alive too, or for a while at least. Two limbs broken. Bleeding inside. You won't have long to get answers if you get any at all.~

Cado nodded. He could hear the man's soul struggling to hold on to body and flesh. There was an edge of cooling iron in the smell of blood dripping from the chin of the mask onto the man's chest. Life dimming drop by drop. Cado crouched next to him.

~What do you wish of me in this, my prince?~ asked Solia from behind him. He could hear the hesitancy in her voice, the plea. She was a shade, an echo of who she had been in life, bound to the iron of the ring. Like all the dead, she was beyond the concerns of flesh, but the weave of her soul remained. ~Is this going to be distasteful?~

He did not answer. Another thick drop of blood formed on the hooked nose of the man's mask. Cado raised his hand; ice breathed from between his teeth. Pale light grew from his fingers. He placed his hand on the man's chest. The light flared and then sank into the skin. The masked head jerked up, and snapped around. Muscles bunched against the ropes and chains. The man's heart was a thunder roll of panic. Then his eyes found Cado, and he became still. Cado could not see a mouth, but he was certain there was a grin behind the mask. The man drew a breath. It sounded wet, rattling. When he spoke, it was in the sing-song rhythm of verse.

'By what twists of fate, mere knaves and beggars do find them-selves in cruel hands, made cold by death's grave smile,' said the man. 'From the *Call of Trisanda*, Vagabond's chorus, second act. Do you know it?'

Cado nodded once. Long ago… players moving between trees, laughter in a lost kingdom. He knew the words and knew that they had been written in an age that only the immortal and the dead remembered. Through the mouth of this man, the Dark Gods were laughing at him.

'I know it,' he said.

The bound man laughed, blood spattering from the mouth of his mask.

'And I know you, Hollow King.'

CHAPTER TWO

The masked man leant his head against the wagon wheel. Blood was seeping freely from his mouth and the edge of the mask. He did not seem to notice.

'I know you now, though I confess I did not before. The Great Sorcerer reveals what is needed to those whose eyes can see it.' He cocked his head. A bloodshot eye fixed on Cado, framed by a bronze eyehole. The iris was yellow, the pupil a slit. When his voice came, it clacked and scratched like scales and claws. 'I see you Cado Ezechiar, last of a line of corpses, inheritor of a throne of ashes. I can see your tears in my thoughts and hear them fall on the pyres of your people. Weakness. Failure. Cowardice. All of it I see, and know, for ours is the Great Knowing.'

~Stars-of-all-the-firmament, but they always like to talk,~ said Solia. Cado could hear the discomfort behind the words. Ever loyal, never judging, she still did not like the necessities of the path he walked. ~His patron is pouring knowledge into him as his life drains. This one was an initiate, my prince. He will have been going through this place with a purpose. He may be dangerous.~

The man's head twitched as though at a sound.

'Is one of your shades here?' he asked, looking around. 'Nine souls stolen back from the fires of your kingdom, carried with you, a court of echoes and failure. The winds of truth tell me of them, Hollow King. Which one is here? Your brother? No, not him, not unless you want to wallow in the pain of guilt. The tutor? Yes… The parent that never bore you. The one who was too weak to do anything but pander to your delusions. Yes, she is here, isn't she? I will meet her soon, when the Changer of Ways claims her soul at last. We will dance in the Veil of Fire and Revelation, won't we, fair rose?'

Cado looked at the man for a long moment, then reached down and hooked a finger under the mask. He pulled. The man gasped with pain. The mask held in place. There was a sucking sound, and then it came free. Blood dribbled from inside. Hooks and toothed spikes covered the inner surface. There was no skin on the face within. Bare sinew oozed blood and yellow fluid from dozens of tiny wounds. There were eyes looking out from cheeks, forehead and jaw. Some were tiny, green or blue orbs with cracked pupils. Others sagged in loose sockets, spiralling with threads of colour. All of them rotated to Cado. The man's mouth opened like a razor slit.

'All is laid bare before the eye of truth,' he said, half laughing.

Cado dropped the mask on the ground; it rocked, face down. He blinked. He could feel the hunger growing inside him. The hunt for this disciple of the Dark Gods had taken him longer than it should – too long – and now the abyss that held the place of his soul was roaring at him to make the kill, to let anger and vengeance tear the throat from this man and let his lifeblood fill the emptiness within.

His eye found a scrap of rag, snagged on a nail in the wagon's side. A drying smear of blood marked the boards beneath. Someone, already bleeding, had fallen against it, trying to stand or fight or get away. Then the wolves had reached them. A moment of pure terror and agony marked by blood-matted threads clinging to a nub of iron. That was this man's fault. He had hidden amongst these people. The wolves had smelled the sorcery and taint on him and come. This man had sacrificed every soul in this caravan. Not in grand ritual, not for the making of some vile magic, but to petty indifference. Cado had seen what creatures like his captive did to those that they used for greater ends. He had seen the sheets of eyes and sinew stretched over blue flames, somehow still able to scream. And the old man, chained in the bottom of a tower, books of stolen truth sewn into his skin so that the pages breathed like fish gills. That was the way of those who turned to the Dark Gods; everything lost meaning beside the demands of their path to glory and damnation. He felt his lips pull back from his teeth.

The man grinned back at him.

'You must be hungry. Your kind only persist on the blood of the living. Why didn't you kill the girl?'

'I have you,' replied Cado.

'Then it is true,' the man said. 'A Soulblighted killer who thinks himself pure because he spares the innocent and eats only the cursed and unworthy.' He laughed. Pupils bloomed wide in his many eyes. 'When I heard that whisper, I thought it a joke. To find that it's true... Oh what a jest to play! How do you set that against your nature, Soulblight? How do you wash the rivers of blood of that ideal? When you have nothing left, at least you have a code to live by?'

Cado had the man by the throat. Neck muscles bunched under his fingers. He could feel blood beating through veins. The man laughed again, forcing the sound out in gasps. Cado's mouth opened. He could see the red of his gaze in the man's nest of eyes. His teeth were dagger points.

~My prince…~ Solia's voice was low, controlled. ~Remember your purpose. He is trying to protect his secrets by dying.~

Cado didn't move, his hand still locked around the man's throat. He felt the cold roar of rage pulling at his limbs. He let the man go, stepped back, closing his eyes as the black storm thundered in his skull. He could hear the man laughing.

He opened his eyes.

'You left Glimmerheart after I killed the rest of your cabal. You are fleeing to another circle of your cult. You shall tell me where you are going and who you would meet there.'

'I will tell you nothing,' said the man.

Cado stood back and reached under his cloak. The cultist must have thought that a knife or blade was about to appear, because he spat and sneered.

'There is nothing that you can do to me. My soul will flow to the Changer of Ways. I shall transmute and return, as shall we all. This is our realm, Soulblight, our dominion and our age no matter whether false or dead gods say otherwise.'

Cado looked down at him, and then began to pull a length of rusted chain from a pouch. A padlock hung from it. The man's eyes blinked, and he gurgled a laugh. Bubbles of blood popped and foamed around his teeth.

'This is a shacklegheist chain.' Cado looped a length of links around the man's neck, then another. 'This is its lock.' Cado joined two of the links with the loop of the padlock, and then held up a key. Corrosion clogged its teeth and haft. 'And this is its key.' The man's eyes fixed on the key, unblinking now. He was very still. 'You know what this is, don't you? Close this lock and far off, the spectres of torment will hear it shut. They will rise and come across land through sea and stone. They will come and grip this chain, and pull your soul from your flesh before you can die. They will drag your soul after them, down to where there is no life, no heat, no hope. Your patron will not remake or consume you. You will be just another scrap of agony, without eyes, without tongue to scream.'

'No...' The word began low, at the back of the man's mouth. It was quiet enough that Cado did not hear it at first. Then it came again, panting from the cultist's mouth as he tried to bite it back. 'No, no. No!' His head was shaking, his body shivering.

~His soul is cracking,~ said Solia. And it was. A part of the man's soul, the part that he had sold to the Chaos God of Deceit, knew that Cado was telling the truth. The chain and lock would do just what he said. An eternity of grey torment without hope of change or release. Perhaps it was fear of such an afterlife that had pushed the man to the Dark Gods. People did not fall to darkness because of the promise of power or strength or pleasure. Not really. Always at the root it was fear. And the man's fear was now at war with the god he had given his soul to.

'I will not...' hissed the man, back arching against the wheel. Muscles bunched against ropes. Spine bones cracked. 'You are grave slime, Cado Ezechiar. You are the Fateweaver's puppet. You sold your soul for a jest, and eternity laughs. The fire illuminates me. I am revealed and eternal. The mud of life shall not touch me. Death shall not claim me.' Cado let the iron of the chain touch the man's shoulder. He gasped, and his head thrashed from side to side. 'Pl– Please–' The words came from the mouth in bites. It was a different voice, thinner; a starved sound. 'Please, I can hear the rattle of them in the chain– I–'

'Where were you going?' said Cado.

'Your kingdom burned, Hollow King.' The man's voice cackled back, spite swallowing the sound that had come from it before. 'All burned, but all the souls inside are still screaming!'

'Where?' snarled Cado, as he began to wind the chains around the man. Ghost voices slid through the air. The cultist's head snapped back. His tongue was writhing behind his teeth. Blots of blood appeared in his eyes. Pink bubbles frothed on his lips. He was panting, fighting. Cado snapped the jaws of the lock around the man's neck. The wind was rising. Cado could taste cold metal on the air. He held up the key that would close the lock. The man's eyes were wide. He shook again, twisted, teeth champing as though trying to bite off his own tongue.

'Aventhis!' The word tore from his mouth. Suddenly his body slumped. Two of his eyes burst and collapsed into their sockets. His head slumped back to his chest. A force had gone out of him. He whimpered, then spoke again. 'I was making for a city called Aventhis. To the south on this road.'

'Where were you to go once you were there?' asked Cado.

'I was to find the tower with the blue-and-red door. Somewhere in the mid-city. That is all I know.'

'You were going to be sheltered?'

'Sheltered…' The man's voice was low now. 'We are the hunted creatures in this realm now. Shelter is all we can hope for.'

'You betrayed this realm,' said Cado. 'It owes you no clemency.'

The cultist looked up at that, coughed, laughed though there was blood and no humour in it.

'I am not initiated in those truths. This was just trying to survive. I was fleeing.'

'Fleeing from what?'

The man gave a bubbling laugh.

'From you.'

~He does not know anything more,~ said Solia. ~You can see it in him. He is filled with knowledge but none of it is completely true. Tiny portions of lies and truths to keep the devoted hungry, that's the poison of the Changer of Ways.~

Cado put the key back in the pouch and unwound the chain and lock from the man's head.

~Are you going to keep me for the next part?~ asked Solia.

'I need your insight, Solia, and there is one question I have to ask him.'

~There is no point.~

'There is only one way to be certain of that.' Cado finished stowing the chain.

~It failed with all the others. Or had you forgotten?~

'I took the man's face I wore.' Cado turned at the words. The cultist was shaking his head. A slight tremor was ringing through his limbs, and his skin was turning pale, his muscles wasting. The sorcery that gave him strength had fled when he betrayed a truth to Cado. He was in a lot of pain now, Cado could tell. The man looked up at him with a single eye. It was bloodshot and clouding. 'The guard. Razored it off with silver when he went for a piss. Pulled it on still warm and spoke the words. Walked back into the firelight, and do you know how many of his friends noticed anything was amiss? People he'd spent days and nights with for years… Not one. A whole life lived and all I needed to do to steal it was a few words and a knife. You think there is right and wrong in these realms, Hollow King? Justice and betrayal? You believe that you are better than me? Well, I at least can see the lie.'

Cado's face went hard, his predator's features fixed.

'You serve the Burning Hand,' he said. The man slammed back into the wheel as though struck.

'I… cannot…' the cultist managed. Muscles were cording in his neck.

'What is in Aventhis that the Burning Hand wants?'

'I… Where am I?'

~The bindings on him are eating his memories,~ Solia said. Cado bent down, face inches from his captive.

'Where is the Burning Hand?'

The man was spasming, and Cado could hear the beat of his heart collapsing.

'I don't know...'

'She spawned you all,' he hissed. 'A thousand cults left in her wake as she crosses the realms. What does she want in this city you were going to?'

The man's eyes rolled back into his skull, eyelids fluttering.

~My prince...~

'Tell me!'

~Cado!~

He stopped, stood up.

Silence fell between them. The man quieted and went still. Cado did not look at him but began to gather up items: a broken toy, a torn scroll that he glanced at and discarded. There might be a horse nearby that had got loose of the caravan and survived the wolves. His own steed had not made it across the boundary into this underworld. He would go on foot if needed, but it was better to ride: swifter and less likely to cause questions if he ran into mortals. Solia was right, of course. There had been no point in asking the captive about the Burning Hand. Even mention of the sorceress would trigger bindings and blood oaths taken by her disciples. Magic woven deep into thoughts and dreams would wake when a disciple broke their vows or spoke a forbidden truth. Memories would unravel, hearts fail, muscles strangle breath in throats – all to protect the Burning Hand and her secrets. That this man had not expired at the question meant he knew nothing. He would not live much longer, even if left alone. Cado needed that last inch of life before it failed, though. It had been a long road and he was hungry.

~Do you need me for what comes next?~ asked Solia.

'We must talk about what this means,' he replied.

~Yes, we must, but *I* do not need to see you…~ Solia's voice trailed off. ~Ancient stars and suns, what is he doing?~

Cado heard a low whimper and turned. The man bound to the wheel was shaking. Tears formed at the corners of his many eyes. He was crying.

'I… I just wanted…' The man shook his head. Broke off, looked confused. 'I was a letter writer once. In Lethis. I…'

~ His mind is collapsing,~ said Solia. ~Just like the rest. He's down to the last memories of what he is.~

'There was no way out.' The man shook his head. The eyes were closing across his face, sinking back. 'We were doomed to work and toil, and if we couldn't then our souls would go to the Throne of Bones and the Lords of Night.'

~Always the same,~ said Solia. ~Just enough intelligence to make a bad choice.~

'I just wanted to make…' sobbed the man. 'To be able to make choices, to have the power to make a choice, to save my family.'

~And where is that family now, I wonder? Screaming in some fire cage most likely. Always the same, again and again. What is it about mortality that makes the living incapable of learning obvious truths?~

Cado squatted down in front of the man. His teeth were knife blades in his mouth. He tucked the wooden toy into a fold of the man's clothing so that it would stay close. His hand was shaking. He was almost blind now. The hunger was a tattered veil across his eyes.

'Reasons do not matter.' He nudged the man's chin up. 'You damned yourself, and so you must pay.'

The man looked up, and for an instant there was a flash of bright blue in his eyes, and a grin on his lips.

'I know,' he said, and then gave a small, wicked smile. 'And so must you.'

Cado lunged forwards and the world became red.

* * *

~You do know that I can't look away?~

Cado wiped the rag cloth over his face and dropped it on top of the remains still lashed to the wagon wheel. There were bits of flesh on the ground, a bit of a foot and a few fingers too.

He could feel a brief calm filling him, warm and whole. His mind felt still. The jab of hunger and anger had faded. Tranquil. Content. As though in this moment everything were as it should be and there was nothing that could hurt. A brief and perfect world found in red.

He drew and let out a breath. The rotten tang of tainted magic shivered across his senses. Stronger than the copper of blood and corpses. Here, as with everywhere, Chaos crawled through everything. It was in the earth and air, and the taste of the magic that moved through it all. He shuddered and spat. The moon was riding higher above the tops of the trees.

~You should leave. Something may come to the bloodshed, and while you are fed, I do not want to have to explain how foolish it is to fight battles needlessly.~

'We need to talk, of what we have learned,' said Cado, ignoring her remark.

~It is simple. Judging from this one's abilities, he was low ranking. As he said, he was just fleeing along a path that others had laid. The Burning Hand and her disciples must have created a way through this underworld's edge.~ He sensed Solia shudder. ~Sacrilege.~

'They violated this realm long ago. There is nothing sacred left to violate, Solia. These are the corpses of the underworlds.'

~While there are the living and the dead to stand, there will always be hope.~

'If you say so.'

Solia was quiet for a long moment.

~You realise that the Burning Hand left this trail for you, don't you? She wants this dance, her running and you following.~

'I know.'

~You remember the first principles of strategy and war I taught you? Never go where your enemy wishes or do what they want you to do, even if it is what you want. Not if you want to win. Not if you want to survive.~

'I remember.'

The hanging gardens on the high cliffs. The sunlight striking the gossamer trees as they scattered clouds of seeds into the air. The eyes of the shades watching him from the cool shadows as Solia moved an amethyst piece onto an obsidian square. He looked across the board again, checked his calculations then made his move. He grinned up at Solia as he moved her architect and priest pieces into the graveyard. The red-bone figures clacked against each other. Solia nodded slowly then moved her messenger. He looked at the board for a second, then knocked his deity piece over in frustration as he realised that he had lost.

'You let me play my game,' said Solia patiently, picking up the piece and resetting the board. 'Never do that, my prince.'

'But I was winning!'

'Yes, right up until you lost. Now, let's try again.'

'I follow the trail to the end.'

~This one was hiding in this caravan. That implies two things – first that he was going wherever they were bound, second that he would need to pass undetected. Amongst these people he would be one amongst many. So these lands and his destination are likely not under the direct dominion of the Dark Gods.~

'Aventhis, that was the name he spoke.'

~Yes. I am not certain, but its name and the connotation of "avian" implies some correspondence to a city I once knew as Corenthis. It was a city of priests and scholars amongst other things. I do not know much else, and even that scrap is from a lost age. What such a place might be now...~

'An outpost of fools, clutching their hammers and believing that a God-King will protect them.'

~Perhaps.~ Another pause. ~If so, they will not welcome strangers who walk from the wilderness alone.~

'If it is where the trail leads, it is where I go.'

Solia did not reply. He could hear the unvoiced arguments in her silence, said enough times she didn't need to say them again.

~It will end in ruin...~

'As all things do.'

~Revenge is not an ideal that kings follow...~

'I am no king now. The only kingdom I had is long lost. And without a kingdom what is a king but a failed idea looking for purpose?'

~It was an age ago...~

'An age and more, but also today, also here and now.'

The fires burning down the valleys. Blue-and-pink flames dancing across the battlements. The screams and the smell of ash. The chirruping laughter as the shadow of daemon wings passed over the light of the sun.

'She burned my kingdom, killed my father and mother, my sisters and brothers. She gave our living and our shades to daemons as playthings and food. A king protects, and I failed. The Burning Hand, Flame of Countless Light, the Silver Crowned, no matter her title she and I have only one end – death, and vengeance. There is nothing left worth continuing for. I have become a horror to see her end by my hand. What else can there be for me but blood and suffering and vengeance on the Dark Gods?'

~And there is the matter of... hunger,~ Solia said finally. ~If it takes long to find the quarry then a city full of the living is not a wise place to starve yourself.~

'I will refill the vials from this wretch,' he said, nodding at the dead acolyte.

~It would have been better to have done that before you ripped him apart.~ That was true too, but he had been famished, and the anger had overruled sense. That was the point, of course. ~Never life taken from the innocent. That is a promise that demands prudence as much as willpower.~

'I know,' he said. Moments passed in quiet as Cado drew blood from the acolyte and gathered objects to burn his body. 'Thank you, old friend. Rest now.'

~As I said, the dead do not rest,~ she called as she faded. ~You should have learnt that by now.~

The iron ring burned cold on his index finger for an instant, and then he was alone.

He took a striker and flint out and struck it to the pitch-covered ropes he had used to bind the man. They caught. The corpse began to cook, charring, fat sizzling and popping. He watched the flames spread to the wood of the wagon. Fire leapt up. The nearby trees stirred as though wanting to pull away from the light. Cado turned and began to walk along the road.

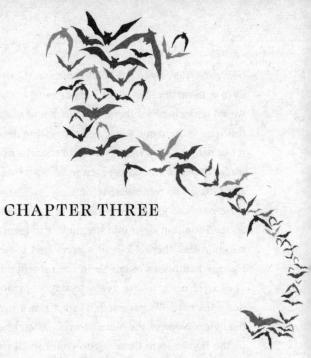

CHAPTER THREE

The moon walked with him as he rode. Above him the trees whispered and rustled, though he could feel no wind. The broken stones of the road gleamed pale under the moon's grin. Even when the surface became dust, or climbed a granite spur, the white stones marked the way. They looked like teeth, Cado thought, great white teeth set in the black gums of the earth. That was the point, of course. Whoever had made the path and set the stones had meant those who passed to have that thought. This was an ossuary road, he was sure. Long ago, the people who lived here would have followed it out from their city to the sacred sites where they took their dead. They would have laid a bone from each corpse on the road and set a stone beside it. So ossuary roads stretched across underworlds as the living passed, their bones ground down under wheels and feet until they became the dust beneath his boots.

That dust still called out to the dead. He could taste it on the winds of magic rattling the trees. The caravan had used the road because it was easy to follow and seemed safer. It was not, though. Even without the acolyte of Chaos drawing the wolves, something would have come for them. The current of magic running along this road was old and thick, and the restless dead moved close to it like fish in a deep river. Nighthaunt, spirits made of the broken pieces of past souls, corpses left to fill with hate and wild magic: all of these and more were close.

He passed a grave, ten paces from the road. A murderer had scraped it a foot deep into the moss and loam. The bodies of a family rotted there. Coils of sorcery had rooted in the bodies. Hunger had begun to curdle in the rot-jelly filling their skulls. They were ready to rise, ready to stagger through the trees and down the road. They wanted to inflict a measure of their pain on the living. None of the humans who passed knew that the grave or the bodies were there. Cado could smell them and feel the ache of their hate in his eyes. He could have called them, and they would have risen to follow him. They could sense his blood, black and cursed, threading his veins. All he needed to do was spill a drop of it and speak, and the path behind him would fill. Spectres and broken souls, a cavalcade of the night, silent under the smiling moon. He kept the black blood in his veins and made no call as he rode on.

Trees gave way to crooked fingers of stone reaching up into the sky. Mist pooled around their bases, as though a god breathed silver across the surface of the underworld. A hazy light came from the sky above as the disc of Hysh pulled higher into the heavens. It was quiet too. The horse whinnied and huffed beneath Cado, as though to break the spell. It did not like the quiet, and it did not like him either. Its instinct to run was pushing hard against Cado's control. He did not blame it. This underworld was a place ill at ease with itself. The white stone markers marched along beside the path as he rode. Some held the worn images of soaring eagles, or stooped crows. Cracks ran through others.

There were bones, of course. Piles of bones clustering around the base of rocks and wedged into cracks. Some of them were human, but more of them were birds – the remains of both jumbled together, as though they had drifted on a sea tide that had retreated and left them caught on the rocks. Empty eye sockets watched him pass. Bleached beaks jutted from piles of human ribs. Teeth smiled half-grins from tangles of grey vines. There were feathers everywhere too, ragged and rotten. Someone had tied strips of fabric and thread around some of the bones, so that white and indigo and violet strands bound them in place. It was a votive practice, one of the ways that the living of this underworld gave honour to the dead. A lot of the threads were old, though, and there were signs of other devotion too.

The first shrine appeared from the mist as he rounded the base of a gully. The horse shied back suddenly, and he fought for a second to stop it bolting. A figure of bone looked down at them. It was humanoid or loosely so, a figure with limbs splayed across the rock observing the path. But there were too many limbs, and its skeleton was not of a living thing. It was a sculpture of nightmare. Copper wires ran through its body, holding together appendages of canine, human, equine and avian bone, and that of many other creatures besides. Its skull was human sized, but its forehead and nose extended into the upper half of a beak. A human jawbone hung open below as though it were shouting. Or screaming. A double set of wings spread behind from its back. The lank feathers rustled and rattled in the breeze, like dry laughter. It was not old. Someone had made it recently. That was the truth that mocked all the talk of reconquest. The Dark Gods were everywhere. This was their land still, despite the dreams and ambitions of others.

Cado forced the horse closer, so that he was looking directly up into the thing's face. Shards of broken blue ceramic had been set in the eye sockets. His skin prickled. Fire leapt up from a burning city in his mind. He thought he could taste ash. He wheeled the horse and continued.

There were more of the shrines on the road. Some were broken already. A few of them had been burned, but there were some that looked more recent or as if they had been reassembled. He passed them feeling as though the eyes of the beaked skulls followed him. The rustle of dead feathers sounded like distant laughter. The mist thickened.

He touched the ring on his index finger. Solia's presence formed behind his shoulder.

~I knew my rest could not last for long.~

'The dead do not rest, you said.'

~We can't, but I like to try.~ A pause. Ahead the road curved between two columns of rock. Skulls and bones dotted the fissures in their sides. Lank threads gleamed with pearls of gathered dew. ~What do you wish of me, my prince?~ she asked, lapsing back into the old formality she used when she was impatient or trying to reason with him.

'We are getting close to the city. It would be useful to know something about how you think this underworld functions.'

~At its simplest, the spirits of the dead become birds.~

'Not a belief I have encountered before.'

~There is a great deal you have not met, believe it or not. You were never one for supplementing knowledge by reading either.~

'You sound disappointed.'

~No, just resigned. Countless lifetimes and immortality do not seem to change people or add to them. They just become more themselves.~

'You are saying that I have become more ignorant.'

~No. I am saying you have stayed as ignorant as you were. The belief that the spirits of mortals live as avian creatures is one that has persisted for long ages. There was mention of the Forest City archipelagos in the spheres of Life whose inhabitants held the belief and would watch for birds in the trees under which they planted their dead – for a sign of what form the departed would take, you see. And in the Condor Tribes of–~

'It is a widely held belief. I understand.'

~Not widely held, as such, but persistent. This is the underworld of that belief, the place where those spirit birds soar in the air. These stone cliffs and the forests are the roosts of the dead. Eventually each bird perishes, and the soul becomes an egg, and then another bird, and on into infinity.~

'Until this place is swarming with birds and there are mountain ranges of their droppings.'

~Was that an attempt at humour, or just a demonstration of a wilful lack of understanding?~

'No doubt both.'

~This underworld was arcanomorphic. It grows and alters with the belief that shapes it and the souls that come to it. The more there are, the larger it grows – the deeper the belief, the more complex its nature.~

'*Was* arcanomorphic, but is no longer?'

~This is a dying realm of the dead. An ironic truth… Can't you feel it? It's there in everything, the wind and leaves and the fall of the light from the moon.~

'You rarely speak in poetry.'

~It is not poetry, it is truth. This place is withering. Chaos poisoned it and the Lord of Undeath leeches away the souls that should make it their afterlife. Much longer and this world of the dead will die.~

'And this city?'

~Made like all the others, far back in the time before Chaos.~

'Mortals coming to settle the lands of the dead.'

~Just so.~

He rode on in silence. The mist flowed past him. The horse's hoof beats clacked loudly on the broken stones of the road.

The first ruin was easy to miss: just a set of steps cut into a rock face and a broken wall of stones on top of one of the lower tors. It might have been the remains of a tower, or a temple; Cado could not tell. More steps and structures began to appear soon after that. Ruins clung to the sides of the stacks of rock. Steps and paths curved up their flanks into the hazed light above. All were broken. Black thorn-vines and blood moss tangled between the tumbled blocks and teetering piles.

~Stop,~ said Solia as they passed an opening in a long face of toppled stone. ~Look there, on the edge of the sky.~

Cado looked and saw a shimmer, like a column of air rising from baking sand on a sun-drenched day. He took a breath, tasting magic.

'I can...' he began, picking his words. 'It is... Something is out of place.' He urged his horse off the road and down the gap in the rocks. After a few strides it would go no further, and Cado dismounted, tethered it to a stone and went on foot. A short way further, the gully opened into a space between a circle of cliffs. He could see the marks where broken steps had climbed the rock faces. The stump of a broken pillar rose from the ground at the centre. Images of birds, and suns, and a skull-faced moon were still visible at its base. Cado stopped, feeling his skin prickle with heat. A beam of pure white light was reaching up from the pillar. No wider than a finger, it faded to a ragged heat haze after six feet or so. It was almost too bright to look at.

'What is this?'

~I don't know. It's not a work of the disciples of Change or some other of the Dark Gods' slaves.~

Cado's eye caught something. He took a step back and tilted his head to change the view.

'Solia, do you see it, the shadow?'

~I do now.~

A shadow spread across the ground at the base of the broken pillar. It flowed in curling lines, as though the light were falling through an intricate grille. It felt like the pattern were trying to push itself into his eyes. He looked away.

~It's a rune,~ said Solia. ~Or a sigil.~

'What does it mean?'

~I do not know, but I can sense what it is doing. This is a place of old magic, and whoever placed this mark here has fixed that magic into a new shape and purpose, like a sluice guiding the flow of water down a particular channel. Before you ask, I don't know what that purpose is.~

'Not the work of the Dark Gods' slaves, though.'

~No. I have not seen this working before, but if I had to guess I would say that it has the quality of one of the kinships of the aelves.~

Cado nodded.

'Not our concern, then.'

~Hopefully not.~

Cado gave a long look at the shaft of light and the sigil spiralling across the ground, then turned away and made for the way back to the road.

He stayed silent as he rode. He had hoped that he could pass through this underworld swiftly. He just needed to pick up the trail of his prey and follow it. He did not want or need complications. Since he had caught up with the caravan, he had had the growing feeling that his wishes might just be fuel for the cosmos to mock him.

The bones of the dead lined the road more thickly now. Old skulls grinned from cairns, their eyes and mouths filled with wilted grave-roses growing through eye sockets and between yellow teeth. There were fresh dead too. People in scraps of armour, the flesh within already rotting when they had fallen for a second time. Deadwalkers – Cado could taste the magic that had threaded their limbs and driven them on. It was bitter and razor-edged, the taste of wild magic. Chests and skulls opened by axes, and rotten skulls crushed by hammers.

The calls of the birds had risen. Above he could hear the beating of wings. Feathered shadows spiralled through the murk, diving down to peck at the remains. Carrion eaters. A bridge between two fingers of rock emerged ahead, spanning the road fifty feet in the air. The remains of towers ran along its edge, broken and eroding to stubs. Rusted chains hung in ragged curtains under the arch, creaking in the breeze. A few crumbling bones dangled in the links. Cado looked up as he passed beneath the bridge. Holes punched through to the sky beyond. Water dripped from vines, and black weeds hung from the openings.

'This place is half-abandoned,' he said aloud.

~A town nesting in the cadaver of a city,~ said Solia. ~It looks as though someone has tried to rebuild and occupy some of these structures.~

Cado looked ahead to where a squat drum of stone blocks rose from a bluff that the road circled on both sides. A jumble of boulders and mortar had been crammed into holes, and a wooden palisade ran around its top.

'Guard towers to watch the road,' he said.

~I do not feel anything watching us.~

'Besides the birds,' he said, and looked up. The carrion eaters were still there, turning in slow circles through the mists.

~It might be best to keep out of sight for now. This is a place used to war. They are more likely to shoot a stranger than welcome him.~

For reply, Cado drew and released a breath. Words hissed in the air. The mist and light folded around him, drawing close like a cloak. He was a blur now, a shadow of grey in a grey world. Mundane eyes would slide off him if they looked in his direction; the sound of his horse and voice would seem like the hiss of the wind. Only if someone focused closely would they know he was there. Or if their senses were more than ordinary.

~The birds might still see you,~ said Solia, as though following the thread of his thoughts. ~There is magic here too. Something powerful.~

'The reek of Chaos and defeat is heavy.'

~No, beyond that. Something deeper.~

He paused and inhaled. She was right. Down beneath the burnt feathers and spice perfumes of the Crow Slaves' sorcery, there was another layer of power. It rolled through the air and tingled between the rocks, dry and cold like frost.

~You sense it?~

He nodded.

'Where does it come from?'

She laughed.

~I have no idea, my boy. If you called the High Councillor, she might be able to tell more, but...~

'No,' he said. He thought he felt the iron ring on the middle finger of his right hand burn for an instant.

~It would be wise. You are going into a place that is at war, filled with the shadows of the unknown. We do not know who rules this city, or what dangers it harbours. I do not know what the source or purpose of this magic is, but I do know that it is powerful. To refuse insight into it is to leave yourself more vulnerable than you already are. A prince or king does not shun knowledge when that knowledge may be the difference between victory and defeat.~

'No,' he said again, flatly. He thought that Solia was about to reply, when the road twisted again and in front of him he saw a stack of rock, taller than all the rest, rising from the mist. Buildings dotted its sides. He could see the lines of roads cut into the rock, spiralling up from a wall that circled its base. Narrow bridges spanned the gap between the higher points of the rock and the nearest smaller stacks. Intact buildings dotted those too, mixed in amongst others that had collapsed into rubble. The broken spans of more bridges jutted from the rock, pointing into the mist like fingers. Towers rose from the top of the rock, some snapped, others crooked. He could see the stones of further roads winding between stacks to converge on the base of the gatehouse in the wall.

There were guards on the gate. They did not notice him until he was only a short sprint away. When they did, they shouted. A quarrel struck the stone in front of his horse. He curbed the animal and inhaled the spell that had hidden him. He touched the ring again and Solia vanished with a hiss of reproach that he had not warned her.

'No further,' came a voice. Strong and firm.

He could feel eyes on him. The tips of arrows and crossbow bolts held steady on him. He held himself very still and made sure his hands were visible. He could hear hearts beating fast. This was a place on edge, that saw dead and predatory things come to its gates all the time. Breathing in, Cado could feel the itch of wards marked on the stones of the gate and walls. There was magic protecting the city of Aventhis as well as swords and arrows.

'Who are you, and what is your business here?' came the strong voice again.

'I am called Cado,' he called in answer. 'I am come to deliver a message to a citizen of your city. That done, I will want to shelter for a night, then I will go again.'

'Where did you come from?'

'The south. I crossed the boundary and have been riding since.'

'You made it alone?' came another voice, loud with surprise. His ears heard a hiss of breaths and mutters.

The boundaries between underworlds were more than water or land. Power divided and bound the patchwork Realm of Death. Mortals and immortals and the undead did not pass from one underworld to another without great will or knowledge, or the help of a powerful ally. If Cado had come across the boundary that meant he was someone of note, or a liar. In fact, he was both.

Cado waited. His answer would either mean that arrows would fly, or someone was going to come and talk to him. He was counting on the second. Curiosity was a powerful flaw. The mortals of the realms were cautious and superstitious, dour to the point of coldness at times. But they were still vulnerable to that oldest need – to want to know more than was good for them.

The sound of bolts drawing back slid through the air. A narrow door next to the main gate opened, and a man in a battered cuirass and purple cloak came out. A symbol of a crow clutching a hammer and hourglass sat on his chest. The man had all the marks of a sergeant-at-arms, or whatever this city's equivalent was. Hard and made harder by surviving as many alley ambushes as shield walls. Two other soldiers came with him. Both had spears and shields showing the same crest.

'Off your horse,' said the sergeant, flicking a hand. He was looking at the road behind Cado rather than directly at him. Cado held still for a second, then dismounted. 'Keep that sword in its sheath.' Cado did not move. Berry liqueur and the smoked meat he had eaten when he broke his fast scented the man's breath. There was muscle under the armour and fat too. A killer this one, and not a noble one. A brawler given authority because his competence stayed ahead of his vices. Just.

'How did you cross the boundary?' asked the sergeant. He flicked a yellow-stained eye directly at Cado.

'The paymaster for my errand saw to it,' said Cado. 'I neither understand nor can say how it was done.'

'And where is your paymaster from?'

'Lethis,' said Cado.

'The Raven City…' gasped one of the spearmen.

'Keep your mouth shut,' snapped the sergeant then looked back at Cado. 'Lucky for you, I am one of the only souls who has seen the four towers of the southern gate.'

'There are three towers at the southern gate,' said Cado. 'The fourth fell and was never rebuilt and is never named.'

The sergeant nodded, but still frowned.

Cautious, thought Cado, *and no fool.*

'Any proof besides your words?' the man asked.

'This,' Cado said, and pulled out a black ring encapsulating a drop of water, which he had taken from the acolyte who had hidden as part of the caravan. He held it out to the sergeant. 'If you know enough to judge my words then you will know what this is.'

The sergeant took it and turned it over in his fingers.

'Black water ring,' he said. 'Made to keep the bearer's soul from being chained if they are killed. Expensive.' The sergeant let the ring sit on the tip of a finger. Cado could read the hunger in the man's eyes, and the touch of his tongue to his upper teeth. In the realm of the dead, the worst fear of the living was that their soul would go to torment and slavery after death. Life could be vile and cruel, but it would end. The tortures of the dead were eternal. People worked their whole lives to earn the chance to die without fear of what came after. Items like the ring that the sergeant was still looking at, represented either peace after death or a fortune in this life. Cado didn't care which made the sergeant lick his teeth, only that it did. 'You say you're a messenger?' asked the man.

'I am to bring an item to someone in your city from my paymaster.'

'Who are they?' asked the sergeant, looking up, eyes still hungering but narrowing.

'Cleopese,' he said without a pause.

'No one I know of that name in these walls.'

Cado was beginning to feel that if he got through this gate then he should try to make his time inside as brief as possible. He was going to have to take a risk and hope that it paid off.

'I was instructed to look for a tower with a blue-and-red-painted door.'

'You'll be lucky to find it,' said one of the spearmen. 'There're more towers here than people.'

'Shut your mouth,' the sergeant snarled, then curled his lip at Cado. 'What's worth sending a sword-bearer across boundaries, eh?'

Again the hunger. Cado shrugged. 'Just a message, but I am not permitted to know what.' This time he took out a sealed silver cylinder. A tiny keyhole at one end. Etched roses twined across the silver. 'Only the key can open it, and the recipient has the key. If I or anyone else tries to open it with pick, or hammer, or charm, the parchment inside becomes ash.'

'I know what it is,' grunted the sergeant reluctantly. Cado was impressed but not surprised. He had acquired the cylinder years ago and had used it to give physical weight to his reasons for wanting to enter or leave cities and settlements. The cylinder did exactly what he had said, but in fact there was no key, or a message sealed inside. Couriers who carried messages between the free cities used such cylinders, and it was a mark of the importance of both the message and the bearer. Only someone with wealth and power could afford to communicate in this way. It was a big lie to tell. Cado reflected that sometimes the larger the lie, the more people wanted to believe it.

The sergeant grunted and looked at the ring. He was almost at the end of the questions he wanted to ask. The man was looking at the story Cado was telling and wanting to believe it.

'I am willing to let you hold that in trust,' said Cado, nodding at the ring. 'As surety of my intentions.'

'Until you leave…' said the sergeant. The hardness and snap had gone from his voice. Now there was just the soft purr of greed.

Cado gave a small shrug. 'My paymaster will no doubt replace it.'

The sergeant nodded, and the ring vanished as though it had never been. 'Open the gate,' he called back, and a moment later the gates began to grind open.

Cado led his horse through. He saw guards on the parapet inside eyeing him, still wary.

'Can't take the horse no further,' said the sergeant. He was still watching Cado carefully. 'There's stabling down there.' He jerked his head at a gap between two half-fallen buildings. 'Give coin and they'll keep him until you leave.'

CHAPTER FOUR

The road climbed from the gate up the spire of rock. In places it cut into a sheer cliff, the stone forming a roof that curved above. In other places the way jerked between buildings and walls. Those buildings stood on terraces or wide platforms that extended from the spire's flank. They were ruins for the most part. There were arches that opened onto heaps of rubble. Halls sitting open to the winds and rain, the beams that had held up their roofs long rotted. The marks of an old majesty were there too: relief carvings of forests and birds, and engravings that must have been words. Cado did not recognise the language. It, like the society that had set the stones of the city, was long gone. And here and there, signs of Chaos. He saw the base of a pillar of iridescent stone left like the stump of a felled tree. Stubs of iron dotted the face of a tower where metal spikes had been. Efforts had been made to remove them, but they were there, like scars left in skin. Cado guessed that the slaves of the Dark Gods had destroyed the city, but never occupied it. A pack of warriors or a vagabond cult might have used it as their nest at times, but it had escaped becoming a fortress of madness like so many other cities had. Before new settlers had made it live again, it would have been a corpse of stone slowly returning to the rubble and land from which it had risen.

He smelled more life the higher he went. Smoke and the aroma of baking bread coiled from bakers' ovens. Pots of piss and excrement sloshed from doorways and ran down the gullies at the edge of the road. He passed a street where the flat stones of a broken temple had become the stalls of a fish market. Long, white eels lay in coils beside violet-shelled crabs, and heaps of small fish with black scales. He had seen no rivers, but that did not mean they were not there. Water flowed deep in the Realm of Death, draining out of the land to the great oceans and seas. In places there were great, black lakes beneath the earth where magic and water gathered. No life swam those waters, but things with fins of bone stirred the surface. If a mortal could dive to the bottom, they could surface and draw breath in other realms. So the stories said.

There were soldiers too. Most were alone or moved in pairs. They wore boiled leather and mail. Here and there he spotted one with a dull metal cuirass. Threads of bird skulls and feathers hung on cords around their necks or from the shafts of their spears. They were a battered lot, with scarred flesh and wary eyes. He did his best to avoid them, and though some watched him, none of them stopped him. People passed by pulling handcarts, heads down as he made the climb. A few looked at him as he passed, but most at least pretended to keep their eyes to themselves. Mercenaries were a presence in every city and settlement across the realms. The curious might notice them, but it seemed that here a sellsword with the dirt of the road on his boots was not worth much remark.

He paused as he climbed. Solia had said that once, the city had extended to all the rock spires that surrounded it, each one linked by bridges, each one crowded by buildings like bird nests atop dead trees. He had presumed that the acolyte in the caravan had been making for the main part of the city, but what if that was not the case? Aventhis was holding half the mortals it was built for, and that was in its main spire alone, but it looked as though a few bridges still linked it to smaller spires nearby. There might be other clusters of inhabited buildings on those spires. What if the tower with the painted door was amongst them?

Another truth had become clear as he searched the streets, too: Aventhis was a half-living city. Newer buildings intertwined with the old. People lived in some of the original structures, but not others. He would walk along one street and see stone and wood climbing the stump of a temple to make a grain house. The buildings to either side would be made of repurposed stone, with the comet-and-hammer symbol carved into them. Then he would turn a corner and find a row of buildings looking down at him with empty windows, their roofs gone and their faces crumbling. Birds roosted in the ruins, great colonies of them. They watched Cado as he passed, and the echo of their calls shivered in his ear whenever the sound of the city faded to quiet. He could feel the curiosity, malevolence and caution. He remembered what Solia had said about this underworld.

~*The spirits of the dead become birds…*~

Behind those black-and-amber eyes, the kernels of souls sensed what he was. They did not think; this form of afterlife did not let most keep that ability. But they felt the current of magic as it flowed through the air. He was not a threat to them, but he was also not of the living. There were far more of them here than there had been out in the forests he had come through. Were they attracted to the living, or was there something else that pulled them to this spear of rock?

A caw shivered through the air as he turned up another road.

This one was lightless and lifeless too. The fronts of the buildings had spilled down onto the street, half blocking it. Water ran down a shallow gully it had cut between the loose cobblestones. He shook his head. There was no tower here, no painted door. He was beginning to feel that it would take days to find the place, and that he might not have that time. He was not sure why, but the feeling had not shifted from where it itched at the back of his skull. It was the kind of feeling he had learned to listen to.

He was just turning to go back down the street he had just climbed when the caw came a second time, louder, and he glanced around at the sound. A huge, pale grey bird sat on the arch of a door in a broken wall. It looked at him, eyes black pinpricks in amber. It cawed again. Cado shook his head and began to turn away, but the bird called once more, and when he looked around, it sat on the top of a fallen block of stone, just an arm's reach away.

He went still. This bird was not just calling to him because he was near its nest or young. It was a sign, and in the underworlds, you ignored signs from the spirits at your peril.

'You wish something?' he said.

The bird cocked its head, then turned and hopped and flapped back towards the arch it had perched on before. It rotated its head to look back. After a second, Cado followed. The bird glided from the arch when Cado reached it, pale wings beating the air inside. Cado paused just inside the threshold. The walls and half-fallen roof soaked the inside in shadow, but his eyes could see clearly. More birds sat within, lining the tops of walls, and the gaps between shifted blocks. Bird droppings lay in a thick, white layer under the bare beams. The great grey bird was on the floor by a doorway at the far end of the space. Cado looked back out at the street behind him, but could see nothing except the rain and the smoke rising from chimneys further down the spire side.

He picked his way across the floor. The bird flapped out of sight as he reached the door.

Cado paused under the arch. He blinked at the dark beyond. It did not recede from his sight straight away, but clumped and drifted back, like a slow retreating tide. He took a small bite of air. There it was: a tang of magic, fading but strong. He was no deep adept of the arcane. The curse in his blood and long years of study meant that he could do many things, but it was a narrow ability rather than mastery. He could feel the winds and current of magic, though. Just as a mortal could smell salt in the wind coming from the sea, or a lion could taste the rot in meat, magic entwined with his senses. Now, in the dripping dark of this collapsed building, he could feel magic. It itched across his skin. There were the textures of death that pervaded all magic in this realm: heavy, like a lead weight dragging the senses down. There was something else though, too, a jaggedness like the edges of a shattered cup.

He slid one of his daggers out of its sheath and stepped further in. The bird cawed. His sight pushed into the gloom. There was something resting against the furthest wall. He took another step. No, not resting. Pinned. He saw fingers, clutched together, then an arm; then the face emerged as though surfacing from deep water. Cado stopped. The eye sockets of the dead face were empty, the jaw lolling on strands of dried sinew. Matted hair hung from the crown of the skull. An iron pin had been hammered through the mouth and back of the skull into the wall behind, presumably while the mortal was still alive. Two more pins went through the shoulders under the collarbone. He could see now where the hands had raked at the wall, fingertips gouging through the lichen on the stone. The remains of robes hung from the body, now reduced to tatters of velvet. Strands of silver thread ran through them like a discarded cobweb. He moved his head closer and pushed the spill of hair to one side with the tip of his dagger so that he could look at the pin in the corpse's mouth more closely. Struck into the top of the iron was a crude symbol of a twin-tailed comet.

He let the dagger drop and touched the ring on his forefinger. Solia's presence shimmered into being behind his shoulder. The grey bird cawed from its perch in the dark above.

He could tell that she did not like being here. Ice prickled over his back, and when she spoke her voice was sharp.

~My prince.~

'Look,' he said as reply. Solia hissed.

~There is magic here, death and the taint of Chaos. Can you feel it?~ He could. It was the aberration in the feel of the magic filling the space. ~The spirit of this one did not go free after death. It was held here, and then ripped away.~

'What could have done that?'

~The cult of the God-King. Witch hunters punishing the disciples of the Dark Gods.~

'Or something else.'

~You must be careful, my boy.~

He looked around, pulled a flask of oil from his pouch, and upended it over the corpse.

~It would be wiser to leave.~

He did not reply but struck a flint until the spark jumped onto the oil soaking the hair and cloth. The flame shrank, then flared up. Cado stepped back and turned. Smoke poured up through the broken building as the flames grew.

The coil of night was drawing tight as Cado walked from the deserted street back into the city. The smoke from the fire he had set climbed slowly, and then thinned in the mist of rain. The blaze did not grow. There was little in the ruins for it to feed on once it had burnt the body. No one cried out or came running to find the source. There was nothing to distinguish it from the smoke of chimneys or cooking fires.

He reflected on what Solia had said. This city was more dangerous than he had hoped and thought. The threat of discovery was high, but there was also an opening. There were disciples of the Dark Gods here, but there were also people who knew they were there and were hunting them. That meant that if Cado could not find the disciples themselves, he could find those already on their trail. It was a risk, but he could walk the streets of this city for days and not find a door painted in blue and red. The more time he was here, the more suspicion would turn eyes towards him; that was how it always went. He thought about it as he walked another street of ruins, then came to a decision.

It was not an inn, not truly. There was no sign to mark it and the building looked as though it had been a counting house. The door at the front was tall and narrow. A slouched guard keeping out of the rain just inside had looked at Cado's weapons but made no move to stop him. Further inside, narrow stone niches lined the walls. A chest-high stone counter was set in each niche for a ledger or scroll to sit on. There were splashes of ink on the sides of some niches, faded but the colour soaked in deep. Dozens of people would have stood here, heads bent over their work as they counted and marked whatever had come in and gone out of the city gates. Counting, bead by bead, quill mark by quill mark: that was what civilisations did, numbering their gains and losses as though it mattered more than a spark in the eyes of the cosmos.

It was called the Candlelight now, and the scratch of quills was long gone. Cado guessed that it had been chosen because it was close to the main gate, still standing and had no other use. The upper floors had slumped into each other. Thorn roses climbed the stones in a thick mat like the hair of a dried corpse still clinging to the scalp.

The ground floor had been reclaimed as a place where the souls of Aventhis could huddle over cups of liquor and do what mortals with only fears and hopes did: talk and drink.

Wooden tables and stools sat in the middle of the two largest rooms just inside the main door. Barrels sat in the niches of the largest room. Candles had been placed in all the others, great clumps of candles. Thick layers of wax covered the stone. Wooden figures holding hammers stood beside the candles. Comets formed haloes behind their heads. They were crude. Cracked paint covered them and wax spattered their faces. The air reeked of alcohol and tallow smoke.

The tables were full in both rooms. He saw men and women in chain and plate just like the gate guards. They glanced at him as he entered. There was no friendliness in the looks, just a cold, low-grade hostility. He took in the other patrons as he walked up to a man sitting on a stool beside the row of barrels. The man blinked at Cado, the gesture as much of a question as he was willing to offer.

'A drink,' said Cado.

The man nodded. Clearly there was not a wide enough selection of drinks to require a clarification. He moved off the stool and went to a barrel set in one of the niches. Cado noticed that the man moved with a rolling motion. There were pale marks down his right arm and on his neck under the collar of his jerkin. They looked like splashes of grey dust. Shade scars, Cado realised, the marks left by the touch of an unkind spirit. The man filled a leather cup from the barrel's tap, turned to Cado and waited. Cado held up a charm-sliver. It was stamped with the hound-head crest of Lethis' charm-makers and had held as good currency in most of the realms he had crossed. The man looked at the crescent of yellow bone and shook his head, then began to turn.

'If you want to pay with totems, it needs to be a bird quill,' said a voice from behind him. Cado turned to see a single amber eye looking up at him from a face that was half scar tissue. The woman smiled with broken teeth. 'They will take lightning iron if you have that, but they are funny about what they accept from people here. And if you can't pay for a drink, they won't let you sit.'

The barrel-man was already turning away, shaking his head and making to pour the cup of drink into a bucket.

'Here,' said the woman, holding out a hand, a small purple-black feather held between finger and thumb. 'I'll take what you were going to give him, and you can give him this.' Cado looked at the bearded man. An eyebrow crooked above the lone eye in the woman's face. The skin puckered under the other, empty socket. She was wearing a rough doublet but had the look of someone who spent their time moving around under the weight of ring mail and boiled leather. Someone who noticed a stranger paying with the wrong coin and who stuck her nose in. Someone who saw things.

Cado nodded, and handed the woman the charm-sliver, took the feather and gave it to the barrel-man, who thrust the cup into Cado's hand. The liquid inside had an oily sheen and smelled of wet earth and herbs.

'Pretty vile,' said the woman. Cado nodded at the stool opposite her. 'Feel free,' she said. 'No one else is going to take it.' He took a gulp from the cup, for appearances, and decided it would be the last. Some of the Soulblighted could not eat or drink mortal food. He could, but it did nothing. He could taste, could distinguish scents and flavours more finely than when he had been alive. But the hunger and thirst it sated in the living was a void in him, the smell and texture of the finest food a mere selection of facts set before his senses. He put the cup down.

'They struggle with what they don't know,' said the woman. 'Stay a week and they will barely look at you. Right now, though, they are all looking at you and wondering if you are trouble.' She smiled. 'I am going with yes.'

Cado shook his head. 'I am just passing through.'

'No one just passes through here,' said the woman. 'People come here, less now than they did, but no one leaves. There's nowhere else to go and no way of getting there.' She took a drink of her own cup. 'So, you might want to change that part of your story.'

Cado nodded, looking at her. He let his senses reach out. The beat of the hearts in the room grew in his ears. The smell of sweat and flesh, the reek of living breath. He let the wave pass and focused on the woman opposite. She had been drinking less than she appeared to have been. Deceptive. Younger, too, than the scars on her face made her seem. Damaged but strong. Blood beating to a broad rhythm in her veins. He let his caution relax a little.

He was alert for his prey coming for him. The acolyte he had taken from the caravan had known who Cado was and that he was hunting them. They were here too, in this city; the corpse he had burnt had confirmed that. Had they spotted him since he arrived? Was this the beginning of an ambush? He did not think so, but decided to voice the question left hanging.

'You are less cautious about whom you speak to,' said Cado. The woman shrugged.

'Foolish,' she said. 'Or bored. Likely both.' She took another drink, the swallow shallower than it looked. 'You are a mercenary, aren't you?'

Cado gave a small shrug but said nothing.

'There are not many of us left, here,' she continued. 'Can't be a sellsword if no one is buying. No trade, no small settlements or expeditions that need watching. So if you were hoping for that, prepare to be disappointed. Amaury, by the way.'

'Cado,' he said. 'If you are a sellsword and there is no one buying, why are you here?'

'I said there was nowhere else to go. Nowhere it's *wise* to go at least. If you came in on one of the roads, you know. The darkness is not ebbing, it's flowing, and this is one of the last islands in the seas. For now, at least.'

'So what is paying for your drink?'

'Militia,' said Amaury. 'Only real payers for a blade. Hungry for people too.'

'And they pay well?'

Amaury snorted. 'They pay like people who are desperate and scared and have almost nothing.'

'Scared?' he asked. 'What are they scared of?'

She tilted her head, looking at him for a long moment.

'A caravan was taken in the woods on the north road,' she said at last. 'Handful of survivors. They said at the gate that there were wolves, but there was something else out there too.' Cado said nothing. Amaury gave her own shrug. 'That's just today. This land does not want us here.'

'And the Old Enemy?' he said. The Old Enemy – one of the ways that people talked about the threat of the Dark Gods without having to name them. The look she gave him was sharp, and with more than a hint of triumph, as though he had done exactly what she had guessed he would.

'No one roams these lands,' she said. 'There might still be a mercenary who dares to, who clings on, but all of the sellswords are from here, came here with the rest or were born here. No one comes from outside or across the boundaries. Someone might claim to be a messenger from one of the great cities, but a messenger doesn't end up in a liquor hall asking about the Old Enemy.' She took a drink, a genuine one this time, and then took out the charm-sliver he had given her in exchange for the feather. 'A fortune in charms from Lethis, an air that says you could kill half this room and not lose sweat or sleep, and the first thing you drop in talk is the Old Enemy... That's not how a messenger or sellsword talks.' She paused. He sensed the beat of her blood rise in rhythm. 'But it is what a witch hunter might ask.'

Witch hunters... Fanatics to their god who killed anything and everything that they judged unholy. He had met their kind several times. He had survived on each occasion. All but one of them had not. That he was one of them was not a poor guess, but even though it was wrong, you would need more than a short conversation and a few observations to reach that conclusion. He looked at Amaury carefully, pieces of what she had said adding to each other.

'You were guarding the gate when I arrived,' he said.

She nodded. 'I was the one that put the quarrel into your path when you popped out of nothing.'

'And you heard what I said to the sergeant-at-arms.'

'I find it pays to listen.'

'It can do,' he said, 'depending on what you heard.'

'And what's on offer,' she said. Cado waited. She was quick, this one, but there was an edge of foolishness in her, of recklessness when caution would have been wise. Where had that come from, he wondered, and how had it survived out here in the last city of a dying afterlife? 'I have more than whispers.'

She paused. She was sincere, he thought, or an exceptional liar. There was something else, though: a hitch in the beat of her heart as she spoke about it. She was not just sincere; she was afraid.

'I want to leave,' she said at last. 'You came from across the boundary, and you aren't going to stay here and stand on a wall waiting for death to come. I go with you when you leave.'

'I work alone,' he said.

'And see how far that gets you in this city,' she retorted. 'I don't want to work with a witch hunter. I want an exchange. I help you here. You help me leave.' She grinned. The scars on her cheek twisted. 'A sellsword's bargain.'

'If you can't help me in what I am doing?'

'Then the deal is off.'

Cado considered the lie that he was allowing her to believe. He would have to honour any bargain he made. That was his rule, one amongst the others he had chosen. Rules defined you; that was what his un-life had taught him. Not the order imposed by others. Not what you could do, but what you chose not to do.

Amaury was still looking at him. He nodded once. She smiled wider.

'Agreed?' she asked.

'Agreed,' he said.

She held out her own cup. He tapped his against it. They both took a drink. The drink was just as empty to Cado as it had been at the first taste. She lowered her cup.

'The Old Enemy,' he said.

Amaury stood, took a last swig, and picked up a sheathed sword from where it leant against the table.

'Not here,' she said. Cado did not stand. 'Better to show you than tell you.'

CHAPTER FIVE

'There,' said Amaury, stepping back. Cado looked down at the patch of wall, then crouched. The chest was small. Pitch soaked its planks so that its shell seemed like the black fossil of a tree stump. The rain dripping from the broken roof burst from the edge of the lid and splashed down into the belly of the box. A mask looked up at Cado from inside. Something had burned the right-hand side. The bronze of the left temple was charred and crumpled, but the hook nose and ragged grin were still there.

'There was a knife, too,' said Amaury. Cado drew one of his own daggers and used it to shift the mask aside. The knife was there. The dim light of Amaury's lamp pooled and rippled in oily colours where it touched the blade. Cado felt his eyes itching as he looked at it. It was like so many he had seen before, no two alike but all the same. It was a sliver of spite, forged into metal and given an edge. His fangs pricked his lips as they started to grow. He suppressed the anger. The needle tips withdrew. He stared at the mask while he caught his composure.

They were in a burnt house partially dug into the rock of the spire. The lower curtain wall was only a hundred paces away. Most of the other buildings around were storehouses, sheds for animals meant for slaughter. Just as many were ruins, or empty. Amaury had led him here by an indirect route. Ready for treachery or ambush, Cado had watched the roofs and shadows, but the few people they had seen had passed by without a word. The only sound had been the tone of bells striking the hours. The burnt building looked like it had been reclaimed. The blackened beams of wood jutting from its skin sat upon the older stones of whatever had stood there before. The fire had gutted the structure all the way back to the cliff face that formed the rear wall.

'You found this here?' asked Cado.

Amaury nodded. 'The dagger and mask. The box was under some of the debris. There was this too, look.'

She shifted a piece of burnt timber to show an opening in the wall. It was small and narrow, and opened into a throat of darkness that went into the rock and down.

'Have you gone in?' he asked.

Amaury snorted. 'I am foolish, but not *that* foolish.'

Cado brought his head close to the opening, drew a breath. There was magic in the dark. Strong magic.

'Where does it go, I wonder?'

'I don't know, but it's got to be the reason the... the person in the mask was here, right?'

'Perhaps.'

Cado straightened.

'Why were you looking here?' he asked.

'Someone had to see what was left after the blaze cooled. I had... vexed the sergeant-at-arms. So they sent me.'

Cado blinked, thinking of the corpse stuck to the wall with comet-stamped pins. A corpse that the birds would not go near.

He put his hand against the rock of the back wall. The soot was thick, and the stone cold. There were no marks of anything, or anyone having been hammered into it. He would have liked Solia's observations, but he could not summon her with Amaury present.

'The dagger and mask weren't burnt,' he said.

'No,' said Amaury. 'I found them buried in embers and ash that were still warm, but apart from the edge of the mask they were clean. Like the blaze had not touched them.'

'No body? No bones?'

'None, and the fire was big but not strong enough to turn them to ash.'

'You are certain?'

'I know enough of fire,' she said.

Cado looked up at her from where he crouched. Her lone eye fixed on him. He nodded, stood, and kicked the chest shut.

'How long ago was this?'

'Five nights.'

The body the birds had led him to had been dead for longer.

'You didn't tell or show anyone else,' he said. 'Why?'

She blinked and there it was again, a stutter-skip of fear in a soul that was not prone to it.

'I didn't think it was wise.'

He raised an eyebrow. 'You know something else?'

'Know?' She shook her head. 'No. But I have not been here as long as others.'

On the outside, he thought, always passing through, always hired but never settled, never part of anything, always looking to move on.

'I listen to what people say,' she added, 'and notice what they do. This is a city of fear.'

'Everywhere is.'

'This is new fear. Something is coming. You can feel it. Four weeks ago, birds flew in from the outer country. Lots of them. More than I have ever seen at once, and there are birds everywhere here, they are–'

'The souls of the dead.'

She nodded. 'And they just kept coming for hours, like they were drawn here for safety.'

When the dead seek shelter so must the living too... He heard the old rule sing through his head like he had heard it sung to children. The wind gusted a fresh wash of rain through the burnt rafters.

'People feel it, and that's without the caravans coming,' she said.

'The few that get through.'

'The few. Fear, witch hunter, it's everywhere. People are looking for something to blame, something to do. I think... some have decided to start looking for who might be to blame.'

He understood then, clear as the light of a new moon. The comet-stamped pins in the corpse. The fire in these buildings with a mask and knife buried in the ashes. Someone was hunting witches, and monsters. They were not doing it openly, but in the shadows.

'People in the militia,' he said.

'Maybe,' she said. 'I don't know. They don't trust me, but there are a few. They talk close, and sometimes there are hints about something they are doing or know. There have been people going missing too. Not many, but some. Here one day then gone, like they were sucked down into the darkness.'

'The rulers?'

'Too busy, too few. There is supposed to be a council, but there are just two. They are up there.' She pointed past the ceiling towards where the top of the city must be. 'If they know anything about people taking matters into their own hands, they don't care.'

'The Old Enemy is here, though.' He nodded at the chest.

'What do you do? I mean, what does one of you do now?'

Cado was about to answer when he heard something over the drum and drip of rain. His head turned and he froze. Amaury picked up on the movement a second later, read it and tensed.

There it was: booted feet on cobbles, moving as though trying to be quiet but not knowing how. He inhaled. The smell of ash and rain stole the scent from the wind. If he had been alone, he might have bounded up and out of the burnt rafters. He looked at Amaury, jerked a chin at the door. They moved towards it. Amaury reached the opening first, looked out, paused, bit her scarred lip, and snarled.

'Get out of sight,' she said, and stepped through the main door into the street. Cado's hand flashed out to pull her back. 'Just me, sergeant,' she called before he could reach her. She had her lamp in her hand, the candle burning fitfully behind the storm glass.

'Amaury?' came a voice that Cado recognised as that of the sergeant he had bribed to get into the city. There was an edge to it now, something cold that he wondered if Amaury had noticed, and that made him slide a second dagger from its sheath. He heard steps coming closer: three sets, leather-shod, moving carefully, like people with weapons.

'Sergeant,' replied Amaury, voice clear.

The steps came closer. The sodden cinders outside the door crunched.

'What are you doing here?'

'Passing and saw a light.' The lie fell hollow. Cado was against the wall, folded into a curve in the rock. He let a phrase breathe silently from his lips and felt the dark cinch closer around him. A figure stepped close to the door, near Amaury. The sergeant. The man did not have a lamp, and his hands were out of sight under the folds of a rain-slicked coat. The light of Amaury's lamp snagged on the man's eyes as he looked across the burnt-out space inside the door. They passed over Cado.

'You were drinking with that wanderer who came in from the road,' the sergeant said, and stepped through the door. Amaury moved out of the way. Another woman stepped in after the sergeant. Cado could see the armour under her cloak. She had a mace held loose in one hand. 'Some at the Candlelight say you and he left at the same time.'

'He went his way. I went mine,' said Amaury.

The sergeant looked at her directly.

'That so?' He turned away before she replied. 'And you were passing here and saw a light.'

'I did.'

'And you thought what? That it was something dangerous? Suspicious? Something worth diverting you from the way back to sleep after a few cups?' The sergeant bent down, stirring the damp ashes with a thick finger. The black chest was just an arm's reach from him, amongst the charred rafters. Only the darkness hid it. All he needed to do was look at it directly to see it.

'I thought it was odd,' said Amaury.

'What did the stranger have to say?' asked the sergeant.

'Not much. Didn't like to talk. Tried to pay with a Lethis charm-token.'

'That right? He is the type that we don't need. Dangerous and not what he says he is.' The sergeant began to straighten. 'Best you didn't spend that long with him. There's trouble enough without you making it worse.'

He was about to turn when he stopped. He was looking down at the tangle of burnt beams. Cado shifted the grip on his knives. The sergeant bent down again, and Cado heard the hinge of the chest open. 'A light, you said?' He was looking at what was in the box. Amaury had gone still. The sergeant rose, fast for a man of his size, a heavy sword in his hand. His mouth was opening.

A crossbow bolt punched into his throat. Blood gushed out.

The sergeant staggered. Amaury turned towards the door, as a second bolt whistled through the dark and hit the woman in the doorway. Amaury jerked back, and not an instant too soon as a third bolt came through the door and snapped against the wall. The lamp fell from her hand. Cado stayed still, wrapped in darkness. Amaury's head came up, as she shifted across the floor. The woman by the door had sprawled forwards. The mace she had been holding had fallen from her grip as she fell. Amaury scooped it up, still low.

'Cado,' she hissed.

Cado did not move. He could hear steps coming close, cautious. He heard a crossbow, still strung, set down on the ground, and a blade slide free from a sheath. A figure stepped in through the door. They wore the same mail and leather as the dead sergeant and guard. The hood of their cloak was high, rain sliding down beside the caul of shadow. He could see the blade, a long spike of steel, held loose in their hand. They paused, eyes moving across the dark, finding the lamp on the floor. The candle had pitched against the glass, but the flame was still burning. The figure took another step into the room.

Amaury came up from her crouch as she swung the mace. The blow was fast, practised. It hit the cloaked figure in the chest. Cado heard bones break from across the room. The figure staggered backwards, hit the door frame and half fell. Amaury brought the mace around again, whipping it into the figure as they toppled. Except they weren't there. They were standing, uncoiling, night and light shearing around them like a tattered flag in a gale. The figure's body grew and stretched. Where the shadow of their face had been, a bronze mask grinned. The knife in their hand had changed too. It rippled now, like a tongue of flame. Amaury was in mid-swing. The rippled blade stabbed forwards, flickered across the gap faster than she could recoil from it.

Cado hit the figure from the side. He stabbed with both daggers as he struck, up under the ribs. That should have been enough – more than enough – to throw the figure's soul into the winds of death. But it wasn't. They hit the door frame. The burnt wood splintered. Cado ripped one of his knives free of the figure's ribs. The man was fast: faster than the disciple in the road had been, fast enough to reverse the knife and stab down at Cado's neck. Cado caught the knife hand and twisted. Bones broke from wrist to shoulder. The figure hissed, and the sound of their breath was the rattle of scales over dry sand. There was blood falling from them. Cado slammed his hand into the mask. The bronze buckled. The figure arched back, then snapped forwards. The headbutt caught Cado on the shoulder as he moved. It was powerful enough to stagger him a step.

The iron head of a mace whistled past Cado and slammed into the mask. The bronze mashed into the flesh and bone beneath. The figure fell back, limbs and body suddenly limp. Cado felt a rustle like bird wings rushing past him. Flames burst from the body as it hit the ground. Tongues of blue and orange blazed from under the skin and clothing. The body collapsed in on itself as the fire reached outwards. The charred timbers were kindling.

Amaury was looking at the inferno that the body had become. Cado reached for her. Her head snapped up.

'We don't want to be here,' she shouted, and was already moving for the door.

The rain was a deluge on the street outside, but the fire grew as they moved away from it. After a hundred paces of running, Cado slowed and began to walk, looking back like someone who had somewhere to be but nothing to flee. Amaury followed his lead without a pause. Foolish in a lot of things she might be but not in this. Soon there were other people coming from doors, other people running, shouts and the clank of warning gongs as the fire reached for other buildings. They did not stop until they were high in the city and the fire was a smudge of light in the distance.

CHAPTER SIX

'Do you know a tower with a blue-and-red painted door?' asked Cado.

They had returned to the Candlelight drinking house. Amaury had said she needed to gather her nerves. That meant two drinks back-to-back with barely a breath in between. Cado nursed a cup for appearances, but there were few left in the barrel rooms now, and those were in no condition to notice anything.

She shook her head as she finished her drink.

'Every other building here is a tower, standing or falling. Not many paint their doors, though. It's not the way they do things.'

Cado nodded, thinking.

'What do they want?' asked Amaury. He looked at her. 'The masked ones. The Old Enemy – what do they want?'

'To enslave the living and the dead. To see everything that is not theirs burn, and to laugh at the suffering they create.'

'I meant here. You must have an idea of what they are doing here. Light of Azyr, but they killed the gate sergeant-at-arms and are inside the militia. All of the killing and the enslaving and the burning, they must have a specific aim for that in mind.'

Cado did not answer. He had not considered that point. Find the tower and the door. Hunt down the disciples he could. Find the thread that he could follow to the Burning Hand. The specifics of what was happening in this city did not figure in his thinking. Or they had not, but Amaury was right; they were here for a reason. If he understood that purpose, he could find them.

'The sergeant, he did not come looking for you, or me. He was looking for what might be happening in that ruin. He knew about the mask. He came to see who had come back for it,' he said.

'The… other one, they were going to kill him there and anyone who was there too.'

'There is a war going on,' said Cado. 'Out of sight. The Old Enemy is here but some know that and are hunting them.'

'Cometsworn?'

Cado almost laughed. It seemed that no idea could persist in the Realm of Death without acquiring a name. *Cometsworn*, the name of any group taking it on themselves to find the followers of Chaos amongst them, real or imagined. Witch hunters were sanctioned by the Order of Azyr, cloaking their activities in the blessing of their god. Cometsworn were the wild breed of the same idea – hunters and killers of what they saw as evil without the sanction of a higher power. That did not stop witch hunters using their feral cousins to reinforce their efforts.

'Something like that,' he said. He was turning the possibilities over in his mind. There was a chance here, just a chance, that he could prise something out of this. 'We need to find them.'

He turned his gaze on Amaury. She shook her head. Whatever partially thought-out idea had brought her to him, it was fading now.

'No. We were there when two soldiers of the city died. We…

you killed one of the others. You have authority, use it. Walk up to the worthies and take charge. Go through the city like a scythe, but without that we are two killers with blood on our hands.'

Part of him wanted to tell her the truth then. Instead, he shook his head.

'Truth is rarely seen in the light,' he said. 'It scuttles into the shadows, so that is where I work.'

She began to shake her head.

You should let her go on her way, said a voice at the back of his head that sounded like Solia. *You are letting her believe a lie. This could end in worse than death for her.*

'There will be someone in the militia,' he said, 'someone who knows. Find them, find what they know.'

She started to shake her head again.

'You want to leave here?' said Cado, and the words were edged with a subtle force that leaked from the void in his soul. 'You want to escape this trap? This is the price, and the price you agreed to.'

She paused. In his mind he saw a blurred flash of crimson as a tall figure bent down to him.

'I will show you.' A finger touched his chin and tilted it up. *'A single drop of truth... All the vengeance eternity can give...'*

'There is someone,' said Amaury. 'They were close with the sergeant. Same type, old friends, and close with the city seneschal, but... I don't know. They might be nothing to do with any Cometsworn. They might know nothing.'

'The only way to find truth is to hear it spoken.'

'And how do we do that?'

'We ask,' said Cado.

The man left the parapet as the dawn light was diluting the black of the sky to grey. A flock of black-and-green-feathered birds was wheeling between the rock stacks. Their calls blended with the dull sound of the hour bells. This was the southern length of the lower wall. The blocks of stone hitched over a spur of crags, and most of it looked new. Wooden beams tied together bits of statue and irregular blocks. Large-lever crossbows sat on stands along the parapet. Poles topped with bird skulls, wing feathers and iron comets rose into the air every ten paces as a ghost fence. Cado wondered how well they would hold against the Nighthaunt. It was a question that had been plucking at his thoughts since he had seen the city. It was defended, yes, but it was large, and the dead should have been drawn to it like insects to a candle. Yet it stood, and from what Amaury said there had been few significant attacks by spectres. When they came, they had not come in a mass, but as individuals. Something was keeping them back for now, and Cado doubted that it was the charms atop the wall.

He watched the man touch one of the iron poles before he took the steps down from the parapet. Another militiaman gave a rough salute as they passed. The man did not seem to notice. He was putting a burning taper to the bowl of a pipe and puffing smoke into the dawn fog. He looked worn and tough. He was called Agen apparently, one of the first soldiers that had come with the expedition that had resettled the city.

The man took a deep pull from the pipe and set off up one of the alleys that led from the wall. Most of the buildings here had collapsed a long time ago. A few still stood, but most of those were empty apart from the birds. They perched in sullen clumps on top of broken walls. Occasionally a flock would take to the air, wheel through the mist, and then return. Cado watched from a door arch two storeys above the streets. His cloak blended well enough with the grey of the morning, but he had other means to make sure that eyes slid off him if they looked his way. The man Agen climbed up through the bones of the buildings, breathing smoke, eyes on the street. Once he was past, Cado began to follow him, sliding from empty window to broken door. Once, Agen stopped and looked around, and Cado went still, wondering if he had seen him. The man tapped the ash out of his pipe on a wall, refilled and lit it, and kept walking.

Cado did not know if the man was heading for a dawn drink or bed. Amaury had not known where he lived, only what division of the wall and militia he looked after. He was a loner, Cado decided, as he watched him continue to climb. One of those souls on the outside looking in, even when in a crowd. Few friends, just people he saw or talked to. There were a lot of living souls like that in the underworlds now, colder than the grave-born spirits. He let himself wonder where the man had come from. Perhaps one of the great free cities of this realm or of the other realms beyond the sky. Had he looked up at the face of his mother or father and thought that he would be a soldier in some forgotten city? Had he stepped out of a gate long ago, bright-faced and filled with the certainty that he was going to play his part in something greater than himself? Had he thought he might come back one day to hearth and home and familiar smiles? All hopes and dreams long gone. The ghost of that self just lines left on a hard face by the retreating tide of time.

Cado held to the man's shadow until he reached a squat building a third of the way up the city. It had been larger once, but the settlers had repaired just a part, leaving the rest in rubble. The street that it sat on jutted out from the face of the rock spire. There was one other inhabited building in sight. The rest were empty shells. Scaffold joists and buckets of hardened mortar sat around some, as though masons had left for the night and never come back. It suited the man. A place on the edge of things, with only the cries of the birds to betray that anything lived.

Agen unlocked a door of pitch-brushed planks. He paused on the threshold to look around, eyes moving across stones, mist and sky. Cado wondered if the man had sensed something, or if this was habit. After a moment, he went in and closed the door. Smoke began to breathe from the chimney a few moments later. Cado watched the street, as much with his taste and hearing as his eyes. He heard Amaury before he saw her and moved through the grey light until he stepped out beside her. She flinched, then caught herself. She was wearing an oilskin cloak and hood over leather jerkin and trews. There was nothing to mark her as part of the militia. Unless, of course, someone saw and knew her face. In a city of thousands, that was still possible.

'I'll watch the street,' she said. 'If anyone comes, I'll delay them. If I can't, well… be listening for a racket by way of warning.'

Cado nodded and began to step out. He heard her draw breath to say something. To ask again what he was going to do. He had told her that he was going to find out if this man Agen was a Cometsworn, and what he knew. She had asked how, but he had only said that he would not harm him. That, for the greatest part, was true. Amaury's spark of trust and hope was flickering though, he could tell. Despite the fight in the burnt ruins, the grey light of day had found her frowning. He could read the doubt in the slight hesitation of her movements. She was beginning to wonder if she had been foolish. She was beginning to wonder if he was someone to follow or to run from.

He looked back at her.

'Keep a clear eye,' he said. She nodded.

He approached the man's house from the side. The ruins of the rest of the street gave a tangle of stone and shadows to move through. The fog had thickened too, and he did not need to call on any sorcery to dissolve into a silent blur. He reached the house and worked his way across the roof and down into the narrow space behind. There he found a small door, barely wide enough for a grown mortal to pass through without crouching. Its planks were thick. Iron bands bound them together and there was no sign of a lock or keyhole. It was what he had thought and hoped he would find: an escape door. A man like Agen did not believe in the strength of walls, small or great. There always needed to be a way out. Cado pressed his hand against the planks. He could feel something push back against his presence – charms nailed to the inside of the door to keep any spirit that got past the city walls from entering. At least any spirit that was not strong enough that walls and doors would not matter. There was a bar too, dropped across the door and held by brackets at either end. Cado could hear it rock in place ever so slightly as he pressed the wood.

He inhaled and pulled the taste of the mist down into the blackness inside his soul. The charms nailed to the door were strong but directed at one thing: keeping something unwanted from passing through. They did nothing to stop someone opening it. Cado breathed out and the breath billowed black from between his lips. The cloud flowed across the planks of the door, found the cracks, and poured in. Cado's fingers flexed. He could feel the iron of the locking bar, as though it were resting in his hand. Slowly, he began to lift. Inside the door, the bar shifted and then rose, slow and silent. Cado felt his teeth clench with effort. There were some of his kind that could have dissolved themselves into mist and flowed through the cracks in the stones and wood. Others could have dissolved the iron to rust and dust. He was not one of them. Sorcery was not the chief gift of his blood, and the greater powers he had mastered came with a price.

As the bar came loose, he pushed the door and reached into the gap fast enough to catch the bar before it hit the floor. He set it down. There was light. The dim glow of a fire in a hearth seeping round the corner of a passage. He slid inside. He could hear the beat of the man's heart as he moved towards the light. He pulled the gloom of the corridor with him as he stepped around the corner. Agen had shed his armour and was bending over a pot hanging in a wide fireplace. Strips of parchment scrawled with images of comets and hammers hung from nails that dotted the ceiling. Bits of mismatched furniture punctuated the space of a room that was too big for one life to fill. It might have been a kitchen for a larger house that had fallen around it. A fur-covered cot sat close to the fire, a table and one wooden chair beside it. Unlit candles dotted the surfaces. It reminded Cado of the Candlelight inn. There was a tinge of incense mingling with the smell of sweat, woodsmoke and living flesh. It reeked of loneliness and bitter faith.

Cado stepped from the passage. The shadows coiled back from him.

'Guard Sergeant Agen,' said Cado. 'I have questions for you.'

The man did not move from where he bent over the fireplace, his back to the room. Cado heard the glop of a ladle stirring what was in the pot.

'I thought there was something following me all the way up from the wall,' said the man. 'Didn't see you, though. You must be good, or something else.'

He turned then, fast. The pistol came up. Its barrel mouth was a cruel circle. The striker poised above the flash pan. Cado sprang forwards and twisted. The man pulled the trigger. The striker snapped down... and bit into Cado's fingers. He clenched the pistol. For an instant he saw shock bloom in the man's eyes. Then he wrenched the pistol free. His other hand gripped the man's throat and lifted him off the ground. He closed his grip on the pistol. The wooden frame and steel barrel broke. He dropped it. Black powder spilled out. A heavy silver ball rolled from the barrel. Cado saw the silver shot and the sigils cut into it in the same moment that the man pulled a knife and stabbed it at his chest. It was wooden, fire-hardened and carved with the same sigils as the silver shot. It could hurt him, Cado realised. It was made to hurt him. He caught the stabbing arm before the blow landed. The man was purple-faced now, neck tense against Cado's grip.

'Witch hunter,' Cado hissed, and threw Agen back against the fireplace with enough force that his body went slack, and his eyes fogged over.

CHAPTER SEVEN

The Order of Azyr. Breakers of the darkness, and bearers of light. Men and women of grim resolve who pursued the foes of Order that nested in the mortal throng. Their agents moved amongst the reconquered lands like a shadow of Sigmar's supposed light. They judged, killed and burnt with impunity. To some they were heroes. To most they were figures of fear.

Cado brought the man to with a touch to his forehead. He jerked upright. The bonds holding him to the chair bit into his arms and legs. He went still, stopped struggling. His eyes focused on Cado, hard knife holes in green irises. Cado felt his mouth twitch despite himself. It was a while since he had looked into the eyes of a fanatic like this.

'You are thinking of how to kill me,' said Cado. 'Beyond that, you are weighing the chances of calling for help. Both are equally unlikely to succeed.'

The man called Agen looked back at him and said nothing. He would not speak, Cado knew. Not willingly at least. This was a soul who saw suffering as a sacrament: whether his own or someone else's did not matter.

'You are an agent of the Order of Azyr, and though it appears otherwise, that puts us into an alignment of purpose.' The man tilted his head to the side. His eyes were sharp points of hate. 'You have found an enemy inside this city. You have recruited others to help you root out that enemy. I am here because I will know everything you know. Then I will deal with the matter, and then I shall leave. You shall live. These people shall live, but I will have what I seek.'

Agen's face twitched, as though he wanted to spit something at Cado, but he said nothing.

'I want you to know and understand this. I want you to consider that this is a kindness to the people and order you serve.' Still the hard expression of hate in the man's eyes. 'Now we begin. I cannot say that there shall be no pain, but pain is not the point. A lesson your order refuses to learn.'

Cado stepped forward and raised his left hand to his mouth. His teeth sharpened. He bit down on the meat of his palm. Blood welled from the wound. It started to clot to ash at the edges. He gripped Agen's face with his right hand and forced his face up. The man fought, twisting in his chair. Cado squeezed the mouth open. The witch hunter was breathing hard now, heart beating fast as he tried to put all his strength into turning his head away, to keeping his mouth shut. Cado kept squeezing. The jaw popped. The mouth opened for an instant. Cado clenched his left fist. Blood fell into Agen's mouth. He tried to spit then, but it was already too late. The pupils went wide in the man's green eyes. Cado heard the beat of his heart stutter. The darkness would be flowing into him now.

The blood of the Soulblighted could do many things. It could give back strength, it could heal, it could bind a weak soul to a grave-lord, and much more things besides. What a Soulblight could do with their blood depended on their lineage, skill and knowledge. Cado understood some of these powers but used them rarely. There was too much risk, too much to lose. In this case he needed insight, and the kind that he would not get by threats or pain.

Agen juddered, convulsing, and then went still, eyes closed. Cado let the man's head go and waited. He listened. The man's heartbeat was low and steady. His eyelids opened. The pupils were starbursts of red in green. Cado could feel the hate fuming off the man like heat from a fire now. At the edge of his thoughts, he saw flashes of images: the street of a city under a pall of red-black cloud; a child trying to shake awake a figure lying face down, oblivious to the wound leaking crimson onto the cobbles; people in armour passing, the screams of slaughter the only sound.

Cado let the images and the hate wash over him. It was a good sign. The man's hate made the bond formed by the shared blood strong. It would not last, though. Soon the curse would fade from his veins. He saw Agen flex against his bonds. The ropes creaked but held. Cado had used three times as much as was needed to hold even a strong mortal. For these moments, this man had a portion of Cado's own strength.

Cado leant down, fangs growing. The false beat of his heart matched the rhythm in the man's chest. He stilled his thoughts, emptied his mind, and bit.

A flood of red.

Then the instinct to feed, to rip and drain.

He yanked the instinct down, felt it roar in anger.

Then came the hate and fear, and all the jumbled flotsam of a mortal mind. He felt the weariness that was growing in the man with every day he woke to. He felt the regrets, small deeds made sharp by loss: the face of a friend never wished farewell, now gone;

a chance to say yes to what might have been happiness; a road begun under a bright sky, never looked back on.

He saw what the man had seen and done. His name *was* Agen. That was no mask or cloak. His father had given him that name, and now it was one of the few things he carried of a childhood that had been brief and ended with horror and death. He saw the reason why he had joined the order: the naive hope of saving others from what had happened to him. He was there when the master-at-arms broke two of the bones in his right arm and told him that the order would never take anyone so weak.

Cado looked into the eyes of a young mortal as Agen pulled them from the ruins of a spell-broken house. He felt his lips move as the young witch hunter – so young, too young – told them it would be all right, that they were safe. The pain exploded in his side as the young mortal breathed a curse to the Dark Gods and rammed a knife into Agen's side. And then he was there, after seasons of fire and sorrow, coming to a city built around a spire of rock and looking up at the first settlers rebuilding the old ruins and thinking that if the darkness was not here yet, it would be soon.

Cado stood back. His jaw was wet. The bloody wound in the man's neck was already closing. They looked at each other. Red eye to red eye. They were almost one now. The blood of each beat in the other's veins. The ghosts of thoughts and sensations hung between them.

'Tell me what is happening here,' said Cado.

Agen looked up. Cado saw an impression of what the man was seeing ghost over his own sight. His eyes were red coals in a gaunt face. Burning. Inhuman. Cado felt the man's will rise to deny the command.

'Tell me what is happening here,' he repeated, with a surge of his own will. Agen twitched, and such was the force of the command that his lips mouthed in time with the last words.

'…happening here.'

Cado nodded, and then, one word at a time, the man began to talk. He did it simply, moving through all that Cado wished to know as though he wanted nothing more than to speak. In a sense, he did. Cado's will and blood had intertwined, and Cado's will was strong enough that it was now Agen's will too. So he talked.

'There is a rot here,' he said. He did not sound like a soldier, but like an old priest, erudite but weary. 'A rot and an enigma. I am the only one of the order in the city. I came alone, amongst a second wave of settlers that arrived after the first expedition claimed the ruins and gave it a name. Hubris, to take a city and give it a name before you know you can hold it. I came because no one had expected them to find a city here. A few settlements out in this land of carrion birds, that's what was expected. There was nothing in the celestial records, nothing that had stirred the eyes of heaven. The geomantic lines converge here from across this underworld, but there was supposed to be nothing at that point. If the powers had known, then there would have been more than the hopeful and the desperate in the vanguard. Once they were here there was no help to spare, and against all odds somehow the city held. Nothing holds forever without knives and swords and blood, though. So I came here. Was sent here to watch. No army of holy might. Just me. Unnamed and unknown. And they were right to send me. Darkness and the weakness to see it flourish, it's all here.'

He paused, and Cado felt the stirring of memories. Disappearances, chance deaths, a body found pinned to a dead tree with crow's wings nailed to the skull.

'Tell me,' said Cado, nudging the man's focus back with a tug of will.

'I am alone, and so there is a method that has to be followed. You must find your own help. You must prepare for anything, and you must keep it all out of sight. Fear, that is the second enemy. A people without fear are weak, but if they fear too much then they become both dangerous *and* weak. They start to destroy the strength they need to fight. The enemy can use that, can hide in it, can even use it to turn people. The third enemy is trust. Trust is a chain that can pull you down into betrayal.' Agen paused. His eyes flickered with amusement, and his lip curled. 'You know that truth too.' Cado had to shut down the memory billowing up in his own thoughts: red fire, and the screams of the living as daemons dived from the sky. 'That's the problem,' continued Agen. 'In the end, the only person you can really trust is yourself. Isn't it?

'I found one of them. Almost killed me.' He touched a scar across his jaw. 'They were a nothing, a grain shifter in the storehouses. Small, weak, the type that talked too much and about nothing that mattered. It was just after I had found a… a shrine. A tortured bird pinned to the rock wall behind a ruined house. They were nearby. I saw them. They were watching, so I followed them, asked a question.' Agen paused. 'They had a mask. A mask under their skin. They were not scrawny either. Altered, powerful, stupid tough. That's another thing people don't understand – the servants of darkness can be foolish and naïve and as incompetent as anyone. If they had watched from further away, if they had played dumb when I asked them what they had been doing, I would have known nothing. Instead, they showed their face and ended with a knife in the guts. I burnt the body. No one noticed the smoke or the smell. People don't like to notice what might make their world break. They were not alone, though. There are others. They are here.'

'You did not tell the city's rulers,' said Cado. The man chuckled as if Cado had made a dry joke over a cup of ale.

'You cannot trust anyone or anything under the stars. That's another thing we both know. Just because someone doesn't wear a mask doesn't mean they are not hiding beneath one.'

'So you recruited a band of hunters to help you fight a hidden war.'

'Hunters...' Another chuckle. Cado felt a heady wave of blurred sensation. The man swayed in the chair as though drunk. The blood bond was making him giddy. His eyes were clear though. 'Hunters... agents of the holy comet and hammer, warriors against the dark...' The laughter drained from his mouth. 'Old soldiers, and boys barely old enough to hold a sword. When you haven't got anyone you can trust, then you use whomever you can. You...' He shook his head, blinked. Cado could feel the man's will pushing against the bond. He was stronger than he seemed. Cado held his own mind firm. The man blinked and continued, his voice touched with a melancholy that bled into Cado. 'You can't be alone. You can't fight alone. Not for long. Not for ever. That's another lie – the lone warrior, strong, needing nothing and no one. These realms make lies like that as swords to cut you and clubs to break you.' He shrugged. 'I found a few people, told them something, showed them other things. Good people, even when they end up with their throats cut.'

The man shivered and became silent. The beat of his heart was getting faster as though it were trying to outrun the matched beat of Cado's pulse. The spell was breaking. Cado wanted to ask more, but once the bond broke, he would not be able to create it again for a long while. He needed to ask the last and biggest questions now.

'What are the servants of the Crow God doing in this city?'

Agen nodded, blinked slowly, and answered.

'There is something in the rock, under the city. I have found places where they have been tunnelling or where walls built into the cliff have been broken through.'

'What is inside?'

'I don't know, but I can guess.' Agen paused, blinked again. The red was fading from his eyes. He shook himself. Cado felt the blood bond between them weakening. He snapped his will taut, and the man's head came up as though yanked by a hand. 'I think that's where they are and where the rot came from. Down there in the dark at the heart of this city is something that the Old Enemy left. They are hiding it, worshipping it – working on it, perhaps. Behind us and under our feet, this city is not ours, it's theirs.'

Cado nodded. He did not have much time now and he needed to make sure that this man did not come after him. 'Do you know a tower with a blue-and-red-painted door?'

'No,' said Agen, shaking his head. 'No.'

Cado's nose flared. His lips pinched tight, but there was nothing he could do. The witch hunter had given him all the answers time allowed.

Cado reached out towards the man's eyes.

A gong sounded. The metallic note rose and reached through the walls. Then another crash and another, and more gongs were ringing, the sound rising from the lower walls. Cado looked around as a fist beat on the door.

'Cado!' It was Amaury's voice. 'Cado!'

He hissed, went to the door and pulled back the bolts. Amaury looked at him, mouth opening to speak, and then looked past him at Agen bound in the chair. The sound of the gongs was louder, echoing through the mist.

'What has happened?' asked Cado.

Amaury looked up at him. He could see the war of questions behind her expression.

'Those are the wall gongs,' she said. 'An enemy is at the gates.'

CHAPTER EIGHT

The lone horseman stood in the mist as the gongs continued to sound. The people on the streets were hurrying back in behind their doors. Strings of bird bones clacked against sealed shutters. The citizen guard were moving down the slope to the walls as Cado and Amaury moved through them. Most of the militia were already on the walls. Torches had been lit and every fourth soldier held a burning brand. There were few of them, Cado noticed. Spread across the circuit of the wall, they were a thin line. That was what the citizenry with their odd coverings of armour and mismatched weapons were for: to fill the wall with warm bodies.

No one stopped Cado as he climbed to the parapet. Everyone's eyes were looking beyond the wall, and with his armour and weaponry he looked like someone who needed to be there. Amaury moved away, going to join her militia comrades or just to distance herself from him. He could tell that she had been disturbed by seeing Agen tied to the chair. More disturbed by the way that the man's head lolled, his eyes rolling in his skull and the fact there was no mark of harm on him. Cado had told her to go out, and when the door had closed, he had reached out and touched the man's eyes. A jolt of will, a breath of syllables and the man's mind was his own. That is, except for the time since Cado had begun to follow him. That went, burned away and running out of his mouth as his head slumped on his chest and a bead of black blood slid from his lips. He would come around and keep nothing of what had happened. Except perhaps a dream that he would wake from when the skull moon was full, but never be able to remember.

Cado saw the lone horseman as he reached the top of the wall. He slowed, eyes straining to pick out the curve of the helm, and shield, and the marks etched into the standard it held. He knew what it was, and what it meant.

'What's it doing?' hissed someone close by.

'Is it a...?'

'Shut up...'

'It's not moving, why isn't it moving?'

It's waiting, Cado wanted to say, but held quiet. Head bowed, mount and body so still that only the discs hanging from the standard shifted in the wind, clicking together. He could feel the fear growing around him. Most of these mortals could not have named what they were looking at. But they knew. In their bones, they knew.

Slowly the horseman raised its head. Polished finger bones reached up in a crest from the crown of its helm. Its face could have been a mask, or a sculpture taken from the side of a tomb...

As am I, so shall ye be. As you are, so once was I...

It raised the banner higher. Dank fabric stirred. The mount beneath it was the image of a horse drawn in stolen bones. The mist gathered in the cave of ribs that was its belly.

'I come for what is due,' said the rider, and its voice seemed to form from the sigh of air. The gongs had quieted. The city listened. 'I come to give you safety. I come to count you amongst the eternal empire that shall never end and shall embrace all. Who shall answer for your debts?'

'We owe you nothing.' The voice came from the section of wall closest to the rider. Cado looked to see who it was. A figure in red-and-ivory robes, head heavy with a headdress that arced like a golden comet above her crown. Guards in plate armour stood beside her. Others on the wall were looking at her. 'This city is free and under the protection of Sigmar, Lord of Heavens, and breaker of tyrants. We will give you nothing. We owe you nothing, and if you come to our walls again, we shall break you and burn you to dust.'

'All that is bone shall be returned once life passes from flesh. So it is marked and so it is. No other claim is truer. You shall bring the bones of the dead from grave and tomb and set them on the spot I speak from. You shall do this by light two rises of the moon from now. The counting of this tithe shall be one hundred and eighteen thousand.'

A murmur ran through the crowd: revulsion, anger and fear, all in hundreds of hissed breaths and muttered oaths.

'We will give you nothing,' said the woman in the robes. 'We owe you nothing. You shall have nothing. Go now and tell your masters that.'

'If the counting is not met then we will claim the tithe from the living. For your payment you shall be protected, for you are the keepers of the harvest and no other shall harm the crop that is yet to ripen. This is the debt and the promise.'

'Shoot it,' said the woman. Along the wall a ballista's arms released with a thump. A bolt the length of a spear hissed through the air. The rider did not move. The bolt struck it on a downward arc. It punched into the rider's chest, passed through and down into its mount with such force that it pinned both to the ground. A ragged roar of defiance went up along the walls. Then the heap of bones on the ground stirred. Rider and mount pulled themselves up to standing, grinding on the shaft of the bolt. The rider gripped the bolt and pulled it free. The crowd on the wall was silent. The rider held the bolt up, pointing it at the walls.

'Two rises of the moon. The tithe shall be given.' Then it threw the bolt into the ground and left it there quivering, as it turned and rode back into the mist.

There was silence after the rider left. Heavy, dense, settling like a fresh layer of fog around the city's spires. Standing on the walls, Cado heard someone cry out, then fall silent. The quiet ached through the grey light.

'Go back to your work and prayers,' came the voice of the woman in red, calling loud. 'We will not submit, and we will not fall. Go back to your prayers and know that Sigmar shall hear you.' None of the mortals on the wall moved for a long moment. Then a few of them began to turn and make for the steps off the parapet. There was no rush, no panic, just a slow draining of people back into the half-broken, half-rebuilt streets. The fear was there in that silence, though, sullen and deep, the beginnings of desperation without hope.

Cado followed them, thinking.

Two days. That was the time he now had. He supposed that the city might pay the Bone-tithe the rider had demanded. But the woman in red had refused. She looked like a member of the Sigmarite cult and a person of authority. That meant that if these mortals were going to pay the tithe, they would have to change who was in charge – which meant bloodshed and mayhem was inevitable. Either the city would be attacked for refusing the tithe or there would be an uprising. He did not doubt that the rider could deliver on its threat to take by force the bones it wanted – he knew its kind and what they were capable of. Two days. Two cycles of light and dark to find the Old Enemy, pick up the trail of the Burning Hand and be gone. It was not much time, and its grains were falling into the past with every step and heartbeat.

'What was that?' Amaury's voice pulled his eyes around. She was standing under the low eve of a house. She had been waiting for him. He had not expected that. Somehow, he had thought she would dissolve back into the city. She had become a risk more than an aid, but for now it was better to keep her close. Better that than give her space to think and unravel the lies she had decided to believe.

'They are the Bonereapers,' he said, as she fell into step beside him. 'The Great Necromancer–'

Amaury hissed and touched a bird skull around her neck. Even alluding to the Lord of Undeath was a curse to many. Call him and he shall hear and come with chains for your soul, that was what parents told children, and many believed it themselves. The truth, Cado knew, was worse by far. The Great Necromancer did not need you to speak his name for him to covet your soul. He would come for you anyway.

'He created them to be his legions. To conquer all the underworlds of Death. They are called the Ossiarchs because they are shaped from bone and filled with souls that want nothing but to create an empire of the dead.'

'It asked for bones…'

'Everything they make is shaped from them. Soldiers, fortresses and the weapons they carry to conquer the living. Without bone they cannot grow the silent empire.'

'Why not attack and kill everyone in the city and take what they want from corpses?'

'Because they need the living. The living grow the bones that the empire feeds on. They want their tithe, and they want cities to rise and prosper, safe and bountiful. In exchange they offer protection.'

'Like a farmer who protects his herd.'

Cado nodded. 'And just like a herd, the farmer has only one reason to protect his cattle – so that he can harvest them.'

'And there are places that agree to that?'

'Many. Even in cities like Lethis there are people who smuggle bones out to the Ossiarchs, in the hope of buying clemency.' Cado paused. He thought of the walls he had seen fall around defiant settlements, and the lines of living mortals lined up, shivering with fear while the Ossiarchs made their calculations, waiting to see how many would need to be culled to pay their bone debt. 'In the end all they buy is a little more time before the debt comes due.'

'They won't agree to it. Cometarian Damascene already refused.'

Cado was silent for a moment, strides carrying him up the city.

'You should go back to the wall militia,' he said.

'We had an agreement.'

He stopped and looked at her. He could see the sneer growing on her face to hide the fear. She had wanted to leave and get back something that this life lacked. Now she just wanted to be gone before the scythe fell.

'Our agreement stands,' he said. He turned and walked on up the cobbles. 'I will find you when the time comes.' Another promise, another risk taken.

'I think I know where the painted door is.' He stopped, looked back at her. There was a defiant look on her face. 'I think I do remember seeing one – blue and red, just like you are looking for.'

'Where?' he said.

'Not totally sure, but I might be able to figure it out from the general area. But that means I come with you.'

He considered. Rain had begun to fall more heavily, sweeping from the iron sky to run from the roofs and cobbles. Time was slipping away and leaving space only for the types of decision that had unseen cost.

'All right,' he said, and nodded.

'What did Agen tell you?' Amaury asked. Cado shook his head, not returning the gaze she fixed on him.

'Enough,' he said.

Three hours had passed since they had left the walls. They had climbed up and around the flank of the city spire to the face that turned towards the northern gates. Towers, both standing and ruined, rose from where their foundations rooted into the rock. Looking out, he could occasionally see the smaller spires of stone that stood close to the city. They slid in and out of sight, as though the cloud and rain were a grey sea, and they were the backs of leviathans breaking the surface of the waves.

'It's close to here, I think,' said Amaury as they turned up a road cut into an overhang. She looked around. A man in the uniform of the militia sat on a barrel under the eave of a roof twenty paces away. He had his hood up and looked like he was trying to make the best of the shelter. Amaury went over to him, and Cado heard her call a greeting. The man waved a hand up the flank of the spire.

Cado had half turned away, looking up a wider street. There were people on the street, bedraggled under the rain. He saw the girl then. The girl from the caravan whom he had last seen under the light of the skull moon as the wolves closed in. She was with a cluster of adults, arguing with a man outside a slumped stone-and-wood building. A rotten sign of a white feather hung above the door. She turned just as he looked at her and froze. Their gazes locked. He gave a small nod, then continued up the road. She watched him pass, then scampered back to the adults.

He glanced back as he turned the corner. One of the women was frowning at the girl as she tugged her sleeve.

Cado turned away quickly. He looked around for Amaury.

She was not there. The militiaman was back to his post, head bowed. Needles ran up his spine. He hurried over to where Amaury had been. He could hear voices from the adults. Every sense and fibre of his being was screaming to run, to get out of sight. Whether by betrayal or discovery or both, he could feel that he was about to become hunted. He started up the road that the militiaman had waved at to Amaury. He turned the corner and started to move faster, calling.

'Amaury?' The chuckle of rainwater running down the gutters was the only answer. He kept moving, faster, mind turning over, senses reaching.

And saw the painted door.

Stones had fallen from the tower's top, and its walls bulged towards the base like a fat man slumping in his seat. The blue and red on the door was barely visible, the paint flaking from thick planks.

He froze. The sounds of human life answered: the cry of a child, the crackle of a fire, and the clang of a hammer striking an anvil. The road was empty for a second. The outer turn dropped away to nothing. The cobblestones ran right the way to a ragged edge where there had been a building that had slumped down the side of the slope. Opposite stood a long building with wide doors. The hinges were new, and a wide chimney breathed smoke and sparks into the rain-flecked air. It was a forge, and a working one too.

He turned back to the door. It looked as though it had not opened in a long while, but looks could lie. He ran his hand down the peeling paint, breathing in as he did. He could taste the sugar-spice tang of magic at once. He would need to–

'Nobody been in that place for a while,' said a voice behind him. He turned. A man was standing on the other side of the street beside the now open door to the forge. He was broad, a layer of fat over muscle, and had a leather apron tied under his gut. Behind the man, Cado could see the glow of a forge fire under a brick hood. The man smelled of charcoal and iron and sweat. He smiled and wiped a rag over his forehead. 'If you are looking for someone, I don't think you will find them there. I come out here every time before I need to clean the clinker from the fire, and you're the first person I have seen even go up to that door.'

Cado's head twitched. He could hear boots on the cobbles coming up the road, just around the bend. The smith's talking had meant that he had missed it before. Many feet, the rattle of chain mail, weapons and armour.

'It's a nice building, too,' said the man, nodding up at the tower. 'But then lots of them are. Their bones are good, even if time's not been kind to them. Someone could make that one good with only a bit of effort. Wonder what it was before? I would say wizards, but then half the town here is towers and the only wizard is Magister Leragrais. Just goes to show that not everything fits with what you think, I guess.'

Cado began to move up the road. Get out of sight and then get up onto the roofs, that would be the best thing.

'I'm sorry, friend,' said the smith, crossing the road and extending a hand. 'I'm talking and for all you know I could be anyone. I am Valentin. This is my forge. You look like you've just come from the road. Was the person you thought would be here someone who was coming here too?'

The man still had his hand out, now just two steps from Cado. Figures in armour came around the corner in the road. They saw Cado.

'Halt!' rose a shout. 'Stay where you stand!'

A quarrel thumped into the door behind him – a warning shot. There were more, a line of crossbows levelled at him with the rain covers pulled from their strings and quarrels set to their nocks. Figures with spears and shields were moving past them, cutting off the road above. The man called Valentin was looking around, shocked and confused, his hand still half raised as though part of him yet thought that Cado would take it.

A woman in pitch-black plate armour stepped from the ring of levelled spears and crossbows. Her face was lean and gaze hard beneath the brim of her open helm. Bird skulls and feathers hung from her baldric and clicked against her cuirass. She held a long sword in her left hand. Raindrops ran down the blade, gathering briefly in the etched emblem of a twin-tailed comet. Holding on to her right hand was the girl from the forest. One of the adults she had been with hung back behind the troops.

The woman in armour looked down at the girl.

'That's him?' she said, pointing the sword at Cado. The girl nodded. 'Take him,' said the woman. Six soldiers moved forwards. Two had lengths of chain and manacles. The others held tall shields, bracketing him as the two with the manacles closed in. The man, Valentin, was backing away now, back to the doors of his forge. 'Him too,' said the woman in armour, pointing at the smith.

'Wait,' began Valentin. 'I don't know what…'

'You looked like you were in deep conversation with our man over here. He hasn't stopped to talk to anyone else. So I want to know, why you?'

The shields were closing around Cado. He could see the fear in the eyes under the helms, but there were scars on the faces of each one: an empty eye socket, a jagged furrow across a jaw, a crumpled nose. They would not break without a fight. There would need to be blood for him to get free. In the back of his mind he saw the acolyte looking at him with dozens of eyes, laughing.

'A *Soulblighted killer who thinks himself pure because he spares the innocent...*' said the mocking memory.

He held still. The circle of shields closed on him. Hands gripped him. Manacles locked around his wrists and ankles. His sword and daggers were pulled from their sheaths. Valentin was still protesting, saying that he needed to douse the fire in his forge, that his family would not know where he was. Cado saw the girl for a second, still staring at him between the press of soldiers as they led him away.

CHAPTER NINE

They took him to a thick tower at the top of the city. There was no doubt that it was a prison, and a strong one. The air inside was cold and damp. Heavy, iron-bound doors closed every doorway. They took his armour and searched every fold of his clothes. He let them. There was no point fighting; the moment for that to be meaningful had passed. The only question was what they intended to do with him now.

They had not tried to end him when they found him. Neither had they led him to a headsman's block with a waiting executioner and a ready blaze to consume his body once the axe fell. No, either they were uncertain about what he was and what to do with him, or they had an entirely different intent. The only course was to wait and see what path appeared from the future. There was risk in that, but if he chose to escape now, he would have to flee the city. The Burning Hand would vanish, and he would have to begin his hunt again. No, he would stay patient, and see how the bones of fate fell.

The soldiers had led him down through narrow passages. The door of the cell they put him in was a foot thick, the stone solid, and when closed sat flush to the frame. The only light and air came from holes cut in the ceiling, each no wider than a finger. It made no difference to Cado – he needed neither light nor air.

He sat, folded his cloak over himself and began to run the chain of sorrow through his thoughts.

Mother that I failed you. Father that I undid all you preserved. Sister that I did not save you... On it went, a chain of words worn smooth by repetition and time.

He almost killed them when they took his rings. He had not been in the cell more than half a bell strike when the door opened again. A withered aelf in a grey robe shuffled into Cado's cell. She had a ball of obsidian in place of her left eye and twitched nervously with every step. Behind her was the armoured woman who had been in the street. She had her sword in one hand, a lantern in the other. The old aelf looked at the woman, who jerked her head impatiently.

'Now, Molufel,' she said.

The aelf called Molufel bobbed her head and edged closer to Cado. She closed her good eye and cocked her head from side to side as she moved the gaze of the obsidian eye across him. Her breath hissed from her mouth in an uneven rhythm. Gold-flecked tears ran from the socket. Cado looked back, unblinking.

'Is there a question you want to ask me?' he said.

The aelf did not respond but raised her hands and ran her fingers through the air around Cado as though feeling the weave of fabric. She took a hurried step back.

'Soulblight,' she hissed to the woman in armour. 'Old, coiled in cold. Seneschal, there are others too, shades that he carries and can command.'

'Carries how?' asked the woman.

The aelf tapped her own fingers.

'Here,' she said.

The woman glanced at the rings on Cado's fingers.

'Give them to me,' she said. He went very still. She moved closer. 'Take them off and give them to me.' The aelf had backed to the door. 'Now.'

She reached for his nearest hand.

Mother that I failed you. Father that I undid all you preserved. Sister that I did not save you...

He was on his feet. Behind her, locking her sword arm. His eyes red. His mouth wide around razor teeth...

He felt the tip of the dagger against his ribs. No matter. A blade point through an unbeaten heart would not end him.

'Pyre-steel,' the woman snarled. 'Flecks of emberstone embedded in the blade, Soulblight. This goes into your carcass, and you burn from the inside.' Cado froze. He could feel the point of the dagger next to his hollow heart. 'That's right. You can rip my throat out, but you will burn. Even if you can come back from that, my troops will grind what's left to dust.'

Cado felt the kill instinct bite into his thoughts. Red, warm and sharp.

No, he willed. Control seeped through him, slowly. He stepped back. The woman held out her hand.

'The rings, all of them,' she said. 'Best chance you have of keeping them is if you hand them over now, believe me.'

He felt his teeth grind against each other, point against point.

He handed her the rings. A flare of pain ran up his arm as each one came free. The woman threaded them onto a length of cord, which she tied. She held out the cord of rings to the aelf, who had returned to just outside the cell. 'You know what to do with them.

'Now you come with me,' she said to Cado, and motioned to the door. 'There are people who want to talk to you.'

Two people waited for him at the top of the tower. He dragged a long iron-and-silver chain with him. Rune-etched shackles bound his arms and ankles. They ached with old magic. Cado could have broken them or got free, but that would have taken strength and time. Time that would have let the seneschal stick him with her ember knife.

The tower top was a platform rather than a room. Rows of pillars supported an arched roof without walls. Mist filled the view. White droppings carpeted the stone under beams thick with birds' nests. Cado could feel dozens of eyes following him from behind hunched feathers. A stone table sat at the centre of the space. It was new, he could tell, because the stone was different – pale grey seeming almost white against the green-and-violet-flecked granite. Hammers, comets and the face of a lightning-crowned king marked the rim of the table. Half a dozen chairs of crow-black iron ringed it, all but two empty. A woman in ivory-and-red robes sat on one. A heavy hood framed her face. Golden thread stitched flowing script across her robes. A golden-haloed hammer hung around her neck. Cado recognised both script and symbols – they were the signs of the Cult of the Comet and the celestial power of the once-man Sigmar. The occupant of the other seemed lost in heavy folds of purple velvet. Silver crow skulls sat on bone-thin fingers that clutched at each other under the chin of a head which seemed almost a skull with a skim of liver-spotted skin. His eyes were bright violet when they looked up at Cado.

'Ah,' he said, and smiled. He had tarnished silver teeth. 'Our reluctant and unexpected guest.' The armoured woman had moved past Cado and leaned down to whisper to the seated pair. 'Speak up, Vaux, for all rebirth's sake. Our guest can most likely hear you anyway.' He grinned at Cado again. 'Advantages of the curse that blights your blood and soul, eh?'

The armoured woman, Vaux, straightened.

'Molufel confirms it, he is a Soulblight.'

'You actually got Molufel O'the Dust into the cell with him? She must have been shaking like a reed in the wind.'

'He had spirits with him, bound to nine rings.'

'Did he now?' asked the man. The grin had not moved from his mouth.

'Was very keen to hang on to them, too,' said Vaux.

'Ah…'

'Very keen.'

'Where is the man he was meeting?' asked the woman in the red robes.

'Still in the cells. He is a smith. He has a forge on the street where we took the leech. In my opinion, sires, he has nothing to do with whatever this creature came here for.'

'Thank you for your opinion, Vaux,' said the smiling man. 'It is as valued as it is irrelevant for now. Bring the smith here.' Vaux's face remained impassive.

The man in purple and the woman in red and ivory looked at Cado. He stared straight back. A pair of white-and-grey ravens flapped from the mist and took their places on the beams above. The clouds of mist coiled beyond the tower-edge.

Cado heard Valentin before the man reached the platform. He was explaining again that he needed to get back to his forge, that the fires needed dousing, that his family would be wondering where he was, that he didn't know what crime he could have committed. There was a pause when he reached the platform and took in the two figures at the table.

'Oh celestial light of my ancestors…' he breathed. Vaux moved him forward to stand beside Cado. The smith looked up at him, eyes wide, his mouth a sag in search of something to smile about. 'Your worthies, I am sorry… I mean, I think there has been a mistake.'

'That is often the case,' said the man in purple. 'So no talk for now. We will deal with you in a moment, smith.' He looked back to Cado. 'I am called Leragrais. I am magister of Aventhis, and a member of this, ah, somewhat limited council of governance.' He gestured at the woman in red and ivory. 'This is my fellow councillor – her holiness Sister Damascene, of the–'

'Cometarian Missionaries of the Orders of Sigmar,' said Cado.

Leragrais' smile crooked up at the edge. 'Just so.'

Damascene shot a hard look at the old man.

'I will speak for myself,' she said. Her voice was clear, unyielding, like the strike of steel. She looked at Cado. Her eyes were the grey of storm clouds. 'You are a leech, and a predator that has come amongst the flock of this city. Your kind bring only ill and slaughter. You should burn.'

Cado gave a small shrug. 'Yet we talk,' he said.

Her gaze did not waver. 'What does one of the Soulblighted want in our city?'

At the words 'Soulblighted' Valentin gave a yelp and flinched back from Cado, eyes wide.

'I am hunting someone,' said Cado. The truth, he had found – or at least a sliver of it –was often the simplest tool to cut through bonds.

'Alone?'

He thought of Amaury, of the way she had been there on the street and then… not. Had she seen the guards coming and got away? Had something taken her?

He nodded. 'Alone.'

'You are not an emissary from some higher power? A legion of the dead does not follow in your wake?'

'No,' he said. Then added, 'I followed my quarry here, and when I have them, I will go.'

Leragrais snorted. 'Will you now?'

'I have no interest in you or your city.'

'And we are supposed to believe that?'

'You are supposed to believe whatever you please,' said Cado. Leragrais' lips peeled back from his teeth. His eyes were glittering dangerously. Damascene spoke before the magister could reply.

'This quarry,' she asked. 'What is it?'

Again, a piece of the truth would have to suffice here. They had yet to reach the heart of what this pair wanted, and though his patience was wearing thin, that would be the key.

'I am hunting servants of the Dark Gods. I overtook one of them in the forests to the south. They were coming here.'

'There are no servants of the Dark Gods here,' snapped Leragrais. 'This is a free city, its people devout.'

'More of a free town than a city,' said Valentin. Everyone looked at him. He shrank back, raising his hands apologetically. 'At least by how many of us there are.'

'Be quiet,' said Leragrais.

'Of course, your worthiness,' said Valentin.

Leragrais frowned as he looked back to Cado. 'You are either a liar or a fool,' he said.

'I am no liar,' said Cado flatly. 'And I am looking at the only fool here.'

Leragrais began to rise. Green and purple sparks gathered in his eyes. The pressure in the room grew. Motes of dust rose from the floor.

'Calm, sir,' said Damascene. 'We must remember corruption uses our faith in ourselves to hide. We should never think that the followers of the Dark Gods are not closer than we think.'

'True...' muttered Leragrais, lowering himself. 'True.'

'I have proof,' said Cado. 'In my possessions.'

Leragrais nodded at Vaux. 'Bring his things here.'

They waited in silence while Vaux sent two guards to fetch his possessions from wherever they had stored them. They came back and dumped them on the floor. He moved towards them, but Leragrais held up a finger.

'Oh no,' he said, and looked at Vaux. The seneschal began to go through the pile, gloved hands moving with care. After a moment she held up the crystal vials. Two were still full. Brown dregs clung to the bottoms of the rest. Damascene hissed. 'Trophies from your victims or food for the road?' asked Leragrais with a sneer that said he did not need an answer. Cado waited. Vaux reached the travelling sack at last and pulled out the bundle wrapped in leather. She unfolded it, looked down, dropped it, and took a quick step backwards. The dagger clattered as it hit the stone and rocked gently in place. The steel of its blade reflected the light in oily colours: cyan, pink, orange.

'Unclean,' hissed Leragrais. Valentin let out a small yelp.

None of them moved to pick up the dagger, which continued to rock slowly.

'This is certainly a thing of the Dark Gods,' said Leragrais.

'But it proves nothing,' said Damascene, 'besides the fact that you have taken it from one of your victims. The Soulblighted do not discriminate when they feed, after all. No, this proves nothing.' She looked at Cado and he saw the hard gaze of her eyes under her hood. 'I think you came here to turn and slaughter us from within when we refuse the offer of the Bonereapers.'

Cado gave a single dry breath of laughter.

'Something amuses you?' asked Leragrais.

'The idea that I or any of my kind would come into a city at the behest of the Ossiarch Empire. That is a jest that reveals your foolishness, more than anything else.'

Leragrais' eyes glittered. 'The same foolishness that kept us from ordering you burned as soon as you were found. It is a foolish man who saws away the plank that is holding him above the abyss. You appear within a day of a herald coming and demanding our capitulation… There are few coincidences that could strain credulity more.'

'Only to the ignorant,' said Cado. He was increasingly certain that he would not survive this encounter if he wished to hold to the tenets of his code. Even restrained, he could get free of the shackles, make for the edge of the platform and dive from the spire top before Vaux stabbed him. He had survived worse, but then there were his rings and the souls that they held. He had sworn to carry and protect them in death where he had failed to protect them in life. He could perhaps take them back, if they were close, but he would have to kill more than a few of the mortals on the tower top. And that would break his vow. They were fools, and ignorant, and might be his undoing, but they were innocent. He could not judge them otherwise. That was the path he had chosen and would not put aside. 'The Soulblight bloodlines and the Ossiarchs do not work together unless in extremity. The Bonereapers are separate, driven by their own needs and jealous of their conquests and domains. There are many reasons why they are here now, but only one reason for me to be, and that is to find the enemy I seek. I am not an agent of anyone or anything except myself.'

'A hunter of the lost and the damned…' said Damascene softly.

Leragrais snorted, but Cado could sense calculation behind the old man's eyes.

'Why? Why does a creature like you hunt such quarry alone?' the magister said.

'My reasons are my own,' said Cado.

'Indeed?' said Leragrais, raising his eyebrows. Cado did not respond. 'Every second of existence you now have is ours, you understand? You persist because we will it, and one of the reasons we do so is so that you might sate our curiosity.'

'Then you will have to consider it sated,' Cado said. 'Because you will get nothing more.'

After a second the magister pushed himself to his feet. He moved remarkably smoothly, Cado noted, as though his withered frame were more cloak than truth. He came close, and Cado could taste a static edge to the air around the old man as he approached. Power rattled in his eyes.

'I will not say that I am not tempted to just watch you burn,' he said softly. 'But my own pleasures must come second to the needs of the many.' He put a hand on the stone of the table as though it were the bedrock of what he was about to say. 'This city persists because of my... because of our will. And it persists because we will not allow the likes of you to destroy it. I know death, my wandering friend – I know its taste, its bliss and agonies. I know that there are worse fates than the torments of life for the dead in a land that submits to the tyranny of the undying. I... *we* will not let this city's living and dead fall to that fate. You understand? I will not let it happen.'

Cado waited. They had reached it at last – what these people wanted.

Leragrais had turned his back on the table and was looking out at the clouds and mist. In the distance a blink of amethyst light washed the murk.

Damascene leaned forwards, her interlaced hands resting on the table. 'We believe that the Ossiarchs have taken one of our outpost settlements. You shall go there and free it, or failing that, destroy their presence.'

Cado looked at Damascene. The Sigmarite missionary had said little compared to Leragrais, but he could feel her directness in the demand, the same force of will that had ordered the Ossiarchs' messenger shot.

'This land is filled with things that could destroy an outpost,' said Cado. He looked around at the shadows of the other rock stacks in the mist. Broken and remade towers rose like the roots of snapped teeth from their tops.

'We are aware of that,' said Damascene. 'But given that the Bone-reapers have come to our walls, it is the most likely explanation. They have been attacked before but always they sent word. The birds carry messages, you see. There have been none. And there have been occurrences – lights, mirages, things that are not of the pattern of threats we have seen.'

Cado believed what she was saying. It was just that what she was not saying was larger by many times.

'They have been occurring more often in the last few days,' said Leragrais. 'People have been retreating to the city and leaving the outposts deserted.'

'Like a rat taken down a mine, aren't they?' asked Cado. 'The spirits take the rat's life first so that the miners can try to flee. Lesser lives sacrificed to warn others.'

'The outposts are part of the future – in time they will be stronger,' replied Leragrais. 'Fortress towns that pin the darkness back. For now, they serve our survival and the survival of all those this city protects.'

Cado gave the man a long look.

'You do not think that I can do anything to help this outpost any more than I do,' he said. 'You are just hoping that it will cause a distraction, perhaps draw off some of the Ossiarchs' strength or delay their attack.' Leragrais and Damascene looked at him but did not answer. 'It will not work,' said Cado. 'Everything falls. Here, the great cities of far realms. All of this is just a final gasp from a forgotten dream. Mortality lost.'

'Thankfully, we don't need your credence, Soulblight,' said the man. 'Only your compliance.' He beckoned to Vaux. She stepped forwards and handed Leragrais a small loop of cord. Three of Cado's rings hung on the loop. Leragrais looked at them, then flicked them with a finger. They clinked against each other. Cado's teeth clamped shut. Leragrais snorted and tossed the three rings onto the table. Cado's hand twitched. The magister's eyes caught the movement. He smiled more widely.

'We all have things we care about, even a thing like you. For my part I have one reason to keep my soul in this shell of flesh. This city. Our city. My city. I will not see it fall. Not to your kind, or to foolishness, or to all the forces that want to break, eat or enslave us. Aventhis has stood and endured in a land that hates it. And you are going to help us keep it that way. Go out and discover what has happened and you get back these soul-cages that you are so attached to.' He picked up the cord of rings. 'Fail to come back from this task, and I can assure you that we will bend all of our skill to destroy those that remain. Refuse and we will not only destroy them, we will lock you in a cell that we will fill with fire. Then we will take your ashes and sink them in a nullstone jar to the bottom of a lightless lake.'

Cado felt the black abyss scream inside his thoughts. A single leap and the magister would be red meat on the floor. He could take the rings from the table. Could kill the others and find the rest of the rings. Except they would not be there.

Vaux had handed Leragrais three. That meant they had deliberately brought only a few of them here to goad him. The rest could be anywhere.

'Here,' said Leragrais, untying the cord and tossing one of the rings onto the floor at Cado's feet. 'A token of good faith.' The ring spun in place and then fell flat. Cado looked at it. It was the ring that held Solia. 'It seemed the one most worn by touch, and so likely to hold a high value to you.'

'Do you accept?' asked Damascene. Cado did not answer but looked at the ring. His fingers twitched, but he did not move. The circle of iron felt heavier than the shackles on his wrists. There had to be another way out without agreeing to this bargain.

'Well?' asked Leragrais, and Cado could sense an edge of desperation buried in the words. He looked up but did not answer. Leragrais' eyes hardened. 'Take them back to the cells,' he said, nodding at Vaux, then looking back to Cado. 'You may have till night-bell to consider our offer.'

'My worthies,' said Valentin. 'May I go now? These things are nothing to do with me. I have my family and forge, and…'

Vaux moved to Cado. Other soldiers appeared; one took hold of Valentin's chains.

'Wait!' called the smith, as the soldiers began to lead them away. 'I am nothing to do with this! You can't lock me up with him!'

CHAPTER TEN

Guards took them down to the cells. Heavyset, and heavily armoured. He could smell fear on most of them, fear and caution. That was what a word like *Soulblight* could do: conjure fear out of ignorance. They watched him all the way back to his cell. Valentin protested the whole time. When they reached the cells with their stone doors, the man was shaking his head, looking around at the guards to either side of them.

'This cannot be happening. It just can't.'

'Be quiet,' growled the biggest guard. This one wasn't afraid, Cado realised. He had something else you sometimes got in mortals – a low-level cruelty combined with petty power that overrode instinct and good sense. The stone door of a cell swung wide.

'The forge is still lit. I must get back. I have children and the forge...'

The big guard slammed a palm into Valentin's back. The smith was big, but his hands were bound, and the guard knew how to throw his weight. Valentin's protests ended, as he stumbled, and half fell.

'I said be quiet,' growled the guard.

'Don't do that,' said Cado, softly.

'What was that?' said the guard, straightening. The man had stubble over a layer of reddish skin. 'Did you say something?' Cado was still. His own manacles weighed his hands. The guard came forwards, close enough that Cado could taste the blight growing in the man's lungs, and the liquor pickling his guts. There was a cloudy film on his eyes as he looked up at Cado. One winter and the man would be blind, thought Cado. Another and he would be rot in the ground.

'Don't do that,' said Cado, nodding at where one of the other guards was hauling Valentin up.

'That's twice you've opened your mouth. Down here that's not for you to do without us saying. Understand?' The guard reached out a hand, fingers thick in a boiled-leather gauntlet. He rested his forefinger on Cado's lips. Brave... No, not brave: too bitter to be brave, too stupid to be wise. 'They say that you're a thing from the dead, but that doesn't scare me, and if down here you want to squeak, you ask. 'Cause I tell you – we've faced it all and are still standing, and the worthies won't care if you or this pile of dung come back to them with less teeth.'

He took the finger from Cado's lips, turned slowly, and as though to make his words real, swung his fist at Valentin's face. It was a hard and fast blow, one that the guard had thrown many times, drunk and sober. Valentin, still blinking and coughing, did not see it coming.

Bones cracked. A scream split the air.

The guard slammed into the wall, as Cado released the man's arm. It flopped like a length of rope. The guard screamed and was still screaming as Cado's hands closed around his neck and jaw. He heard the shouts gather breath in the throats of the other guards. Swords began to pull free of scabbards. The chain of his manacles was up under the guard's jaw. The man's face was turning purple under the stubble. Cado looked into his eyes, smelled terror and the reek as the man's bowels emptied.

'Quiet now,' said Cado.

A burning point touched the back of his neck.

'Let him go,' said Vaux's voice just behind him. She was good, he thought. Good enough to get that close. He looked at the guard's eyes, wide in purpling skin. He let him go. The man fell to the ground, screaming again as he landed on top of his shattered arm. Vaux held her dagger point on his neck.

'Get him out of here,' she snapped at the other guards. 'In,' she said, jerking her head at the open cell door. 'You too,' she said to Valentin. The smith was wide-eyed, staring at Cado. He began to shake his head. 'In!' snarled Vaux, and something in her expression must have cut through whatever the smith was thinking, because he scrambled through the door. Cado followed. Vaux took the dagger from his neck as she swung the door closed. The locks clattered behind the stone.

Valentin became quiet as soon as the door closed and the key turned. Cado moved back to the far wall, as far from the smith as he could, and sat. He closed his eyes. Every now and then he heard bits of words come from the man's mouth: 'It's not real... This is not...' After a while the words ran out, and then there was just the sound of Valentin sucking breaths. That quieted, too.

Cado considered his options. He did not have many choices, not real ones anyway. They had his rings and with them the souls bound inside them. They thought that they were valuable to him, but they had no idea how much they meant. Nine souls taken from fire, saved from the pyre of his lost kingdom. Nine out of tens of thousands swallowed by the daemons as they danced, and the flames of betrayal leapt higher. Nothing, a few tears held back from a river of suffering. Nothing. And yet everything. He had to have them back. He had promised all that time ago that he would keep them safe and give them vengeance. He had lived many mortal lifetimes for the first promise and had never failed in the second. He would have to agree to what these mortals asked, for now at least, until he could find a way to get the rings back.

Slaughter them, whispered a voice at the back of his thoughts. *When they open the door – that will be your chance. Kill the one with the knife first. She is deadly but not deadly enough. Then the guards. Call to their flesh and bones as their blood cools. Then the rest. All the rest in the tower. You will have a horde at your back before they know what is happening.* The voice was a shout in his skull. *Kill! Let the blood flow and the skies boil! Slaughter until they are kneeling in the gore of those they love, pleading for you to have what they have taken. Like you once would… Like you should again…*

He could see it. Charred black and bone white and red running on stones. The cries were a song to echo the roar of the storm as he stood atop the city spire, and around him the risen dead raised their blades.

'Why did you do that?' Cado opened his eyes. Valentin was looking at him. The man's eyes were wide in the thin light coming from the holes in the outer wall. 'To the guard, I mean. Why did you do that?'

Cado shrugged, then realised that the man could not see the gesture. 'He was strong, and he used that strength to bully the weak.'

'But you are a… a Soulblight. You kill and hunt the living, you…' Valentin's words broke as though he did not want to say "feed", or mention blood. Cado did not answer. 'I thought, I mean, the stories… nobles in castles, armies, thralls… terrors that come out of the night and see the living as cattle… But you are alone.'

Alone… Alone for long ages of mortals, watching the dreams and hopes of gods and kings unravel. Living an un-life, separated from all that made life real: home and love and kinship. An existence filled with absences, shadows on the tapestry of life, burned in place, inescapable, never to return. No place to call safe or to rest, just ruins and battlefields and the long road always under his feet.

'You don't seem like a… like the stories. You just seem like a person. I mean, you could have… when the militia came, you could have… Soulblights are supposed to be able to… You don't seem like a, a…'

'Like a monster,' said Cado.

'Thank you,' said Valentin. 'For what you did, I mean.' Quiet pooled in the place where Cado could have answered. In truth, he was not sure why he had turned on the guard. It had been foolish. He needed to be free, and showing what he was capable of would not help that cause. Valentin's revulsion at being in a cell with him was right; they should be terrified of him, that was how cattle responded to a predator. That was the truth, but the truth would not help him.

Valentin shifted, coughed. Cado could hear the man's heartbeat settling. The smith shook his head, drew breath again to break the silence.

'I hope that they are all right,' he said, looking up at the light coming through the narrow holes in the wall. Cado realised that the man was talking to himself as much as anything or anyone else, talking for the sake of talking. 'Sigmar's light and strength, but I hope…' He looked at Cado, as though responding to a question that no one had asked. 'It's got worse in the last few months. A lot worse since winter. The city, it's safer than most but… they say that things are moving in the land. Nighthaunt, other… things.' He bit his lip and shook his head. 'I have two children, a boy and a girl. They are supposed to help me in the forge, but only the older one does. The younger, well… I shouldn't have brought them here, but here we are. Light of comets, but all I worry about is what will happen to them if I'm not there, you know?' He glanced at Cado and then caught himself. 'Of course… I am… sorry.

'It wasn't my idea. To come here, I mean. It was hers, my wife's. I wanted to stay where we were. It was safe. But she said that people needed to reclaim the lands and that staying where you were did nothing for the future.' He smiled. 'She was not good at accepting other points of view. She was normally right, though. So we came out here. In other places, they call them crusades, you know, but that was not what happened here. The city was already built, you see, ruined but serviceable. No need for dragging stones through the sky, or a cohort of warriors and spell-weavers. So it was, I don't know, an expedition. Soldiers, a few priests, people. They made it, re-set the first stones, beat back the first enemies, and marked the wards. Made it a home. None of the holy warriors or their lightning, just people without a choice but to make it work.'

'Were there ever any of the Stormcast here?' asked Cado.

Valentin blinked in the dark, surprised at the question.

'No,' he said. 'I have never seen one. I don't think our problems are big enough for the God-King's warriors. There must be places that have it worse, even now.'

Cado thought of the wolves on the road, the Nighthaunt drifting through the trees, and the shrines to the Crow God of Lies not half a league from the city. One small place where the mortals huddled against the dark and the claws of Chaos, alone, always alone, while demigods and would-be legends played games with the suffering of the living. He felt his lips pull back from his teeth.

'No doubt,' he said.

Valentin frowned but did not reply, and lapsed into silence, and then into a fitful sleep. Cado waited. The next step on this path was set, his decision made. As ever, there was no choice, not really. That was the truth he had known since he was a mortal child: there were no real choices, only consequences. Now he just had to wait.

The seconds passed in a slow fall, like sand gathering into hours at the bottom of an hourglass.

The locks in the door clanked open and it swung. Vaux stood in the opening, a lamp in her hand.

'The worthies want to see you again,' she said. Valentin came awake, blinked, confused as the dream he had been having faded. Cado stood, nodded.

Vaux led them back up from the cells. A vein beat hard in her temple, and her gaze fixed, never touching Cado.

It was daylight as they emerged. The low clouds and mist had diluted the sun to a grey glow. The magister and cometarian broke off a conversation as Vaux led Valentin and Cado across the tower top. Cado thought Leragrais looked aged by the passing of the night. The life held in his bones was leaching out into the life he lived.

'You have considered our offer?' asked Damascene. Cado gave a slow nod. 'And you agree?'

'Yes,' said Cado.

'Good, worthy of celebration if circumstances were different,' said Leragrais. He looked at Valentin. 'I am told that you went to attend the metal works at the western outposts, smith?'

'Yes, your worthy, but I–'

'Good! Our friend Sire Ezechiar will need a guide to show him the way, and someone to… ah, calm any nerves of the people in the outpost.'

'I… What?' Valentin looked aghast. 'I'm not… I mean…'

'You are perfect. While your craft is of immense value to our citizens, it is currently of less value than keeping our militia on the gates and walls. You know the paths. You know our… ha, associate now. You are trustworthy, yes?'

'Well, yes, I have always–'

'Indeed, and you will be our representative in this, a reassuring presence all round. Besides, this small service will balance your crime on the scales.'

'Crime?'

'Of association with our friend here.' Leragrais smiled at Cado. 'A dangerous outsider.'

Damascene stood and handed Valentin a bronze ring set with the device of a bird encircled by a twin-tailed comet.

'The seal of the council and the city,' she said. '*You* bear it for us.' Cado noticed the smith blink and stand a little straighter at the words.

'Excellent,' said Leragrais. 'Leave by first bell after dawn.' He looked at Cado and pointed at the weapons and gear on the table. 'Yours,' he said, 'and ah…' He took Solia's iron ring from his pocket and rolled it across the stone top of the table. It hit the hilt of Cado's sword and clinked flat. 'As promised.'

Valentin was looking at the signet ring, running it through his fingers. Cado picked up the iron ring from the table. The flare of pain in his hand was cold as the metal slid over his finger.

Leragrais and Damascene were already moving away. Vaux remained for a second, her doubts and contempt clear on her face.

'I'll be by the gate when you leave,' she said, then she too turned and left them to the gaze of the roosting birds, their eyes amber flickers in the light of the single torch.

CHAPTER ELEVEN

'You'll want to stay back. The heat can take your skin off and the sparks can burn if you're not careful.' Valentin nodded to a heavy workbench on the other side of the room. Cado walked to it and sat cross-legged on its top. Valentin moved about the forge fire. Every now and then he would prod and stir the coals with a poker, then stare at them and frown. He picked up tools, rearranging them so that they were in easier reach of the anvil sitting in the middle of the floor. A girl, his daughter, whom he had introduced as Leire, stood close by. Her eyes flicked to Cado and then away. She was frightened. Not of Cado, at least not consciously – younger mortals reacted strangely to him, even if they did not know what he was. Some sensed some wrongness about him and were wary. Others were more curious, just like a child might be to get closer to a sleeping wolf.

They had come back to Valentin's forge after leaving the high tower. Cado had not wanted to go, but the tower with the painted door would be close by, and he thought it likely that Vaux would have sent watchers to make sure that neither he nor Valentin fled or went into the rest of the city. If he went with the smith, then he could slip out and explore the tower when night fell. Besides, this mortal was going to be his companion while he tried to get his rings back; he needed to understand how much of a burden he would be.

Leire had been there when they reached the forge. She had smiled with relief when she saw her father, and looked with caution and suspicion at Cado. She was tall – almost as tall as her father – and there were burn marks from forge sparks on her forearms. She looked wary, on edge, a child of this city-that-should-not-be, and full of its quiet sense of dread. Valentin had told her that there had been a misunderstanding with the militia but that he and Cado had a task to do for the city. She had not accepted the lie completely, Cado could tell, but her father had said they needed to finish some work in the forge for the next day. Cado had glanced at the painted door of the tower opposite. The rain was still falling.

'It's a lot warmer inside,' said the smith, 'drier too.'

A sign of trust, thought Cado. Valentin was showing Cado he trusted him by inviting him in. Rare and brave, or very foolish.

Cado had turned from the painted door. He was not going to be able to examine the tower yet. So he went into the ember-warmed dark and watched as the smith put the metal into the glowing coals. Leire began to pump the bellows. The flames rose. Sparks spat from their edges. Valentin looked down at the fire, shifted the metal. His gaze was calm, his movements sure and relaxed. The agitation of the man in the cells, who had seemed terrified in the presence of the city councillors, was gone. Here was a soul fitted to what he was doing, at peace in the heat and sparks. That was the point, Cado realised. Here, the smith was king of his realm. Here he could find a way to be at peace with the fact that a monster was sitting within feet of him. Here, Valentin could put Cado into a place where he was no threat and where going outside the walls with a Soulblight was all right. The smith was doing the things he did every day because that was how he made sense of the world, even when it refused that sense.

He shifted the metal bar again, pulled it out and set it on the anvil. The girl slowed the breath of the bellows. Valentin picked up a hammer and began to strike. Sparks scattered from the struck steel. Grey flakes of impurities fell away. The sound of the hammer rang clear, a steady rhythm.

Cado watched as the metal changed, Valentin hammering and forming it between spells in the fire. Neither the girl nor the smith spoke, just the odd glance here and there, a nod or a shake of the head that somehow governed the heat of the air, the tools used and the song of bellows and strikes. All the smith's words had gone, as though replaced by the rhythm of his craft. It was, Cado was surprised to note, almost comforting.

'May I?' he said as Leire turned back to the bellows. She shot him a surprised glance, then looked at Valentin.

'Da?'

Valentin smiled. 'You ever worked in a forge?' he asked.

'No,' said Cado.

'Best leave it to her,' he said and nodded to the girl, who went back to the handle of the bellows. 'Would take a while to tell you how you need to be doing things, and then a while longer still for you to get the truth of it. I don't doubt that you can do many things, but smithing is not just fire and hitting hot metal. There is a world in here.' He pulled the metal from the fire and began to strike. 'Everything has a place and way. It's not big or mysterious. It just is the way it needs to be. Let the fire burn wrong and the metal won't heat right. Leave the metal in too long and it will burn, crack, flaw and spoil. Strike wrong and you can hit the strength out of it. It's not complicated, just needs to be done with care, that's all.'

He lifted the glowing piece of metal off the anvil and looked at it. The glow shimmered in his eyes. After a long moment he nodded and plunged it into a trough of water. Steam leapt into the air. 'There's some around that like to wonder after the things that might be done with magic, what we might do or make or dream, but that's not for me. There's magic enough in heat and hammer.'

He took the piece of metal, now black and dripping, from the water, tapped the back of his hand against it, and hung it from an iron loop close to the fire hood.

'Take this to Mother Clay after light-bell,' he said to Leire. 'Her nephew will want to have the fitting of it to the lock, but don't let him or it will be jammed in a week. All right?'

'Yes, da.' The girl nodded, straightening. She flicked a look at Cado then away. 'When will you be back?'

'Not long,' he said, and smiled. 'I have got a job to do for the council worthies, but I won't be out more than a night or so.'

'Outside the walls?' she asked. Cado could hear the catch of fear at the edge of the words.

'Yes,' said Valentin. 'I'm going with Ser Ezechiar here, so don't worry. He's a great soldier, come from a long way, and seen a lot more than our little fold of life has to offer. He's got all the means to keep us both safe and more.' He looked at Cado, who hesitated for a moment, uncertain how to respond.

'Your father will be safe with me,' he said at last.

The girl glanced between them. Her eyes were both fearful and sharp. She did not trust him, Cado could tell.

'They say that there are Soulblights in the woods on the north road,' she said.

Valentin glanced quickly at Cado and then back to his daughter.

'There's no Soulblight on the north road,' he said, and began to busy himself with shifting the tools on their racks. 'And we are going west, towards Innoth Eyrie.' A moment of quiet formed.

Leire did not look reassured. Valentin was frowning, his hands fidgeting as they moved where they had been slow and sure before. 'Sweep down, get the clinker out of the fire, then get to bed,' he said. 'I'll be up and gone before light, but no need to stir. Try to keep your brother out of the ruins and rookery towers.'

The girl tutted and muttered something that was not clear even to Cado's ears. The tone was obviously familiar enough for Valentin to catch the drift.

'That's enough,' he said, firm but not harsh. 'I know it's a lot on top of a lot more, and that you asked for none of it, but Ama will grow out of it – for now he just needs to know that it's wrong and dangerous. I've no more been able to stop him crawling through the city than any has, so the chances of stopping him short of a chain are small, but he needs some rule even if it is one he ignores.'

Leire shook her head, glanced at Cado then stuck out her chin.

'A chain would be a start,' she said. 'It's dangerous, da. People go missing, even off the streets, even guards. Ama will get himself hurt or...' The words trailed off and Cado heard the fight drain from her voice. She glanced at him again.

'Just try, Lei. I'll be gone a night, two at most.'

She nodded, stopped, then pulled up the thing she had wanted to ask.

'Is it about the Bonereaper?'

She didn't need to explain what she meant or how she knew about the emissary who had come to the walls. The whole city would know by now. The truth would have added to the stories so that its shadow would grow with every telling. You did not need to have seen the rider or heard its words to feel the weight of its promise. He always wondered why people just continued when a force like the Bonereapers came to their door. Running was no better a strategy, it was true, but it held out hope where simply standing was to make a possibility into a certainty. He had seen it many times, though, people just carrying on, as if pursuing the mundane needs of life could shield them from doom.

Because when you are powerless you hold on to what you have, and hope and pray that it is enough to live a little longer, said a voice at the back of his thoughts. *That's what being mortal in a realm of gods and monsters means.*

Valentin put a hammer down, let out a breath to try to explain.

'No,' said Cado. Leire and Valentin both looked up at him. 'It is not the Bonereapers. Your father is helping me do something for the city. It's dangerous, but all will be well.'

The girl looked at him. He held her gaze and at last she nodded.

Cado pushed himself up from his perch on the table. The night would have deepened to true darkness now. He went to the door of the forge.

Why did you tell that lie? asked the silent voice. *These mortals will die soon, and their souls will either go to their idea of afterlife or to the black mouth of the abyss. To you, to your vengeance, to this realm, they matter not at all.*

'I will see you at dawn,' he said to Valentin, and walked from the forge into the night.

The darkness on the street was cold after the heat of the forge. The rain had stopped but there was still a sheen of water on the cobbles. A portion of the sky had cleared, and stars blinked at Cado from the dark heavens. He paused, pushing his senses out and drawing the scent of magic and life in. There was no one watching him that he could sense. There were mortals, close by, but in a city, even a half-populated ruin, there were always mortals. He could hear the tap-tap of their sleeping blood like the raindrops falling from the edges of the roof. There was nothing else, though, no tang of magic or sound of a foot shifting on stone to give away a watcher. If they were there, they were more subtle than his senses. That was possible, of course.

He moved up the street to the tower with the painted door. Even before he touched it, he could tell it was not the same. The tang of magic had gone. He pushed on the painted wood. It held firm. He traced his hand down to where a bolt would likely be and gave a single sharp shove. There was a crack of shearing metal. The door lolled in. Cado pushed it with his boot. Nothing moved. Raindrops had begun striking on the road. A grumble of thunder rolled in the night sky. He went through. There was nothing there. A spiral stair wound up the inside of grey stone walls. A tangle of sodden and rotten planks lay in the space in front of the door. Rain spattered down from holes in the wall and roof above. It smelled of damp and rot. No one had used it or been here for a long time. That was not right, though. It was too neat, and there was something else out of place that it took him a moment longer to identify.

There were no birds. They were always present in this underworld, and if they were not there themselves the signs of them were. But not here: no nests placed on the broken steps and beams, no droppings covering the floor. He climbed up to the tower top, swinging and bounding. If anyone had seen him, they would have thought they were seeing a wolf, or a bat, anything but a man. He was not a man, of course. He just wore the shape of one.

He crouched on the broken parapet when he reached the top. The tower sat amongst the jumble of its fellows: some just as old and dilapidated as it was, some repaired, smoke winding from their chimney stacks. Below, the slope of the city plunged down, near sheer. Torch lights flickered on the wall ringing the base. Above, the rock rose to its pinnacle. The mist of the day had cleared and so he could see the bridges spanning the gaps to the nearby stacks. A few were stone, but several were rope and wood slung across the gaps left where the old bridges had fallen. He could smell the life seeping from the city as it slept and dreamed. Small dreams, fearful dreams, hopes and worries all wrapped up in night. That was what all these new settlements were like, whether they built on the bones of the past or were raised in the middle of nowhere: small, desperate dreams of a world that did not exist any more. That could not exist. It was only a matter of time before the truth swept them away.

He dropped down through the tower. The followers of the God of Lies and Change had been here, but they had gone and scraped any sign of their presence from the place. They would still be close, though, in the city. The disciples of the Dark Gods did not retreat, they simply dug deeper into the flesh of their host.

He landed on the ground floor, rose and was making for the door. He froze. Someone was there. Crouching in the shadows. He could feel a heartbeat, smell the sheen of sweat on skin. He whirled, daggers drawn.

'Please, no!' said a high voice. Cado froze. A boy, likely no more than ten years old, was staring at the point of Cado's dagger. 'I'm sorry. I...'

Cado's eyes flicked across the boy's face as his lips worked for words. He saw the lines in the jaw and eye sockets, still forming but recognisable. He noticed the edge of coal smoke and iron in the boy's sweat. Iron, blood iron beating fast in veins... And the abyss of hunger and slaughter opened its jaws in the shell of Cado's soul. For a second it roared, and Cado thought it was about to move him, to send daggers and fangs flying forward and blood spraying.

Why? Because we can! laughed the hunger and darkness. He forced the roar to quiet, the hunger to a growl as the chain of his will snapped taut.

He sheathed his daggers.

'You are Valentin's son,' he said. The boy nodded. 'Why are you here?'

'I saw that the door was open on the tower,' said the boy quickly. 'It's never been open before. I wanted to see what was here.'

A half-truth, not a whole lie.

'You noticed the door was open during the dark hours?' asked Cado.

The boy began to nod then turned the gesture to a shake under Cado's gaze. 'I went to the forge, to… to look for you.' There was a long pause. 'You are a mercenary, aren't you?'

Cado shook his head. 'A mercenary fights for pay.'

'What do you fight for then?'

Cado looked up at the rain dripping down from the rafters. He felt the taste of the acolyte's blood in his mouth and saw the moment of fear bloom in the man's many eyes as the last instant of life loomed close, sharp and cruel.

'What is your name?' he asked.

'Amandus…' said the boy. 'I mean, everyone calls me Ama.'

'Do you know what justice is, Ama?'

'Making the wrong balance with the right.'

'That's what I fight for.'

'Why are you and da going out of the city? Is that to do with justice?'

Cado straightened.

I've no more been able to stop him crawling through the city than any has,' Valentin had said.

'Did you ever try to get into this tower before, Ama?'

'Once, but the door wouldn't give, and I couldn't find an opening higher up.'

'You climbed all the way up?'

The boy nodded. 'You can climb or squeeze through most of the buildings. Almost everything has a way in.' Ama gave a guilty grin. 'Even if the people who live there don't know about it.'

'You never saw anyone else come here?'

Ama shook his head.

Cado gave a nod. He had not expected more, still…

'Best get back to your family, Ama.'

The boy began to move towards the door, then paused, biting his lip.

'You are dangerous, aren't you?'

'Yes,' said Cado.

'But not to my dad?'

'No, not to your father.'

'But being around you… that's not safe, is it?'

'No,' said Cado after a moment. 'You see a lot, don't you, Amandus?'

The boy shrugged. He had a serious look on his face. 'Da being hurt… that wouldn't be fair,' he said. 'Wouldn't be just.'

Then he ducked through the door, and left Cado to hear the seconds pass in the slow beat of the rain falling through the broken tower.

Cado stayed in the tower until the night faded to grey and a distant bell struck the fourth hour. He had not expected anything to happen. There was a chance that someone else might return or a spell would fade to reveal a clue. Cado had not held much hope of it. Nothing had happened. The stones of the tower had stayed cold, through the dark hour. Crouched in the silence, all he could feel was the thrum of magic that lay over the city, leaden and stifling.

When it was time to go, he did not wait to see Valentin but went down to the stable where he had left his horse. A new sergeant watched him as he went. He saw the man spit and make the sign of the comet with his hand but did not come close or say a word. Valentin arrived later. His horse was smaller than Cado's, an animal made for travel rather than battle. No doubt the worthies had provided it. The smith had packed bags and an oilskin roll that hung behind the saddle. He looked to know what he was doing with the beast, too. It should not have been a surprise; almost everyone in this place was a pilgrim to this new life in a reclaimed land.

Cado saw to his own kit, ignoring the stare of the sergeant and the glances of the militia by the gate. A thought struck him, and he turned and walked directly to the sergeant. The man's hand flinched towards his weapon, and he took half a step back. No matter what lie the worthies had told the militia, it included the fact that Cado was dangerous even if it did not include the truth. Cado raised his hands, placating. The sergeant didn't relax but didn't move either.

'You are new on the gate,' Cado said. The man grunted and nodded. 'I came in two days ago, and the sergeant of the day watch was different. What happened to the man who was in charge before?' Cado kept his tone low but edged with a little of the force of someone who is used to command and being obeyed. He knew, of course, the man was dead, but had that fact reached the rest of the militia? The sergeant sucked his lips.

'No one's seen him since night before last,' said the man. His eyes went up to the walls, where the gate guards stood in the half-light. 'Won't be the first, won't be the last,' he said, half under his breath. Cado nodded thanks and was about to turn away when another question surfaced in his mind. 'You have a militia soldier called Amaury on the gate.'

The sergeant snorted. 'No I don't.'

'She is missing too?'

The sergeant looked at Cado with narrowed eyes. 'There is no militia soldier on the gate of that name, nor has been, ever.'

Cado held the man's gaze, thoughts clicking around in his mind.

The sergeant shook his head. The command of Cado's tone and the worthies' warning were clearly fading to a sense that he was talking to a fool.

'Cado.' A small voice made him turn. The boy Ama and his sister Leire were standing next to their father. Valentin was mock growling something about how they should not have come but was clearly delighted. Ama came towards Cado.

'He said he had met you after you left,' said Valentin. 'Wanted to give you something.'

Ama came closer and held up an open hand. On the palm was a small piece of black iron shaped into a comet. A loop extended from one of the twin tails so that it could hang from a buckle or length of twine. It was simple work, but neatly done.

'For you,' said Ama, holding it higher. 'To... ah, keep you safe, so that you can keep da safe.' The boy bit his lip. Cado looked at the small talisman for a long moment, then took it. The iron was cool in his fingers. No magic echoed in its heart.

'No magic but heat and hammer,' said an echo of Valentin's voice in his mind.

He nodded.

'My thanks,' he said, and found a leather thong on his gear and tied the talisman to it. Ama stepped back, suddenly shy in that way that only children could be, shifting from lightning to silence in an eye-blink. He went to his sister and Valentin hugged them both, then climbed onto his horse.

'I don't know whether I should be worried they are staying, or we are going,' the smith muttered.

Cado did not answer but turned his horse. In front of him the gate was opening.

CHAPTER TWELVE

The mist came as the light of the day grew. It seeped up into the air from the dark ground, slowly swallowing sight from around them. The shadows of the great spires of rock fell through the haze. For a while, the sky above was clear so that it felt as though they were passing through a veiled world. At first, they had followed the pale road between the rock pillars, but after they passed a slumped pile of stone blocks, the smith led them up onto a path that wound through narrow gullies and across low humps of ground. He seemed to be navigating by landmarks and by counting the strides of his steed.

The clouds covered the sky after what must have been an hour or two more. Valentin kept them moving until they crested a ridge and found the stones of a road beneath them. It was narrower than the road they had followed before or that Cado had followed to the city. The earth had swallowed its edges and its slabs had crumbled to gravel in places.

'There were grave-roses growing when I came this way before,' said Valentin, when they forded a patch of bog that had swallowed the path. Cado looked down into the water of a pool and saw a skull without a jaw. Black weeds tangled its eye sockets.

They rode on. The clouds growled rain down on them. The broken stones of the road gleamed with water, white and grey. The birds were there, of course, watching from nests on stone walls and in the branches of trees. Occasionally, some of them would drop low out of the rain and cloud, pale grey wings beating slow and silent as they passed overhead. Valentin would watch them, murmuring sometimes. He had begun the journey looking uneasy. With every league they went further from the city, he looked more nervous. Cado paid it little attention and kept his eyes on the road and the rain-smudged world they passed.

'How long…?' began Valentin, then hesitated.

Cado looked around. 'Yes?'

He watched the smith bite his lip.

'How long have you been…?'

'A long time,' Cado said and looked back at the road.

A moment of silence broken only by the sound of the horses' hooves.

'The… the people… the enemy that you came here chasing… what did they… do?'

Cado stared at him. Valentin flinched, but the curiosity in his eyes was stronger than the fear there. Cado turned away.

'They destroyed everything and everyone I cared for,' he said.

Another pause passed that Cado did not fill.

'What were… before you became… before you are as you are now, what were you?'

'I was a king,' said Cado.

Valentin did not speak for a long while after that.

* * *

'Something is not right,' said Valentin as big, grey birds glided across their path. 'Those are sorrow-wings, supposed to be old souls, ones that have been born, believed, flown these skies, lived, believed and done it all over again. They keep to themselves. Seeing one means that something is out of true. Seeing this many...'

Cado did not answer. He didn't need the lore and insight of birds to know what Valentin said was true. He could taste the wrongness in the rain mist. The magic of death was everywhere in the underworlds. It was thick on every false breath he took, and in every bite. That magic threaded the curse in his blood, and he could sense it like a living soul could feel the change in the taste and texture of the air. Sometimes it was thin, or stagnant, or curdled with the taint of Chaos. Here on this road it was... He was not certain he could describe it. Split, stuttering, as though a wind had divided into ridges of hot and cold. He could not smell the scent of the living and the unliving either. Both were always there, even if they were faint. Now it was as if something had scraped the land clean of both life and un-life. He had not felt anything like it in the underworlds.

'How far to the outpost?' asked Cado.

Valentin looked around. 'I am not sure... I only came this way the once, and it looked... You could see more. I think we are close, though.'

'Leragrais said there was a garrison. Did they have lookouts on the road?'

'I don't know. Maybe.'

'Start calling a greeting,' said Cado.

'What?'

'We don't want to end with a crossbow bolt.'

Valentin looked at Cado for a long moment as though trying to detect a joke. Cado kept his eyes on the road and mist. Valentin shook himself, took a breath and called.

'Messengers on the road… from Aventhis… Messengers…'

The words vanished into the rain and echoed back in cracked pieces. No reply came, and no bolts either.

They had just climbed a rise and turned a shoulder of rock when Cado saw the light. He reined up hard. His horse whinnied in protest. Valentin, who had been looking behind them for a second, almost rode into them. He squawked, struggled with his mount, then looked up and went still.

'Sacred comet of the sky…' hissed Valentin.

Ahead of them, the broken road curved down the side of a valley. On the opposite side sat a cluster of towers moulded out of spears of dark rock. A shaft of bright sunlight poured down from a break in the clouds above. In the rain-heavy air it was dazzling. Cado flinched away and then forced his eyes to focus on it. The light touched the stone towers but nothing else. Clouds and mist frayed around it, and gloom pooled in the valley beneath. It was as though the light were a great and shining spear blade thrust into the grey body of the air.

'It's…' Valentin faltered. Cado glanced at him then back at the light. 'I was going to say beautiful, but it's not, is it? There is something…'

Curves of rainbow light flickered at the edges of the shaft. Cado's teeth grated against each other. Migraine pain popped at the back of his eyes.

'What are those?' asked Valentin as a gust of rain gleamed with colour, every drop a jewel burning with multicoloured fire.

'Splintered magic,' said Cado. 'The fabric of the realm breaking into its eight parts.'

Valentin flinched and made a gagging sound.

'I can't…' he said. 'I can't look at it for long… It's…'

'Don't try,' said Cado. His skin was crawling. Of all the things he had thought he might find at the end of Damascene and Leragrais' mission, this was worse than he had imagined. The worst thing was that he did not know what it was.

He inhaled. It was like breathing in broken glass. Beyond the aetheric rainbows, a shape swam in the column of light, a heat-haze impression pressed into the air. It kept moving in and out of sight. It was a rune, he realised, a rune painted in the air.

Go, said a voice in the back of his head. *Turn your horse and leave now. Find another trail to follow to vengeance, but go now.* He could do that. It would cost him time… but he had a life that would not end. Across the thought swam Leragrais' smile, and the other eight iron rings that had been on his fingers. He could not leave them behind, not again.

'Those… specks, inside,' said Valentin. The smith was heaving as he forced himself to look at the light. 'I thought they were birds, but they look like they are floating, and… they don't look like birds. What are they?'

Cado blinked. His eyes were stinging. He dropped his gaze.

'Debris,' he said, and nudged his horse down the slope towards the illuminated outpost. 'And bodies.'

The towers sat atop a rock crag. There were three cylinders set close to each other, each kinked around the spurs of rock that formed their roots. They were old, and before now, must have remained largely intact through the long ages that had cast down so many relics of the past. Cado and Valentin rode up the road to the towers and tied their horses to a post to climb the rest of the way on foot. The animals shifted fitfully, tugging their necks at the tethers. They did not like being this close to the towers or the light shining on them from the sky. Valentin looked ready to stay with them, then shook himself and followed Cado up the road to the gatehouse. The only sound he made was an intake of breath as details resolved from the glare.

The remains of birds covered the ground and walls. Bones and feathers had melted into each other. Shrieking beaks jutted from stone. A single quill turned in the space above them, burning. The smoke was an oozing smear above it.

What had happened to this outpost had been overwhelming, a moment of cataclysm, but there were no signs of battle. Cado doubted that anyone inside had had the chance to do more than raise a sword.

'What happened here?' asked Valentin. Cado did not answer. In truth he was not sure of the specifics, but he knew the cause: magic. Breathtakingly powerful magic. They moved under the shadow of the gatehouse. The gate itself had blown outwards – was still blowing outwards, in fact. Splinters hung in the air, rotating with treacle-slow momentum. Brilliant light filled the space beyond the gate.

'Am...' The sound rose and faded.

Valentin stopped, head snapping around. It came again, sliding up and down, just on the edge of hearing. Cado nodded towards the tunnel beyond the broken gate.

'Am...' The sound shivered through the air as they moved forwards. The tunnel led through the rock wall into a courtyard between the towers. Cado could see the light blazing in the open space. A shiver was building under his skin. The false beat of his heart was becoming fainter, as though his stolen blood were trying to retreat as deep inside him as it could. Magic was not just thick here; it was a hammer blow to the outside of his skull.

Ahead, a woman hung in the light. She was on her side, half folded, arms and legs trailing, as though the whip-crack force that had sent her flying were still passing through her. She was rotating slowly, tumbling. The light poured down on her. The noise they had heard faded as she turned away from them.

Valentin made to step into the light towards the woman.

'Don't.' Cado held the man back. Valentin turned, eyes angry. 'Keep out of the light,' Cado said and jerked his chin at where shadow pooled under an intact arch. Under it they would be only an arm's-reach from the woman as she rotated towards them. Valentin nodded and edged across the bridge of gloom towards where the woman hung in the air.

'Mistress,' called Valentin, his voice shaking. Cado saw him swallow.

'Am… Amena…' The woman's cracked call came again. Valentin shifted closer to the edge of the shadow, closer to where the woman's face would be as she turned. 'Am… Amena…'

'Mistress?' called Valentin again. 'We have come from Aventhis, mistress. We have come to help. Can you hear me? We have come to…' The words caught on the smith's tongue, because the woman's face had just come into sight. Half of her skull had been torn away by a chunk of stone. Splinters of both the stone and her skull spread to the side of her, turning with her as though both it and she had been frozen and set revolving like a spindle at the end of a tangled thread. The blood and meat of her brainpan was curved in a flat arc. Her lips were still moving, repeating the last words she had shouted. The eyes were open too, gazing into the light. 'Am… Amena… Am… Amena…'

Valentin stared, mouth open, then made to lunge across the gap to her. Cado's hand fastened on him. Valentin twisted, but Cado held him back.

'Look,' Cado said and gestured out past the woman. Another shape hung in the air five paces from her. Smaller, much smaller – just a bloody bundle of cloth hanging in the light, no clear sign that it was a human, and no need for one either. And up and out beyond that, more: a figure tumbling, back folded to a sharp angle, limbs already slack; a young woman, shield strapped to her arm, a shard of stone halfway through her torso, yet to hit the ground. A murmur of last breaths and words cut short came on the breeze.

'Don't go into the light,' repeated Cado before Valentin could move. The smith tensed as though he were going to do it anyway.

'This… they… they are not dead.'

'No,' said Cado. He understood what he had felt earlier now. 'They are balanced on the edge between life and death. Trapped.'

'So they can't… What could do this?'

Cado looked at him. 'We must get back to your city.'

Valentin looked up at the shaft of light hung with people. He gagged, trembled. 'What about… them? There must be something that–'

'There is nothing we can do.'

'We have to try to–'

'There is nothing.'

Valentin looked at Cado, and there was a flash of forge fire in the man's eyes.

'Soulblighted,' he growled. 'Soulless is closer to the truth, isn't it? The living as cattle or pieces in a game.' Valentin held his gaze steady. Cado could hear the drumbeat of blood in the man's heart rolling fast. Then Valentin shook his head. 'Sorry, I am sorry. I… You are right. We need to let the city know what has happened here. Maybe they can do something for them.'

Cado looked up at where the woman they had found pivoted slowly in place, the veil of blood and bone shards trailing from her skull, the gasp of her last cry pulsing through her over and again.

'Perhaps,' he said.

The rain struck them when they reached the horses. The valley was grey-smudged by falling water. Behind them the shaft of light engulfed the broken towers. The rune pinned to the air at its heart shimmered. The storm clouds turned around the light. Thunder snapped. Lightning touched the rain with silver.

Cado pulled the hood of his cloak up against the deluge. Valentin was quiet. His eyes were wide, as though still seeing the people in the broken tower, dead but yet to hit the end of life. Cado steadied his mount and looked at the iron ring on his index finger. He needed counsel, and not from a smith who had not ridden further than a handful of leagues from his city in years. He would need to warn Valentin. Solia was a hidden presence to most, but not to all. Some people without a speck of apparent magic could see or sense her, even hear her words just as he did. He would have waited until he was alone, but there was no time to wait.

'You should prepare yourself,' he began and glanced from the ring to Valentin. The smith was in the saddle of his horse, his hands in the middle of gathering the reins. He was looking down the valley, frowning, eyes squinting against the rain.

'What is that?' he asked.

Cado followed the man's gaze.

Pale blurs, swift against the ground. Glints of silver blending with the falling rain.

'Ride,' he said, then louder, 'Ride, now!'

He spurred his horse down the slope. Valentin followed a heartbeat later.

Their horses were not bred for swiftness, but they were running with fear. They plunged down into the bottom of the valley and forded the stream in a spray of icy water. Cado could see the pale riders more clearly now. Some were on horses, with shield and helm and long spear. Others rode beasts with long necks and slender tails that bounded on their hind legs. They were wind-fast, their feet barely touching the ground with each stride. Cado saw high helms on the riders' heads and bows in their hands.

Cado spurred his horse harder. Valentin was breathing hard in his saddle, eyes locked on the way up the valley side as though he could will the ground to pass more swiftly. Cado glanced back.

The riders on the bounding beasts were outstripping the horsemen and splitting into two groups that reached to either side of Cado and Valentin. They were going to cut them off, and then the horsemen would be on them. He had time to think this, then the first riders were past them, circling. Cado could see coats of silver scales and cloaks of ivory. He wheeled his horse, looking for an opening. A line of arrows struck the ground just in front of his horse's hooves. It reared back. The riders were all around them now.

CHAPTER THIRTEEN

'Who are you?' called Valentin. His eyes were still wide, flicking between the turning circle of riders.

'The very question I would ask of you,' came an answer. The voice was clear and strong, pitched to cut through the growl of thunder and the drum of hooves. A rider broke from the spiral. Their armour was pearl white. A cloak of pale blue and pure white snapped behind them. They had a sword drawn, the blade low. Rain ran from the cutting edge as their mount came to a stop. Valentin glanced at Cado as though expecting him to speak. Cado kept his eyes steady on the figure beneath the curve of his cloak.

'You are from the Granite Eyrie, from the resettlement called Aventhis,' said the figure into the silence. Raindrops shivered from the azure plume and crest on their helm. They sheathed their sword and pulled the helm from their head. Valentin gasped, then stifled the sound. The face beneath was slim, like an arrow tip that had re-formed into cheeks and chin and brow. Black-in-black eyes looked out from either side of a blade-edge nose. Silver rings held a thick coil of black hair against her scalp. An aelf, thought Cado, but not one of the types that he had met before. He could taste danger and sharpness bleeding from her stillness. She looked at Valentin for a long moment. The man looked dumbstruck. She shifted her gaze to Cado. He felt that dark stare fizz like the heat of the sun. 'Tell me your names,' said the aelf.

'Tell us yours,' said Cado. The other riders were still circling, though more slowly. There were other figures coming down the valley, too. They were on foot but moving fast. Spear and sword tips glinted. If they did not break out of the riders now then they would be facing encirclement by foot troops as well. These did not look like a force raised from an enclave or city, they looked like a warhost: skilled, disciplined, dangerous. They would not be able to break through. Even if he were alone, it would be impossible. With Valentin it would be a brief jest and swift end. Under the edge of his cloak, he brought the fingernails of his left hand to his palm. The points bit.

'I am Lotharic,' said the aelf. 'Regent by the Light of Lord Teclis, bearer of a Sword of the Sun. I come as emissary to all who would see an end of the night, and the return of hope. If you are such that have dwelt under the shadow of despair and the fear of death, then I am here as friend and ally to you.' She bowed her head, the gesture small but heavy with control and formality. When her gaze came up again, her eyes were on Cado. 'Now I would have your names.'

'Cado.'

'Valentin,' said the smith. He was trying to keep his voice steady, Cado realised.

'Where are you bound?' asked Lotharic. She was still only looking at Cado. He could feel his skin prickle. He dug his nails into his left palm and felt blood well onto his fingers. The infantry was joining the cavalry now. Spear and swordsmen slid between the riders, formed up, eyes and weapons levelled. He could see high helms, shields, arrows already nocked to strings, swords drawn and ready. A figure came through the lines. He wore blue, white and ivory robes, and a conical hat. The rain beaded on the fabric. He held a crystal lamp on a tall staff, and his knee-high boots tapered to long metal spikes under each foot so that he stood almost as tall as the riders' mounts. His eyes were pale grey, almost white, with ragged pupils like ink splashed onto paper.

'We–' Valentin began to answer.

'We are bound where we please,' said Cado, cutting him off. He shifted the shadow of his hood towards the newcomer. 'Who is this?'

'Atharion,' said the aelf. He had begun to circle them. His stilts made his stride into swift cuts, like the snick and cut of shears. His gaze was like the noon sun. Cado shifted, despite himself. The smell of magic was billowing off Atharion; it tasted of burning sand.

'What are you doing here?' asked Cado. 'You are not of this realm.'

'We bring light to the darkness,' said Atharion. He had yet to blink.

'And that is your doing?' asked Cado, turning his head slightly to where the shaft of light shone on the outpost settlement.

'They were given warning,' said Atharion.

'Warning?' It was Valentin. The smith's face had flushed under his beard. 'Warning? Have you seen…? There are people… They…'

'They were warned,' said Lotharic. 'They knew what would happen. It was known to them. They chose to remain. Believe me that we wished them no harm.'

There was no edge of sorrow in the words, just the clarity and conviction of a razor's edge.

'No harm?' spluttered Valentin. 'No harm!'

'They resisted,' said Lotharic. 'The fear and darkness within them did not allow them to embrace illumination. Their lives ended because of that blindness, but still we saved them. Their souls will not suffer the fall into the utter-dark. They will not suffer the chains of un-life. We have given them to light. We have set them free.'

Valentin's mouth was open. His head shook.

'Did they ask for that freedom?' asked Cado.

Atharion had returned to stand beside Lotharic. He tilted his head. Cado could taste magic in that gaze, hard, like light focusing through a crystal. He felt the blood oozing across his left hand. He ran his tongue across his teeth. Atharion looked at Lotharic. For the first time her gaze moved from Cado and Valentin.

Cado squeezed his left hand into a fist. Blood welled between his fingers. He formed a word on his tongue.

Atharion's fingers danced through the air. Glowing lines trailed from the fingertips, forming a rune. Lotharic's eyes went wide.

'*Kel'ylan!*' she hissed. Her sword was in her hand, a shining blur of sun and silver.

Cado threw his bloody hand wide. Blood scattered from his fingers. The word on his lips rasped from his teeth. Lotharic was across the space in a single bound of her mount. Cado felt the blood scatter into the rain and wind. The word he had spoken howled up to the thunder cloud. It was a call, a cry to the world of graves and death that echoed through the magic of Shyish.

'Soulblight,' she spat, 'your last grave will be here.'

She raised her sword arm, and then whirled.

Valentin was still wide-mouthed and wider-eyed. Cado grabbed the man's reins and yanked both of their mounts back as Lotharic's sword sliced towards them. It was a cut of murder made poetry, fast and simple, distance and force balanced precisely. Cado jerked back in his saddle as the sword passed a handspan from his face. Its blade was blazing. Heat radiated from it as though it had just come from a forge. The skin of his cheek prickled. He twisted, controlling his mount with his legs as he held Valentin's reins and drew his sword with his free hand. It was not a cavalry weapon, but the craft and magic of its forging made it leap in Cado's grip. He did not try to parry the next blow, which was already coming. He struck. Lotharic was fast beyond the reach of most humans. But Cado was not human, and his sword hissed as it sliced at the aelf's neck, and now it was her turn to arch back, bringing her sword up to turn the blow.

The weapons met. Force jolted up Cado's arm. The marks on his sword shone silver as the burning blade kissed it. Lotharic coiled and a fresh wave of force rippled through muscle and sword. Cado's blade vibrated and almost jumped out of his grip. Lotharic lunged into the opening. Cado wheeled his horse and the blow missed. He lashed out as they came around, and the tip of his sword found the join of an armour plate below the right shoulder. Lotharic reined back. Blood was seeping down her arm, staining the white of her armour. He saw a flash of pain and rage in her eyes, a blink of fire breaking through a shell of control. The whole exchange had not lasted two heartbeats. The rest of the Lumineth were reacting now. Valentin was slack-faced, shock still unfolding in him. There were bows rising. He could see the tips of arrows pulled up to shoot. Boots flexed in stirrups as spears began to lower. Magic gathered on the fingers and tongues of mages. It was all just a heartbeat. All so fast, but still to become the present, as though time were a cresting wave yet to break.

Far off in the distance, he heard the first howl answer his call. Then another, and more, shivering higher than the living could hear: the hunting cries of the dead. Light filled the world. Flashing. Green and white. The colour of sun falling through emerald water to the edge of darkness. Then the thunder crashing, out of time with the flashes, a roar that splintered into shrieks.

Cado alone could see. The aelves were blinking, trying to steady their mounts. Valentin was shielding his eyes. Cado kicked his own horse into motion, and whether it was the Soulblight's force of will or because it was on the edge of flight already, it jumped forwards. Cado yanked the reins of Valentin's horse, and they were going for a gap in the cavalry. One of the riders had enough of his senses to see him and lower his spear. Cado hacked through the shaft, backhanded the pommel into the rider's helm, and then they were amongst the ranks of cavalry.

They were not free, though. There were spear and swordsmen running up the valley. The cavalry were turning to follow. The light that had been shrieking through the air was draining. The scream of thunder vanishing.

Then the dead came. The first of them appeared through the rain and storm cloud, ragged shapes of shroud, fizzing like black ball lightning. Ghost hands reached from cloaks. Shadows of skulls with broken faces opened their mouths. These were Nighthaunt, cruel spirits tormented by their own sins, now set loose on the realm of the dead. They came with no purpose but to torment the living and drag the life from their bodies. Cado's blood and call had brought them, but they were not his to control, and now they fell upon the aelves like saw-fish swarming a bleeding cub. Arrows flew, spells loosed from lips, and suddenly the air was howling with light. The spells and silver bit into the descending spirits. Streams of black un-substance ripped free from hands and cloaks. A sound like shearing glass cut through the drumming of rain.

Then the dead reached the living. A crackling smear of black-and-white ghost-light struck a rider. The rider reeled back. Their armour shone as the magic in its forging tried to hold back the pressure of the Nighthaunt. Then the rider was falling, and the horse was crying out, and the Nighthaunt swept on. Another struck, then another. A smell like dank water and grave-mould filled the air.

Cado saw a figure rise above the aelf ranks, floating. He had his eyes closed, but his hands moved, snapping through patterns, fingers gripping. Stone shards burst from the ground, reached up into the air and enveloped half a dozen spirits. The mage's hands clenched into fists. The shards fused into spheres. Heat glowed through the stone as the spirits trapped inside each tried to break free. The mage opened his hands and the spheres of stone dropped into holes in the ground that opened to receive them.

Cries rose from down the valley as the spear and swordsmen that had been hurrying after the cavalry joined them. They flowed into formation as they charged, shields and spears rising as one. More Nighthaunt were falling from the clouds. A Nighthaunt with the blurred shape of a figure weighed down by ropes of stolen coins hit a swordsman right in front of Cado. The aelf's sword slid through the gossamer black of the spirit. Babbling howling boomed out. The Nighthaunt split like a torn rag. Silver coins fell from the ropes hanging from it. It shivered, dissolving into a black scorch mark on the ground. The swordsman saw Cado, stepped forwards, sword rising to cut.

A ragged black shape swept from the rain. The tip of a silver sickle punched through the swordsman's mouth and wrenched him up into the air. He writhed, scattering blood as the hook bit deeper.

'Light of Azyr...' gasped Valentin.

'Will not save us now,' Cado said, and urged the horses into the chaos. The coming of the Nighthaunt had bought them moments, but the aelves were rallying and their steel and spells could cut even the dead.

Another swordsman turned as Cado forced his way on. Cado kicked him in the face before the sword could rise. Steel crushed into bones and flesh. He kept going. There was no opening between the clashing sides.

A bellow rolled up the valley, rattling with breath drawn through a giant, rotting throat. The spirits of the dead did not respond, but some of the aelves who had just made it up the valley turned to face the way they had come.

The spirits of torment had come quickly, but now the creatures of the grave had arrived to take their due. Wolves and rats, and corpses left in swamp-thick ground. They came in a ragged tide. Death-light shone in their eyes. Teeth rattled in broken skulls. Hands dragged broken swords. There were more of them than Cado had thought would come at his call. Many more, as though a storm cloud of unquiet and bitter souls had found its lightning path. Souls set adrift by the spite of the Lord of Undeath, pieces of fractured ghosts in shells of bone and rotten skin… all and more.

Behind them, heaving itself across the ground, came a broken giant. Its bones and meat must have lain in the earth for an age. Worms coiled through it. Roots of blood-seeking trees threaded its ribs. Its fists were knots of skin and beetle-chewed bone. Its head a lump of rot, bellowing without air through a cave of splintered teeth. It was a gargant, a monstrous child of destruction that had risen from its unquiet grave.

It began to run. Its strides scattered walking corpses and dead creatures. Arrows rose to meet it. Then the tide of dead hit the first of the aelves. The dead giant swung its arm low. Horses and beasts and bodies flew into the air, tumbling like leaves kicked by a child. Another stride; the tide was pouring over the living, gnawing, ripping, tearing the souls out of their shells of flesh and bone. The giant reared up, a rider and horse in its grasp. The rider was still alive, hacking at the gargant's huge, putrid fingers, while the horse's legs kicked a death dance. The giant closed its fist. Rotten joints creaked. The rider and horse burst into blood and jelly. The gargant threw them aside and took another step. A beam of light struck it in the chest. The light bored through in an eye-blink and punched out of the behemoth's back. Burning bits of skin and rancid fat fell from the edge of the wound. The gargant roared. Atharion was walking towards it, each stride of his stilt shoes a dancer's step between the blows of walking corpses. The beam of light was shining from a rune that burned in front of his fingers.

The giant twisted, then lunged forwards. The beam of light sliced down and through its gut. Ash and embers fell from it. The aelves close to it drew back as it raised a hand.

Cado saw an opening.

'There!' he shouted at Valentin. 'Ride! Now!'

They charged forwards, right at the giant. Their horses running from fear as much as their urgings. The giant swung and the blow passed over them as they sped past. A thing with a collapsed skull and bone hands lunged at them. Cado kicked it back and crashed the flat of his sword into the head of a silver-clad spearman trying to block their path. Then they were out of the circle of swords, out and galloping up the valley side towards the road, while behind them the rain fell on the dead and the living.

CHAPTER FOURTEEN

They rode until the horses could take no more. Cado did not ask Valentin if they were on the right road. The smith was silent, slumping in his saddle, eyes staring. Cado slowed as they came to a place where a foot-beaten path led up a rocky slope. He dismounted once they were out of sight of the road. Valentin stopped but did not get off.

'We need to rest and feed the horses,' said Cado. 'By my reckoning we are only a league and a half from Aventhis, but we won't reach it if we keep going as we have been. There are things out there, but I can keep us safe.'

'Is that what you were doing back there in the valley?' asked Valentin. His voice was flat, cold, like iron dropped into quenching water. He looked at Cado. His eyes were wary.

'We are alive,' said Cado.

'Alive...' Valentin gave a chuckle that held no humour. 'That aelf, the one with the stilt boots, he pegged what you were, didn't he? *Kel'ylan* – that was what the other one said before she pulled her sword. I am guessing that's not something good in their tongue, something about you. Soulblight… Never seen one of you before, just heard the stories… Blood and horror and slaughter, but then I meet one and I think "stories can't all be true otherwise they would be called truth" and I think maybe they miss something, that one example is not a story.' He looked at Cado again. 'But you're not different, are you? The stories are true. Blood and horror and slaughter. If you hadn't been there, she wouldn't have pulled the sword, if–'

'They would have killed you.' Cado let the words hang. Valentin blinked. 'They didn't need me there as an excuse to do what they did to that settlement. People like that don't need reasons. They bring their own reasons, and night help anyone who is on the wrong side of them.' Valentin blinked again. Cado moved to deal with the horses. 'If they hadn't killed you, they would have sent you back to your city with a message.'

'A message?'

Cado nodded. He was looking out at the night. Lightning flashed across the high roof of clouds. 'They want something here. They knew where we had come from. They know this underworld. And an army does not come to a land that they know without purpose.'

'Purpose aside from killing and destruction.'

'They weren't there to destroy that settlement. That was incidental.'

'Incidental?'

'Yes. That shaft of light and the rune – it was like an arrow pinning the air and land in place.'

'What? Why?'

'I don't know, and the soul who would know, I can't talk to.' He looked down at his hands. The fingers were empty apart from the forefinger of his right hand. A howl echoed in the distance. Valentin shivered and opened one of the leather pouches from his horse. He shook pieces of rough material into his hand. One of them fell onto the ground with a metallic clink. Valentin gave a muffled curse and then a plea for pardon. Cado could see them clearly, but in the dwindling light, the man must have been working blind. Cado bent and picked up the chunk of metal. It was rough, cracked and bubbled in places, but also flecked with specks of crystal. It had a shape too: an irregular comet with twin tails and spiked halo. He held it out to Valentin. The smith looked around, took it, nodded thanks. He was frowning.

'Lightning-struck iron,' he said.

'From when Sigmar's light strikes from the heavens,' said Cado. Valentin looked surprised. 'Yes… They are to keep us safe.'

'Do as you want, but the dead will not find or harm us for now.'

'Because they fear you,' said Valentin.

'I have ways.'

Valentin nodded, uncertain, turning the piece of iron over in his fingers.

'I have faith,' the smith said and glanced at Cado. Even though the man could barely see in the gloom, his eyes were wide, watchful.

'Is some of that faith that Sigmar will protect you from me?' asked Cado. The smith did not answer. 'Keep your faith if it gives you comfort, but you should fear your god before you fear me.'

'You can't mean that,' said Valentin. Another flash of lightning and roll of thunder. The man's eyes were dark mirrors in the night.

'I will tell you something. I have existed for longer than this age and the age before it. I have seen people put their faith in gods that are now dust and ashes. I have known creatures that were more powerful than those gods, and I have seen them rise and fall. In all of this I have learnt one thing. They do not care. They have their concerns and their games, and if they do have higher goals then those exist at a point of view that is so distant that ages and cities and souls are less than grains of sand in a desert. Everything dissolves in their sight – the tears of the father over a lost child, the pain of the warrior who realises she will die without seeing home again. All of it is less than the great truths that only they can see. Good becomes an idea that they pursue through cruelty and indifference. You are nothing to them, as am I. We are not a damned soul and an innocent, and they shall see us both broken before they help either of us.'

Valentin was silent, the iron comet still in his hands. 'It gives hope, though.'

'You have yourself and hope only makes you weaker.' Cado moved away, looking out at the sky flashing above the cairns. 'Get some rest. We will need to ride soon.'

Cado stood and watched as the man slept. Out beyond the ridge and the crags, the sky flickered with light. Pale blue, golden yellow, ochre: all the wrong colours for lightning in this realm. He could taste the magic now, more bitter and dry with every breath. It was wrong, very wrong and becoming more wrong with every flash of light on the horizon. He needed to understand how. He looked back at the sleeping man, and the horses. He touched the iron ring on his finger. A flare of cold pain and then the shimmer of cold light just behind his shoulder.

~Something is wrong,~ said Solia, before he could speak.

He told her what he had seen at the outpost, and about the aelves and the wild undead he had summoned to evade them.

~My boy, but you know how to cause trouble.~ He could imagine her sigh, and almost see her shoulders move. ~Not least for yourself.~

'I think the aelves are the strand of their type called the Lumineth.'

~I cannot confirm from personal knowledge, but from what I have gleaned that would be a reasonable inference. The aelf children of the Realm of Light… they are powerful, my prince.~

'I have witnessed that. The question is, what are they using that power for?'

~Geomantic lines,~ said Solia. ~That is what they are interfering with. That is what is causing this shearing of the arcane fabric.~

'How?'

~Lines of magical resonance cross the realm. Power flows along them. Some have unique characteristics. Strands of bright power flow more strongly along some, or the jade fire of life, adding and mixing with the amethyst tides that seep and roll through everything. Where the lines intersect, you have confluences, points of great magical potential. Arcanomorphic features mark these confluences – spirals of cloud, great trees that dream and sing, holes that breathe dreams into the air. Many cities, temples and the works of mortal hands have risen at confluences. A work of power at such a place can achieve incredible things, but everything works in balance. Everything influences every other part. Magic and power balance across the web of geomantic lines. Change the flow in the lines and confluences and you change the nature of magic. You change the realm.~

'That is what these aelves were doing. That outpost was a confluence. They cast their rune to change it. To pin it in place with light.'

~That would alter the flow of magic across this world.~

'To what end?'

~My knowledge is only theoretical. If you call on the Speaker, then he would give you greater insight.~

'I do not have his soul-anchor, Solia,' said Cado. 'The rings were taken.'

Solia did not reply, but he felt her presence fizz behind him. He felt the weight of the silence. The rings were the last of the souls of his kingdom. His duty beyond even his oath of vengeance was to protect those souls in death. Now only Solia remained in his care. She would know the weight of that failure, but was there a rebuke in her silence too?

~The mortal is awake.~

Cado turned and saw Valentin's open eyes looking at him.

'Who are you talking to?' the smith asked.

Cado turned his head slightly. Solia shrank away from his glance.

'It is good that you are awake,' Cado said, and moved to the packs and horses. 'We need to move and quickly.'

'It's still night,' said Valentin. Above, a flash of cyan lightning blinked in the distance. Cado knew what the man meant. As the rictus moon rose, the cruel and unquiet dead slid out from earth and sky. Creatures of wild magic and Chaos shed their daylight hides and hunted for souls and skins. Nowhere was safe in these lands, but danger rose with the moon. People did not travel unless they had to and when they did, they avoided the night.

'We can move faster than in the day, and–'

'Your powers are stronger,' said Valentin.

Cado nodded. 'Lotharic and her kind are creatures of light. It will be more difficult for them to follow and find us.'

'If they lived.'

'They lived,' said Cado. 'Be ready to ride. Rest now. We need to get back to your city before night passes.'

Valentin slipped into sleep, exhaustion dragging him down into dreams that twisted his face as he fell deeper. Cado had sat unmoving, letting his thoughts rotate through his skull.

He wanted no part of the knot of trouble that was binding tight on this underworld. He would do no harm, but the justice he sought was his own. The suffering of mortals was as universal and certain as the falling of rain. This place was one amongst many he had passed through, and many more would follow. Injustice and cruelty filled the realms too thick for any response other than indifference. Aventhis might become a ruin in days or stand for years. In the end it would fall, and all those who clung to the false hope of its stones would die. He could not prevent that. He had his road to walk.

A light glimmered at the edge of sight. He felt it a second before he saw it. Heat prickled the skin of his face as though a candle flame had brushed over his skin. Then it was there, dancing in the distance in a gap between two crags. He watched it, his hand still on the hilt of his sword. Feelings and impressions arrived in his mind without words. He could taste dry sand and warm air. The light was an invitation, edged with assurances of safety.

After a long moment, he stood up and walked slowly to the light. It shifted behind the rock crags as he got closer. He followed. A figure waited for him in a circle of rocks. It shimmered like a mirage caught in a heat haze, blurring and smudging as it turned. Cado could feel the magic creating the image as a prickling heat on his face and bare skin.

'Is this an opening for an ambush?' said Cado to the image of Lotharic.

The Lumineth leader shook her head once. 'A parlay.'

'You do not parlay with my kind. You made that clear.'

Lotharic gave a slow nod. 'True, yet that is what this is.'

Silence.

'If that is so, it is customary for an offer to be made.'

'Withdraw from Aventhis. Whatever your concern is, abandon it, and we will not prevent your leaving nor pursue you.'

'A generous offer,' said Cado, allowing his lip to curl with the words. 'What could make you believe that it would appeal to me?'

'Of all the vassals of Nagash, the Soulblighted are the most way-ward, the most self-serving. You believe you are free of the power of your necromancer god, and so this offer has value. You may leave without loss. You may even take some of the humans with you as... as recompense.'

Cado held the mirage-figure's gaze for a long moment.

'Is that so?' he said. 'Such generosity, particularly from those who drew their swords as soon as they knew what I was.'

'In time we will illuminate you all. This does not change that. It is a stay of execution that serves a greater end.'

'A greater end...' said Cado carefully. 'A higher purpose that eclipses the suffering of other mortals. That is indeed–' His hand lashed out. 'Illuminating.' His fingers were talons as they sank into the mirage. He felt his anger reach across whatever magic linked this image with the living Lumineth. His fingers dug red tears in Lotharic's neck. Blood welled from sympathetic wounds. Cado tasted it. Sharp iron and hot copper. Wherever she was, Lotharic staggered.

Cado caught himself as he reeled. Steam and frost formed before him. There was blood foaming in the air, real blood. Around him the fractured tides of magic were suddenly twisting like a cyclone. He had not intended this. The magic of the Lumineth's conjuring and his curse had formed a bridge between them.

Emotion burned across his senses. He tried to shut it out, but it was too powerful, and he was unprepared. The aelves felt emotions more deeply than any other mortals. He had felt it before, in the blood he had taken in older, less controlled times. They knew love and hate and fear, but their experiences were far more intense. A human might taste the same joy for a single morning of wonder and then never have it return, or touch the bottom of despair in the darkest of moments. For the aelves, hate and joy and despair were always at such extremes, rising higher and plunging lower in a single day than others might experience in half a lifetime. Such tides of feeling could sweep them into waters of elation or despair for long ages before they passed. It was said to have brought them ruin when their kind were born into being, and even now it drove them to some of the greatest and worse excesses. If not controlled, emotion could consume them, cruelty lying over their souls like the snow of a long winter, languor dancing in their blood like the heat of a summer that never seems to end. Cado had learnt that to touch these currents of feeling was to risk being overwhelmed. And that was what had happened now.

Pain came first, cold and razor sharp, slicing into his core, opening his mind and soul to spill him into the dark. He was not Cado. He was Lotharic.

She was falling and flying and tumbling. She was a spark, a star falling through a nebula, folded in burning clouds of dust. She did not have a name, not one she could remember. And there was pain. Pain that skewered her through and through. It rose and fell, changing shape, like laughter, like the pulse of a monstrous heartbeat, like the teeth of a saw snagging as they cut through bone. There were others too, countless others just like her, all trying to scream, all wrapped in silence and starlight. Secrets filled her. The pain of them was the worst of all. She knew that her mother had never been proud of her and had lied when she said she was. She knew that the love of her life had never felt the same. She knew that when she had drawn a sword for the last time, the death that followed was meaningless. She knew other secrets too, vast flows of them scattering from the lives of mortals like sparks from a falling fire arrow. All of it was there and she could not separate herself from the pain or the knowing. It just went on, past the point where she knew who she was. Excess, an eternity of excess, her soul slowly eaten by secrets.

Then light. A hand of sunlight reaching into the abyss and pulling her free. Bliss. The kind of bliss that comes from the first gasp of air after suffocating. Pain drained away. The light filled the darkness. The secrets screamed at her, faded. Silence wrapped her. She slept without dreams. She had no name. No memories, but she was free. Then she opened her eyes and found that she was alive.

The cruelty of the moment was the embrace of ice after warm sunlight. The bliss faded. She woke to anger. When she touched the stone of a balustrade, it was there telling her to shatter it. When a smiling face placed clothes for her to wear, it told her to burn them to ashes. When she bit into sweet fruit, it told her to cut the trees they had come from and salt the ground in which they had grown. It was all she could feel. It was the only thing that was true. She had existed in torment, then bathed in oblivion. Now she had to live.

Control, learned bit by bit, crafted like a mask. That was what came next. Cold and unyielding as steel, as harsh as noon sunlight. She became a veneer of learned actions layered over the rage. She took a name and a role and chose a purpose. Glory, truth, righteousness. Every twilight she would say her name silently and list the virtues she served. Lotharic, warrior, regent in war to the Lords of Light. Far-seeing, wise, deadly and true: that is who she was. That is what life was. She had been saved. She was free. She lived in light.

It was always there, though, behind her eyes – a scream without sound or end. Down in the red depths, where the light could not reach, a single belief nested like a secret pearl. None of it meant anything. None of it mattered. All of it was empty, and the life she had been given was just a shadow, without dimension or truth. Her name, her mask, was a brittle covering over the rage that wanted to grind everything into dust and let the silence of windblown ashes drown all. Sometimes she dreamed she was falling into annihilation, and when she woke wished she were still asleep.

And that gave her shame. Cold and simple shame at the lie she wore as a mask.

The grip of sensation slackened. Cado felt his senses become his own again. He wrenched himself back. The image of Lotharic was smeared across the darkness. He saw the shame and loathing in her eyes, before the mask of control snapped back into place, and the conjuring vanished.

He stood in the circle of tors for a long moment before going back to the horses and shaking Valentin awake.

'Is something here?' the man asked as he scrambled to his feet. 'Has something happened?'

'We must go now,' was Cado's only reply.

The rain began to fall again as they rode. It tasted of metal and minerals. Whenever lightning flashed, Cado could smell burnt sand and flint. Apart from the flashes in the sky, there was no light. Cado could see, but Valentin was as good as blind. Cado had attached a rope between the smith's mount and his own so that the beast could follow. Valentin was staring into the dark as though it would suddenly clear. They were not following the direct road now. Cado was leading them, following the tug of the realm heart in his senses back towards Aventhis. They picked their way through gullies and over spurs of jagged rock. It was slower than it would have been on the road, but he had an idea that the way between Aventhis and the outpost followed a geomantic line. He did not want to follow such a path. It did not seem wise.

Cado felt the breath in his mouth cool. The taste of grave-incense and dust filled his senses.

He reined in his horse and put out his arm to halt Valentin's mount.

The smith drew breath to ask why they had stopped. Cado touched the man's hand, and the gesture was enough to silence the question. Cado held his gaze still on the gap between the stone tors they had been about to pass. A figure rose into sight. Without light, his eyes had pulled fragments, had shifted cold green and grey: the sight of a predator. The figure moved up onto the slope. It was tall, its back straight, its limbs spindle thin. It held a spear in one hand, a shield in another. Layered armour hung loose on its shoulders. It stopped. Then another followed, and more, each marching in lockstep. They rattled as they moved, metal on bone, a dry sound that pushed through the drumming of the rain.

Valentin couldn't take it any more.

'What is it?'

Cado turned, looking back in time to see spear tips and shields close the path behind them.

'Trouble,' Cado said, and slid his sword from its sheath. You could ride the underworlds for days and find only the feral dead and the desperate living. Now, the powerful and the ambitious were seeking him out. It did not augur well.

Ahead, the line of figures parted. A horseman rode into sight between them. At a distance it might have seemed a cadaverous mortal, but the resemblance was a mockery. Its armour was bone, as was the beast it rode. Its limbs and face were a sculpture of a skeleton. The crest of its helm were human ribs. Ghost-light gleamed as distant stars in its eye sockets. It came to a halt, its gaze fixed on Cado. It inclined its head in acknowledgement.

'I am Xericos, Liege-Kavalos of Lyria,' it said, its voice arriving at the back of Cado's skull. 'This by my command is the count taken and the reaping made. We come to gather tribute from these domains. I did not realise the Court of Blood had set a claim here. This error will be resolved before it results in disorder of transition.'

'I was not sent by the Court of Blood.'

'It is known that the children of the red night do believe themselves free of the bonds of authority. You are of their line and curse, and you are here. Therefore, the Court is part of this transaction. That their hand is as renowned a general and warrior confirms the need for this matter to be clarified.'

'I am no general.'

'You are Cado Ezechiar. You led the Crusade of the Red Banners in the rising against the followers of the Gods of All Corruption. You burned the Three Cities of Gorvael. Two hundred and seventeen passed from the ranks of the living in forty nights. So it is marked and accounted. You are the Hollow King, whose thirst cannot end, and who gives no mercy. Your name and deeds are marked.' The Ossiarch pointed at the twin-dragon crest on the hilt of Cado's sword and its ghost stitched into the fabric of his cloak. 'You still wear the sigil that you bore in battle. You are of the line of Highness Neferata. You are a creation of the Undying King and shall ever be.' It gave a single nod. 'It is marked.'

Valentin was staring at Cado. The Ossiarch moved its hand through the air, the gesture smooth but artificial, like the movement of a puppet. 'This part of the Lord of Bones' domain will return to his protection,' it continued. 'The bones of its living shall walk to war against those that threaten it. This is marked. You understand that this must be, Hollow King.'

'What are you talking about?' Valentin's voice was edged with fear, but Cado could hear an iron edge just behind it; the man was angry.

The Ossiarch looked at Valentin.

'Two hundred and six,' it said. 'Six cracked in the left hand, fused but with imperfection. Strong, of higher grade.' Valentin shook his head, not understanding. 'Postural errors. The position of the ribs and blade from carrying an infant.' Valentin froze, blinked. The Ossiarch tilted its head around its gaze. 'I correct, from carrying two infants. Four hundred and twelve of unknown quality.'

'What?' asked Valentin.

'Bones,' said Cado. 'It is talking about your bones.'

'All bones belong to the Lord of the Tithe,' said the Ossiarch.

'Two hundred and six,' said Valentin. 'Four hundred and twelve, that's–'

'Your worth,' said Cado. 'Your bones and the bones of your children.'

'My children?'

'If they are of an age where they still grow, theirs and yours are a single counting. When it comes to barter for tithe, you may draw markers for their count.'

Valentin just looked at Cado.

'Markers that you can exchange for influence or protection, or spend in place of your own debt if you were subject to the tithe.'

'In exchange?'

'If the tithe is not met, the empire takes its due from the living.'

'You are a crop left untended in the wilderness without protection from the forces that may damage the bounty you grow in your skin. This will be corrected.' The skull face leaned closer to Valentin. The gleams of green fire in the eye sockets grew brighter.

'All will be placed into order,' it said. 'We are here to save you.'

Then it sat back and pivoted its gaze to Cado.

'Do not dispute our claim, Hollow King. You are protected by your place in the greater order, but if you stand against us, we shall take you back to the Blood Queen in chains or as ashes.'

The Ossiarch bowed its head, then turned its steed and rode back between the line of spearmen. Cado watched it go. The spearmen followed, bone and armour clacking against each other as the rain fell.

Valentin stared after them, then looked back at Cado.

'You–' he began.

'We need to get back to your city. We go back to the road, and ride hard,' said Cado. He untethered his horse from the smith's mount. Valentin did not move but gazed in the direction that the Ossiarchs had gone. Then he turned. Anger and confusion pinched his brow. He was a man who did not know how any of what he knew fitted any more. 'Valentin,' said Cado. The sound of his name snapped the smith's eyes around. 'We ride now.'

Valentin blinked in the dark. What was the man seeing at that moment, Cado wondered – the silhouette of Cado against the storm-touched night, a thing who had burned cities and stained his banners with the blood of his enemies, a pale face under a ragged hood, or a man who had come with him this far? Something else, or none of these?

Cado waited. The rain poured down. Valentin nodded and took up his reins.

'Stay close,' Cado said, and began to ride.

CHAPTER FIFTEEN

The air was howling with the voices of the dead. Green-and-ochre light flashed across the sky. Balls of lightning crackled between the spires of rock above the road. The wind was heavy with magic. Nighthaunt shimmered at the edge of sight, before vanishing like scraps of cloth caught in a gale. Cado could feel the gale tugging at him too. It had changed since they had left Aventhis. The winds of death were pulling at the abyss inside him and the stolen blood in his veins. He could feel the magic that sustained him unravelling even as it renewed. They were not just riding to a city, they were riding into a growing hurricane of magic.

Cries of challenge came down to them as they reached the outer spires. There were militia on the bridges and towers now. Valentin called in reply and showed the worthies' seal when a wing of horsemen flanked them. The riders followed them all the way to the gate. Birds cut the air above them.

Vaux was waiting as they came through. Word must have passed from the watchers on the outer spires to the gate, and Cado remembered the birds following them as they had approached. The seneschal was grim-faced and said nothing as Cado dismounted. Valentin levered himself from the saddle and slid from his mount.

'Follow,' Vaux said, and turned. She began to stride up the road towards the spire top. Guards fell into step beside them. They looked grim but reeked of fear as much as the people who looked from the cracks in the doors as they passed. The curtains of grey-and-black cloud flashed at intervals. Cado could still hear the rustle and hiss of spirits clawing towards the spire only to vanish. Birds wheeled in the air, their cries filling the quiet between the crashes of thunder. Vaux glanced out occasionally. Valentin glanced around constantly, somehow more nervous now that he was closer to home. Up they went, step by step through the fold of cloud and the flash of lightning.

They reached the spire top, and then ascended the spiral steps of the tower to the platform. Dry whipcracks of lightning greeted them. Damascene and Leragrais were waiting again, standing over the table rather than seated.

Vaux raised her hand and pointed where Valentin and Cado were to stand. The guards hung back, but all of them were ready to level spears or draw swords.

'What did you find?' asked Leragrais.

Cado looked at the pair, then at Valentin. 'Tell them,' he said.

Valentin hesitated. Cado looked away from the smith. These mortals needed to understand what was coming for them and why. They might listen to him, but they would believe the smith.

Valentin licked his lips and then recounted what they had found. The man only hesitated when it came to the point where the Lumineth host had attacked.

'They attacked without warning?' asked Leragrais.

'They attacked me,' said Cado, before Valentin could answer. 'Their mages sensed my nature and that was enough for them to try to kill me.'

'Understandable,' said Leragrais.

'But you escaped?' asked Damascene.

Cado nodded. He thought that Damascene was about to press the point further, but Leragrais spoke first.

'And they are coming here?'

'Yes,' said Cado.

'Why would they do that?' Damascene asked Leragrais, but the wizard did not answer.

'In time of need,' the magister said, 'we may have an ally.'

'No.' They looked around. Valentin was shaking his head. Leragrais frowned at him, face wrinkling as annoyance built within. The smith shook his head again. 'They will not help us. They will destroy our home.'

'Be quiet,' snapped Leragrais, looking at Cado. 'Where were they last?'

'They destroyed the outpost,' said Valentin, his voice beginning to shake with anger. 'They told the people to get out and when they would not leave, these aelves destroyed it, and…' His voice faltered then, and Cado knew he was thinking of the woman with half her skull ripped away, pivoting in the air, the last cry from her lips rising and falling again and again. 'People… it is as though the people were nothing.'

'They trapped the souls of those inside,' said Cado. 'They will always be there, neither living or dying.'

'What would such a thing achieve?' asked Damascene. 'It's barbaric.'

'Not to them,' said Cado. He thought of what Solia and he had talked of, and the geomantic lines that led to the spire of rock they were standing on now. He let those suspicions stay inside his head.

Leragrais' eyes were flicking from side to side, focused on something that was not there.

'Where are they likely to be now?' he asked.

'No,' said Damascene, nodding in deliberation. 'The smith is right. These are another enemy.'

'So we turn over the bones and souls of our dead to the Reapers?' snarled Leragrais.

'We hold our walls,' replied Damascene. 'We defy the choice.'

'And lose everything,' said Leragrais.

'And hold firm to the only thing that matters.'

'There is no comfort in purity!' snarled Leragrais, and Cado could tell that this must be an argument that had been growing between the worthies. 'When the souls of the dead are dragged into the abyss, the principles we hold to will not save them. Eternal torment, your holiness. Souls sent back to cut the living. That is what will become of you, of me, and every mortal in this city. They may breathe for a few more seasons while they pay the Bone-tithe, but that life will end and then we will have given them to that fate.'

There was real fear behind the man's words.

'We have talked of this, and the decision is both of ours. We make no bargain with lesser evils.'

Leragrais bristled and looked as though he were going to spit a fresh retort. Then he looked around at Valentin and Cado. His eyes glittered, his lip curled, but he turned and walked away, his robes dragging over the damp stone.

Damascene looked as though she too were about to leave, but Cado raised a hand. 'My rings,' he said.

Damascene began to shake her head.

'We had an agreement,' said Cado.

'I know,' she said, and he was surprised to hear weariness rather than anger in her voice. 'I would honour it, but I cannot do that alone.' She glanced at the spot where the magister had stood. 'You see how it is. Once there was a Council of Worthies to make these decisions. Now there are just the two of us. It is easy to reach agreement as a pair and twice as easy to become mired in an argument.' She gave a snort of dry laughter. She turned and sat on a seat beside the stone table, then reached up and lowered the hood that covered her head. Her hair was blonde, with strands of grey winding into the plaits that coiled at the base of her neck. The lines around her eyes had only just begun to spread. She must have carried no more than forty winters. She pulled the comet crest from her scalp. She looked at it for a second, then placed it on the table. Cado saw the tiredness in her then.

'Why did you come here?' he asked.

'Because it is here. Because people are here. There does not need to be another reason.' Damascene hit the table with her fist. He studied the hardness in her face. There were supposed to be others here with her. The greater crusades sent from the great cities into the wilds took small armies with them, Stormcasts, wizards and warriors. Whatever strength had come to Aventhis, it had gone now. Now there was just this woman, the last symbol of her God-King's intent to reclaim the lands of the dead for the living.

This is the strength of this city, he thought, and the weight of it bears down without relenting. She does not sit on a throne, but she might as well. The burden is the same because they try to do what only a fool would do – rule and protect in a cosmos that is defined by cruelty.

Damascene tapped a large sand timer that sat amongst the rolls of parchment and paper on the table. All but a pinch of sand had drained from the top to the bottom of the glass.

'I am sorry,' she said simply. 'It seems that for all my suspicion you keep your word, and we, the pious mortals, only fail to keep ours. I do not have your rings. Leragrais is keeping them. When he returns, I will… talk to him.' She looked around at them. 'I cannot promise, but I also cannot say that part of me is not glad that the bonds of our bargain remain. We are a city in need of all the help we can get.'

'This is not my fight.'

'You are a mercenary, any fight is yours for the right price, correct?'

'What are you offering?'

'The same as before – the return of the rings, and to that I will add my help to find whomever you are looking for in the city, if they are here. All I ask is that you fight for us when the time comes.'

'You do not have the rings, and without them you do not have the means of paying me.'

'I have two of them, and Leragrais will not give the rest back to you without my help. So we are at an impasse. I, and this city, need your help to survive what is coming. You need my help to get what you want. That's a fair exchange, I feel.'

'You said I should burn, and now you want my help?'

'You all but said we are doomed, but you are going to fight for us. Things change.'

She stood and moved around the table, to where rolls of parchment gathered damp from the passing mist. 'You do not have much choice unless you want to relinquish what you care about. And neither do I.'

Cado held still. She was right on all counts.

'I may go free about the city?' he asked.

'Within reason, yes. Vaux will see to it. But you will not harm any of the people here. Not for *any* reason.'

'You trust me to do that?'

'I trust that you understand our agreement, and the consequences of breaking it.'

'You can't do that.' It was Valentin, all but forgotten beside the two as they talked. Cado looked around at the man. The trust had gone from his eyes. There was anger there now. Simple, direct anger. 'You can't do that. First he…' The smith jerked his head in the direction Leragrais had gone. 'First, he begins to think about those aelves, those… monsters as allies, and now you are going to give *him*' – he shot half a look at Cado that did not connect – 'freedom so that he can fight for us? Do you even know what he is, what he really is? Because I don't think you do. I think you have heard about the blood leeches and the night-kin like the rest of us, but you have no idea.'

Cado stayed silent. The man was frightened. Very frightened. His world had been simple, and his worries scaled to fit. Cado had seen it that night in the forge. Heat and hammer, that was the logic of Valentin's world; skill and patience applied with slow care. He was alone with two children to raise in a city surrounded by things that would kill them all. But if he could hold that danger at a distance and make the world stronger one tap of the hammer at a time, then that was enough. That was gone now. He had seen and understood, and the trust and naivety that had somehow lasted this long was gone. The cosmos had brought its hammer blows down on the smith, and his soul was cracking. Cado did not blame the man. It was fear and guilt. He had let Cado into his house – had let a creature who could call the dead talk to his children. And now he was hearing that armies were coming for his home, his family and all their souls. Given that, anger was almost the best response he could have had.

'I saw,' said Valentin. 'You know how he escaped the aelves? The dead came to him. He pulled them from the ground and air. The Bonereapers know him. They warned him that this city was theirs, not his. The enemies you fear think that he is a creature who wants to make us cattle, and you think you can hold him like a dog on a chain?' He stopped, blinking as though surprised that the words had come from his mouth.

Damascene looked at the smith. 'As a loyal follower of Sigmar, I thank you for your service,' she said. 'You are released and may go about your business with the thanks of the city.'

Valentin looked as if he might say something, but the fire had gone from his eyes and tongue. He fumbled a bow and walked away. One of the guards went with him. Damascene waited until their steps had faded.

'He is right,' said Damascene at last. 'I should kill you or drive you out. That is what the witch hunters and the fanatics of the Sigmarite creed would say. That is what every part of my mind and soul are telling me to do now.' She sighed. 'But missionaries and those of us on the edge of things have to learn to see things differently. Sigmar is said to have once called the Lord of the Dead an ally. Is our need any less than his was? So now, what will you say? Will you serve us and yourself?'

Cado was still for a long moment. Events had boxed him in, he knew. This follower of Sigmar had judged him well and placed just the right pressure to get what she wanted. She was desperate, it was true, but there was something else.

'You and Leragrais agreed with each other before…'

'We agreed for many years, on many things.' She gave him a keen look. 'I understand – I wanted you imprisoned before and now I want an alliance. What has changed?' She looked levelly at him, and there was no attempt to hide the tiredness in her eyes. 'Necessity. Our great Lord Sigmar made many alliances to secure the Mortal Realms. As he did, so it seems his servants must.'

Cado did not respond. She gave a tired smile. 'You think that we are playing you, Soulblight? That our disagreement was a way of creating a way to coerce you into doing more than was agreed?'

'It had crossed my mind,' he replied.

'And it crossed my mind that despite your protestations, you might be here to claim the city for your own before the Ossiarchs and now these aelves of light. That does not make either of those thoughts true.' She shook her head. 'Leragrais is a great man and has done more to protect and build this city than any other, but he is old and afraid. He spends more and more time alone, in whatever private sanctuary he has for himself. He was high in the Arcane order, you know? A scholar of magic and how it bound the realm together. Why he came here to a settlement on the edge of nothing… I wonder if sometimes he wishes that he had not come at all.'

Cado felt himself blink slowly.

Why he came here…

He thought of the mask in the ashes, and the words of the witch hunter.

'*You cannot trust anyone or anything under the stars.*'

How could the disciples of the Burning Hand be here, and have killed and wormed their way into the people, militia and spire without a wizard like Leragrais noticing something?

Pieces began to slide into place in his mind.

He knew the answer, or the beginning of it, and he knew what he had to do. He just needed a little more time.

He nodded to Damascene.

'Very well,' he said.

Damascene reached into her robes and pulled out a silver chain. Two of Cado's rings hung from it. She put them on the stone table.

'Yours,' she said again. 'Returned as promised.' Cado looked at them and then at the cometarian. She returned his gaze and gave a small shrug. The hard set of her lips flicked the grim beginning of a smile. 'It was what was agreed. You kept your word, and I keep mine. For my part, you are free.'

Cado nodded. He picked up the rings and slipped them free of their fastening.

'We are all made of fire and the wish to destroy,' she added. He looked up again. Her face was set sincere, as though she were speaking from a need that had nothing to do with the organising of walls or people.

'Even creatures like me?' Cado asked.

'Above creed or curse there are our choices, and in those there is always a way to be more than others' judgement of us.'

'I have met many of your faith who would disagree with you.'

'And I have never met a blood-tainted warrior of the night who would begin to listen.' The flicker of the smile returned for an instant. 'It seems that often things are not as we assume they will be.'

Cado gave a slow nod. He slipped the rings on. Pain flared up each finger at the touch of the iron.

'What are they that they mean so much to you?'

Cado closed his hand and looked at the black metal circling the pale skin of his fingers.

'Family,' he said.

Damascene raised an eyebrow, but then shook her head. 'I am afraid I have no idea where Leragrais has gone or why – we share responsibility for this city but little else. He vanishes often. That is a wizard's prerogative.' Cado saw something flash in her eyes, a hard snap of emotion quickly controlled. Anger? Bitterness? Fear, even?

'I wish you fortune. May stars and comets light your path, and Sigmar guide your way,' said Damascene.

'I doubt the blessings of your faith are intended for the likes of me, mistress.'

'Perhaps not, but take it all the same.'

'Thank you,' he said.

Damascene nodded, pulled up her cowl then turned and walked towards the stairs, her twin guards falling in beside her. And far down on the walls of the city, the gongs began to sound. The cometarian looked at the sand timer that was draining its last grains. 'The Bonereapers have come for their reply. I shall go and give it to them.'

'No,' said Cado. 'I will.'

CHAPTER SIXTEEN

Cado rode from the city before the sun rose.

~Family.~ Solia's voice reached after him as he rode into the fog. ~Or vengeance. It's the old choice, my prince.~

Behind Cado the shadow of Aventhis sank into the bruised light of dawn. The horse tried to turn back as they curved around a spire of stone. He pushed the beast on with will and reins. Above, a clack of dry lightning flashed ochre light through the murk. The magical distortions were getting worse. Time was running down to the last grains. He had lost the trail of the Burning Hand. He had lost his rings. He had lost the protection of anonymity, and he was losing the time he needed to get them back.

~The city might hold,~ said Solia, when Cado did not reply.

'It will fall,' he replied.

~So certain? What did I teach you about outcomes and will? If—~

'It will fall, Solia, and when it does the trail will be lost. Everything will be lost.'

~There could be ways of salvaging the situation. If the Ossiarchs' controlled the city, you could negotiate. They might even help you sift through Aventhis for the Burning Hand's disciples. They would return the other rings to you.~ He did not reply. ~You will have considered it, I know. It would be a king's choice – the least terrible of the options available. Make the move now. Their herald agrees you give them the city and they help you. They deny the Lumineth, and whatever magical horror they want to commit is averted.~

He thought of Valentin striking iron in his forge. It all meant nothing in the end. That was the great lie the Sigmarites spread: that there was space in existence for hope, and the small acts that made that hope. Hammer blows on iron, buildings repaired, children fighting about who had hit whom, rain and crops and things made for unborn generations. All a lie. All a skin of false hope over the truth that the darkness had won long ago. The gods warred not over the future but the scraps of the past: dead souls spooled into darkness, worship, and power over the patches of resistance. There was no future, not for this city, not for the greatest enclaves of mortals. Those that stood for longer were just delaying the inevitable. Death or damnation, those were the only futures that would come to pass for the mortals hunkering behind their walls and hoping. Solia was right. Better that he make the king's choice, the choice that followed the contours of reality rather than dreams.

'Do you believe that is right?' he asked. Around them the dawn fog flew past as he rode.

~I serve. I advise. I lay out the choices you know already and perhaps some you do not. But I am dead, my prince. I do not believe anything.~

Cado saw a shadow in the fog ahead.

'Thank you,' he said.

~What have you decided?~ asked Solia, but Cado touched the ring and her presence folded out of being.

The rider came out of the fog. Its banner rattled with each stride of its steed. It was not Xericos but another of the Ossiarch constructs. It halted. Cado slowed his own mount. The spire's lower walls were a quarter of a league behind him and hidden by mist and the bulk of one of the smaller spires. They were far out of sight or earshot from the walls. The rider cocked its head. Perhaps it was an affectation or a memory echo from the soul that animated its shell; either way it seemed inhuman. The surprise was clear, though. The rider had neither expected Cado to be there or to meet so far from the walls.

It gazed at him. The fingers of the hand holding the banner tapped the pole. Cado wondered, as he had before, if the removal of mortal habits from the Ossiarchs was as efficient as they thought.

'I am the herald of Xericos, Liege-Kavalos of Lyria. I come to receive the tithe from the city yonder. You are Cado Ezechiar. You are known to our lord and our legion. To what end do you come to meet me, grave-lord?'

'The city has gathered no bones for you,' said Cado.

The rider nodded once. Vertebrae creaked in its neck.

'The judgement was that their compliance was unlikely. The legions will come, and the tithe shall be taken.' The rider fixed Cado with the star glow of its eyes. 'But why are you here to relate these facts, Hollow King?'

Cado held the rider's gaze.

A king's choice…

'You will take no tithe from this city. It is not and will not be part of the empire.'

The light in the rider's eyes flared brighter. Its finger clacked on the banner pole.

'Grave-lord,' said the Ossiarch. 'You were warned not to press claim to this–'

Cado leapt from the back of his horse. His sword was in his hand as he arced through the air. The rider's mount reacted faster than it, rearing up to try to meet Cado with its fore claws. It was not enough. His sword struck the rider. The magic in the blade met the bone and sliced down through breastplate, ribs and on through the spine of the mount beneath and out through its back. He landed. The split halves of rider and mount scrabbled and twitched as ghost-light bled from them. Then they collapsed. Cado wrenched the rider's head free from its spine, looked up at the enfolding mist. Arcane lightning crackled in the distance. He held the head up. Emerald sparks were already flickering in its sockets as the magic inside searched for the rest of its body.

'Here is your Bone-tithe,' he said and threw the head towards where unliving eyes would be watching.

'We will come for you and for them…' came a dry breath of a voice from the distance. He sheathed his sword. He had picked his path. Now he just needed to walk it.

'So be it,' he said without looking back.

'No,' said Vaux. Cado looked at her, unblinking. She met his gaze and smiled. Coldness bled from the expression.

'Damascene agreed that you would help me find the followers of the Dark Gods in your city.'

'The cometarian has made a bargain with you, not me, and to say that I argued against it does the act a disservice. You are dangerous, you are not to be trusted, and you will get no help apart from what Worthy Damascene has ordered you receive. She may have bought your help, but you have not bought ours.'

They were in the shadow of the gate. Men and women lined the parapet top. Most had the barest semblance of armour and uniform. Some held their weapons as though they were holding a snake that was about to twist and bite them. Others clutched them like they were their salvation. They had started pressing the people to bulk the militia. Cado wondered how long any of them would stand when the Ossiarchs attacked, or the Lumineth tore the world apart with sunlight. All of them were staring out beyond the walls. They were waiting for the Bonereapers' herald to appear, a herald to whom Cado had given Damascene's reply with the edge of his sword. It was already one bell past dawn, but neither a rider nor an army had appeared.

Cado looked up at the people on the parapet. A muttering of voices was beginning to replace the silence. He could hear the tone of questions and the beat of rising hope.

'They have not come…'

'Maybe…'

'It was a bluff…'

'…won't come back…'

'Sigmar be praised.'

'They will come soon,' said Cado, looking back to Vaux. 'When night comes. And once they start, it won't end until the walls are broken. Use the time you have carefully, seneschal. You have the advantage of the spires and bridges. They will come against the walls on the ground and in substantial numbers. The more you can slow or damage them before they reach you, the longer you will hold.'

Something flickered in Vaux's eyes that Cado could not read.

'You know them well,' she said. 'I can't help but wonder if it hurts to betray your own kind, but is there such a thing as loyalty amongst you?'

'They are not my kind.'

'They are. No matter what you claim, this realm is the battleground between the living and the dead.'

Cado looked at her. Fire and defiance shone from the darkness of her eyes.

'You lost someone,' he said. 'Before you came here…'

Her cold smile peeled back from her teeth. She looked like she might turn away, but then stepped closer.

'Five families, five houses on the edge of a town on the moors close to the Lethis. They had all nailed the wolf tails to the doors and windows like they should. Besides, they were part of the city, and nothing that would go through a wolf-marked door would attack the town. Walls and soldiers and Stormcasts all there to keep them safe. There was an agreement, an understanding with a brood of your kind. We kept to ourselves. Them to theirs. Except they must have grown bored of it, or maybe they just wanted to deliver a message.'

Vaux's eyes were hard.

'Nailed to the walls of their houses,' she said. 'All of them. Five houses. Five families. They did not even feed on them, just left them like vermin kills.'

He blinked.

Nailed to the walls of their houses...

'Your family?' he said, carefully.

'No. None were my family. I had never met them before, but I was the one who found them. Two of them were still alive. Held my hand and shivered as they prayed that the Lord of the Undeath would not take them. I learnt enough of what the promises of the blood leeches are worth and what they buy.' She stepped back. 'Maybe you will fight. Maybe you will help us when it comes to it. But until then you will stay where I can see you. And I can see you everywhere. Understood?' One of a cluster of militia in cloaks hawked onto the cobbles. They were staring at Cado with hard eyes.

Cado felt his face settle to a mask. Vaux's words had pulled a recent memory into sight.

A corpse nailed to a wall, its flesh long rotted from it. Birds watching from the rafters. Amaury, the person who had appeared like an answer to a wish, and now was gone, unknown like she had never been...

Vaux gave a snort of laughter that held only ice and sharp edges.

'Nailed to the wall like vermin...'

'Get out of my sight,' said Vaux.

Cado nodded and turned away.

'Don't forget, my prince – this is their territory and they have had who knows how long to worm their way under its skin. In this city, they are no one and they could be anyone...'

Over on the wall, the waiting men and women had begun to look around at each other. Some of them were leaning on the hafts of weapons, relief clear on their faces. Cado turned back. Vaux looked around from where she was talking with a sergeant in a steel skullcap.

'They will be coming at night, seneschal. Remember what I said. Be ready.'

Her lip curled, but she said nothing and turned back to the sergeant without a word. Cado left and began to climb up into the city. Behind him Vaux's watchers would be following. He was sure they would be the best she had, and they knew the city. He would have to be careful but cursed himself as a fool for the thought that he might just have seen a hand of truth reach for him out of the fog of lies. Leragrais would come later. For now, he could smell the scent of prey. Above him flocks of birds rose from the city roofs to wheel against the growing dawn light.

CHAPTER SEVENTEEN

The birds crowded the roof spaces just as they had before. They watched him as he approached and entered but did not move. Just watched him with amber-and-red eyes. It felt as though they had been waiting for him.

He had returned to the building that he found on the day he first arrived in the city. The building where the birds had seemed to lead him to a corpse nailed to a wall, a corpse that had been touched by Chaos. He had forgotten it until Vaux's use of words had brought it back to mind, and he realised that it was one of the only traces of the disciples of the Burning Hand he had uncovered. He had thought the birds had led him to the corpse to cleanse their eyrie, but now he thought they might have been trying to show him something else.

He crossed the floor until he reached the section of the ruin where he had set the fire. No one had attempted to put it out and it had consumed the body and the remains of deserted nests in the vaulted ceiling above. Scorches and soot marked the stone. The fire had reduced most of the body to ash and the rain that had come through a crack in the ceiling had turned the rest to a black-grey slime. The odd tooth glittered amongst pieces of clothing. Bits of hair gave fibre to the mass. A stub of bone remained snagged on one of the spikes still driven into the wall. The birds shifted as he moved closer.

He paused, breathing the reek of the place: charred hair and meat, bird droppings and damp. It had taken him longer than he had wanted to get free of the eyes Vaux had set to watch him. He could have used blood sorcery, but they might have realised that he had got away from them deliberately, and he did not want that. Vaux was ready to try to hunt him down if he gave her any reason. He did not need that problem, not on top of the others he was facing. She was suspicious. Him losing her trackers would make her more so. Overt magic would put an end to her doubts about obeying Damascene's command. That was if she was following Damascene's orders. That was if she was what and who she claimed to be.

Either way he was not going to risk being followed or becoming an enemy of the militia. So he had used ways that took longer. He had folded out of sight faster than a mortal could move as he turned corners, jumped over walls, and hung silent and still in the broken gables of buildings. He had watched his hunters pass, become panicked; had listened to their hissed oaths and let them go by him. One had passed a hand's breath beneath him after he swung up into the beams of a roof that hung over a street corner. The man had blinked, then continued up the curving alley at a run. Cado had listened to his steps and huffing breath recede and then had lowered himself to the street and walked on. A few people had seen him, but the eyes of the city were either looking down in fear or out at where their fears gathered in the fog and flashes of light. It had not taken him long to retrace his steps.

He looked down at the rings on his fingers. A fraction of the nine that were his to keep and protect. There was Solia, her band also worn to a shine. The two others sat on the little finger of his left hand and the ring finger of his right. One was fine, almost just a loop of iron wire. The other was thick, heavy and pitted. He had not called on the spirits they held for a long time. Maybe he never would again. He looked at where the heavy ring sat, close to the knuckle of the ring finger of his right hand. It was broader than Solia's, and the sigils cut into it were almost invisible against the dark metal. He did not want to do this, but he needed insight and knowledge that was not his.

'Idyon,' he breathed and touched the ring with his thumb. Sharp pain snapped up his arm. A mote of grey-white light formed in the air. It fizzed, and split. Tendrils of light traced through the air as though a stylus were sketching with silver in shadow. Light smudged. Shadow blurred. For a long moment there seemed no pattern to the unfolding light, then it settled, and the head and shoulders of a man hung in the air.

The man looked young, though when Cado had last seen him alive he had seen over a hundred summers. A smooth scalp above sharp features, eyes as piercing in the ghost-glow of his presence as they had been in life. The folds of his clothes and the lowered hood blurred as the frayed light of his shade faded from the chest down. He looked at Cado, shook his head and regarded the remains of the corpse on the floor.

~Ah,~ he said, eyebrow arching. ~Another disaster or another tragedy. How much of this one is your making?~ The shade shook his head. ~Don't answer that. The less we have to talk, the better. ~

'Hello, old friend,' said Cado.

The spirit flinched and then shook his head once.

~My friend and king died a long time ago. You wear his face and memories well, I have always thought, but no... let's not start this unfortunate exchange with fancies and lies. Better the truth no matter how bitter. I am your captive, and whatever you will, I must do. No choice or way out. There is a word for that, I am sure...~

'I keep you only so that you are safe.'

~Ah, yes.~ Idyon's voice rose, projecting as though he were a priest rousing a crowd. ~If you did not keep me and the rest tethered to our soul-cages then the winds of death would carry us into the dark and hungry abyss, into the heart of Nagash to feed his terrible majesty.~ His lip curled and he shook his head. ~Pathetic. A bit of truth used to cover the ugly lie. Yes, Nagash could wind in our souls and eat them up like the monster he is, but there are other ways of keeping us safe. Yet you don't use them, not just because you like to keep us close, but because it lets you flagellate yourself so you can feel better about what you have become and what you have done. Oh, and of course it lets you summon us up like the court of lackeys that every king must have, even one without a throne.~

Cado shook his head. He'd had this argument many times and knew that it would not change any more than the shade of his friend could change. Both were preserved just as they had been when they crossed the threshold of death. He knew that, but he could not help trying.

'None of them would protect you from her,' he said.

~The Burning Hand wants nine souls from a kingdom she reduced to ashes in another age?~ Idyon laughed, the sound like the crackle of wind through a burnt forest. ~You hunt her and the disciples she creates, but you still refuse to admit the fact that what was done to you does not matter any more. No one even remembers that your kingdom existed. The Burning Hand is no longer one person. It's a species of the Change God's followers. They and she – if she is even alive and not burning in a daemon's gullet – don't care about what happened. My death and your kingdom were barely a step on whatever road they are on. You know what they do care about? The future. That's what they care about. Power and dominion and undoing all the things that are in their way. They aren't hunting us, and they don't care about you.~

Cado let the words finish.

'I need your help.'

~When do you not?~ Idyon winced, shook his head. ~But you have only summoned me now because your need is great enough to overcome your discomfort that I see you for what you are – a leech, a parasite soul-feeding on the living while my true friend and king rots under your skin.~

Cado heard the edge in the words but did not respond. He could not say that what the ghost of his greatest friend said wasn't true. They, like the road he walked, were his penance.

They had always been friends when both lived, or at least since both had been old enough to remember. A lot of others had shared his childhood. There had been the sons and daughters of his mother's and father's advisors and ministers, and the children of the guard cadre. There had been few divides of status or station, at least while they were truly young. Cado had just been Cado, quick and quiet, and Idyon had been clever and loud, and always the first to laugh when he did something foolish. The structures of the adult world had crept in as they grew older. Cado could still remember the day when Grelao, the daughter of a guard captain and two years older than him, had been about to grab Cado's ankle and send him sprawling in a game, only to whip her hand back. There had been a look in her eyes as though she had been about to put her hand into a fire pot. She had been the first but not the last. One by one he went from just another child and friend to the First Heir. Unspoken rules built walls where there had been simple understanding. Formality took the place of friendship. Not with Idyon, though. He had remained just the same. Clever, mocking and loyal; never afraid to take him down a peg or many; never stepping back from the kind of loyalty that made the years between childhood and adulthood bearable. A friend. A loyal friend all the way to the end. But not beyond.

~What do you want?~ asked Idyon.

'This corpse. I burned it three nights ago.'

~How very imaginative of you.~

'The birds led me to it.'

~They did?~

'This underworld is created by the belief that the dead live as birds. Here the birds hold the spirits of the departed.'

~I know. I can feel them. I was just doubting that they led *you* here. We who have gone beyond don't often like blighted souls.~ Idyon turned to look up at the rows of eyes staring back at them from the perches. ~Have you tried talking to them?~

'No. Without a voice to hear or binding them to me, I can't–'

~A good decision,~ Idyon cut in, and looked round, smiling. ~They would rip you apart if you tried. A thousand beaks... How much of you would be left after that? Enough to scrape into a bag perhaps and send back to your Queen of Blood.~ He turned away before Cado could reply. ~They are afraid. Afraid and angry. All of them.~

'Of what?'

~Of what is coming. There is a...~ Idyon broke off and the image of his head turned as though he were trying to hear a very faint noise.

'A geomantic disturbance,' said Cado.

Idyon nodded. The distaste on his face clear.

~Yes, but that's not all.~ Idyon reached out a hand, palm open. The birds around the room shifted. Feathers rustled. Then a grey bird took flight, dived towards Idyon. Its wings splayed open just before it would have touched his apparition. It hung in the air, wings beating. Time thickened. Cado felt the beat of the wings in his ears. Idyon still had his hand out. The bird's wings beat again, but the movement was slow as though running to a different time. Its beat touched Idyon's fingers. Cado felt a crackle of lightning charge. Cold shivered across his skin. He thought he heard the distant sound of water falling drop by drop into a still pool. Then the bird's wings were beating fast again. It cawed and flew up to its perch in the roof. Idyon lowered his hand. The arm below the elbow dissolved into nothing. He pivoted to look at Cado.

~This death was not just a murder. It was a ritual.~ Idyon glided close to the pile of burnt remains. ~The spirits that come are the birds of this land and not just the dead in avian form. They do not think or understand like the living, or even as I do. Concepts, ideas, information mean nothing to them. Anything that happens fits into a world of food, of seasons or predator and prey, flight, and territory. They are the flock. They did not bring you here because they wanted this gone. They brought you here because they watched you on the road and in the forest before you reached the city. They saw what you did to the acolyte. They know what you are. They wanted to bring you here because they thought you would understand. They are not here for shelter, they are guarding this place. This is not just a city. It is like a lake in the flow of magic across these lands. It flows here and vanishes, and that keeps the balance of the underworld and those close to it.~

'How?'

Idyon laughed. His image flickered.

~You think that I can just know everything in an eye-blink? Whatever this city is, and whatever it is hiding, is just that – hidden.~ He looked up at the birds and down at the mass of ash and shards of bone on the floor. ~Whatever it is, we are not the first or only ones seeking it.~

'The Burning Hand – they will have a reason to be here, and a reason to stay out of sight.'

~Just so.~

'What did happen here?'

~A crime against the living and the dead. That is what the birds feel. The details are not clear.~

'Can you make it clear?'

~Perhaps,~ said Idyon softly. ~That is why I am summoned to your *majesty's* presence.~ The words were edged with bitterness and scorn. ~There is nothing I have said that Solia could not have told you. I am here to mediate with the dead for you.~

Cado nodded. Idyon had been his First Speaker, the strongest wielder of magic in the kingdom Cado had lost. Even in death he still held a depth of arcane knowledge and power greater than Solia or Cado.

~I will need help, though. Solia, and the others.~ He nodded at the rings on Cado's fingers.

'No,' said Cado, sharply.

~If you want me to find out–~

'Solia, yes. The others...' He shook his head. 'No.'

Idyon flashed a bitter smile.

~Ashamed to show them how far you have failed to come?~ He shrugged. The gesture sent motes of ghost-light spinning into the air. ~I am a shade. My power is limited. If you won't let me have the help I need, then I cannot do as you ask. Simple. Even you should be able to understand that.~

'I will help you.'

~You were always a poor student of the arcane even when you were alive. Death has not improved that.~

'But it has given me power.'

Idyon looked at him. The holes in light that were his eyes met Cado's gaze.

~And there is the only thing that matters.~ He shook his head. ~I cannot refuse you. So it will be as you command.~ Then he gave a bow, the gesture so stiff that contempt radiated from every part of the movement. ~My king.~

Cado drew the knife across his palm. The blood that welled from the wound was thick. Black as tar. The eyes of the birds were circles in the gloom. Solia's presence glowed from behind him. Idyon hung in the air. The burnt ashes lay on the ground between them. The dead wizard opened his eyes.

~Call them,~ he said.

Cado squeezed his hand into a fist. A blood drop formed. Whispers hissed from behind him. His fangs were sharp in his mouth, his eyes red. The moment balanced. He clenched his hand. The blood fell.

'Rise,' Cado said.

The birds exploded from their perches. Caws and cries split the air. Beating feathers and the voices of Idyon and Solia calling from beyond their graves; calling, demanding, singing as their hands plunged down into the abyss of oblivion. Dark and shadow became light. The marks scratched into the floor were black. Then the heap of ash and hair and bone stirred and began to rise. It made a shape like a person, the kind of shape drawn in soot on cave walls by the light of a fire. Thin lines as limbs. Scratches for hair. The smudge of a head came up last. Cado could hear rasping, the sound of flames trying to breathe, to burn. The figure opened its eyes. They were two holes into an inferno. The birds froze where they flew. Their wings were a dome of feathers.

A weight seemed to fall on him. Leaden, crushing. He fought to stand. His heart was beating thunder. Stolen blood screamed in his ears. Then blackness, and the silent roar of heat washing over him. He could not see.

He was blind.

There was a sound, a shriek, that rose and wound through itself until it was a rope of pain.

Then sudden quiet, and just the aching thrum left as an echo by pain.

'Speak,' commanded Cado.

The laughter that answered was low, growling, heavy, inhuman.

'I called you, and you must answer.'

~Burn,~ came the reply from next to Cado's ear, in a voice that was not Solia's or Idyon's. And he felt fire pouring into him, flesh charring, no more space for a scream, no more time for anything but a single moment of terror.

~*This is a risk,*~ *Solia had said when they had prepared the summoning.*

~*He knows that,*~ *Idyon had replied.* ~*He does not care. Risk, harm, hurt, he can barely know what those things are, let alone feel them. He wants. He wills. He gets. And we obey. I sometimes wonder why you even bother trying.*~

~*The same reason you cannot forgive.*~

Idyon had snorted. ~*Solia is right, though. It is a risk, a bad one too. This was the site of an unclean ritual. Whoever this mortal was, they died as part of it. Their soul would have been consumed, mutilated. Whatever was left will be a shadow of their death. Scraps of agony and emotion that are seeping slowly into the earth and air. What you call up will most likely want one thing – to inflict its pain on whatever part of the world it can reach. At that moment that will be you.*~ *Idyon had shrugged.* ~*Come to think of it, forget what I said. It's no risk at all.*~

'Speak. I command you to speak!' Cado forced the words from his lips.

The laughter of fire was the answer.

'How did you die? I need to know.'

There were hands on his cheeks. He could feel bone poking through rotten skin. Pain poured into the abyss of his soul. It was strong. So strong.

'Tell me.'

The hands were gripping tighter on his face, and he knew that a face was moving closer to his, a smile opening to show teeth. Everything gone, all of life and hope. All the futures never lived, cut off. Ashes and burning and pain. And in that, the one question that no one asked the dead or the damned. The one question that no one had asked him in a lifetime.

'Who were you?' he asked.

Stillness. A pause. Then the hands were gone from his face. The leaden weight shifted.

~I...~ growled the burnt voice, but it was crumbling to something human ~I was alive...~ it said.

Cado recognised the voice. Shock flooded him.

'Amaury,' he said aloud.

~No... I...~ The voice came in starts. 'I do not know you. I...'

'I need to know what happened here.' A wall of force slammed into him. He staggered. The crushing force piled onto him. He felt joints pop. He could feel cords of air wrap around him and constrict. There were few things that could undo him. The hurts of the mortal world were temporary at worst. Blood renewed all. Except that here, in this ritual, he had called a broken spirit up. It existed by his power. Here and now it was as powerful as he was. And it could hurt him. He could dispel the spirit, but then it would vanish and there would be no answers or justice for the dead.

'Amaury,' he called. 'Show me. Please.'

The pressure grew and then released. For an instant there was just stillness, and then something struck him, enveloped him, drowned him and he was gasping backwards through the last moments of Amaury's life.

Gasping... breathing, somehow still awake despite the pain.

A monster stood in front of her. A monster with a mouth but

no eyes, a monster that was holding a knife in one hand. Blood was charring to soot on its edge.

'There,' the monster said, and held up what looked like a rag. A small and bloody rag. They pulled it taut with one of the fingers of the hand holding the knife. 'A good fit.' There were holes... Holes in the cloth. Eyeholes, and an opening for the monster's mouth to grin through. Except it was not a cloth. The monster lowered the flayed face and sheathed the knife. 'You know, what is it you call yourselves – the Mask Breakers? Mortals trying to peel back the lies that hide the truth. But you really don't understand the nature of masks.' The monster put a long finger on her chin. The pain of the touch was like a lightning bolt inside her skull. The monster tilted its head as though looking at her, even though there was just skin where its eyes should have been. 'The point of a mask is that it can be changed. And what can be changed cannot be broken.'

The monster took its finger away and rubbed it against its thumb, as if the smear of blood on it was distasteful. 'You see, we are not going to destroy you or your, what would you call them – comrades? Friends? Witch hunters? We are going to use them. Starting with you and this wonderful mask you have given me. All I need is a few more details to make it perfect...'

And the monster had put on her face. It spoke a word as it pressed the skin to its skull. Blue-and-cyan fire wreathed its body. Steam billowed from the edges of the flayed face. It stuck and squirmed. Skull and skin re-formed into features. Hair uncoiled from the monster's scalp. Its shoulders and body pushed into a new shape. It looked up at Amaury and smiled at her with her own smile. Then it raised a burning hand and plunged its fingers into Amaury's mouth. Heat poured into her throat and down into her chest. She felt the fingers close. She was choking, smoke filling her lungs. The monster yanked its hand back. Amaury felt something in her mind or soul snap. The pain was all-consuming now.

She could not breathe, could not make a sound. She was falling away from the world in front of her eyes. The monster held what looked like a tongue and lowered it into its mouth. It swallowed then looked around at her as sight splintered into fire and agony.

'Well, isn't this just the perfect fit,' said the monster with Amaury's voice. Then there was just the fall and the fire and the roar of death coming to claim her soul.

Cado shook himself as the vision drained from him. Blackness filled his eyes. He could feel the spectre of Amaury around him. She still held him immobile. Anger and hate and fire. He had summoned it up, and now he needed it to let him go.

'I will give you vengeance,' he said.

~Ven... geance...~ said a voice like the hiss of flame. The pressure holding him tightened.

'Yes. You deserve it.'

The pressure built again. He could feel the blind hunger in that. The anger that was now so much of the spirit wanted to pass on its agony. No matter that he was not responsible. He was here, a reality rather than a promise. Then the pressure lessened. The fire on his skin cooled. His eyes cleared in time for him to see the outline of a figure move back from him. He could feel her fading. The rage that held her in the world had gone. In a second, the tides of death would sweep her away. Nothing else was moving. The halo of birds still hung in the air. Their wings stretched in mid-beat. Idyon was similarly motionless. The image of his mouth was open. Only Cado and the shadow moved in this frozen world.

'Come with us,' he said, half on impulse. The spectre of Amaury flickered. 'You can see your revenge.' The spectre did not reply, but it held still. Then the shadow of its head gave a single nod. Cado reached out and pulled the metal spike from the wall where it had pinned an arm in place. He spoke. The words shimmered in the air, grey and gauze-like. The spectre twisted. Cado felt the power he was calling on pull on the blood in his veins. He kept speaking. The spectre began to fold, one part over another. Cado flicked the metal spike into the air. It tumbled. The collapsing image of Amaury's spectre soaked into it. It glowed orange and red, hanging before him. Then the heat faded from it, and it fell. Cado caught it. The iron was cold. He felt the spirit stir inside.

~Was that pity or weakness?~ asked Idyon. The shade was opposite Cado. The birds fluttered up to their perches. Cado put the metal spike into a pouch.

'It was what she was owed.'

~Imprisonment in a lump of iron with only hate and pain and your promise for company… Quite a payment for dying in agony.~

'A sorcerer took her face,' said Cado.

~One of the disciples of the Burning Hand,~ said Solia from behind him. ~The person you met in the drinking house was one of them.~

'No one knows who Amaury is… Not the drinkers in the inn or the militiamen.'

~All memory of her eaten by sorcery,~ Idyon said, then laughed. ~They found you and played you without you even expecting it. Oh, how history does love to repeat itself.~

'She led me to evidence of the cult in the city…' said Cado. 'Why?'

~Why indeed?~ said Solia. ~Added to which was the killing of another one of their number in the fight in the burnt house.~

~No doubt a flourish to remove any doubt about his new ally from our king's mind,~ said Idyon.

'But to what end?' asked Cado.

~Also obvious,~ sneered Idyon. ~To direct your attention. You are looking for them, so they show you that they are here. You want to know where to look and so they point you in the direction they want.~

~He is likely correct,~ added Solia. ~Though his mode of expression is coloured by emotion...~ Idyon made a *tsking* noise. ~The analysis fits. The disciples prompted your hunt for them.~

Cado felt the cold truth of it settle on him.

'Every mark and trail I have followed must be treated as suspect.'

~And they were hardly generous with them: a painted door, the existence of a secret hunter cell in the city, and the idea that there is something hidden underground. They set you looking for them in the places where they almost certainly are not and added in the fun of getting you to tangle with another of their enemies. Elegant, it has to be said.~

~The birds knew,~ said Solia. ~In whatever way they understand the living, they knew even if they could not speak it.~

~They led you to the truth, but you could not see it.~

~The question is – do the disciples know where you are now? Do they know that you have found out?~

~So far, they have been one step ahead,~ said Idyon. ~They will have wanted to be close to you, to keep you within reach. They are stealing faces, that means they could be anyone you have come across since you got here. If you are following a trail they set out, then any of the people who just happened to be on that path could have been one of them.~

Cado shook his head. He had heard enough.

'There is one person who cannot have been false,' he said. Idyon frowned.

Cado turned and walked away through the ruined house. The birds cawed at him as he passed.

~My prince, that is not wise. Idyon is right. The disciples have led your steps. You should wait, consider options...~

'This city will be lost before another night passes. They know that. Whatever they are doing, they are running out of time too.'

~My prince...~ began Solia.

'Thank you for your counsel,' he said, and felt the two shades fade out of being. The rain and growing storm greeted him on the street. He raised the hood of his cloak, striding quickly.

They were right, Solia and Idyon. He had been led by the nose and diverted into tasks that had taken him away from the true goal. He knew where he needed to go now, and to whom. When lost in a storm of lies, the truth was the only shelter, even if that truth came from an enemy.

CHAPTER EIGHTEEN

Cado could smell the blood before he reached Agen's house. Thick iron and copper, still warm from the vein. He felt his thirst rise, bit it back. The front door was locked and barred as it had been before. He moved to the small door at the back. It was open, hanging on its hinges. He drew a dagger and went inside. The smell of blood was a hammer here. His senses lit and sharpened. He could feel a single fading heartbeat, could taste and smell the fresh blood touching the air. A moment to close his eyes. Then he moved, step by slow step, controlled, dagger ready.

Agen had been nailed to his chair. Iron spikes pierced his forearms, knees and torso under the collarbone. Blood leaked from the wounds, but most of it had come from the cut that ran across his gut. A wide pool of gloss red covered the floor around the chair. The fire in the hearth was still burning. Freshly cut logs cracked and spat in the flames. Cado held still, clamping down on the hunger spinning through him. He could feel the points of his teeth, and knew that his eyes would be red. It was as though

Agen had never moved from the place where Cado had questioned him, but Cado had set him free and nights had passed since then. Cado had expected to find Agen alive, and to use either sorcery or a simple offer of alliance to find out what the witch hunter knew about Amaury – or rather what had been wearing Amaury's face. He had not expected to find the man mutilated and dying. Worse, Agen looked like he had been placed in a deliberate echo of his position during Cado's interrogation. It was a calculated act, as though whoever had opened the witch hunter's guts were leaving a message – *We are ahead of you,* it said. Cado considered leaving then, simply turning and going back into the cold embrace of the city.

Then Agen twitched. The wound in the man's belly opened with the movement. There were coils of gut in that red smile. Very carefully, Cado moved forwards. Agen did not move. Cado stopped a pace from the witch hunter. The blood was a thick pool around his boots. He squatted down so that his eyes were level with the man's closed lids. He looked at the red pool at his feet, dragged a finger through it and raised it to his lips. The life was already fading from the blood, but it was strong enough to make the darkness within snarl with hunger. Cado bit down on that, focused on the salt taste of life, and spoke.

'Agen,' he said. The man did not stir. The flow was slowing from the wounds. The link between blood and life was weakening. Cado would need more. He scooped a palm of blood from the floor and brought it to his mouth. '*Agen,*' he said, through bloody lips. The blood sorcery in the name was a hammer blow of will. The man flinched and sucked a breath. Cado put more of his will into the next command. 'Wake,' he said. The man's eyes opened. The pupils were pinpricks.

'What did they want?' asked Cado. The man's head lolled, his eyelids already drifting shut. Cado brought his own hand up to his teeth, bit down and forced a bead of blood from the bite. Then he pushed the man's mouth open and let the single drop fall between his teeth. The man's head snapped upright. The pupils bloomed wide in the eyes. Flecks of red gleamed in the irises.

'I...' said the man, forcing the word out. Just like he had before when he had been fighting Cado's will. Now he was fighting for his life, its last moments measured in slow heartbeats. The wound in his gut had stopped bleeding, but this was just a pause, a stolen moment balanced between last breaths. Cado's blood was keeping him here. 'I... know... you.' It was Cado's turn to rock back at the words. 'They... said you would be coming.'

Cold, cold down his spine. This scene, this exchange of questions had been laid out like the elements of a play or a picture, a picture painted for him. He knew he should flee, but he did not.

'Who?' he asked, his own voice a thin growl.

'The face thieves...' The man was slurring slightly, as though drunk. He blinked slowly. 'Bronze masks... knives.'

'What did they want?'

'Want? They have everything they want. They have won... or close to won... Out of time... Sand running too fast.'

'How have they won? What do they want?'

'You know... You do know. Power... Under the city... They have it now... Should have stopped them... could have stopped them... Too late now... no salvation for me. Or you... not that there ever was.'

'Why did they do this? What did they want to know?'

'Nothing. Didn't even ask any questions. Just cut and talked...' The man shook his head and his head lolled onto his chest halfway through the movement. 'Loose ends to cut... spite and suffering to see done.'

Cado gripped the man's head and held it up. There was delirium dancing in Agen's eyes now, oncoming death in the breath coming from his teeth.

'What are they doing?'

'Under… always under… Under our feet, under our sight…' The man's shoulders lurched and a mass of blood came from his mouth. His pupils were shrinking. The red flecks fading. 'They told me… They knew… you would come.' Cado was still. Then something hammered at the door. Shouts rose. The bolts jolted in their settings.

'They knew…' Agen's head sagged onto his chest. The last words a wet sigh.

'Who?'

'Them…' gasped Agen, and the last flicker in the man's eyes reflected a movement behind Cado. He whirled as a twisted knife descended into the space where his neck had been. He had an impression of a cloak, and a bronze mask under the shadow of a hood, grinning with hooked teeth. He slammed an elbow into the mask. The cloaked figure cannoned backwards. Something heavy hit the door. Wood buckled. The stone of the frame shook. The masked figure rose from where they had landed. Cado was halfway across the room towards them. The shouts were rising from outside. The masked figure whirled, cloak scattering light as it dived for the passage leading to the door at the back of the building. The front door gave way. A metal bolt sheared. A last impact, then the thunder of splintering wood.

Cado snapped a look over his shoulder. Vaux came through the door, two of her militia with her. She saw the blood and Agen's corpse nailed to the chair. The masked figure was out of sight already. Vaux's gaze snapped up and met Cado's. Then he was running for the back door and bounding through it after the cloaked figure as shouts chased him into the rain. He had been set up, pulled by strings that he had not seen being tied, and now he was no longer just a hunter in this city, but the hunted. It almost felt reassuring.

* * *

Cado chased the cloaked figure up and through the city. He moved by scent and instinct as much as sight, a hunting beast loosed after its prey. The militia had not been watching the door at the back of Agen's house, and by the time they reached it, Cado was already out of bow shot. They had pursued, but he was a predator intent on his quarry. Still they might have caught him. They might have flooded the streets with soldiers, raised a mob, stolen every shadow with torches and fire. At a different time that would have been what happened. Now fear boiled through the city, and Cado moved under its shroud.

People bustled past him, climbing as if fleeing a rising tide. Every now and again he would catch a glimpse down the side of the spire. Fog coiled around the lower levels, grey and bruised purple. Light spidered through the murk, crackling and fizzing. Rain poured from roofs. The strings of bird skulls and feathers hanging from the eaves whipped in the rising wind, clacking and snapping. He could taste the magic in the wind and storm. Rose scent and sharp mineral. Out there beyond the clouds, the Lumineth were reshaping the web of power around the city. It would not be long now before they and the Ossiarchs came for their prize, or until the Old Enemy snatched it from them.

Behind, he thought he saw an occasional militiaman with a torch, searching the faces of the crowds and looking to the rooftops. He kept moving, sliding between the buildings and the bunches of people climbing the steps and streets. The scent of the prey was thick in his mouth. Hunger rose with it, until the two were knotted together, spiced and sharp. He was close and getting closer.

He stopped, turned, drawing air but only smelling the rain and the reek of mortal life. A press of people jostled past him, carrying bundles of possessions. A child wrapped in a sodden cloak cried out. An old man coughed. A pulse of white light spidered the fog not far below. Someone muttered a plea for protection. The rain rattled and spattered on grey stone.

He saw it only briefly then, a blink of an impression caught at the edge of his eye as he turned. A ring on the finger of a hand pulling a red cloak close against the rain. The glint of a sapphire set in the palm, a bronze hand haloed by tongues of fire. Then it was gone, and the press of people moving up the steps was flowing on. Cado was still for an instant, and then he was pushing the people aside, vaulting down steps, cries and curses following him. He saw the figure half turn to look back at him, face hidden under a red hood. They were still for an instant, and then they were jumping down the steps as Cado followed. He knew that sapphire ring. He had pulled one from the finger of the false guard on the caravan, and before then in a dozen places across the realm of the dead.

He broke from the crowd. The figure in the hood was at the bottom of the flight of steps. Cado leapt. All thought of the mortals around him drained to nothing. He landed on the wall above the steps and leapt again. A cry went up from behind him: shrill shock and surprise. The figure in the hood sprinted out of sight at the bottom of the steps. Cado landed on the bottom step and twisted up the road that the figure had taken.

Cado knew where they were. Fifty paces up on the skyward side, smoke rose from the chimney above Valentin's forge. The crumpled remains of the tower with the blue-and-red door stood opposite it. No one else was on the street. Cado saw the tower door swing, and the edge of a red cloak vanishing inside. He lunged for the door, each stride a wolflike bound. He reached the door and went through it without stopping. Wood splintered. He landed in a crouch, sword drawn, fangs bared.

Stillness and quiet, except for the fall of rain through rafters. It was just as it had been before. No… There was something different. At the edge of the floor there was a crack running up between the stone blocks and across the ground. Cado moved over to it, sword levelled. He could taste a new strand to the magic in the wind now: burnt spice and ashes, jagged and bitter, the scent of sorcery and corruption. The crack moved as he stepped closer, altering in his eyes, until he saw that it was not a crack, but one edge of a door set into the floor. When pulled shut it would have been invisible. The weight of the stone would mean that you could walk or stamp on it and not hear a hollow knock. If it had closed properly, he would never have detected it at all.

He gripped the edge and pulled. The trapdoor did not move. He tried again. Muscles stood out like ropes on his neck. Still it did not move. He stopped, forcing his instinct for rage to calm enough for him to think. He took out a knife and ran it along the edge of the crack, feeling for a catch or a point of leverage. There was none. The stone was immovable. He could feel a dull numbness in his hand. There was nullstone worked into this trapdoor. Clever, a physical door too strong to lift or break without knowing its secret, made so that magic could not help finding that secret.

He felt his lips snarl back from his teeth with frustration. Inside him, the black void of hunger opened its maw. Hunger billowed up, using his anger to climb into his thoughts. He had left it too long. He could feel the hollowness under his skin now, in his stomach and soul. He needed to keep his mind clear. He needed to…

Feed.

Red warmth pouring into him, taking away all the anger, all the pain; filling him, giving strength. Bliss and serenity… No guilt. No need to chase redemption. Only the call of the hunt and the release of the kill. Not redemption but purity… The living were nearby… hundreds of them. Fresh life filling all of them, beating, warm…

He reached for the vial of blood he had taken from the acolyte on the road. His fingers rattled against the glass. The blood had clotted brown inside the glass. He took the stopper out and raised the vial to his lips.

'Cado?'

His head turned.

Ama was standing inside the splintered door, eyes wide.

CHAPTER NINETEEN

The thud of a heart.

Life sliced into beats.

He had a device that measured time in the click and turn of cogs. Cog-wrights had made it in a realm where the rain was gold and the fruit tasted of iron. The merchant who had shown him the device had said that it measured time perfectly: each second a copy of the one that came before, each hour a flower of brass-counted minutes. Cado had shaken his head and left the merchant to find another customer for her fancy of cogs. It was a wonder, no doubt, but it held no truth. The slide of sand through the neck of an hourglass told the same lie: that time existed outside of living. It did not. The long afternoons of laughter under the sun, and the instant of waking to the sound of screams and the smell of smoke did not divide into cog teeth or grains of sand. It passed swift or slow, idle or urgent, but always by being lived. And its measure was the beat of blood. The drumbeat of the heart.

'Cado?'

He could hear it. The rhythm beating inside the mortal's ribs, so loud, so close, getting faster, slicing time finer and finer.

'Are you all right?'

He felt his teeth against his tongue. Needle points against skin. No pulse in his own chest, no rhythm of blood, no time.

'Are you hurt?'

Ama took a step closer. Grit scraped underfoot.

No time of his own but what he stole.

'Cado?'

Cado turned his head away. Then slowly, with effort, he raised the vial to his lips. The clotted blood tasted of rust on his tongue. He heard the hungering void open wide… and then shrink. The blackness retreated. He took a breath, closed his eyes, smelled the rain on the air.

'What are you doing here?' he asked. His voice was thick. The blood thirst was trying to pull his lips back from his teeth.

'I was looking out, at the storm and the…' Ama glanced back at the doorway. Outside the rain glittered in the grey daylight. A fizz of light cracked through the air. 'Da came back, said he needed to go up to the city top. He went and said to bar the doors and stay in. He said that you had already gone there.'

Cado nodded, only half listening. So close, so close again. They were here. The disciples of the Burning Hand were here. He snapped his knuckles into the stone of the closed trapdoor.

'That's a door,' said Ama. Cado looked up sharply. The boy had come close and was looking down at the crack at the edge of the trapdoor. He bent down and ran a finger along the gap. 'I have seen broken ones, but the rest you aren't supposed to be able to see unless you know they are there.'

'There are others?' asked Cado.

Ama smiled. 'Yes. They are supposed to be as old as the first rocks of the city.'

'Where do they go?'

Ama shrugged. 'Into the rock.'

'Under the city?'

'Under, behind, above – the tunnels they lead to go everywhere.' He looked suddenly wary, like he had said too much. Cado could hear the boy's heartbeat rise.

'You have been into the tunnels?'

'Da told me not to go where I shouldn't be.'

'Is there another hidden way near here? One that you can get through?' The boy looked at the ground, frowned. For an instant he looked just like his father. 'Could you show me?'

The boy was still for a moment and then looked at Cado. His gaze was open, his face serious. 'You are a Soulblight, aren't you?'

Cado almost flinched. He paused, then nodded. 'Yes,' he said.

'There are stories…' the boy began and trailed off. 'About what the Soulblights do – are they true?'

'Yes.'

'But you are not like the ones in the stories.'

'But you're not different, are you? The stories are true. Blood and horror and slaughter,' Valentin had said.

Ama blinked. 'You saved da, he said you did. You kept him alive, brought him back.'

'I have done a lot of things.'

The boy looked at him for a long moment. Then he smiled. 'You are not like them. I can tell.'

'How do you know that?'

'You could be worse,' the boy said, shrugging, 'but you choose not to be.'

Cado moved across the roofs. The sky beat at him with rain and tugged at him with wind. He kept his cloak around him and breathed a spell into the air that smudged his outline as he bounded and scrambled across broken walls and tiles. The spell was weak, and it was taking effort to keep it in place. The effort was thinning the blood in his veins even with the draught he had taken from the last vial. He kept Ama in sight as he moved. Every now and then he saw figures moving up the streets. Their flaming torches rippled in the wind. Mail and swords gleamed under cloaks. They saw Ama but did not stop him.

Cado followed the boy across the curve of the spire until they reached a street that followed the edge of an overhang. Pieces of the overhang had collapsed at some point in the past and taken part of the road with it. Cobbles and sections of buildings sagged and teetered over the drop. The buildings next to the rock of the spire were empty and looked as though none of the settlers had tried to claim them. Walls slumped against each other. Roofs had fallen inwards. The white spatter of bird droppings covered the stones, and Cado could see black-plumed birds perched on the exposed beams tucked inside the ruins. Ama paused on the street and looked around. Water was running from the hood of his cloak. Above, the lightning and thunder snarled.

Cado let go of the strand of spell he had been breathing into the air and dropped from the roof to the road. Ama looked around, startled. Cado saw a flicker of fear in the boy's eyes. Then the fear was gone.

'Over here,' Ama said, and moved to one of the buildings. It was little more than a pile of rubble contained by the outer shape of its walls. The boy slid down the gap between the two collapsing walls. Cado followed. It was tight and he could only move by shuffling. The space he came out into felt like a cave. Walls and ceiling had slid and fallen on top of each other, leaving a pocket of space between them. The air smelled of mould. Painted plaster covered one of the walls that leaned in to make the ceiling. Figures dragging comets and bearing hourglasses walked in flaking gold leaf across a heaven of chipped blue. A grey shaft of light fell from a crack in the debris ceiling.

'There,' said Ama, pointing. Cado looked. A section of the wall had broken free from the rest, forced out when the structure collapsed above. It was octagonal and, like the trapdoor in the tower, when closed it would be invisible. It was thick enough that it looked like it could have taken a blow from a giant and still stood. A narrow gap opened behind it on one side, no wider than the span of two hands.

Cado crouched beside the opening. The dark beyond was absolute.

'Have you been inside?' he asked.

Ama shook his head quickly. Cado looked at him steadily. The boy gave a small shrug. 'Once, but not far. It was dark and I couldn't see, and...'

'What?'

'It was...' He shivered. 'Cold...' he said, the word trailing off in search of one that fit better.

Cado looked back at the opening. He thought of Leragrais and the rings he still had, of the souls they held. He had chosen to follow the trail of the Burning Hand rather than find the wizard. It had been an instinctive as much as a considered decision. That same instinct had him wondering if the two paths might not intertwine.

'Go,' said Cado to Ama. 'Go back to the forge and do what your father said. Bar the doors. Wait for him.'

He moved to the gap behind the hidden door.

'What about you?'

'Tell your father where I have gone, but no one else.' The boy frowned. 'Will you do that for me, Amandus?'

His head came up at the sound of his name. His eyes were dark mirrors to the faint light. He nodded.

'Good,' said Cado. 'Go now.'

Ama hesitated for a second more and then went back to the gap between the collapsed walls and scrambled out of sight. Cado looked back at the space beyond the door, then went through.

'Cold' the boy had said. He had no other word for what he had felt beyond the hidden door. It was understandable. Only some mortals could understand the raw magic that touched every stone and filled every breath of their existence. Almost all of them could feel it, though.

Cold... Cold like frost on a blood rose. Cold like the inside of a mausoleum. Cold that crept through flesh as the warmth of life faded... Magic. The magic of death and the grave. It breathed past Cado on the still air. He felt it run fingers over the back of his neck. He heard it chuckle in the silence filling his ears.

In the underworlds of Death there were places where the magic of the grave gathered, pooling like water in a lake. That was what this was. Down in the heart of Aventhis there was a source of magic as powerful as any he had felt. He thought of the nullstone worked into the hidden doors – not just to keep them closed to magic but to contain the power inside them.

There were steps on the other side of the door, sloping sharply down between walls so narrow that they touched Cado's shoulders. There was no light, but Cado's eyes saw through the dark as though moonlight fell past him. Everything was silver, a gossamer world. He followed the staircase down until he put his foot onto the next step and found a floor there instead. He looked around, surprised to find himself in a space that looked like a chamber. Its walls were roughly circular. Veins of pale crystal ran through the rock of the walls, floor and ceiling. The cold surrounded him, flowing over his skin like an ice wind. But the air was still.

He touched the ring on his forefinger.

'Solia,' he said, and she was there, a shimmer behind his shoulder.

The light of her spirit flickered like a flame struggling against a gale.

~My... prince...~ she said, and her voice shivered in his skull.

'There is a source of magic in the core of the rock spire.'

~Yes... I can feel it... It's radiating through the stone. Souls and stars, it's powerful! This is what the geomantic ley lines in this underworld converge on. These tunnels and walls, they are like channels to guide the flow of power, to turn it back on itself over and over.~ Solia's ghost presence fluttered. He imagined her shivering.

'This is what has kept the feral spirits from the city. This convergence of power.'

~Yes...~

'The Burning Hand are here for it. That will be why they are in the city. This is their lair.'

~They would... hunger for it, yes, but I cannot feel any taint in the tide. Just power. Cold and dark and without end... This catacomb is made to protect itself as much as it is to channel it... There is a heart to it. There are... living souls down here too...~

'More than one?' he asked, thinking of the figure in the cloak who had vanished in the tower with the blue-and-red door.

~Perhaps,~ she replied. Her voice sounded thin, like someone forcing words out while standing in a freezing wind.

'How can you tell?'

~They are like shadows. Their life makes the...' Solia paused, and he could feel the effort as she spoke again. ~Their life distorts the flow of magic.~

'How many and where are they?'

~I can't... I can't tell... Further down.~

The feeling of standing in the water of an icy river was growing stronger.

He looked between the passaged openings. A stone skull capped one arch, a tangle of roses and thorns another, an hourglass in skeletal hands the third. The spaces beyond each opening were black and blank.

He took a step forward. His foot sent something skittering across the floor. He looked down to see a human thigh bone. Dried strips of flesh still clung to it but dissolved into dust as he picked it up. Then he saw the rest of the bones, lying under the roses and thorns: ribs, skull and vertebrae jumbled together like flotsam discarded by a river. Lying on top of them were bronze masks.

~Starvation,~ said Solia. ~I can feel the agony of it eating them… They were down here for a long time… Lost… and the echoes of their deaths are still here…~

'How could they be lost long enough to starve?' asked Cado as he looked between each of the passageways.

~The currents… The tide of magic… It… protects itself… It did not let them go… I…~ Solia's spirit voice was a whisper. ~The currents are getting stronger… I… Please… I can feel them… pulling… me away…~

Her presence dimmed. Cado felt an icy breath on the back of his neck. She folded out of being, leaving him alone.

'Solia?' he asked and touched the ring that held her. She did not appear.

The sound of distant footsteps came, shifting in the silence. He went utterly still. The false beat of his heart stopped. His senses reached through the dark.

Cado looked at the heap of bones on the threshold of the rose-and-thorn passage, then back at the skull-capped arch. His eyes fixed on the hourglass passage. He went to it, looked through and paused. No bones or phantoms marked this way, but he could feel the cold flow of magic surging out of the opening.

'Are you trying to show me where they hide or lead me astray?'

he asked to the dark. He held still for a long moment, then he stepped over the threshold.

CHAPTER TWENTY

Steps sloped down into the thickening dark. Cado moved by touch. His eyes could see in the deepest black, but this was not simple absence of light. The darkness was almost physical, a void pressed against his eyes. There were carvings on the walls: faces, figures, hands. He could feel the chisel marks under his fingers as they traced the wall.

He had been walking for a long while when the walls were suddenly not there. One second his hands were touching stone, and the next there was nothing. He stood perfectly still. He could feel the empty dark going out and out around him. If he were to step to the side and fall, he would just fall and fall and fall… He took a breath to speak a spell of flight, but there was now no air. He was standing in nothing. Had he been living he would have suffocated, but if that were the case he would likely not have got this far anyway.

He took a step and his foot hit a solid force. It was not physical. He could feel emptiness in front of his face. He tried to move backwards. The force slammed into his back. Then it was all around him, crushing him, squeezing his flesh. Voices rushed into his skull. He heard a man gasp for air through fluid-filled lungs; a child cried out as they tumbled through the air.

'No... No... Oh...'

A woman sighed as the fog of blood loss smothered the pain for the last time.

And more, all passing and not returning. The last sounds of mortals as they left life. Out there at that moment all these instants of ending were happening. He was hearing the tidal surge of death. It pulled at him, and he felt its force grow when it felt the void where his soul should have been. The sounds became a roar. Words formed in the cacophony.

'Liar...'

'Cursed...'

'Abomination...'

His empty heart felt as though a fist were crushing it. Thorns of ice ripped through his veins. A huge weight pressed down on his head, trying to crush him to the floor.

No, he tried to say, but his jaw would not open. *I am trying. I wish you no harm. I am...*

The crushing force grew. Pain cut off his thoughts.

Just let it happen, said a voice that was his own from the depths of his skull. *Let go and let the anger of the dead tear you apart...*

'No,' he said, and the word forced from his lips. 'I am one of you. I am not living. I have nothing.'

The pressure, pain and babble of voices ended. Silence and stillness filled Cado as though the assault had never been. He felt that he had passed a test or perhaps turned a key in a lock. He waited for a second. The echoing dark still surrounded him. He took a step.

* * *

The blackness ended suddenly. He felt a shift, like ropes snapping. His foot had settled on stone. He stood on a ledge that jutted out into a dark space in front of him. He turned his head. The frame of an arched door stood proud of the rock face behind him, but the space inside it was blank rock. He turned his head. He was high on the wall of a large cavern, he could tell, but he could not see the floor or other walls. There was a sound like… water, but not. It was lower, grittier; wind blowing dust across dry stone, perhaps. He took a breath. There was air in this cavern. The ache of hunger in his heart rose, sudden, furious, a red migraine. He staggered and half fell to his knees.

The feeling passed, draining out of him. He felt his arms and legs shake as he pushed himself up. He felt weak, empty, shivering cold. He found the edge of the ledge and moved along it by touch. The stone felt like ice. He stopped when his fingers found steps cut into the rock face and leading down from the ledge.

'*Nulus… meyon… altuss…*' A voice. Cado froze. He had heard a voice, an echo of a whisper, dying on the air as soon as it rose. And there, down in the dark, was a light – pale green and mauve flames flickering as they kindled. He could hear movement, the swish of fabric and the scuff of boots.

He began to climb down the steps. The flames were still there, gleaming but unmoving in the centre of the cavern. He reached the bottom of the steps and dropped into a crouch. His eyes were wide, black spheres now, pulling in every scrap of light. He could see the cavern more clearly. It was vast, a natural dome scooped out of the rock. The stone of the walls was smooth and rippled, as though it were water frozen at the instant a breeze passed over it. Crystals glinted in the rock. The floor rose in irregular tiers to where a single pillar of rock reached between floor and ceiling. The firelight came from the space beside the pillar. Cado slid his sword from its sheath and moved forwards. The light of the flames grew in his eyes, step by step.

He could see that the light came from fire dancing in a bowl of oil. There was a figure next to the flames, too, half out of sight. Cado could just make out the faint impressions of fabric, of a hood covering a head.

'*Shy'su... ish...*' The sound of the voice rose above the rustling hiss that filled the cavern. He knew the voice. He felt a shiver of weakness pass through him again, but forced it down.

'Tell me,' Cado said aloud. The figure's head jerked up, hunting the dark as the echoes spread. 'How long have you served the God of Lies?' He stepped from the dark, sword in hand. His eyes were red coal lights of hunger and anger. The fire poured shadow into the recesses of his face. The figure whipped around. Heavy robes rustled. 'Magister Leragrais.'

Leragrais stepped back, hands raised. He looked shocked. Cado took a step forward, sword levelled at the wizard. The invisible currents of the river were strong now; he could feel ice seeping into his flesh. Leragrais took another step back.

'No further,' said Cado. Leragrais' indigo eyes gleamed black.

'You have made a mistake,' said Leragrais. His mouth twitched. 'More than one, I think. But thank you. This, believe it or not, will make things simpler.'

Leragrais' left hand twisted in the air. Crystals glowed in the stone pillar beside the magister.

Cado felt the ice currents shift around him. He lunged. The point of the sword reached towards Leragrais' chest, and–

Slid downwards, falling, the weight of the sword dragging on Cado's arm as he staggered. Cold flooded through him. Sensation drained from his body. He was on his knees, trying to rise, trying to make his limbs move. Leragrais moved his hand through the air as though gentling an animal. Cado buckled. The current of magic in the cavern was roaring through him. The wizard looked down at him, his mouth hooked into an apologetic smile.

'To a man with a hammer, every problem is a nail. To a predator, everything is prey. You think I am a slave to the false gods? Oh, but you are a fool. They are here, make no mistake. Did you think that you tipping a mask and dagger out in front of me was a revelation? I know they are here. The Old Enemy have been trying to get into the heart of these catacombs for some time. Only the magical barriers the ancients created have kept them out. What? You wonder why I didn't tell you, why I didn't come blurting out with the truth that this city is rotten? You may hunt them, but you do not understand the enemy. The only way to survive against them is by holding power close and secrets closer. While you have been running around bleating about your hunt, they have been using you to find a way in here.' He shook his head in disgust. 'And now you have shown them how and broken the wards that were keeping them out. Well done. Very well done.'

Cado forced his leaden tongue to move in his mouth.

'What...?' he began.

Leragrais curled his lip. 'What is down here that the disciples of the Dark Gods, and legions of death want? Look,' he said. He placed his hand on the pillar he had been standing next to, and the grey stone became transparent. The inside of the pillar was a geode. Amethyst crystal formed a hollow funnel that narrowed and then ballooned out again, so that it resembled an hourglass. Pale green light gleamed on the edges of the purple crystal. Grey, metallic sand slid down the throat of the funnel, gathering in the bottom in a pile that did not grow higher. He knew what it was, and the realisation took his breath away. It was grave-sand.

'Everything is magic,' Solia had once explained to him. 'The soil and stone, the air, the thoughts in our heads and the stars that wheel through the heavens. All of it. Magic is one, but when it blows through existence it divides. Just as white light falling through rain splits into colours, magic divides into a spectrum. Death, light,

shadow, life and more. Each of them pools in places where those elements dominate. The winds of death blow strong where the dead lie and life ends. Tides of shadow are strongest where darkness hides the world from sight. It is a cycle – the magic changes existence, and existence pulls magic to it. The cycle becomes so intense that magic becomes physical. Just as salt forms on the edge of seas and lakes, so realmstone forms in the places where magic touches existence most closely.'

'What is it, though, this stone?' he had asked.

'Physically, it has many forms. It can be liquid, or a glowing mist or a lump of amber. In the realms where death blows strong, it runs as granules of grey stone. Grave-sand, most call it. But that is just what it looks like. What it is... It is power, my prince. Pure power.'

'This is the heart of Aventhis,' said Leragrais. 'A soul-cascade. A naturally occurring nexus of the magic of death and immortality. All the geomantic lines in this underworld lead here. All the currents of magic lead here. The fall of this sand is this place's magic made visible. Reverse it and you end life or break time. Stop it and its gathered power rips through the underworld as a storm. It has kept us alive in the wilderness, and now I must keep it from those who want to take it.'

CHAPTER TWENTY-ONE

'At first I thought that you had come here for this,' said Leragrais. 'That the soul-cascade had drawn you just as it had the cultists of Change. But no, you were just a petty creature hunting for your own wants. Easily used by all, it seems.'

'You are…' began Cado.

'I am what I am and what I seem – a rarity, I know. I have spent my life to protect this city and its people. Death is cruel.' He gave a small smile, as though at a joke. 'Strange for me to say perhaps, but it's true. Once we mortals feared death because it marked the end of existence. What waited beyond the grave's doors was a void of mystery. Faith and stories told of paradises and torments, but always it remained behind the curtain of the unknown. Even in the face of phantoms and miracles, people could cling to the idea that a different end awaited the dead. That comfort is long lost. We do not only see the afterlives of the living but live in them ourselves.' He shuffled forwards, and slowly bent down. Cado tried to move away but couldn't. Leragrais reached out. Cado showed his teeth, hissing like a dying cat. Leragrais hesitated and then placed his fingers on Cado's cheek. 'We see the torments and the creatures that prey on the dead – creatures like you. I will not see the souls I have tried to protect become slaves or playthings for your kind.'

He let his hand fall and stood, turning away.

'I thought that when the lights appeared in the sky it was the hand of the Great Necromancer reaching out to take us at last. I confess I was terrified. What could we do? Damascene, poor faith-blind Damascene. She thought we could use you, that we could tame you by your pitiful attachment to your soul-cage rings.' He held up a chain of rings and swung them, so they clinked. 'But that idea was foolish, wasn't it? The soldiers of your masters' approach even now. You met with them before returning. We have seen their riders on the road, following in your wake.'

Leragrais shook his head. His smile was cold.

'I cannot destroy you. Even here, with all the power of this confluence, something of your vile nature would remain in the dust. I could do what I threatened and sink your ashes into a lake or bury them deep, but you are a creature of vengeance, and I cannot risk that you would find your way free. You are a thing of death. The grave-sand that gathers here both empowers and binds and wards against the dead like you, depending on the intent I place into it. The amethyst tides bind your curse to you, and so I cannot break them with that same power. I cannot destroy you.' He paused, smiled more widely. 'But others can.'

Leragrais peeled open the fingers of his hand. Cado felt the black night swirl inside. The magister closed his fist and darkness snapped through Cado like a rope pulling him down into the dark.

A blink of lightning. Cold light. Far away, like a crack in the night.

'He is alive?' a cold voice said.

'That which is dead cannot live and cannot die,' came an answer.

'His eyes are open.' The cold voice again.

'This far from the confluence, I cannot keep him subdued.'

'No matter. We have strength enough to take him further.'

'You are certain you can destroy him?'

'Oh yes.'

He could see a blur. The white light was dissolving to grey. He felt pain. It surrounded and flowed through him. Sudden, black and red, edged with sharp hunger. His jaws snapped wide. He could hear hearts beating close to him. Three of them. Alive.

The narrow faces looked down at him.

'He perceives us.' It was Lotharic. The Lumineth shifted her head to look at him from different angles, but her gaze stayed steady. She did not blink once. 'Strange...'

'What?' Leragrais shifted into sight. He looked older than he had under the spire, skin loose and grey over his bones.

'There is an air of nobility to him.'

'He is a leech,' snarled Leragrais. 'He killed one of the city's guard this morning.'

'He has not fed,' said Atharion. 'The furnace of his curse is burning low.'

A frown on Leragrais' face, then a shake of the head.

Thunder shook the air. All three looked up. A jagged bolt of lightning had crossed the sky above them. Another had flashed into being before the first faded, and then another from that bolt, and on, so that the light was stitching the underbelly of the heavens. They were moving south, towards Aventhis. Streaks of amethyst afterglow remained after each flash. The two aelves and old human looked at the sky for a long moment.

'The time required is approaching,' said Atharion. 'We must be at the nexus and paint the runes when it comes. The confluence will not last.'

'It is a good thing that I came to you then,' said Leragrais. 'Or you would have to fight your way in.'

'What needs to be done would be done,' said Lotharic, her voice metallic and cold. 'If you had not come to us, your people would have perished without need. As it is, many may survive.'

Leragrais blinked as though he had not heard it put so baldly before. He frowned, as if he were about to object or ask a question.

'You did right and serve a higher purpose, magister,' said Atharion. His voice was steady and smooth. 'The Ossiarchs will be at your walls come night. The Soulblight was within your walls. If they did not take your city now, then its walls would fall on another day. The power of the nexus, the power that has protected you until now – it would serve only the Necromancer. It is not enough power to stop them. As it is, it will become a weapon against the march of the cold legions. The lines and magic will shift. The bridges of bone that span the lands of the Ossiarchs shall break, and the Nighthaunt will flee before the light that will shine across the realm.'

Atharion's eyes were shining, and Cado could tell that he was not seeing the old human in front of him.

'And some will survive?' asked Leragrais.

Atharion blinked once.

'Some shall,' he said. Leragrais looked uncertain for the first time since Cado had met him, but more he looked tired. How long had he worked his craft alone in the dark beneath the city? Decades or more, long years of never trusting, always fighting to keep the dead from coming close, always working to keep the power secret. Failing, growing old and more tired, and waiting for something, *anything*, to take the burden from him. In the end, time was the weakness of all mortals.

'The place is ready,' came another voice. A third Lumineth, whom Cado recognised as the mage who had commanded the earth in the fight in the valley. The aelf's voice was deeper but still melodic, like an instrument turned to a bass register: harmonious but heavy. Lotharic shot the newcomer a look, and Cado wondered at the flash of fire in her eyes. Anger, or something else? If the others had noticed it, they showed no reaction.

'Come, bring him a little further. It is not far,' Lotharic said, and turned and began to walk away. Hands lifted him. Fine hands that felt like steel left out in frost. Cado saw now that he had been lying on the ground at the base of a rocky tor. Steps had been cut into its side and spiralled up to the finger of rock. He tried to struggle but his movements were weak, and the cold grip of magic was still a crushing force in his chest.

They carried him up the stairs. The steps were narrow and worn by ages and feet. Crumbling faces leered from the stone: hooded skulls; great birds with hooked beaks and blank, chiselled eyes. Grey clouds flowed across the sky above. The top of the pinnacle was a flat circle of stone, rough and slick with rain and red lichen. A wind gusted a greeting as they set him down. Lotharic nodded to the warriors that had carried Cado. They left.

'You have his weapons and the soul-cage rings?' Lotharic asked Leragrais. The magister nodded, glanced at Cado. A frown flickered over his face.

'Yes,' he said.

'Give them to him,' said Lotharic.

'What?' said Leragrais, looking between the two Lumineth.

'Place the weapons beside him and the rings on his fingers,' said Lotharic.

'You are going to destroy him. His chattels–'

'End with him,' said Lotharic. She placed a hand on Leragrais' shoulder. She was so much taller and the magister so stooped that she barely needed to raise a hand. 'These rings hold souls that mean everything to him, souls that have been imprisoned for ages upon ages. That bondage ends with him. Besides, this is not about punishment, magister. This creature is a thing of darkness, and can never be otherwise, but it feels and thinks, has cares, and feels pain. This is not about cruelty. For light to prevail, it must banish the shadows. That is not without a price or suffering. It is simply that they are small when balanced against the greater matter.' She lowered her hand from Leragrais' shoulder and gestured at Cado. 'Please,' she said.

Leragrais nodded, still frowning.

'I am...' He shook his head. 'I am just not sure that it is wise.'

'It is right, though,' said Lotharic, 'and as to wisdom, that is not a judgement you have the insight to make.' The last words came from her lips, clear and unyielding as stone. 'Place the rings on his fingers and his weapons beside him.'

Leragrais blinked, then bent and did as she asked. Cado felt the cold fire as the rings slid back onto two of his fingers. Two, only two... He wanted to speak, to call out that Leragrais had only given two of the rings back, but his mouth would not work, and the only sound that came from his lips was a hiss. Leragrais placed the sword and daggers beside Cado and stepped back.

Then Lotharic stepped forwards and knelt beside him. The scales of her armour clinked. She was close, her black-in-black eyes wide above him, her gaze still like the sun.

'There is no hope for you,' she said, and there was sorrow in her voice. 'You cannot be saved. Your existence is a curse on the living and the noble dead. Your continuance will heap only more suffering on that which you have already caused. You are not to be feared – no monster of the night is to be feared in the light of day. No... you are to be pitied, Hollow King of a lost kingdom.'

She stepped back and nodded to Atharion. The other Lumineth stepped forwards. Eyelids dropped over grey eyes. He raised his hands. A yellow glow wreathed his fingers. For a long heartbeat he was still. Then he began to slide his hands through the space above Cado. Shining light painted the air. A shape formed, brush-strokes of white and blue and sun-blinding yellow. Cado felt his skin begin to itch.

'You are certain that he will be destroyed?' asked Leragrais. 'I have heard of no art that could do such a thing.'

The shape forming in the air coiled and rippled. Cado could feel heat on his face. The clouds high above parted. A thin shaft of sunlight speared down, struck his eyes. He closed them reflexively.

'He will be no more. The light will pour into his body and into the shadow where his soul lived. Illumination – total illumin-ation. His existence is darkness and things hidden in the night. The light will burn through all of it, layer by layer. There will be nothing left – no mote of memory, not a grain of dust to grow a body. No resurrection, no echo left in the wind of death.'

Cado could still see the rune Atharion wove in the air, shining through his eyelids.

'Will he feel anything?' asked Leragrais.

'Yes,' said Lotharic. 'He will feel the pain of all his life and the un-life which followed it. It will be agony beyond what a living soul can know.'

A shaft of light struck down. White fire filled the space behind Cado's eyelids. His skin was charring. He could hear a hissing rattle. The cry of a bird? Then he realised what it was. It was a gasp coming from his lips, the call of a creature staked out and feeling the first tongues of fire lick their flesh.

The rune was an expanding knot of light. The light was beyond bright.

'Good,' said Leragrais.

CHAPTER TWENTY-TWO

White.

Bright beyond blinding.

Silence.

A black line of pain drawn across time that never ended.

The beat of a heart but not his own. Memories boiled up from the abyss, old times and old voices.

'You remember what you did once for vengeance?' said a voice-echo from the edges of a fever dream.

Sissendra... he tried to say, but his voice was silent.

'Yes, sire. You remember the slaughter some see again...'

A memory of red...

Warm red flowing between teeth and across his tongue. The taste of iron and copper. Life, stolen life. Filling him, giving him a heartbeat.

Cado threw back his head. The throat of a dying man came

away in his jaws. He opened his eyes. The burning fortress of brass unfolded beneath him. The body he was holding twitched, shivering. Blood gushed from the hole torn in its throat. Its eyes rolled back in its head. It was still holding on to its axe. Cado looked at the knot of warriors on the parapet. Red-crusted armour, burnt bones on chains, scar-knotted skin, hooked iron teeth snarling under blood-shot eyes.

Cado grinned back. Blood poured from his lips, down his chin.

'Where is your God of Skulls and Slaughter now?' he asked.

They came at him. He dropped the corpse and leapt to meet them. Axes cut the air, but he was past the blows, amongst the throng, sword slashing. Guts unspooled from slit bellies. Limbs cracked. He punched his fingers through the bare chest of one, hoisted the warrior into the air and ripped the heart through his ribs as he threw him at those behind him. He was bloodsmoke and darkness, a whirl of claws and fangs and sharp edges. He rose from the slaughter, slick, crimson, lacquered in the glow of the fires.

Above him the higher battlements of the fortress rose in tiers of scorched iron and crude brass. In the space between the inner and the outer walls, he could see the skull mounds. Smoke still rose from some. Jellied puddles of fat and burnt flesh dotted the ground where the Slaughterpriests hooked heads from the pits and shook the slurry of cooked meat from the bone.

Behind and around him his legions pressed forwards. Firelight glinted off spears that still held the rust of the grave. Burning coals exploded amongst them as the fanatics on the inner wall sections rolled fire cauldrons down ramps into the attackers. The phalanxes of skeletons did not pause. They moved in great rattling blocks of armour and weapons. The bones of those that had fallen re-formed as the front ranks passed over them. When they reached the walls they climbed one over another, building a ladder of bone that reached up to the wall-edge. Axes and shields and swords threw some back, but they kept going. The magic that animated them drove them on.

Behind them came the rest of the Soulblighted. They waited for the dead to surround the enemy before closing to kill and feed. Cado knew that they would have preferred to be loose on the battlefield, able to do as they pleased. He had ordered their restraint, and his will was stronger than their instinct. For now at least. Most were blood-cousins, used to doing as they pleased and taking what they wanted, but he was their lord and the razing of this citadel his to order as he willed. He would leave nothing to the chance of a pack of Soulblights' blood hunger. This abomination and everyone in it would become blood and ashes. They would not even raise the bones of the enemy dead. When they had finished, they would summon the Nighthaunt and let the spite of the tormented dead drag away any of the souls that lingered. Not just destruction, but true annihilation.

The skin on his back prickled as he watched one of his winged kin land in the middle of a clump of enemy. Blood rose in a ragged spray. The presence at his back came closer.

He felt the echo of Sissendra's voice before she spoke.

'Not long, I think,' said Sissendra. He felt her anticipation buzz through his senses.

He turned. There was a thick layer of blood on Sissendra's armour. Heavy rivulets ran down the silver plate. Droplets gathered in the eyes of the snarling faces moulded into her vambraces and greaves. Only the twin dragons on her cuirass were unsullied, as though she had somehow kept them clean while bathing in gore. She met his gaze, then bowed, the gesture somehow both perfect and edged with mockery. She was his only surviving get. Vestus had become ash on the road to the Endless City. Merro had not been seen for long enough that they were most likely lost too. Only Sissendra remained, the last and only Soulblight of his creation. In another life, he would have called that a mistake, but she was a creature perfect for this age.

Spiteful, ingenious, clever, and with a thirst for blood and vengeance that was the equal of his own; she was a punishment loosed on the Dark Gods and the mortals that followed them.

'These barbarians will not be able to resist much longer,' she said. 'Once we have taken the inner wall, it's just going to be about herding the survivors together. They will make quite a herd. Keep us entertained and feasted for months.' She shrugged, reconsidering the point. 'Or maybe for just one especially luxurious month.'

Cado shook his head.

'Keep one in ten alive,' he said. 'Take their hands and feet. Leave them their eyes and tongues. Kill the rest.'

'Yes, sire,' Sissendra said, and smirked. The needle points of her teeth hooked over her lip. The fires had dyed the silver of her armour gold. Her white-in-white eyes were wide with laughter.

'But why not keep all of them? We could feast here for months, let the children and cousins play.'

'One in ten,' he said again. 'Any more will slow us down.'

Sissendra pouted, then shrugged and grinned. 'Some night you will let us enjoy ourselves, Cado.'

He was in front of her, eye to eye, red gaze to cold white.

'I did not make you for joy,' he said. 'We are the revenge of the dead on the damned. There is war and punishment, and nothing else.'

Sissendra shrank back, head dipping as though forced down by an invisible hand.

'Yes, sire,' she said.

He turned away and felt her linger for a second before spilling into the air in a billow of mist.

Down on the causeway leading to the next gate he could see a figure amongst a tightening circle of animated skeletons. Almost twice their height, the man whirled a spiked ball on a chain. Scars and brands covered his skin. Muscles surged under the jagged marks. He was *bellowing, calling out in a broken tongue to his god to witness him. Cado stepped to the edge of the parapet and dropped to the ground. The skeletons parted as he came forwards. The muscled warrior saw him and did not wait but swung. Cado ducked the blow and cut in reply. The silver of his sword took the warrior's right hand at the wrist. The ball and chain flew free. Blood scattered to add to the clotting mud. Smoke was thick in the air. The warrior staggered, shock cutting through his frenzy. He reached for a knife at his waist. Cado's cut took the fingers from the hand just above the lowest knuckle. Then he pivoted and kicked the warrior high on the chest. Ribs shattered, and the warrior was falling. He hit the ground. Cado's sword skewered him through the collarbone into the ground as he tried to rise. Cado looked down at the warrior, tilted his head. There were tattoos of fishhooks under the jaw. He wondered if that meant this man had been a fisherman, pulling a pale catch from one of the dark seas, worrying about storms and the winter ice.*

'Blood... for the... Blood God...' he gasped. 'My skull will sit beneath the Throne of Skulls.'

Cado shook his head.

'Your blood is mine,' he said, and looked up at the next wall of the fortress. Ball cages of fire rolled down from the parapets above. Arcs of ghost-lightning burst on the brass crenellations. 'There will be no death in battle for you. Your life will end one drop at a time to feed the warriors that shall tear down this fortress and the next. And if your soul should find its way to your false god, it will be nothing worthy of glory, only of pity.'

The warrior began to laugh. 'Khorne cares not whence the blood flows, only that it does.'

Cado yanked his sword free, spun it up and lashed it down to slice the warrior's legs beneath his knees. And his world began to crumble to black all around him, and the memory or dream was turning into—

* * *

No sky or ground or fortress. Just him and the blur of the sword-edge descending and the warrior grinning up at him through bloody teeth.

~So much suffering and yet it brings you no peace,~ said a voice behind Cado. He straightened. The warrior sank into nothing. His face, with its frozen snarl, was the last thing to vanish. The blackness around Cado was squirming and vibrating like the skin of a struck drum. Over his shoulder a pale shadow hung. He could half see the impression of a face.

'How are you here?' he began. 'I did not summon you.'

~I am ending, my prince,~ said Solia. ~Just like you. Annihilated by light. Stripped down to nothing, spirit blasted into oblivion.~

Somewhere, far away but just here, he lay on a bed of stone under a shaft of light. Pinned in place. Burning.

'This is the past...' he said, then shook his head.

~The past, yes. The present, too.~

'It seems like...'

~This is where you always are, my boy. In the past. I would say that the light is killing you, but that's not possible. It is destroying you. Like the aelf said, layer by layer, down to the core.~

'This is my core? This?'

~The blood and slaughter and vengeance, you mean? No, it's not. That is just what it became.~

He stood. He looked at his hand. It was a blur, fingers sketched in charcoal blending into night. The light behind his shoulder was receding.

'I am alone. Your voice... It's no more real than what I am seeing.'

~I am here, my prince. Truly.~

'How can you be?'

~The five rings on your fingers. The rings that hold me and

some of the others. The light is washing our spirits from them. We are all ending, and we are here with you.~

He opened his mouth to answer, and the charcoal blur of night poured in.

A memory of shadows...

His father looked down at Cado, eyes hard chips of amethyst and obsidian. The line of his mouth pulled taut. Behind the king, the Council of the Beheld hung in a loose arc, their images faint in the brightness of the morning sun.

'We will not talk of this again,' he said.

Cado opened his mouth to reply, but his mother had already turned away.

'Father...' he began and took a step to follow. His father pivoted. Cado saw the flash in the eyes, felt cold pass through him. He faltered, stepped back. The spirits of his mother's council flickered. Cado saw Xanus' face manifest clearly enough for the dead Arch-Votive's face to curl its lip. Cado bit his lip, straightened to formal alertness, then bowed.

'My king,' he said.

The king, his father, held his gaze for a long moment, and then turned and left the room. The black-lacquered doors closed softly. Cado screwed his eyes shut and let his breath out between his teeth.

'Well... that could have been worse.'

'Not now,' he breathed, and rubbed his temples.

'I mean there were ways that you could have botched it more... just not many.'

'Jakinda, please...' He looked up. His sister raised her eyes and hands innocently. Cado sighed. 'Just don't...'

'As you wish,' she said, half under her breath, and moved to one of the windows. They were in one of the palace's high wings, hanging from just below the western cliff-edge. From here you could see all

the way down and up the canyon below. The silver thread of the river plaited between the trees and towers. Clouds of pollen from the forests hung in a shimmering layer beneath them. Above, the bowl of the sky was the hard blue of summer heat. If the wind changed direction, you could sometimes smell the dust from the plateau. This wing had always been the family's retreat from the kingdom's business. Here the duties of the throne receded, and simpler things took their place. Laughter, stories, a king laid low by the wooden swords of his children, a queen kneeling to a solemn court of dolls and asking if she might join their number. Those times had slowly become part of the past, set aside and replaced. Cado came there most out of all of them now.

'Talking to him here… that might have been a mistake,' said Jakinda.

'Please just–'

'I mean here, this does not really fit with serious talk about succession and continuance of rule.' She flicked a hand over the room. It was small by the standards of what the palace held. A wide, square space, under a wooden-beam roof. Worn dragon heads grinned and snarled from the beam ends. Low stools sat in a loose circle on a worn rug that coiled with more dragons, some indigo, some violet. Steam rose from the dew-tea poured and untouched in its clay cups. The shutters on the shadeward side were open and the breeze sent the soul-flutes piping and swinging.

'That was what I was trying to…' He shook his head. 'I thought that maybe here… he might be different, you know?'

'What? Because of memories of happier times?'

'Something like that.'

'Oh, my poor brother, you really don't see all the angles of this, do you?'

She came and sat down opposite him. She was a shade taller than him, a fact that had been true for most of their lives, and she never *failed to remind him of. It was part of fate trying to balance out him being born half a turn earlier, she said. Younger by the blade stroke of midnight: she was his twin, tormentor, ally and the first and last person he wanted there just then. There was just too much truth in her for comfort.*

'Tell me,' he said.

'You do not want to be king.'

'I don't,' he snapped.

She held up a hand. 'So you bring our father here to tell him? Here? To the place where he and mother came to pretend we were like any other family?'

'Where we were a family.'

She shook her head. 'A dream, my brother, a lovely dream that was given to us to dream, and now must fade.'

'Do you honestly try to talk like a page from the prophet books?'

Jakinda sighed. 'All right, here it is – you are saying that you don't want the throne you have been raised to. You are saying that you will not take the responsibility you are being raised for, and you are doing it in the room where our mother played at heroes and monsters with her children. You are saying that you don't even begin to rea- lise the gravity of what you are asking. You are saying that you are a child, Cado. A child who wants to stay a child.' She picked up one of the cups of dew-tea and took a sip. 'Is that plain enough for you, brother?'

He closed his eyes, shook his head. 'How would you have done it then?'

'I wouldn't be so naive to try, but… It's the throne, Cado. The rule of this kingdom of shades, all the way from the Silus Mountains to the Sickle Sea. Dragons rise to the call of our line. The dead sit and give us counsel. Truth and justice sit in our hands. I would have tried to make my…' She shut her eyes. 'My act of supreme foolish- ness feel like a decision made with deliberation. The decision of a

prince, who could be king. I would have done it in court, kneeling before the whole lot of them in the armour of our ancestors. I would have made them respect what I was asking for.'

'You could do it for me.'

Jakinda snorted. 'I won't. For starters it would not work. Second, I am not about to enable your idiocy, and third, I am not going to make myself as much of a fool as you.'

He flinched, and felt his face harden. He stood up. His face was flushing. He could feel hot anger behind his eyes.

'Maybe you're right,' he snapped. 'Better I am king than you having to sit on the throne yourself. I mean, what would you do then? You couldn't watch and snipe and give advice whether anyone asked for it or not. And what would you do when you had to decide rather than comment on everyone else's choices? It's easy when it's not you that has to... has to...'

'Be a king.' *The words were cold.*

Cado shook his head. Jakinda had gone very still.

'I am sorry. I didn't mean...'

'Yes,' *she said, voice still cold.* 'Yes, you did.'

She stood and went towards the door.

'You would be better than me,' *he said, suddenly. She looked back at him, face unreadable.* 'I mean it. You would. You are second in line by moments. It could be you. It should be you.'

A smile flickered across her face but did not reach her eyes.

'Thank you, brother. Nice to hear you say so. Kind, but... You know what I have learned being second for all these years? That a throne is a curse. This kingdom, its line, all the power, it leeches the life from whoever rules it. Once I thought, I don't know... that we could both bear the crown, split the rule... but no. That's not the way it works. I saw that a long time ago.' *She gave a mirthless laugh.* 'I don't want to be you, Cado. I pity you. This is your kingdom, brother, and you are welcome to it.'

Cado heard the door open but did not see his sister pass through. The sunlight of the past mottled to black.

This time he did not think the memory was real as it faded.

'I was such a fool,' he said aloud.

~You were only fourteen summers old,~ said Solia.

He shook his head. 'I did not realise…'

Solia was silent in the swirling dark.

'What now?' he asked, but something caught in his throat. He coughed. Solia was not there. Just the swirl of black. He could not tell if his eyes were shut or open. He felt air rake into his lungs. The blackness of the night was thick, swirling, cloying. He forced his eyes open, and–

Woke with the smell of smoke thick in his throat.

He was older now. That was the thought that clung to him. Older… A king. A king yet to see a full circuit of the seasons. But older… a king… a king whose first breath was full of smoke.

'Majesty,' came the cries. Doors opening, footsteps clacking on stone. 'Majesty, the southern forests are burning.'

CHAPTER TWENTY-THREE

A memory of fire…

The great drake folded its wing. Cado swung up into the saddle. Muscles shifted under scales, tensed. Then Herezai launched into the air, wings unfolding to beat the smoke-filled sky. They curved up. The clouds were silver-grey and dark blue under the dome of the night sky. They were moving too, boiling and spiralling, fizzing with blue lightning. Cado could feel the charge in the air, the burnt-sugar taste on his tongue. Magic, great and terrible magic. He turned towards it. Around him, others of the royal guard and household followed. They rode a menagerie of creatures. Shades followed them, fluttering in the wind.

Only he rode without an entourage of the dead. The iron rings lay beside his throne, still, empty of the spirits that would attend him through his reign. One more task that he had to complete but which remained undone. So much undone that he should have made time for…

'His majesty must choose a court,' Udio had said, in that delicate brittle voice that held as much scorn as deference. 'And tradition is our protection against repeating the mistakes of the past.'

'My father,' Cado said.

The major-domo inclined his head. 'Your father, glory to his living reign, moved beyond only two seasons past. It will be seen as an unseemly brief time to let his spirit rest before binding. Besides, it is not considered wise to include in the court a monarch who sat upon the throne within two generations.'

'So I may only take advice from a relative if I don't know them.'

'Only if they sat on the throne, sire. There is good reason to it.'

'What are those good reasons, Udio?'

The ancient major-domo smiled slightly at the irritation in Cado's voice.

'That the rulers of the past do not try to recapture their rule by influencing the living monarch.'

'My father was–'

'A most wise and just king, and a noble man who understood the importance of continuity and restraint in all things.'

'I have advisors – Solia, Idyon, my mother. Drake's teeth, I have more people who can give me advice than I have moments to talk to them in.'

'And all those people have their place, but that place is amongst the living. A king must have the wisdom that only the dead can know.

'So that one who sits on the throne does not fail to see something that they should.'

'Talk to me,' Idyon had said. 'Not as a king but a friend.' He had waited until the rest of the royal council had gone. The heat of the late-summer day had been draining from the air. The breeze stirring the window hangings was cool and touched with the promise of rain. Cado had not moved from the throne since the start of the council.

'Kings do not have friends,' Cado replied. 'They have advisors and enemies and allies.' He rubbed his eyes. He was bone-and-blood tired. His thoughts would not settle.

'Now you are just talking piss and dung,' said Idyon. He smiled.

Cado gave a weak smile back. 'How do you do it? Keep so sharp and clear. You are Speaker. No one else has greater responsibility, but you... It's like you are carrying nothing.'

'I think the Marshal, and your mother, and my king – if he would pull his head out of his arse – would all make a good case that they carry more responsibility than me.'

'All our heritage of arcane lore.' Cado began to count on his fingers. 'The care of the spirits who make this realm. The training of all those who would learn our traditions of magic. Chief intermediary between the unspeaking dead and the living. I forget how many of the best and most powerful in this kingdom answer to you, but I know it's a lot. Oh, and you must help your old friend not make a ruin of it all from his throne. I would say that you can't argue out of that being a great weight of responsibility, but something tells me you could both make that argument and win.'

'No, you are right,' said Idyon dryly. 'Honestly, I am just very, very good.'

They both laughed.

'You should talk to me,' said Idyon, his expression grave again, 'but I can see you won't. That is your prerogative.'

'As friend or king?'

'As both.' Idyon drew a breath, and Cado noticed there was something about his friend's nature that he had missed before: a kernel of shadow in the orange embers of his eyes. 'You do not need to talk to me, but I need to talk to you.'

Idyon held his gaze steady. Cado frowned. 'Something you didn't want to say in front of the council?'

'Everything I didn't want to say in front of the council.'

Cado raised his eyebrow, gestured. 'Well? What?'

'I...' Idyon hesitated now.

Cado noticed then that his friend had closed his hands tight. His soul-rings were glowing deep red at the edges as though still cooling from the fire.

'Idyon,' said Cado carefully. 'What is going on?'

'There is magic at work, magic like I have never heard of. It is changing things, altering memories and truth.'

'What do you mean?'

'That... name I said. Can you remember it?'

'Name? What are you talking about?'

Idyon nodded. 'I told you a name. Just a moment ago.'

'No, you didn't. You said that you knew...' Cado felt the words falter on his tongue. He blinked. Idyon and he had been laughing, and then... He could not–

Idyon gripped Cado's hand. The iron rings on his fingers were burning. Cado snarled and yanked his hand back, but Idyon gripped harder.

'I told you about troubles in the south, about cults of masks, and the vanishing messengers, of people who we are forgetting.'

Cado stood up then, eyes wide, tiredness gone.

'Idyon, what is this? Tell me now!'

'I told you a name,' said Idyon, pressing on as though he had not heard Cado's command. There were spirits peeling from Idyon's rings, tattered images spiralling through the air in a sphere around them. Cado could feel pressure inside his skull, and behind his eyes. The spirits were a blur of ghost-light now. He couldn't see past them. Frost sparkled on Idyon's skin. He was breathing hard. 'There are monsters amongst us. They are called the Burning Hand.' He closed his mouth as though biting the end of the words off before they could slide free. 'They are here. They may be many. They may be one.'

Cado felt his head swimming. 'What are they?'

'Sorcerers. Worshippers of something that we have all forgotten, something outside the circle of the cosmos. Their magic... It's old, Cado, old and dark and powerful, and it's everywhere. It's cutting reality to hide them. There are spells that eat memories and vanish names. Even the dead. They have eaten souls to protect their presence.'

'How did you find them?'

'Chance, patience. They are moving. Inside the holes they cut, they are moving.'

'To do what?'

'I don't know, but they are getting close to what they want. I think I have told you this before. I think we have lost a lot of time.' The pressure in the circle of spirits was crushing. Cado could barely draw breath. 'Above all, you must remember what I have told you, Cado. You must remember.' Idyon was reaching for the ring on his small finger on his left hand. 'I found a way to hold on to the memories – a dead soul bound and shielded who holds it for you and pours it back into your mind as it vanishes.' He pulled the ring from his finger. The sphere of spirits flickered and thinned. Idyon staggered as though trying to push himself up against a great weight. He held out the ring.

'Take this and remember.'

'Whose soul does it hold?'

'A strong one, new from life.'

'Who?'

'Your father.'

'No.'

'Take it. I cannot hold our thoughts outside the world for much longer. When this circle collapses, only the one with this ring will remember. It must be you. The Burning Hand are a long way along the road to wherever they are going. If they know you know, they will either steal your memory or move sooner.'

Cado did not move.

'Take it!' shouted Idyon. 'Take it, Cado. You are our king, sire. Save your kingdom.'

Cado took the ring. Idyon fell back. The halo of spirits vanished. The warm air filled his lungs. He looked around. The curtains were stirring across a view of the sun setting over a late-summer day.

'The Burning Hand...' whispered a voice in his skull. 'Remember...'

He looked down at the ring in his hand, a narrow circle of iron. He could feel the past sliding away out of sight. He pushed the ring onto his left little finger. The iron was cold against his skin. He blinked. Sharp memories filled his mind. His head snapped around, part of him expecting to see masked figures standing in the shadows. There was no one there. Only Idyon, groaning from where he lay on the floor.

'What happened?' he asked.

Cado looked down at him. He felt his mouth open.

'If they know you know, they will either steal your memory,' *Idyon had said,* 'or move sooner.'

Cado closed his mouth and forced a smile. 'I would have thought that slipping and falling over your own feet would be something that was beneath the dignity of our worthy and wise Speaker.'

'Worthy and wise?' said Idyon, rubbing his scalp. 'Are you sure you didn't somehow hit your head too?' Cado held out a hand. Idyon looked at it. 'Talking of dignity, I am not sure that the king should be helping one of his councillors up off the ground.'

'I won't tell if you don't.'

Idyon grinned, gripped Cado's hand, and hauled himself up.

'What were we talking about before I fell? The floor must have shaken it out of my head.' Cado felt the smile fix on his face.

'Nothing of note.'

'You have chosen a soul-ring?' said Idyon, pointing at Cado's left hand. 'When did you do that?'

'Just today.'

'Udio will be pleased. Or at least his disappointment will shift to why you haven't chosen the other eight. Smallest finger of the left hand. The Unnamed Companion. No one royal, or important. Unusual to choose that member of the spirit court first. I am intrigued.'

Cado shrugged.

Idyon blinked and frowned. 'Are you sure there was nothing important we were talking about?'

'Nothing,' said Cado.

'Then I will wish my king goodnight and retire.' Idyon gave a bow and made for the door.

'Goodnight, my friend,' Cado said, and watched Idyon until the door clicked shut after him. 'Goodnight.'

He had sat on that throne alone afterwards. What could he do with fears and suspicions? In the days that followed he wondered if it had been a dream, or a jest, some dark conjuring from Idyon's sense of humour to jolt him out of his depression. He had hinted and tried to cajole Idyon into owning up. His friend had frowned at him, but shrugged it off, and no release had come.

Days went by, then weeks and the shadows gathered. He felt as though he were moving through the world separated by a sheet of crystal. When he had become the crown-anointed prince, and then the king, he had felt something similar. People had talked to him differently, expected him to be different. He had become aware of new things; of smiles that did not reach the eyes, and the guarded words of old friends when they spoke to him. The past had become separate, and the patterns of the world had become unfamiliar. Now though, it was not just a feeling; the separation was a literal truth.

He saw things, heard things, and then watched as the rest of the world turned away as though they had neither heard nor seen. There had been shadows of truth, stories from towns in the south;

gatherings of people who spoke of strange gods, secrets, masks. A traveller had come from a land just beyond the boundary and told of a tower seen shimmering on the horizon at dawn. The traveller vanished and only Cado could remember the tale they had told. Spring had barely passed when the vanishings began. It started in the cities and towns close to the borders. Messengers were the first. Sent from one place to another, they never arrived. After several of these disappearances, road-wardens had been sent out to find the missing messengers. They found nothing. That had been three weeks ago. That was the point that Cado should have talked to his own court of the dead. Except that the other rings still lay empty on the arm of the throne.

All those moments and chances now lay in the past. The future was ahead, burning like a poisoned dawn beyond the pall of smoke. He heard the other riders shouting to each other about what was happening. None of them knew. Cado knew. He could feel it in the heat on the wind. In the back of his head, the memory of Idyon's voice sounded like a promise:

'The Burning Hand are a long way along the road to wherever they are going.'

The peaks of the Broken Spine Mountains cut through the clouds of smoke ahead. Herezai banked. The cavalcade of beasts followed. The spire of a mountain slid past. Ghost spectres danced across the ice clinging to the rock. Their shrieks were needles on the wind. The ground dropped away. The light of fire filled the world beneath him.

Blue and pink and orange tongues of flame coiled into the air. Herezai's wings curved them into a gyre without Cado willing it. The dragon didn't want to fly above the flames, he could tell. The rest of the beasts were banking away from the fire too. Cado felt the heat in the air as he drew breath. There had been a forest here once.

From the mountain passes, the green of the leaves in spring had reached to the horizon. There had been cities too. Two great cities and towns dotting the roads between them. The spirits of the dead walked beneath the boughs when autumn turned the leaves to silver. Now the trees were burning torches. Fire leapt from their crowns. Trunks exploded as the sap inside them became steam. Plumes of smoke coiled through the air. The blaze was moving, flowing across the land as fast as a horse at full gallop. It was no simple fire either. Magic billowed from it. The air above the blaze shimmered. Cado thought he could see rolling eyes, and teeth and claws whenever he blinked. His head ached from the eyes to the back of his skull. The smoke was sweet, like fruit cooking to tar in a cauldron.

How had this happened? He had been trying to find the Burning Hand, had tried to find a way to tell other people and not have them forget. He did not have Idyon's arcane skill, though. He had tried to get his friend to give it to him, but without explaining why, it had not been possible, and the closer any reasons were to the truth, the quicker they would vanish from Idyon's mind. Whenever he had tried to grip the truth, the further it had moved into the darkness. The truth was here now, though. Nothing would remove this from memory.

One of the riders shifted closer. Their mount's wings beat swirls in the sparks. Shock showed on the rider's face, clear under their helm's cheek pieces.

'What is this?'

'War,' Cado said and urged Herezai around and back to the mountains. Beneath him the flames leapt higher as though to catch the riders as they turned in the air.

He had ridden back across the mountains to the canyon-city and the palace, and the sounds of warning horns already sounding. That had been what had happened then.

But now, in the space of this dream, he was falling, and he could feel his skin burning.

'It will be over soon, my prince,' came a voice that sounded like Solia's but wasn't. 'Do you want to see your mother? One last time?'

No! he wanted to shout, but the fire of the past was reaching up to take him in its grasp.

The fires rising through the streets of the canyon city. Cries and shouts from the guards. The sweet smoke of sorcery and meat cooking from bones…

He had landed on the palace, and it had already been burning. There had been people on the roofs, trying to get away from the inferno. Skin peeling from flesh, parents clinging to children in the last moments of agony. And there were things dancing in the blaze. Shapes that blurred with the fire, grinned with teeth, bounded and spun and hooted.

Ashes… all of it ashes…

His mother, clad in armour, framed in a doorway, backlit by the blaze.

'Where is Jakinda?' he had called.

Cities burning, always burning…

A whirl of ashes. His mother's cry as the sorcerer's knife opened her from throat to thigh. Blue fire. Blood becoming smoke.

'I… did not realise.'

Cinders falling on his face. Pain, a lot of pain, more pain than he could overcome.

Cold and darkness took the place of fire, but the pain remained. He was alone in an abyss, curled into a ball of limbs and memories and shame.

'Are you there?' he called, then quietly, 'Please, are you there?'

He felt the ghosts then. Ice in the fire. Close enough to feel their breath as they answered.

~We are here,~ came Idyon's voice.

~We come with you,~ said Solia. ~Always, and to the end.~

'And that end is here?' asked Cado.

~Yes, my prince.~

He closed his eyes, and felt the peace of relief wash through him.

A memory of ashes…

Cado lay on a bed of embers and ashes. He could taste. He could not see. His eyes were open, he could tell, but the world was blank. The last thing he had seen had been the fire rolling to meet him. Herezai had swept her wing up to try to shield him. The dragon had been bleeding, her wings tatters. The fire… It had taken his sight, he realised. His face and left hand felt cold, as if they had been resting against snow. That was the burns, he decided, scorched to numbness. The pain was there, though, waiting far behind the cold. He raised his right hand to his cheek, hesitated and then touched it. Soft, blistered flesh, weeping fluid. He began to shake, then stopped himself. He had to move. He was somewhere on the plateau away from the canyon city. He had to get back to it, had to find…

Figures vanishing into the inferno… Blue coils of flame strangling the trees. Daemons grinning and spinning. Towers collapsing into a sea of flame…

He stopped. His burnt hand was shaking. There was pain coming from the distance, crackling behind the numb cold.

'Herezai?' he said. The word brought a rasping breath from his lungs. He gasped, coughing. He could taste metal in his mouth, blood. Something was bubbling in his chest with each sip of air. He reached out, gasping. His fingers touched the dragon's scaled bulk. 'Herezai…'

'The beast is dead.' The voice froze his hand in place. 'You will be soon too.' He heard a soft rustle of fabric like dust on the wind, and a low, dry clink. He tried to rise, but his legs gave out and sent him sprawling back to the ground. A laugh danced around him.

'What… do you… want?'

'A king does not ask. They proclaim. They speak and reality obeys.'

'Do not mock me, daemon.'

Daemon... A word whose meaning and use had come with the fire and the death of his kingdom.

A hand was around his throat, and he was lifted into the air.

'Such things are not said to a queen,' said the voice. It was serene, utterly calm, as if it did not belong to the hand that clamped tight on his neck. He could not breathe. 'We understand, though. You are without sight, without knowledge, and so we will forgive you.' The hand opened, and he tumbled to the ground. Pain stabbed through him. He tried to draw breath. Thick bubbles gurgled in his throat.

'You are a king yourself, though your throne is ashes,' said the voice. 'We have watched you. I have heard your whispers and pleas. You let the weakness of this age infect you. Young, naïve, kings and queens on thrones that are no older than a blink of eternity's eye – none of you know what it is to rule. You don't know what it requires or what it demands. You are a hollow king, and so... here you are.'

Cado tried to force out a snarl of defiance, but a clotted burble was the only sound he could make. The voice laughed, the sound as beautiful as it was cutting, like the hiss of a silver knife.

'No, do not spoil your beauty with profanity. It does not please us, and it serves no purpose. Once I was going to offer you freedom, Cado Ezechiar, freedom and beauty and eternity to be the king you wanted to be. Now... You have no throne, no kingdom, no power. You are a burnt piece of meat clinging to the last of your mortality. Pitiful.'

He felt that she was suddenly close.

'But to be a monarch is to see beneath the skin. I would still offer you something, hollow king though you are. Not beauty or power, though you would have those too. Such things do not hold any value to you now. I offer you vengeance. The slaves of the Dark Gods suffering under your hand, their blood soaking the ground, their *waking and dreaming filled with dread, and the last terror in their eyes there for you to see.'*

He wanted to shake his head, to get away, but...

Another thought was in his head, unfolding as he heard the words. Vengeance. He could hear it growl with hunger. But it could not be... He was dying, blinded, choking on his own blood.

'It can be,' said the voice, as if in answer to his doubt. 'I will show you.' A finger touched his chin and tilted it up. Pain shivered through him. His lips parted. 'A single drop of truth...'

Something splashed between his lips. Iron, copper, the taste of fire and swords. He felt his body judder. He tried to pull back, but the fingers holding his chin held him. A chill unfolded through his body, pouring out from his throat through flesh. Pain dimmed. The darkness of his eyes clouded to silver fog, which thinned and then drained back from a world cast in silver and drawn in red fire. Above him, a face looked down into his. It was shining, luminous. Its eyes were spheres of night in features carved of moonlight. The mouth smiled. There were needle points behind the red lips.

'If you die, there can be no vengeance,' said the queen.

'Vengeance... what vengeance can I have?'

She smiled. 'All the vengeance that eternity can give.'

He looked at her. Inside his chest he could feel the strength fading again, the pain welling up. His vison was clouding, blindness returning. All over now. All of it gone and burnt. He was nothing. All of it, all the years of his childhood had been a golden lie. He had grown thinking that he was special, that his choices mattered. Even when he had tried to reject the throne, he had been thinking that his life and what he wanted mattered. It didn't. Hollow. It was all hollow. Life was a skin of lies and hopes and dreams wrapped around a void. You matter. You are special. You are a king. *Now the skin had burnt away, and there was just the empty truth, bitter on his tongue.*

'I am no one,' he said.

A laugh like breaking bells.

'Aren't we all? But we can do something about that.' A pause. He could hear the hiss and burble of his breath getting quieter. His thoughts were becoming dilute, slipping away into a grey current. 'I am not without patience,' said the voice, 'but the time you have for this choice is down to the last grains of sand. I could make that choice for you, but that rarely ends well. Choose now, Cado. Live and make life bleed for what it has done, or go and suffer as a shade.'

Cado could feel the beat of his pulse. It was faint but somehow as loud as thunder in his skull. He could not even taste his own blood any more. He could not feel. The woman with the red smile might no longer be there. The moment might have passed.

'Time is up,' she said.

The last breath he drew was cold.

'Yes,' he said.

CHAPTER TWENTY-FOUR

'So you gave it all away for a lie?' Cado opened his eyes. Orange light met him. He felt heat on his face, stepped back. Coals were glowing. Tongues of heat reached up, breathing brighter and brighter. 'You took what was offered,' said the same voice. 'Let your soul go.'

There was a figure by the fire, bare-armed and bearded. He turned, lifting a length of metal out of the flames. It glowed. The eyes above the beard were black pebbles reflecting the light.

'Valentin,' Cado said, and heard the uncertainty in his voice.

The smith laughed, the sound a growl without humour.

'There's nothing and no one here but you, Cado. I am back in the city that is either going to burn in the light of the Lumineth or become a bone-farm for the Ossiarch Empire. I'm trying to make sure my family is safe.' He turned away from Cado, rested the glowing metal on the anvil, and began to hammer. The strikes rang through the dark, a heartbeat of iron and steel and sparks. 'You are pinned out under the light of the Lumineth's runes. Light is pouring from the sky. Your eyes have already boiled in their sockets. Your skin has cracked. Bone is showing through.' The hammer blows fell between the words. Cado found that he was flinching to the sound. Valentin turned back to the forge fire and plunged the metal back into the hot coals. The breath of the bellows took the place of the hammer strikes. 'The aelves didn't lie. You are burning – body and what's left of your soul. Layer by layer peeled back to the light. That's what this is. Your past, memories, all of it – by the time it's over... well, there won't even be the lies left.'

'I should have left when I could,' said Cado.

'No,' said Valentin. 'You should have died when you could.' The smith turned and the forge light was bright in the darkness of his eyes. Cado could feel the heat of the forge on his face. 'You chose to become a blight in the world, because you could not bear the idea that your suffering and loss was no different to anyone else's. Your pain had to matter, had to daub life red. It had to be that way because otherwise it would mean you were not special, were not a chosen prince, king of all you saw. You thought you deserved vengeance and that was all that mattered. You would not pay the price of it after all.'

Cado tried to step back, but there was no space behind him. The heat of the forge was growing. His skin was prickling.

'I...' he began.

'What?' snorted Valentin. 'You never caused anyone else pain? You never let others die because it didn't matter compared to what you needed?'

'I know what I am.'

'Yes, you know that you are a monster. You know that you have done terrible things. That you do not deserve even to live. Yes, yes, all of that and more, but really, down under all of that is just a mewling, self-pitying princeling wallowing in his own pain.'

Valentin grinned, the expression merciless, and when he spoke again it wasn't his voice but a whining mockery of Cado's own. 'I don't want the throne. No one ever asked me what I wanted. I have lost everything. Existence has no meaning. I am not worthy.'

The forge was bright. The metal in the smith's hand was a streak of burning red between the hammer and the anvil. Cado raised his hands to shield himself.

'What happened to you is not special. Countless have suffered worse. At this moment in Aventhis, thousands will see the small piece of life they have fought for vanish. To you that means nothing because it isn't your suffering.'

'I have a code.'

'A code? A code of what? That you will only murder and slaughter people who you decide are damned? If that code means so much then why have you not turned on your own, on your blood-siblings? Why not work to end yourself?'

'I have a task I must see done.'

'No.' Valentin shook his head. 'The real reason is the same one that made you go pleading to your father to spare you the duty of the throne, the same reason you accepted the offer of undying life.' Valentin pulled the metal from the forge fire, and for the first time Cado could see what it was that the smith had been shaping. It was a sword. White heat bled from the tip down the blade, fading from red to black. 'You do not have the courage to make the other choice.'

Heat was pouring into Cado's hands and face. Valentin's eyes were mirrors to the glowing blade.

'I…' he started.

Valentin rammed the sword into Cado's chest.

The world burned white. Edge to edge. Every direction. A hammer blow of light and heat that never ended.

'Cado!' A shout, close by.

Where was he?

Where he always was: on the bed of ashes, folded under the shadow of Herezai's wing.

She would be here soon, the queen with her red smile and promise of vengeance.

'Cado!' The voice again, but not hers.

A grey shadow fell through the white. Something was pulling at his arms. He was burning. He knew it with total clarity. The skin of his face and hands had gone. The bones of his cheeks were black and crumbling. His flesh was falling as grey embers onto the cloth of his cloak. Ribs were collapsing. The ivory grin of his fangs was broad between charred lips.

Another tug at his limbs and a muffled cry. Pain, but not his own. He could hear hammer blows now. Then a grunt of effort and he was moving, rolling, rising, carried like an ember on the wind. Someone was biting out words, a prayer, each sound pushed through clenched teeth. The white fire grew as though it were trying to keep him in its embrace. Then it was gone, draining to a bright scar in ash grey.

'Cado? Cado! Can you hear me?'

Valentin. It was Valentin's voice, hoarse and urgent.

Cado tried to move his arms, but he could only feel the fire still burning. He…

'Lightning's truth…' swore Valentin. A part of Cado's thoughts, floating free of the rest, could imagine the smith looking at him. A burnt cadaver, cooked flesh sloughing off bones, bloodsmoke steaming off the meat. He tried to draw a breath, and something must have moved in the ruin of his flesh because Valentin gasped.

Cado formed a word. He felt something that had been his tongue shift behind his teeth.

'Blood…' he said, the shallow breath hissing out.

For a second there was quiet, and stillness as a decision was made.

Movement, a hiss of suppressed pain, and then a splash against his teeth.

Red. Iron. Life and warmth. Just a drop. An explosion. A lightning bolt reaching down to kindle light. Another drop fell and then another, spattering against his teeth, seeping in. The pain was retreating. He could feel his limbs, his tongue, the withered claws of his fingers. His hands lashed out, gripping Valentin's arm. His head rose and his teeth sank into the meat of the wrist.

The world went from white to red.

Beat by bloody beat, strength flowed into his flesh. The husk of his soul swelled. Flesh grew. Wounds closed. His eyes came last. Skin unfurled across muscle. Sight shimmered into being, swam and then focused.

Valentin lay on the ground next to him. Cado still had the man's wrist in his teeth. He could feel the smith's blood beating, an echo of his own, stolen pulse. He wanted to keep drinking. He wanted to drain the mortal's veins and feel the thread of life snap with the last thud of an empty heart.

He let the man's arm go and scrambled back. Valentin moaned but did not rise. The bite in his left wrist was still weeping blood onto the stone. Cado shut his eyes. He felt the hunger roar at him to finish the kill. He forced it down and knelt.

There were burns on Valentin's face and arms, pale marks like the inverse of shadows. Blisters were growing on the patches of skin. Cado looked around to where the blinding column of light poured from the sky to strike the place where he had lain. He could only glance at it before he had to shield his eyes. Valentin had gone into that, had hammered the chains till they broke and then pulled Cado out. He looked back at the man. He was alive but would not be for long. Cado bit his left hand. Thick, almost-black blood seeped from the wound. A heavy drop formed on the tip of his finger. He held it above Valentin's mouth. Not much. Not enough to be anything other than a small gift, life returned to where it was stolen from. He let the drop fall. It splashed on the man's lips then trickled into his mouth.

Valentin's eyes snapped open. He gasped and jerked to his feet, staggered. Cado's hand snapped out and gripped the man's arm. Valentin whirled, eyes wide and wild.

Cado willed stillness. The man froze. He turned to Cado. His gaze was steady, calculating, the look of a predator gauging a rival. A spark of red light clung to his eyes. Cado shook his head, and Valentin blinked. The light went from his eyes and confusion replaced the wary calculation.

'Valentin,' said Cado carefully.

'What…?'

'All is well,' Cado said, and let go of where he had grabbed Valentin's arm at the wrist. Where the bite had been, a glossy scar puckered the skin. Valentin touched his face. The blisters had gone, the pale burns faded so that they were almost invisible.

'How…?'

'A gift.' The man blinked, shook his head as though trying to clear it. 'Valentin,' said Cado again. The man looked up. 'Thank you.'

Valentin nodded, still uncertain.

'It was Ama,' said Valentin. 'He followed you, down into the passages. He saw… He saw Magister Leragrais. He fled, found me, told me what he had seen and heard.' The man's eyes were hard. 'I could have killed you myself then, but he said that you had told him to go.' Valentin shook his head. 'Wilful, stubborn, just like his mother. But he told me, and I knew then that the magister must have seen a way out by making a deal with the light aelves or whatever they are. There was only one way he could really leave alone, by the high gate over the bridge to the northern spire. So, I went out and waited close to the way down from that spire.'

'How did you get out of the city?'

Valentin held up the seal of the worthies that they had been given.

'I still had this. I waited, saw the magister come down riding one horse and leading another with a shrouded body on it – you.' He shrugged. 'I followed.'

'Why?' asked Cado.

'Why? I don't know really. I suppose because you got me out of that fight in the valley. I was angry before, afraid, but that was not fair. You got me into it too, but you could have left me behind. I believe… Everything is empty to you, I know that. You are just like the rest. You have this… end that you thirst for. You will do anything to reach it. It's not conquest or slaughter, but it's the same… Soulblight, a blighted soul. Says it all, doesn't it? But I don't see things that way. I see light and hope, and the only way we hold on to that is by acting as if it matters and is true.' He shrugged again. 'It was the right thing to do. Besides, I could not have told Ama that I knew and did nothing.'

'Thank you,' said Cado again. Valentin did not respond but nodded at where Cado's sword and rings lay on the ground. Smoke was rising from them.

'I got those out first.'

Cado picked up the rings and slid them onto his fingers. Their touch was ice cold. He looked down at his hand and blinked. Small facts and details aligned in his mind. He stared into the distance for a long moment. Lightning flashed in a strobing sheet across the sky. Raindrops began to fall, heavy and freezing.

'You have horses?'

Valentin nodded, began to ask a question.

'We have to get back to the city,' said Cado.

'What? They will do the same to you again if you–'

'Leragrais is going to give the city to the Lumineth. They will have given him time to get some of the people inside the walls out, but the Ossiarchs are coming and the Lumineth will not wait. What happened at the outpost, Valentin, that is what will happen to every man, woman and child in Aventhis.'

'If the… Bonereapers reach it first?'

'Then they will take it,' said Cado. 'Then the Lumineth will fight to stop them. A battle of light and undeath, Valentin. There is no room for survival when such powers fight.'

Valentin held Cado's gaze for a second and then nodded, but then shook his head again.

'But what can you do?'

Cado turned and made for the steps down the crag.

'Everything I can,' he said.

CHAPTER TWENTY-FIVE

They rode under the roof of a growing storm. Daylight was fading to night behind the clouds. The rain fell without pause, cold heavy drops that tasted of lightning and tin. They didn't need the sun or land to guide them. On the horizon, visible behind the veil of rain, light flashed and stuttered. The horses shivered as though they did not want to turn, but Cado hissed at them, and they kept on. Valentin was quiet in his saddle, eyes fixed on the flashes.

'Leragrais will get people out of the city,' he said, half to himself.

'He may try, but the Lumineth will not wait. They know the Ossiarchs approach. The city is a keystone in a game that goes beyond Aventhis and this underworld. They will not let their design fail because there are mortals inside. What they have begun is shifting the currents of magic across this underworld, and per-haps beyond. Leragrais' help simplifies matters for them, but they do not need his consent. They will take the city, paint their rune in the sky and–'

'Don't,' said Valentin.

'When we are inside, you find your family. Get everyone you can into the catacombs, as deep as you can.'

'Not out of the city?'

'If there are armies close, then it will be the safest place for them.'

'All right,' said Valentin, raising his voice over the hiss of the rain and roll of thunder. Cado could hear a grimness that had not been in the man's voice before. He looked at the smith. Valentin kept on looking straight ahead. 'Your blood,' the man called as though sensing Cado's gaze. 'You gave me some of your blood to heal me.'

'Your life is still your own,' said Cado. 'To become like me requires… more.'

'I know. I know the shape of my soul well enough to know that it is still mine.' He paused as another blinking series of flashes lit the night sky. 'I saw things, for a moment after… I saw things. They were not from my life, or my dreams.' He looked at Cado. His gaze was clear and hard, and in that look Cado imagined that the forge-light gleamed with judgement. 'I hope you can help us.'

Then he looked back to the horizon, and they rode.

In the silver blink of light, Cado could see skulls and spear points in the dark, rank upon rank. Valentin followed Cado's look.

'There are hundreds of them,' called the smith.

'There will be more,' answered Cado. They were close now. The spires of rock stabbed up at the sky around them. He could hear the cries of birds blending with the sound of rain and growl of thunder. 'Which gate are you making for?'

'The south gate,' said Valentin. 'It's smaller, a cart gate.' Cado looked at Valentin as the man pulled the seal of the council from under his cloak.

'The militia are hunting for me.'

'I know, but we might be able to confuse them.'

Cado shook his head. 'The high gate that Leragrais took – we take that.' Valentin looked as though he were struggling with the words for why that was not a clever idea. Cado felt a cold smile form on his lips. 'I am a Soulblight,' he said. 'There is a reason we are feared.'

'Let me pass! In the name of Magister Leragrais, let me pass!' The guards almost loosed their bows, but Valentin shouting Leragrais' name gave them pause. Then Valentin was closer, and the lightning flashes must have shown he was alone. The seal in his hand gleamed. He shouted again. 'I come from Magister Leragrais!' The arrows and bolts did not fly, but neither did the gate open.

'The magister sent you? Where is he?'

'I do not have time for questions. I have to get to Cometarian Damascene.'

'You are the smith that set out with the wanderer they are now hunting.'

'I am the man with the magister's seal.' Cado heard the strength in Valentin's voice. Where had that come from? Had it always been there, or was that what heroism looked like – not an inheritance, but a quality that came from inside like metal tempered by heat and hammer?

The guards hesitated and then were calling for the gate to open. Gears ground. A split appeared in the doors, barely wide enough for Valentin to lead his horse through. In the dark, on the edge of sight, Cado inhaled. The magic filled his chest, needle-sharp and cold. There was so much power in the wind... Valentin was off the horse and at the open gate.

A flash of lightning. A heartbeat of the storm. Then utter black.

Cado breathed out as thunder shivered through the rain. Darkness folded around him, and he was walking, flowing in Valentin's wake, clinging to the space he had just left as a ragged shadow.

Valentin was almost through the gate. The guards were staring into the rain and night.

Cado saw the man's head twitch to look behind him.

Don't look... he willed. *Keep moving.* He could feel the storm inhaling. Another flash of lightning was coming.

They were through. The gate began to shut. The sky blinked white, the rain silver.

'Wait!' called one of the guards. Valentin looked at him. The darkness poured back into the space the lightning had left.

'Yes?' said Valentin, iron in his voice again.

'I thought there was something behind you.'

'We all have shadows, don't we?' Valentin said and hurried to climb the spiral road up the side of the rock stack. Above them the beams of the bridge linking the stack to the city spire creaked in the storm.

Cado let the spell fade. His head was ringing. Red veins spidered his sight. He stepped out of Valentin's shadow and staggered against a wall. Water was churning down the channels at the side of the street.

The smith turned then looked up as three swift blows of thunder shook the air. Seen from here, the light of the thunderbolts was the purple and green of bruises. Valentin had done as they had planned and not stopped moving until they were across the bridge and on the street with Valentin's forge.

Cado pushed himself away from the wall. The effort of holding the spell around him was fading, but he could feel his hunger growing.

Valentin glanced at Cado.

'Go,' he said, and started down the street towards his forge. 'Do what you must, I'll find Vaux.' They had left the horse at the high gate. Inside the city it would only slow them down. Cado straightened and looked after the smith hurrying down the road. There were no lights in the windows of the buildings to either side, nor the rest of the city. Anyone who was not on the walls would be huddling behind locked doors, waiting as the night shook. The forge was just as dark and quiet as the rest. No smoke rising, no light seeping from under the doors.

They had talked about what to do once back inside the walls. Valentin was going to find his children, then he would go to Vaux. The seneschal must know about Leragrais and the Lumineth. She might not believe Valentin, but she certainly would not believe Cado. For his part, he needed to get to the spire top. He blinked again. His sight was swimming, as though an afterglow of the storm flash had caught in his eyes. He half turned, then stopped. There it was again, something on the edge of seeing…

He started down the street after Valentin. The smith was at the door of his forge, knocking, calling. Cado was next to him as the door opened and Leire looked out.

'Father? Father!' she said, going to him, but then recoiled as she saw Cado.

'It's all right. Where is your brother? We need to go now.'

'He… went out.'

'What?' Valentin had gone pale, staring at his daughter.

'He looked out of the door once, saw something. He was not making any sense, kept saying it was important that it hadn't been there before.'

'Why didn't you stop him?'

'I tried, but I couldn't. He ran out of the door and when I reached it, I couldn't see him.'

'I know where he went,' said Cado. Valentin whirled, mouth opening. 'I will go and get him back.'

'What…? How?' began Valentin, the panic stealing the words before he could get them back. Cado could feel cold calmness spreading through him now. He knew what he needed to do.

'Both of you, go and find Vaux. Tell her everything. She will not want to listen, but she must. Leragrais, the nexus under the city, all of it. I will get Ama. Go now. There is not much time.'

'Where is he?' asked Valentin.

'In the tower behind me,' said Cado. 'The tower with the blue-and-red door. That is what Ama saw, and that is where he is.'

'It's just a ruin,' said Leire. 'There is no tower.'

'But there is,' Cado said, and turned. The lightning blinked. He took a step. At the edge of his sight, in the crack between light and dark, a shape loomed above, a crooked finger scratching the heavens. Cado drew his sword. 'Go now,' he said.

Cado took a step. The lightning was pulsing, the thunder a roar to drown any words that Valentin called after him. Another step, another flash. Magic… magic tearing through the air, blowing reality ragged. The storm was reaching its height. All the lines were crossing, all the desires of mortals and immortals aligning over this place. One step after another, one in light…

Flash…

And one in dark.

And there was a broken door hanging open at the base of a broken tower…

Flash…

A stump of stone set into the side of a rock face…

Flash…

But there in the smeared light after the fading glare, there was a tower, rising to the sky, caught on the edge of seeing, balanced on the edge of impossibility. It was tall, impossibly tall. The rain glistened on its stone and held the thunder flash so that it shone silver-white.

No darkness came to fill the second in which the thunder echoed. Cado was at the door. It was blue and red, and at its centre the shadow of a hand was burnt into the paint. He paused. He knew that if he looked back, he would not see the city. He was on a boundary between the magic that mortals called reality and the truth. He had been here before. He had seen the like of this tower many times, in many places. It was there and not, a thing forgotten as soon as you saw it. It was there the first day he arrived in the city. It was there when he sat in its ruins through the night. It had always been there, a parasite worm with its jaws fastened to the flesh of the Mortal Realms.

He pushed the door open. It creaked but did not resist. There were stairs inside, a great coil of steps going up and plunging down. He began to climb. He knew that the tower was welcoming him. He knew that this was a trap. He kept climbing until there were no more steps. A platform with nine sides opened under a sky of frozen lightning. There was no parapet, just a drop down into the dark where the city lay. There was a stone table, black and flecked, and a figure stood beside it. Small objects sat on the stone: crystals, a feather, bits of iron. The figure was rearranging them. She was calm, unsurprised by his presence. He knew her face.

'Hello, Cado,' said Amaury's voice as she looked up at him.

CHAPTER TWENTY-SIX

'Where is the boy?' asked Cado.

Amaury's face smiled.

'Ah, the boy. A perceptive one, him, and that is a rare quality. There is a spark of talent there, you know. He might have done remarkable things.'

'What have you done with him?'

'Nothing,' she said. 'Yet. But maybe soon. He came running in here as soon as I let him see the tower. You know you should not have let yourself get close to the smith. From all I know of you, you should have learnt by now that sentiment only makes you vulnerable. As soon as I knew that you had survived and come back to the city, I knew the only way to stop you making real trouble was to bring you to me. The smith would bring you here, and the boy would compel you to step into my realm.'

'I am here. Let him go.'

'And why would I do that?'

'Amusement.'

She laughed, bringing her hand to her mouth.

'You do understand us,' she said. 'At least in part.'

She tapped a finger on the table. A shape folded into being on the floor. 'Here. He has performed his purpose, and why not let him see what comes next, yes?'

Ama pushed himself up. His eyes were wide with terror before they found Cado.

'It's all right,' said Cado, holding his gaze on the figure of Amaury. 'Go down the stairs, Ama. Go until you reach a door. Go out. Run. Do not stop, do not look back.'

'Cado,' began Ama. 'I–'

'Run,' snarled Cado. Eyes red, face hollowing, teeth bared.

The boy ran.

Amaury's face laughed. 'Ah… what a delight to see people show their true faces. If only more did that, life would be such a simple and dull thing.'

'Is that why you hide behind the face of a dead woman… Cometarian Damascene.'

The figure's face showed no reaction. Then its features became fixed, a perfectly painted likeness cast in wax with glass for eyes and dead teeth for a grin. She reached up, gripped the face like a cloth, and pulled it free. Change rippled over the figure from head to foot. Heavy red cloth unfolded in place of worn leather; gold comets and hammers gleamed in place of worn buckles. Damascene nodded slowly, grey eyes dancing with appreciation under her cowl.

'How long have you known?'

'Not long.'

She smiled. 'How?'

'The rings,' said Cado. 'The Lumineth told Leragrais to destroy the rings. He set two rings beside me in the light. You said he had kept them all, so he was either lying to the Lumineth, or you were lying to me. He was a man who was going to give up a city and all the power it hid – such a man does not lie to keep a few rings. That told me you were not what you seemed. After that it was not a great distance to cross with a guess.'

'Ah, so simple, but I think you underestimate that man's pettiness. I am sure all the reasons he gave for what he is doing were high and mighty – refusal to bow to the dominion of the King of Bones, better for the living to burn in the light of agony forever than… and so on and so on. All lies. Most of them he believes but lies all the same. The truth is that he is doing all of this because he is bitter and tired and afraid. He has power, but he was sitting on top of a locus of magic that would make the students of the arcane soil their robes in excitement, and he couldn't do anything with it. Deep down all wizards want to be lords, and he had the power and, well… found he did not have the ability. Worse, he can feel the sand of his own time running fast. He can feel your rattling lord in his pit of night sucking in his life just like all the rest of the wretches in this realm. He does not want to defy the powers of death. He wants to run from them.'

'They always want to talk when they believe they have won,' Solia had once remarked of the followers of the Crow God of Change, *'as though the pressure of secrets held in their souls wants to find a release.'*

'Tell me,' said Cado, 'are you actually Damascene?'

'Or am I just wearing her face? Is there another face under this one, another truth under the lie? If I am her, did I fall before, or after I came here? If I am not her then what did I do with the real Damascene? Did I eat her soul and shrink her body to a pinch of dust? Did the Burning Hand find me and teach me the truth?' She grinned broadly and gave a shiver of pleasure. 'The possibilities are dazzling, and the answer to them all is "yes".'

Cado held still while her last words faded.

'The Burning Hand,' he said, 'your master. Where can I find her?'

Damascene laughed. The hammer amulets hanging from her headdress jingled.

'That is why we are talking rather than spitting spells, isn't it? You think that I can tell you where the Burning Hand is and then you can hunt her down and kill her.' She smiled, cruelly. 'Peace and redemption, peace and redemption... somehow yours after all your lifetimes. What a delightfully simple notion.'

'You will tell me now, or with the last breath of your life,' said Cado. He was almost close enough that a single leap would carry him across the gap between them.

'Come now,' she laughed. 'That is hardly a fair offer. You are going to try to kill me anyway, no matter what I tell you.'

Cado shifted forwards.

Damascene raised a hand and stepped back.

'Ah now, let's not do anything regrettable.' Cado saw now the rings on her fingers. His rings. She followed his eye and tilted her head as though to admire how they sat on her hand. 'Lovely, four souls trapped and plucked. Would you like me to suck them out one by one or eat them all at once?' She raised an eyebrow and smiled broadly. The expression seemed too wide. There was a blue gleam in the grey of her eyes. 'So, it seems that I have two things that you want, and that hardly seems fair. Let me rebalance matters. The Burning Hand – the great sorcerer that burned your kingdom, the Shadow of Deceit who you have hunted past the bounds of mortality... Dead. Long dead, in fact. You have been chasing an illusion, Cado Ezechiar. There is no one Burning Hand any more, it's a mask worn by many. I am the Burning Hand.'

'You lie,' said Cado, but inside he felt his fears echo what Damascene had said.

'Lies are the truth,' she said. 'That's what the Great Changer reveals. Down beneath everything, there are only lies. So they are the ultimate truth, and the ultimate power.'

Cado felt the temptation to believe her scream inside him. All the doubts gathered over the years since his kingdom fell, all the moments when he thought he saw that he was on a road that would never end, all of it whispered to him now.

A black blade of will sliced the thoughts away. Lies used as truth, truth as lies – that was how the slaves of the Crow God worked. There was only one way this ended now, but he needed to be ready, and he needed to be closer.

'You will give me back the rings. If you do, I will let you live and leave the city.'

She laughed, shook her head. 'You are a poor crafter of lies, Cado.'

'You have no choice. The Lumineth are coming and the legions of the Ossiarchs. You will not survive, unless I let you flee.'

'Narrow thinking, disappointing really. They are here *because* of me, Cado. Who do you think nudged Leragrais to bargain with the Lumineth? Who made the case for you to be used to antagonise and confuse matters? Who do you think made sure that the Ossiarch Empire knew that this city stood filled with bones for the harvest and on a nexus of power? I have made all of this.'

'To what end?' Cado found himself asking. He glanced at the ring on Damascene's right forefinger. A path was opening in his thoughts.

'Mayhem,' said Damascene. 'All of the enemies of the Way of Change at cross purposes, change and power and confusion all blazing on a pyre.'

'You will lose the city.'

'You know us so well but so poorly. We *never* lose. The city falls, I win. It does not fall, I still win – it will burn just the same, and from the flames I will ascend. The Lumineth have forced the flow of magic into a flood tide. Thousands of souls cluster here for safety... firewood and kindling set atop the furnace just waiting for the spark.'

'The nexus,' said Cado. 'You were not using it or hiding in the tunnels, you were trying to reach it.'

Damascene nodded. 'I have spent years trying to break through the wards and charms around the deepest part of the catacomb. This tower sits above one of the first doors I could open into the passages. I tried subtlety and violence and trickery, but even though Leragrais never realised who his enemy was, the nature of the catacombs kept me out. Old spells and power that knew that I and my servants were a threat. So what I needed was someone with the power of death to break those spells. You did that for me, and now the way is open.'

Cado did not react.

Damascene opened her hand. Blue fire leapt between the fingertips. The slabs of the floor slid, shifting as the opening to the stairs stretched wider. The steps spiralled down into night. Cado thought he could hear falling sand whisper from the depths. Above, the frozen lightning in the sky was spreading like cracks through ice.

Damascene looked up.

'The moment approaches. Look, the other fools gather to play their parts.' She waved a hand and the view beneath the tower-edge flexed as though it were bending through crystal. Cado could see ranks of soldiers with spears marching through the outer stacks of rock. Each one a sculpture of bone with dead light in the holes of its eyes. And as he shifted his gaze, he saw riders and spearmen coming from the west. Silver shone under lightning flare. Ivory-coloured silk streamed in the wind and rain as they ran, feet barely touching the ground. At their head rode Lotharic, face grim, and behind her came Leragrais, clinging on to a steed.

'You see, all ends, all changes. Even your road, Hollow King. I admit that I am pleased that I will be the one to drag your blighted soul into the fires of change.'

Cado began to move. His first stride pushed him into a leap that would carry him across the space between them. His sword rose. Damascene closed her hand. The stones of the floor moved. Blocks slid and flipped. The circle of the tower rotated. Cado landed. Damascene was on the opposite side of the building.

Cado leapt again. Fire breathed from Damascene's mouth. The folds of her robes burned. Skirts of armoured scales flickered into being in their place. Where there had been velvet, now there was bronze and silver. The skin of her face fell in grey ash. Beneath, the flesh was the colour of a seashell pulled from poisoned water: iridescent, shifting between the shades of a polluted rainbow. There were no eyes, ears or nose, just a mouth and the gleam of teeth. Blue fire haloed her.

Cado's first blow struck as he landed. The sigils on the sword blazed as the blade met the magic surrounding her. Pain jolted up his arm, and somehow he was still in the last second of his leap, his strike still unfolding, but now Damascene was not there. A dagger flashed towards his chest. He saw it in time and jerked aside. He felt heat skin his face as the blade passed by. He struck again, but again the blow stuttered in time and Damascene was now behind him, and he felt the dagger punch under the edge of his armour.

No pain. Just cold, and numbness spreading as the blade pulled free. Ash fell from the wound in place of blood. He half fell, half jumped back from the next thrust. Grey fog was filling the bottom of his sight. The hunger in his chest roared as his body tried to heal the ashen wound. Everything was slow, the speed of life reduced to the heartbeat of a dying man.

He needed time. He needed help.

'If you die, there can be no vengeance,' said the voice of a queen.

Vengeance… a promise as much as a desire.

'I will give you vengeance,' he had said. His hand found the pouch next to his belt.

Damascene came forwards, flame-flicker fast. Cado's fingers touched the spike of burnt iron.

'Amaury,' he called, and her spectre unfolded into being.

Blackness stole the light from the world. Fire and heat turned white, flesh the red smear of blood. Amaury's spectre was a ragged outline of night. It struck Damascene. She screamed. The spectre was flowing over her, swallowing the blue halo of fire. Now it was the sorcerer that was burning. Skin and muscle twisted as she tried to get free. The spectre squeezed tighter and tighter, hissing curses. Only Damascene's mouth was visible now, biting the air as though to chew off the scream coming from her throat. The sound stopped. The mouth closed. The darkness flowed over the gap. Cado stood, sword raised, and began to move closer.

A sphere of orange-and-blue flame exploded out. The spectre tore into shreds of shadow. Damascene stood amidst the flames. Cado lunged. Fire blazed up in a ring around Damascene. Teeth and claws formed from heat and snapped at him. He backed away and spat an oath into the air that howled in the gale of magic. The spell died before it could form, and the fire arced towards him. He dodged again, faster than a mortal blink but slower than the treachery of magic. He saw Damascene behind the wall of flames. She held her dagger loose. Cado's iron rings were black circles on her fingers. Her mouth was a smile of razors. She came forwards. The flames withered as they tried to catch Cado. He coiled and leapt high. His body was shredding to shadow as he arched towards Damascene, high and fast…

A coil of fire caught his ankle. Skin and flesh charred. Pain snapped through him. He heard a rustling laugh like the chatter of crows. The slowed world shattered. His spell vanished. He fell, twisting as he struck floor. Damascene was above him, dagger plunging down at his chest. He cut. There was no opening or time for a death blow, just as he had known there would not be. The edge of his sword sliced Damascene's forefinger from her right hand. Cado caught the iron ring as it fell from the severed digit. The sorcerer's blow faltered. The ring slid onto Cado's finger. The iron was burning cold.

'Herezai,' he called.

A beat of silence and shadow. Lights dimmed. Sounds stolen. Then a roar and rattle as a spiral of bloodsmoke and bone-dust unfolded from the air above Cado. Bones shaped in emptiness. Torn flesh pulled across desiccated muscle. A great arc of vertebrae formed. Then wings – great sheets of tattered and burnt skin stretched between spars of bone – unfurled.

The downdraught of the dragon's first wing beat crushed Damascene to the floor. She tried to rise. Blue fire wreathed her hands. Herezai opened her jaws. Green light and black smoke poured from her mouth. The cloud struck Damascene and flowed over her. Silver armour tarnished. Flesh withered. Bones crumbled. The sorcerer screamed as her skull began to dissolve. Somehow, she was still moving, blue light falling from wounds and mouth as her blood burned. She raised her hand towards the dead dragon. An eye opened on her palm. A lick of fire blazed at the centre of a black iris. Cado could feel the magic winding tight around them. The fire speared towards Herezai. Then the beast's head lunged forwards. Her jaws snapped shut. The sorcerer staggered backwards, burning blood scattering from the stump of her arm. The dragon raised her head to the sky, wings spread to the storm. Rotting muscles worked in her neck as she swallowed.

Cado was across the space, reaching beneath his cloak to the pouch on his back. Damascene raised the dagger in her remaining hand, still whipcrack fast even as the armour and flesh melted off her bones. The loop of chain whipped around her neck as Cado released it. Black iron links circled her arms, coiling like a snake. She snarled then choked, falling. The links tightened, pulling her down. The manacles clanked shut on her arms. The lock closed. Ghost-light was already fuming off the black links of metal. Cado slowed, stopped. Behind him the storm roared up into the sky, but even over the crash of thunder and magic he could hear the cold rattle and creak coming closer, waiting.

Tatters of darkness coalesced behind Damascene. The outlines of fingers gripped the sorcerer's shoulders. Cado felt heat prickle his skin, as the shade of Amaury looked at him from behind Damascene.

~My vengeance...~ rasped the shade.

'It is yours. Go with her and see her torment.'

He looked at Damascene. She was still alive. Even as he watched, there were fresh fingers growing from the stump of her arm, pink digits writhing between the loops of chain like the feelers of a crustacean emerging from a shell. He held up a silver key.

'You will end lost and damned, Hollow King,' said Damascene. The chains clinked tighter. Bones crunched under the pressure. Cado put the key into the lock hanging around her neck.

'I am already damned,' he said. 'But not lost.'

He turned the key.

The clank of turning bolts and cogs rolled into the sound of thunder, rising higher and higher. The air was vibrating with the clank of winches and hoists and wheels turning. Shapes flickered in the air beside Damascene, hunched and hooded shapes of tattered cloth and pale light. Metal masks encased their heads. Locks and chains hung from them. A keening dirge, half pain, half mocking chuckle shivered from them as they gripped the chains holding Damascene. If she had had eyes perhaps they would have shown fear then. The spectres' grips tightened and then they were pulling her away, and they and she were folding out of being. At her back raged the shadow of Amaury clinging to Damascene, scorched fingers cradling the sorcerer's head as she shrieked.

CHAPTER TWENTY-SEVEN

The tower began to shake as Cado turned away from where the sorcerer had been. Its stones and substance creaked as the magic holding it together bled away. The frozen sky was moving again, the pulse of lightning and the clouds churning in the magic gale. Herezai was flicking her head as though trying to shake herself free of a chain. Cado took a step forward and put a hand on the dragon's flank. She twisted, jaws wide, eyes boiling with ghost-light. Cado could feel the death agony in the creature, the moment of her demise stretched out beyond life into torment.

'Herezai,' he said. The dragon froze, and the blaze dimmed in her eyes. Cado felt a tremble under his fingers, a pulse of emotion that ran through his blood. An echo of loyalty held in dry bone and tattered skin. Herezai's wings folded, and her head dipped. Cado held out his hand. The dragon shivered, bones clicking. Her mouth opened again, and she coughed iron rings onto Cado's palm.

A flash of ochre light ran through the clouds surrounding the platform. Thunder shook the stones. Hail began to fall, smashing into the stone. Cado could taste the magic boiling in the air as the geomantic currents twisted. There was no more time. Spears and swords and the rattle of bones, all around. He could leave. Could go now with the souls in the rings safe.

He shook his head and put his hand on Herezai's neck.

'I am sorry, my friend,' he said. 'I must ask you to carry me again.' Then he was swinging up onto the dragon's back and her tattered wings were opening. Another flash of light above, Herezai rose, wings beating through the falling hail. Cado saw fire shimmer beneath the clouds at the platform-edge. He smiled, grim, as though at a joke that he could not escape. Herezai tucked her wings and they plunged down through cloud and thunder.

The storm boiled around Cado. He could feel the frayed magic in the air: white and amethyst, blinding light and purple gloom, coiling, bubbling and flashing in the clouds. Aventhis was below him. There were troops on the walls, rain running from battered metal, storm flare catching spear points. He could see soldiers racing along the wooden bridges to the closest spires. Down in the gullies between the fingers of rock, darkness flowed like the currents of a flood tide. A light flared on top of one of the outer spires as a pitch-soaked hay bale lit. Cado could see the faces of militiamen, grunting as they pushed it to the edge of the wall with pitchforks. Then they sent it tumbling down from the parapet. Another bale lit, and then there were more, light flaming red from the walls and bridges. Down they went, scattering sparks and burning stems. The first bale hit the ground and burst into shards of fire. Red-and-yellow flame cut into the dark. Another landed and another, and now the ground between the city and the spires was glowing with a thousand jewels of light. And there in the dark and sparks were figures, advancing as one. The firelight gleamed from polished bone and high shields. Great war machines came in their wake. Horsemen rode with banners the colour of falling night. On they came, through the pools of fire without pause, every one of them in lockstep, a legion of the remade dead. The Ossiarchs had come, just as they promised.

Arrows began to fly from the walls and parapets. The Ossiarchs raised their shields as one. Steel points rang off hardened bone. Arrow shafts shattered. Cado heard a shout go up from the walls between the roar of thunder. People were rolling boulders to the edge of the bridges. The lumps of stone teetered and then fell. The boulders struck the shells of interlocked shields. Shaped bone splintered. Rock crushed skeletons to powder. Shards of stone whickered through the Ossiarchs. The arrows flew again, skewering into the holes opened by the stones. Skeletal figures stumbled under the impact. Spiked shafts pinned them to the ground. Others fell, but most rose again, and marched on.

Cado saw the war machines at the rear stop. The bones of god-beasts and drakes were their frames. An arm rose from each of their backs, like the limb of a murdered giant clawing at the sky. They had walked into position, crawling on dozens of legs made from the bones of lesser beasts. Now those legs braced. Clawed feet gripped the mud. Pulleys and ropes of dried sinew flexed as the arm drew down. Lumps of glowing stone and cauldrons of ghost-fire sat in the cupped claws at the end of each arm.

Cado fixed his eye on them.

'Down,' he called, and Herezai stooped into a vertical dive. Rain whipped past. Down along the bridges, the faces of men and women turning towards him as they passed by. Down past the spires of stone surrounding the city, their flanks still gleaming with motes of burning pitch. Down as the arrows hissed around them and the ground came up to meet them.

Herezai opened her mouth and roared. The sound rattled with fury. The bone warriors riding with the war machines looked up as the dead dragon's cry shook the air. Ropes of sinew released. Herezai struck the first machine. She did not slow but went through it. Her wings sheared through a catapult arm. Her head snapped down, and her jaws closed on the bone warriors on the war machine's platform. Ghost-light and glowing liquid arced through the rain as a cauldron tumbled from the wreckage and fell amongst a block of spearmen. Screaming faces formed in the blast wave. Spectral hands tore through bone. Herezai banked. Her claws reached down from her belly and ripped through the ranks of warriors like a plough through soft earth.

Cado pulled the dragon up, and she spiralled high, wings beating. They climbed, arrows chasing them. He heard shouts, and what might have been cheers from the parapets. He climbed higher. Looking down he could see that the ranks of spearmen were re-forming. Figures were standing amidst the ruin of the war machines. Ropes of ghost-light stretched from their hands and mouths, pulling the broken frames back together.

He urged Herezai up further. He was looking down, eyes searching for the Lumineth. A spear of lightning reached from the clouds, and in its flash he saw them. They were on a fallen bridge linking one of the outer rock spires. The flare of energy reflected from spears and swords, and a long column, white and silver in the dark, moved like the flow of water and the breath of air. At their head, mounted on a grey horse beside Lotharic, was Leragrais. Even across this distance the magister looked broken, a hunched figure, his purple robes lank in the downpour.

The lightning was coming faster, now. Blazing forks of electricity shook the dark. Cado saw the Lumineth reach the edge of the broken bridge. Once a tongue of stone had linked the great tors that surrounded the main spire of Aventhis. Now most had fallen. The Lumineth had climbed one tor and were making for the gap where a bridge had been. It was as though they intended to cross from one tor to another and then use the human-made wooden bridge to enter the city. But there was nothing linking the two tors, just a long drop in empty air. Lotharic was at the front, her mount a blur of fluid speed. She did not stop but leapt. The air flexed. The broken stone of the bridge broke apart. Blocks of it split into many pieces and slid back together. Lotharic landed, and galloped on as a new bridge formed under the strides of her steed.

Cado banked, diving for the rock tor the bridge was reaching for. A second wooden bridge still linked that tor to the main mass of the city. The re-settlers had taken most of the stones from the ruins to throw a rough parapet around the spire's summit. There were few soldiers on that wall, a dozen at most, and until this moment they had been looking down at the Ossiarch advance on the ground. Now some of them were shouting, pointing at the stone bridge reaching towards them. Cado pitched Herezai into a dive. He could see the soldiers hesitating.

'Let us pass!' he heard Leragrais shout. The magister's voice boomed across the gap. The air twisted with magic to carry his words. Cado saw the soldiers on the parapet falter at the familiar voice. The Lumineth kept coming across the gap. 'I am Magister Leragrais! You will let us pass!' The men and women on the parapet did not move, caught between the words of one of their leaders and the sight of whom he rode with. They would never have seen such a thing. These were the children of places where realms beyond the heavens were the stuff of stories and songs, not living truth. The magic of the dead, and the cruelty of life under the shadow of torment – that was mundane to them. This, though – a shining host moving like the wind, stone forming under their feet and hooves, spear tips sunlight bright against the night – it was enough to stop the breath in their lungs.

Cado and Herezai plunged down onto the parapet facing the Lumineth. The dragon roared. The soldiers looked up. Terror filled their eyes. Herezai landed. She coiled, wings beating. Cado had his sword drawn. His eyes were red stars.

'Flee,' he said, and the word caught in the magic swirling the air. Spears dropped from human hands, arrows dropped from bowstrings, and then the soldiers were running back over the wooden bridge towards the main city. The Lumineth's bridge of stone had almost reached the parapet. Arrows flew at Cado. Herezai's wings swirled up. Silver barbs struck rotting scales. One pierced the skin membrane of her wings and passed within a handspan of Cado's head. He willed the dragon down and she dropped from the parapet into the air. Arrows chased them. Herezai's wings snapped out. They rose, spiralling. Above, the Lumineth's bridge touched the parapet. The first riders were almost across the top of the rock and onto the wooden bridge that led to the main city. How long for them to cross? A handful of heartbeats.

Once they were in the city, they would stamp their rune into the air. The nexus of magic beneath the city would become inert. The nature of magic in this underworld and beyond would alter. A component in a cosmic power game would shift in the Lumineth's favour, but here, in this city, the souls of the living and the dead would be trapped, frozen on a precipice between life and death.

Herezai's wings beat, pulling them up. The face of the rock spire rushed past them. The Lumineth saw Herezai rising out of the dark. Arrows whistled down. The first rider was on the bridge leading to the main city.

Herezai struck the wooden bridge from below. Her wings beat just before the impact then folded over Cado and her back. Her skull hit first. Bone and horns rammed through beams. Planks became splinters. The bulk of her body followed. Momentum drove her through the bridge. Right through. Like a hammer hitting a dry branch. Cado felt the force judder through him as he held on to her back. Then they were out the other side, wings spreading to catch the air.

The bridge held for an instant, and then folded down. Ropes and beams twisted, splintered and broke. The Lumineth riders who had begun to cross tried to stop. Their mounts sprang from plank to plank as they began to fall. Cado could see Lotharic, Atharion and the other spellcrafter looking up at him from the edge of the broken bridge. Lotharic's mouth was a snarl, the mage's eyes black pearls of loathing. The splinters of the bridge were still falling. Cado could see the stone mage behind Atharion. The mage had closed his eyes, and only his hands moved, fingers pulling and twisting. Blocks of stone ripped from the cliff. The mage's palms slammed together, and the blocks met in mid-air. One palm smoothed over the other and the blocks became a smooth road growing where the wooden bridge had been.

Cado dived at Lotharic and the mages. Atharion raised his fingers. The first stroke of a glowing rune began to flow through the air. Rain flashed to steam. Atharion finished the last stroke of the rune. Herezai spread her wings, caught the air, and slammed to a stop. A beam of light flashed through the space where the dragon would have been. Cado felt heat skim his skin. The dragon twisted her wings and plunged towards the Lumineth, spiralling around the shaft of light. The mages and Lotharic on her mount seemed frozen. Leragrais' horse reared and sent the magister tumbling onto the stone. The beam of light blinked out. The rune vanished from Atharion's fingertips. Herezai opened her jaws. Cado braced. Ghost-flame poured from the dragon's mouth. Lotharic's steed leapt like an arrow released from a bow. Atharion swept his hand through the air. Cado felt and saw it all unfold. A blink-fast movement as Lotharic on her charger sprang over the fire towards him, sword drawn. The ghost-flame spilling towards the Lumineth from

Herezai's mouth. Atharion standing in front of the other mage whose hands were pulling a bridge of stone out of nothing. The ghost-fire hit Atharion's barrier of light. Stone cracked, crumbling under the touch of flame. Cado saw this all in the space it took his heart to beat once.

Then Lotharic rose from her saddle. She took two strides up the neck of her mount and jumped. The steed landed on the stone bridge below. Lotharic landed on Herezai's neck, sword rising, its edge a razor slit cut into a furnace. Cado sprang forwards. Lotharic cut. The sword-edge touched Herezai's neck. Dead flesh flashed to ash. Cado rammed into the aelf, and they tumbled from the dragon. Herezai twisted, wings thrashing. Ghost-flame scattered into the air as she roared in pain. The sword had not just cut. The magic in the blade was burning her soul in its shell of dead flesh.

Cado and Lotharic hit the bridge. Stone broke under the impact. He heard breath leave Lotharic's lungs. He punched a hand up to her throat, his fingers talons. She twisted, whipcord strong, and pushed back out of his grasp. She kicked him as she moved. Her boot hit him in the jaw with enough force to stop him following. Her sword shrieked as it came around. He met the blow with his own sword. Silver and burning gold ground against each other. He spat a silent sound into the air. The rain turned red. Drops hit Lotharic's armour. Metal steamed. Crimson rain poured into the aelf's vision slit, burning, blinding.

Cado came out of the red downpour. His sword pommel struck Lotharic in the face. Metal crumpled. She was faster than him, and she could end him, he had no doubt. But her strength was control, and he knew how to break that. He felt the spell he had breathed seep into her. The impressions and images he had stolen from Lotharic in their encounter in the wilds was in the rain, pouring wild rage into her with every drop: a scream without sound that never ended, the ghost of a nightmare just inside the eyelids, the eternity of agony that would always be with her like a shadow on her back.

'You will never be free,' he shouted. 'You are an echo of a dead dream, and it means nothing.'

She staggered, and he cut. She went under the blow. How she sensed it coming, he would never know. She spun back, an armoured warrior moving like a dancer. Cado followed. One blow following the next, cutting air and meeting her blade in reply to each strike. Then she parried one of his blows, turned with the flow of his force, and struck back. Her sword flicked inside his guard and the tip went through his chestplate. It was white hot as it cut. Blood flashed to steam. He felt a jolt of pain pass through him – a pure pain, like a single note of a scream held past the point of bearing. He flinched back, and the movement was just enough to pull him out of the next cut. Black and yellow spots bubbled in his eyes. Red screamed at their edges. His sword was parrying, but now he was going back, and Lotharic was flowing from thrust to slice, coming from every angle without pause. He could feel the ash in the wound in his chest. The pain there was still ringing. He could fall here, rendered down to ash, grey dust blown in the wind, soul scattered and screaming.

The Lumineth were moving past Cado, running for the growing bridge. Herezai was nowhere in sight. They were simply going to occupy Cado and bypass him. He thought he saw a cold smile in the gap between Lotharic's cheek guards: knowing, calculating, superior. The Lumineth did not even see him as an enemy, not really. Loathing defined an enemy. It took a force of hate and will and action. There was nothing of that in the Lumineth, or in this fight with Lotharic. Pain might fill her, but he was nothing to her, merely an obstacle to bypass on the way to a higher goal. That was their truth. Disdain and cosmic arrogance.

'You are a fool, Hollow King,' she said, and cut. He drew breath. Red had swallowed his sight. She cut again.

He breathed a last word of power. The sword sliced down. Cado exploded into shreds of night. Black and red mist billowed out from where he had stood. He felt the burning blade pass through him. Pain again, like a white-hot needle pushed into muscle. But it was distant, and he was spiralling past Lotharic as the mist congealed into wings. His mind was hundreds of needle teeth, his will the beating of the stretched skin of a swarm of bats. He boiled across the space towards where Atharion and the stone mage stood. The Lumineth were as fast in mind as they were when they moved, but in their minds they had won. That was the flaw of the mighty, those who wore a crown but did not understand that a beggar on the road saw the world true where they saw only what they wanted.

He broke in a flock over the two mages, surrounded them, drowned them. Teeth and claws drew blood in hundreds of cuts. Bats fastened onto Atharion's hand, chewed his fingers as they tried to draw a rune in the air. Atharion attempted to call out a sound of power, but the bats were on his mouth, tearing and biting at lips and tongue, and he was tottering on his stilt boots. The stone mage could do nothing to help. His will and attention were all that was holding the growing bridge of stone in the air beneath the feet of the spearmen and cavalry charging towards the city. The cloud of bats poured into a spiral and Cado stepped from it, bat wings folding into the ragged edge of his shape. His sword came around once. Blood scattered into the rain. The stone mage's head fell. His body followed. A boom of sound rolled through the air as magical forces released. The half-bridge of stone collapsed. Blocks came apart. The charging Lumineth went forwards for an instant and then began to tumble. Cado heard them begin to scream. Part of him thought he could hear an edge of disbelief in the sound of terror.

He felt the heat of the sword just before it would have hit his skull. He turned, brought his sword up, met the blow and the next as Lotharic came at him. There was no superior serenity to her now, no grace. There was just lethality and rage. He went backwards, and she followed.

'You are darkness!' she spat. Another blow and another, and he was at the edge of the parapet, the drop from the rock spire a step away. He did not have the strength or anger to pull magic from his blood. He could not stop her now. He might parry the next blow and the one after, but she was a whirlwind. He had unlocked the darkness and the hate in her, and she would come for him until it faded back behind her mask of control.

Behind her, he saw the body of the stone mage and the slumped form of Atharion, bloody and ragged.

'You claim to be just!' she spat, and their swords met again.

'I claim only to choose my own path,' he said, and leapt back into the air.

A second of falling. Then a horned head and neck caught him. Herezai rose, wings snapping out to catch the storm wind.

CHAPTER TWENTY-EIGHT

Cado turned as Herezai banked between the spires and stacks of rock. The dragon was bleeding cold light and beads of cooked flesh. Lotharic's blade had cut deep.

'Stay with me,' said Cado, leaning down as the dragon's wings went still and they glided through the night. It was suddenly quiet, sounds swallowed by the hiss of rain and wind. The ground below was dark. The city lights hid behind the cliff as they flew past. He was a league at least from the walls and outer spires. They were turning west, arcing back around to behind where the Ossiarchs moved towards the main gate. The anger was surging in him now. His blood was shrieking in his ears. His eyes shone with the memory of the city and the fires. Swords and flames and the terrified look on the face of the militia soldier, all caught in the blink as Cado had passed them. He wanted to kill now. He wanted to bleed the guilty until they did not have the strength to scream. This was not a city, this was *all* cities. All that had faced the choice of fire or surrender.

He would not let it become like the rest. It mattered. Suddenly it mattered to him a great deal.

He had delayed but not broken the Lumineth. The Ossiarchs would be at the walls now. Once there they would fight without trying. Even if the walls of Aventhis held, even if the magic at the city's heart blunted the legion's sorcery, even then the mortals on the walls would tire, and break, and fail. He would not let that happen.

They came around a cliff face and there it was: the city, its walls lit by green fire. Pale ranks of spearmen were almost at the foot of the wall. The warding poles on the parapets were red with heat. War machines stalked forwards. Howling spheres of green flame streaked through the air from skeletal siege engines. Cado could see faces on the ramparts, human faces, eyes wide, knuckles white on swords. Sections of the wall were already burning, stone melting into smoke as emerald flames flowed over it. Lumbering shapes like puppets made from the bones of broken angels lumbered next to the ranks of warriors. Cado looked and saw Xericos atop its steed towards the back of the advancing army. They had not seen Herezai yet, and now the dragon swooped, silent as a bat, without a beat of wing or growl of warning.

They were almost on their prey when one of the riders beside Xericos twisted in its saddle. Glowing eyes fixed on Cado as the dragon struck. Cado's sword took the rider's head. Xericos drew its own blade, but Cado's hand took the Ossiarch under the chin and yanked the creature from its mount as Herezai beat her pinions and wheeled into the air.

There was a moment where the only sound was the movement of dragon wings. Then fire began to chase them across the night. Balls of howling ghost-fire burst around them as the war machines turned their fury from the walls to try to bring Cado and Herezai down. Cado held his grip on Xericos as Herezai fought to reach the protection of the maze of canyons around the city. Fire was bursting over them as they struggled to rise. The dragon's flesh was unravelling as green fire crawled over her scales. Her claws caught a crag of rock. They spun over. Herezai's wings were fraying sheets caught in a gale. The dead beast tried to roar. Her neck twisted. Xericos was not fighting. The lights in its eye sockets were small sparks.

'The end is inevitable,' it said, its voice clear and emotionless.

Herezai pitched sideways, wings beating for purchase on the air. Another tor of rock loomed ahead. She tried to avoid it, wings straining, rotten muscles snapping. The rock caught her left flank, and suddenly they were tumbling. They hit the wet earth. Wing bones broke. Cado flew from the dragon's back. He hit, rolled and came up just in time to avoid Herezai's bulk as it skidded across the ground. He could feel the shattered vertebrae in his back crunch as he straightened. His right arm was a lank bag of torn muscle and splintered bone. Blood was leaking in his chest. He would heal. His curse would remake his flesh, but it would take time. He turned towards Herezai. The dragon was trying to rise. Her wings and limbs scrabbled at the dirt. Cold light flared in her eyes. He could feel the soul in the flesh trying to move the failing body. Pain, so much pain; not from now but from when she had died for him. That was what her soul was now, a last long exhalation of loyalty and pain. This was what death meant in this age: not peace, or reward, or justice, but suffering.

He limped to her side. She tried to rise again. He put his left hand on her flank. The light flared brighter in her eye sockets.

'Thank you, old friend,' he said. 'Rest now.'

He forced his broken fingers to touch the iron ring on his right thumb. The dragon reared up, neck arching, broken jaw trying to form a roar. Then the scales began to crumble. The rotten muscle dissolved to mist, and her bones to dust. In his heart, Cado felt her roar and closed his hand on empty air.

Xericos was standing where it had fallen. Herezai had crushed the Ossiarch as she rolled. Its body had shattered. Glowing green light wound around it as it moved, spilling from cracks in limbs and armour. Splinters became shards, shards bones. The bones fused, one after another, stacking themselves on top of each other like the parts of a puppet pulled to standing on strings. Cado watched. He could have tried to strike Xericos down, but he did not move. The Ossiarch's head came up last. A wide fissure ran down the face and crown. Light shone from the hollow inside. Then the edges of bone fused, and Xericos was looking at Cado. The rain was still falling. The lights of the city were a blur behind the curtain of water. Around them the great tors of stone stabbed up at the sky.

'You cannot win,' said Xericos. 'You were warned, grave-lord. You are spent. You turned away the Lumineth and that cost you much. Even if you break my shell, I will return. Our legions will not stop. There has been a counting. Our numbers are sufficient, and the mortals will pay their bond when no more than two nights pass. All has been measured. All has been weighed. The bones of this place are ours.'

Xericos raised a hand and pointed. Ranks of spearmen marched into sight. Cado could see the larger shapes moving behind them. He tasted their souls as he took a breath of dry sand and dust.

'You have interfered in the collection of the tithe,' said Xericos. 'You have worked against the ordained order of all things. There must be consequences.'

Cado nodded. He knew what they would do; he had seen it once before. Grave-beetles would eat the flesh from his bones before they were ground to powder. Packed into nine jars, his remains would be dragged across the underworlds by a procession of skeletons, who would cast them into the great abyss at the heart of the realm, there to fall, and fall, and perhaps never touch the bottom.

He took another breath. The strength in his blood protested. Broken ribs cracked.

'I understand,' said Cado.

Xericos bowed its head. 'It is as it must be.'

Cado looked up. A star was pushing through the cloud layer, a shaft of light. He smiled, a fanged and bloody smile. There was no way he could defeat two armies, but he could bring them together to destroy each other, and that is what he had done.

'If you wish to judge me,' he said, 'you will have to fight for the right.'

Xericos looked up then, too late. Cado leapt back. Pain flooded him. A beam of burning light struck where he had stood. A rune burned in the air above. He looked up in time to see Atharion and Lotharic floating down from the night sky. Blood scattered from the tips of Atharion's broken fingers as he carved them through the air. Lotharic landed behind Cado and levelled her sword at him. Its edge was a shard of the sun.

'He's mine,' said Lotharic.

Xericos began to charge. The ranks of Ossiarch spearmen broke into a run. Shields locked together. A high cry rang out, and from above Lumineth came, bounding down the broken paths on the sides of the rock spires, the feet of their mounts dancing from broken stone to stone. Then they were amongst the undead constructs, silver edges flashing through bone, spear tips stabbing up at the eyes of the riders.

Cado saw Lotharic come for him. The hate in her eyes was pure now. He wondered what the stone mage he had killed had meant to her. A comrade? A valued friend? Something more? A true enemy. That was what she was to him now. All the ideals swallowed by a bright soul that had lost too much.

We are kin now, he thought. Her and I.

Her sword reached for him.

'I am sorry,' he said, and with the words he breathed the blood spell into being. The world became mist and wings, and he was rising, up and up, as a cry of rage followed him, and the sound of battle grew to meet the thunder.

Cado landed on the pinnacle next to the bridge that the Lumineth had tried to cross. Leragrais lay on the stone nearby. A few scattered militia clung to the ruin and battlements. One had the courage to whirl towards Cado with a spear. The man's eyes and mouth were wide with terror. Cado broke the spear shaft and kicked the man back. That was enough. The man ran and stumbled away.

Cado turned back to Leragrais. The magister was alive but unmoving. Cado gripped him and hauled him up off the ground by his robes. The man's head lolled. Cado spat a fragment of a curse at him. It flashed crimson. A cut opened on Leragrais' cheek. His eyes opened. He twisted, then met Cado's red gaze.

'This city needs you, magister,' he snarled. The man began to splutter. Cado twisted and launched himself and Leragrais out into the drop where the bridge to the main city had been.

Spell-light flashed across the ground below. In a blink Cado could see one of the Ossiarch bone creatures wading forwards as Lumineth scattered before it. Scythe limbs struck shields and sent bodies tumbling. A sun-bright flash passed clean through a block of Ossiarch spearmen. Bones crumbled to ash in an eye-blink of light. He thought he saw Lotharic and Xericos amongst the churn of weapons and magic. They were not duelling; they were trying to destroy each other. Aelves and bone soldiers fell around them. Lotharic's sword cut through two Ossiarch spearmen as they tried to block her path. Xericos met her and sent her reeling with a blow that drew thunder from the air.

Cado landed on the pillar of rock that had supported the bridge and leapt again. The city spire rose to meet him. He felt an invisible tide of power rise to oppose him, then pull back. Arrows flew from battlements as he landed. He spun past them, half carrying Leragrais, half dragging him as he moved. He was up and bounding over the walls above the bridge even as cries and more arrows chased him.

'What are you doing?' gasped Leragrais.

'Ending this.'

They landed behind the wall of the third tier of a ruined building. Cado gripped the magister and thrust his face so that they were eye to eye.

'Take me to the nexus,' he demanded.

'No...'

'You are a coward, but you have a chance to actually save this city. The aelves and Bonereapers will not be occupied with each other long – they must be dealt with before it's too late.'

'It is impossible...'

'Do as I ask or it and everything in this underworld will be lost,' said Cado. 'You are a coward.'

A mote of amethyst fire lit in the magister's eyes. Cado felt a prickle of charge run through his fingers where they gripped the man.

'I gave everything until there was no real hope.'

'Then you have not given enough, not yet,' said Cado. The fire flickered in Leragrais' eyes. 'Get me to the cascade.'

'What do you mean to do?'

Cado told him.

'That is impossible.'

Cado's smile was as cold as the grave.

He hauled the magister up as the arcane storm crazed the dome of the sky above and the din of battle rose to touch the thunder.

* * *

'You don't know what you are doing,' said Leragrais. The words echoed in the cavern. Cado did not reply. He could feel his strength fight against the silent gale trying to rip it from his body. He held still, gathering will.

They had hurried down into the passages through a hidden door beneath the buildings at the city's peak, led by the magister. The currents of magic in the tunnels had crushed the old man to his knees as they crossed the threshold. Cado had had to carry him, following the ghost current and Leragrais' directions. Now they stood in the cavern next to the pillar that held the grave-sand nexus. Everything came down to this point, this power that so many wanted to hold in their hands or turn to greater ends. But it was not theirs. It belonged to the dead. It was the heart of this underworld, the headwater from which souls were reborn to the air and by which it held together. He was going to halt that flow. The power of death would reverse, flowing out from Aventhis rather than in. That would break the Lumineth's geomantic web and send the spirits of Ossiarchs flying back to the darkness at the heart of the realm. At least it might. It was not a rite or piece of lore that he knew would work, it was an act as simple as putting one's hand in a stream to dam the flow of water.

'No one can claim this power and survive,' Leragrais said as they stood in front of the grave-sand nexus.

'I am not going to claim it,' said Cado. 'I am going to set it free.' He gave a cold laugh. 'Besides, I am already dead. Survival is a curse I am happy to risk.' He took a breath and felt power fill him. 'Do it,' he commanded.

Leragrais put his hands either side of the cascade. Cado brought his palm to his teeth. Blood welled as he tore open his flesh. He pressed it into the stone pillar. The cave was glowing. Veins of crystal lit. Purple and indigo light shrieked through the air. Cado could hear voices howling and the cry of birds.

'This will destroy you!' gasped Leragrais. The grave-light shining from inside the pillar lit his face. 'This will destroy us all!'

The stone of the rock pillar turned transparent. The grave-sand was pouring down its core. Past to future. Life to death. Cado put his bloody palm on the stone. The iron rings on his fingers flared ice cold. Pain leapt up his arm. Leragrais clamped his eyes shut. Cado breathed a soundless word. The blood on the rock became fire, became mist. He pushed his hand through the stone and into the cascade.

Grey.

Edge to edge in his sight.

Echoing silence except for the sound of…

Sand running through his fingers…

Each grain a second of life. Each one a part of a soul.

No pressure or power tearing his mind and body apart. Just the sand falling, carrying away thought and time. He was drowning in hissing quiet.

'No,' he said, but he could not hear the word come from his lips. He forced his hand up against the cascade. He felt his muscles, blood and body shake with the effort. Sand was filling his palm, pressing down with the weight of mountains. For a second, he thought he might have screamed. He wanted to take his hand out, but his will held it firm. It was a simple act, no grand ritual – a hand placed in a stream, held against the current until it turned.

The flow of sand stopped. Time balanced on the edge of the next second. Then the sand was flying up out of his hand as the direction of the cascade reversed. Up became down. In became out. All the converging power of death flew up and away. It yanked Cado's mind with it.

Silence struck, echoing through him, pushing his senses out of the shell of his body and through the spire of rock, up to the sky and the cobweb of amethyst lightning.

The tides and winds of magic flowing into the spire met the surge of invisible power radiating from the nexus. Across the city, birds took to the air as one. They soared. Wings caught the arcane winds. Shrieks cut through the roar of thunder. The clouds trembled.

Outside of the city walls, the Ossiarchs juddered as they moved. Bone joints ceased. The death-light in their eyes flickered. The Lumineth reeled as the cries of the birds filled their skulls with nightmares of eternity in the gullet of a god. A wave rippled across the clouds, peeling them back from the night sky and the skull grin of the moon.

Then the birds fell on the forces that remained. Cold light feathered their wings and shone in their eyes. Beaks struck Ossiarch constructs and ripped the spirits from their bone shells. Claws tore the runes of the Lumineth from the air. The ground heaved as they passed.

Segments of bone fell from the Ossiarchs as they struggled to stand. Xericos turned to Lotharic and stepped towards her, its body crumbling with each stride. A hiss of lost words came from its teeth as the last part of the Ossiarch fell to the ground. Then the birds were amongst the Lumineth, passing through them like wind through grass. Aelves fell, limbs slack, their death screams clutched in the ghost talons of the birds come to avenge the violation of their afterlife.

The last thing Cado saw as the magic tide drained from his mind was Lotharic and Atharion making for the cover of the rock tors and the land beyond as the flocks wheeled up into the sky. Then the grey of falling sand filled his sight. He felt himself blink and open his eyes on the dark of the cavern under the city. Leragrais had fallen to the floor. Blood and saliva flecked the old man's lips. He was still breathing. The sand had resumed its fall through the nexus. The crystal of the pillar was fading to opacity. Cado could feel the city and the underworld breathe out as it settled back into resting. In the skies above, he knew that the birds would be returning to their perches and roosts, the death-light dimming in their eyes.

Carefully, slowly, he let out a breath and let a beat of time pass in silence and peace.

CHAPTER TWENTY-NINE

Vaux stood beside the stone table. Objects sat in neat piles: rolls of parchment, a reading glass, boxes of brass and wood. A pair of ravens stood atop an unlit candelabra, regarding Cado with amber eyes. Vaux's armour was clean, the dents hammered out and the rents mended. The repairs had been made in dark steel, Cado noticed, so that they remained like healed scars. She looked around when he stopped. Eyes hard.

'You have taken control of the city,' said Cado.

'I have taken the principal position on the Council of Worthies,' said Vaux. 'You are leaving by first light,' she added. Cado nodded. It was as he expected, as it always was and would have to be. 'There is no place for you here. Half of the living are terrified. More than a few would like me to make you ash. The rest… well, I have heard one bad song about the deathless saviour already and I'm not going to let there be reason for more. You understand, I am sure. No matter what you did, you cannot remain, not even

317

for a day. We are on our own out here. The sooner people realise that they must be their own saviours, the better.'

'I understand,' said Cado.

Vaux gave a curt nod.

Cado began to turn away.

'We have not been able to find any of Worthy Damascene's possessions,' said Vaux. Cado turned back. Vaux frowned. 'Her chambers looked as though they had been ruined for years. No trace of anything, as if she had never been. People are starting to struggle to remember her face or what she said.'

'You will not find anything,' said Cado. 'Soon you will not even know who I meant if I told you her name.'

'You will remember her, though?' asked Vaux.

'I am not mortal. My memories are part of my soul, and what has been sold cannot be stolen.'

Vaux's frown hardened for a second, then she nodded.

'There is something that I do remember.' A half-smile formed for an instant on Vaux's mouth. 'A messenger came and talked with her, no more than a dozen days ago. I remember that, but I can't remember what they looked like or what reason Dama… Dama…' Vaux's voice faltered. She frowned and shook her head as though trying to force out something that was slipping away as she spoke. '*She* received them personally. What reason she gave for them coming here I don't know. We do not get many travellers from across the boundaries of the underworld. I never saw them again. But I did find this – it dropped from their saddlebags.' She opened a metal box and took out a vial of black crystal. A leather thong wrapped the neck just under the stopper. The device of a skull with skeletal hands pressed over its eyes had been etched into its side. Vaux handed it to Cado.

'You know what it is?' she asked.

'It's Night's Tears, water taken from the Black Lake and poured into a vial by a blind mortal under the light of the moon. It's a charm against the senses of the Nighthaunt.'

'Made in the city of Lethis,' said Vaux.

Lethis… But he could not go back to Lethis. Not now, perhaps not ever. Except if this came from there then that was where the road led. He almost laughed.

He looked up at Vaux.

'Thank you,' he said.

She gave a small nod and went back to the maps laid across the table. He was about to leave when a pair of guards came up the steps; between them was Leragrais. The magister looked crumpled, older even than he had been before. He was rubbing his wrists, and Cado could see the red marks of where the manacles had been. He glanced up at Cado, flinched and then dropped his gaze.

Cado turned back to Vaux. 'This man betrayed you and all the people of this city.'

Vaux looked at him, irritation spreading across her face.

'He also helped save it. Without him we would still be facing whichever of the enemies had triumphed outside the walls. Besides, Magister Leragrais is still a member of the Council of Worthies,' she said.

'A council of which only he is left,' said Cado.

'That matter will be addressed.'

Cado looked at Leragrais as the man shuffled to the table.

'All I have done is to deny the forces that would destroy us,' said Leragrais. 'I will continue to do that.'

'Enemies will come again,' said Cado.

'And when they do, this city will need all the strength that it has,' said Vaux, her tone final. Cado looked at Leragrais again. The man did not meet his eye.

'He cannot be trusted.'

Vaux shrugged. 'Who can be?'

Cado stood for a moment and then turned and left. Behind him he heard the murmur of conversation between the two.

The skull moon was high in the star-pocked sky as Cado led his horse out of the city gate. The guards wound the iron doors back to let him through, but none said a word to him. He wondered if Vaux had ordered them into silence, or if it was instinctive. Every mortal in the city knew what he was now – he was not one of them, not mortal, not living; a thing of hunger and bloodshed. He could see that knowledge in the eyes of the few who looked at him directly, the same cold wariness that you would look at a wolf or lion with.

The gate began to close as soon as he passed through.

'Wait!' The shout came from up the road leading to the gate. Cado heard feet slapping on the stones. He turned to see Valentin running towards him, hands raised. Ama was with him, his stride shorter but quicker. The guards hesitated, hands still on the handles of the chain drums which pulled the gates closed. 'Wait,' called Valentin again, 'keep the gates open.' One of the guards looked ready to argue, but the smith rattled the bird-skull medallion hanging around his neck, and the gates stayed open.

Valentin stopped just through the open gates, panting, hands resting on his thighs as he breathed.

'Where are you going?' said Ama.

Cado looked at the boy. There was a defiant gleam in the eyes that looked back.

'I have a long journey that I must continue,' said Cado.

'You...' panted Valentin, straightening. 'I know what the seneschal said but...' He lapsed into a coughing gasp for a moment. Cado looked at the amulet around the smith's neck.

'You are one of the Council of Worthies now,' said Cado.

Valentin nodded, coughed again, and found his breath. 'Vaux is not this city. You saved us. You can stay. You have earned that.'

Cado swung up into the saddle and turned for the gate. He turned once as he rode under the arch and looked back to where Valentin and Ama stood.

'Live well,' he said.

'Until we meet again,' answered Valentin.

Cado turned and passed through the gate. Ahead the pinnacles of stone rose against the night sky. The wings of pale birds flicked across the stars, and their cries rose. He did not look back. Not when he heard the last calls of the boy or the smith, or the sound of the gate shutting. Before him, the stones of the road shone white under the light of the skull moon, beckoning towards the edge of the world hidden behind the fold of night. Cado nodded to himself and walked on.

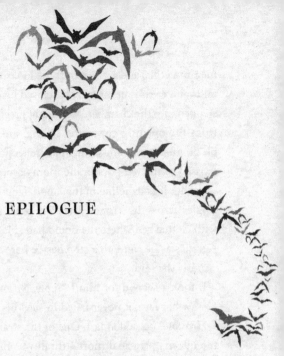

EPILOGUE

Aurelias paused to catch his breath on the threshold of the sanctuary. He knew that his queen would hear the rattle of mortal weakness in his chest, but a spark of pride made him want to come before her composed and without the weakness of age so obvious. She would grant him a draught of elixir soon, he knew. She never let his decrepitude reach a point where it interfered with his duties. Still, he knew that watching him struggle with his mortality amused her. That she would likely never raise him to the Aristocracy of Night was a fact that he had come to terms with long ago. But there were other routes to immortality, and he had watched the intrigues of the Soulblighted for long enough to know that their un-life was a curse more than a gift. No, better to be as he was: a servant, despised by all but protected by his queen's power. Yes, better to live in the shadow of a throne than sit on it.

His breath was coming smoother now. He resettled his robes over his shoulders and forced the latter back from the hunch they had been assuming. They had once called him the most handsome man in Lethis, and a ghost of those looks still lingered under the folds and creases of his face. He closed his eyes for a second then stepped into the chamber. Moonlight greeted him, pouring down from the opening cut in the ceiling. The walls and floor were black, mirror smooth so that pale reflections followed him as he crossed to the red pool in the room's centre. The queen sat at its edge, her legs dangling in the liquid, languid kicks sending thick ripples across the surface. The edge of her ivory robe was crusted with clotted red where the liquid had splashed. She looked up at Aurelias as he came to a stop beside her.

'Yes?' she said.

It took a second for him to reply. No matter how many times he saw her face, it never failed to steal his thoughts.

'Trouble,' he said at last. One of the strange privileges of being the queen's principal mortal thrall was that he did not need to address her with any of the formality or deference that her court did. No bowing, no titles or obeisance. That was one of the reasons her blood-children loathed him, of course.

'They have sent an emissary,' said the queen. She dipped a finger into the pool and stirred the surface. 'And they have moved forces into the fastness on the boundary to the south.'

Aurelias nodded. She knew already, naturally. A great, blood-bloated spider at the centre of a web of secrets, that was what she was – ancient and terrible and as beautiful as the silver smile of a knife.

'Some amongst the court are already saying that the only option is to raise the legions, and that an example must be made.'

'Do they?' She smiled. 'In a way they are right. The positions have become clear, the pieces set, and only the predictable moves remain...' She flicked her hand at the pool. The gesture was small, but the surface churned. Red splashed into the air and spattered the queen's face. She stood, rolled her shoulders and stretched as though she had just woken from a pleasant sleep. 'We must upset the balance of this game.'

'You mean to introduce an unpredicted element,' said Aurelias. She smiled at him and patted his shoulder. Her touch sent a shiver through him and left a crimson handprint on his robes.

'Just so,' she said, and turned away. 'Bring our Hollow King to us. It has been too long since I saw him.'

Aurelias opened his mouth to object, but Neferata, Queen of Blood, looked over her shoulder at him, and the ivory needles in her smile closed his mouth.

'It will be done,' he said.

ABOUT THE AUTHOR

John French is the author of several Horus Heresy
stories including the novels *The Solar War, Mortis,
Praetorian of Dorn, Tallarn, Slaves to Darkness* and
Sigismund: The Eternal Crusader, the novella *The
Crimson Fist,* and the audio dramas *Dark Compliance,
Templar* and *Warmaster.* For Warhammer 40,000 he
has written *Resurrection, Incarnation* and *Divination*
for The Horusian Wars and three tie-in audio dramas
– the Scribe Award-winning *Agent of the Throne:
Blood and Lies,* as well as *Agent of the Throne: Truth
and Dreams* and *Agent of the Throne: Ashes and
Oaths.* John has also written the Ahriman series and
many short stories.

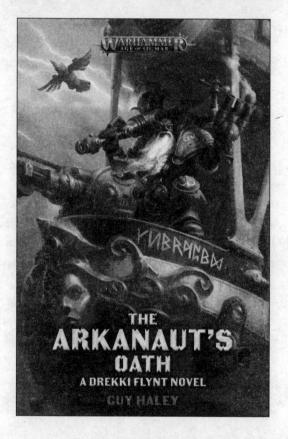

THE ARKANAUT'S OATH
by Guy Haley

Captain Drekki Flynt is in trouble. Finding himself at the mercy of his nemesis, Rogi Throkk, Drekki and his crew are sucked into a conspiracy that could see an ancient empire rise again, or fall forever to Chaos…

An extract from
The Arkanaut's Oath
by Guy Haley

A poet spoke. This is what he said:

'Rain pounded. Cold gathered against the tops of the Fourth Air. Bavardia suffered bad weather as a matter of course. For those abroad on the street, atmosphere wrapped meagrely about the body, failing to warm, failing to nourish labouring lungs. Everything was thin there – air, prospects, life, love. Only the rain was thick, thicker than beards, thicker than oaths, thermals thrust up from the lower airs, flattened by the chill into thunderheads that lashed the town with oily, unpleasant waters.

'Drekki Flynt, Kharadron privateer, came into port. His crew weathered the rain like rocks do, grey, silent and stoic. They were grim. Nobody liked Bavardia.

'Bavardia was a young place, a lawless place, one of a dozen towns budded off great Bastion, the last remnant of ancient, shattered Achromia. If hope for the future had established Bavardia, despair of the present ruled it. Heirs to a venerable empire, the citizens brought ambitions with them that they could not fulfil. Their dreams were beyond their grasp. A young place with an old soul,

Bavardia was filthy as infants are, soiling itself, unsure of its limits, creeping up one crag, then up another, always on the verge of catastrophic tumbles, never settled, uncoordinated, wild with the potential and vulnerabilities of youth. Built upon ruins, reminders of what had been, sad, lost, and yet full of hope. Bavardia! A town of–'

'Oh put a sock in it, Evtorr Bjarnisson. On and on all the bloody time with the bloody poetry!' Drekki Flynt said.

The flamboyant ancestor face that fronted Drekki's helm was known across the Skyshoals. Then there was his drillbill, Trokwi, skulking head down on his shoulder. He usually gave the game away, and if the little automaton was still insufficient a clue, the massive axe Flynt carried on his shoulder was equally unmistakeable. For the truly unperceptive, the ogor plodding through the water in front of him cinched the deal. No one flew with Gord the Ogor but Drekki Flynt! Say Drekki's name aloud of a night and astound a bar. *'I've fared with Drekki Flynt!'* was a common enough boast. But just then, there was no one to see. No one to hail Drekki or to curse him.

To call the streets 'streets' was a generous lie; they were yellow streams pouring from the hills behind the town. The flood cut the earth of the unpaved roads, leaving hollows and rounded stones to take feet by surprise. Tall Gord was untroubled, the water foaming about his tree-trunk legs. For him this was fun. The others struggled on in his wake in varying levels of misery.

'Do we really need the running saga about how filthy this weather is in this filthy town, when it's all running down my bloody trouser leg?' Drekki went on. Rain rattled so hard off his closed helm that he had to shout over the noise.

'But, captain!' Evtorr protested. 'I'm chronicling your latest adventure. It helps to say the words out loud, so I'll remember.'

'Thanks, but no thanks. No amount of poet's polish is going

to put a shine on this bilge pit, so stow it in your deepest hold, Evtorr, and keep it there,' said Drekki.

'I'm supposed to be *Unki-skold*,[1] protested Evtorr. 'Couplets and rhymes is what I do, captain.'

'You're ship's signaller, too. Stick to that. You've more talent there,' chided Drekki.

The others in Drekki's party chuckled. Evtorr's verses were an acquired taste, one that no one had yet acquired. Evtorr's helm drooped. He had spent good money having its moustaches inlaid with silver, so all would know he was a poet. Never had his metal mask looked so woebegone.

'Yes, captain,' he said.

'Now now, don't sulk, write it down later, and torture us with it when it's finished,' said Drekki. 'You never know, you might pen a good one yet.'

'Doubt it,' piped up Evrokk Bjarnisson, ship's helmsduardin, and Evtorr's brother. 'He's been trying all his life. Not got there yet!'

'He left me out and all,' grumbled Gord. 'All stout duardin. I'm stout.' He slapped his massive ogor's gut. 'But I ain't no duardin!'

He laughed at his joke alone. The crew were too busy avoiding being swept away to find it funny. Being duardin meant being shorter than a human, broad across the shoulder, with powerful, stocky limbs and large hands and feet. Beards. All the usual physiognomy of the children of Grungni. Their form was suited to life underground, as ancient history attested, and surprisingly well fitted to life in the sky, as the more recent Kharadron nations had proven, but rather poor for swimming. Heavy-boned duardin sank and drowned more often than not, and a duardin weighed down by aeronautical equipment most certainly did. It was a fate they were at some risk of just then.

---

1 | Kharadrid: Ship's poet.

'Come on, stunties,' Gord said cheerily. 'Not that hard. Push on now.'

'Not that hard!' said Kedren Grunnsson, ship's runesmith. A unique appointment on a sky-ship. He was no Kharadron. You could tell by the way he moved. The crew wore aeronautical suits of design so similar they were virtually indistinguishable, but Kedren stuck out. He walked stiffly, as someone who had become accustomed to the gear rather than born to it.

'Over there! Way up's on that side,' said Gord. They waded to the side of the street.

'Look at this. Ropes!' Kedren said incredulously, tugging at the lines anchored to the buildings. They were at human height, for it was mostly humans who dwelled in Bavardia. 'What good are ropes? What about paving? What about drains? What about choosing a better site for their town rather than this piss-filled bathtub!' He grabbed hold just the same.

'You're no fun, ground pounder, too *grumbaki*[2] by half,' retorted Adrimm Adrimmsson, who was dragging himself along behind the smith.

'Is that me you're calling grumbaki, Adrimm? The grumbliest duardin alive? There's a cheek!'

'Now now, my lads,' said their captain, who had it a bit easier, being safe in the ogor's lee. 'We'll soon be out of the rain and into the dry. Ales all round. Some meat! That much I can promise.'

Adrimm didn't take the hint to shut up – he rarely did – and continued to moan at Kedren.

'I could have stayed on the ship,' said Adrimm.

'What, and miss all the fun in this sewer?' said Kedren. 'That's the fourth turd that's slapped into my gut.'

'I keep telling you aeronautical gear has its benefits, Kedren,' said

---

2 | Khazalid/Kharadrid: Old grumbling duardin.

Otherek Zhurafon, aether-khemist, and Kedren's long-standing friend. 'Sealed in. Turd proof.' He rapped a knuckle on his chest-plate.

'Proof? Pah! It will take forever to get the stink out,' said Kedren. 'I hate this place. I hate this *funti*[3] weather.'

'Listen to the oldbeard,' said Drekki. 'Evtorr was right about one thing, at least – *nobody* likes Bavardia.'

Offended, the rain redoubled its efforts to wash them out, and they were forced to cease their grumbling for a while.

'Keep on, stunties, keep on!' bellowed Gord. 'Nearly there.'

The crew reached a set of steps that led off the road to a raised pavement.

'I suppose we'll be dry now,' said 'Hrunki' Tordis, who would have had a monopoly on optimism in the crew, were it not for Drekki.

'Dry? Dry?! All this pavement is is a shoddy substitute for good civic planning,' said Kedren.

Gord stepped aside to let the duardin up. Buffeted by the flow yet untroubled by it, he shepherded his crewmates with care. A good job too. Although Drekki mounted the steps all right, Gord was obliged to catch Kedren to stop him being whirled away.

'Grungni-damned, Grimnir-cursed stupid *umgak*[4] city,' growled Kedren as Gord deposited him on the pavement. One after another the crew scrambled up, shedding filthy water. Buildings covered the pavement over, forming a sheltered area, though to duardin sensibilities it looked like it had been done by accident rather than by design. Buildings of stone leaned on buildings of wood, propped up over the pavement on wonky timber posts and rusty iron girders.

---

3 | Kharadrid: A common Overlord curse. Best left untranslated.

4 | Khazalid/Kharadrid: Human-built. Also: shoddy.

'This place was surely built by *grobi*,'[5] said Evrokk. There was a sense of wonder in his voice. 'You couldn't design a collapse better than this if you tried.'

'You say that every time we go to an *umgi*[6] town!' said Evtorr, still peevish at his brother.

'Worth saying, that's why. Unlike your verse, brother,' said Evrokk.

'Come on, come on, beards straight! Keep your aether shining,' said Drekki. 'Umgi build as they will, and bad weather we have, but good beer awaits.' Even Drekki didn't swallow his own bluster. His jollity was entirely forced.

There were a few folk around up above the flood but they hurried on by, heads down, eager to escape the weather, and not one recognised the captain, to his chagrin. The crew trudged into tottering alleys as water and shit surged down the streets below. A rat's maze to be sure, but it could not defeat their beer-sense. A duardin can find his way to a pub all turned about and blindfolded.

Drommsson's Refuge was the sole duardin-built place in town, with four square walls and a roof of precisely engineered bronze plates. Old Drommsson hadn't trusted human foundations and had cut his own right through the clay until he hit rock. Old Drommsson didn't like human beer, so served only the best duardin ales. Old Drommsson didn't like humans at all, but always seemed to find himself among them. Old Drommsson was a host of contradictions. Old Drommsson was a lot of things, but most of all Old Drommsson was dead.

'Fifty *raadfathoms*!'[7] Drekki said, recalling the old publican's words. 'Do you remember that?' He elbowed Kedren. 'He boasted long and hard about the depth of the pilings he had to put in. He

---

5 | Khazalid/Kharadrid: The common species of grots.

6 | Khazalid/Kharadrid: Human.

7 | Kharadrid: Standard measurement of distance.

always used to say that, remember? Fifty raadfathoms! Good old Drommsson. Eh, lads?'

He turned about. His duardin were subdued, aetherpacks steaming, rain plinking loudly from the brass.

'Well, a more miserable line of skyfarers I never did see. Show some spirit! You're Drekki Flynt's swashbuckling crew, not a bunch of half-drowned skyrinx. I've got an image to think of!'

Nobody spoke.

Drekki sighed into his helm, a noise like a night wind teasing the rigging. For a moment, he wished he were back out at sky. 'All right, lads. First round's on me.'

The crew perked up remarkably.

Behind the Refuge's roof the great copper sphere of the brewery vat swelled invitingly, not dissimilar in appearance to a Kharadron aether-endrin globe.

'Now there's a promise of beers to be drunk, eh, lads?' said Drekki.

They reached the doors. They were sheathed in bronze, and decorated in beaten, geometric designs of the sort that once graced the gates of the ancient mountain karaks.[8] Very inviting, but Drekki stopped, and turned to face his crew.

'Hold it right there, lads,' Drekki said. 'Before we go in…'

'Can we at least get out of the rain before you give us one of your interminable pep talks?' Adrimm moaned.

'Eh? Interminable? Pep talks? You stow it, Fair-weather,' said Drekki, using the nickname Adrimm hated. 'This is important. We've got our rivals. We have our friends. There might be either in here tonight. We've a delicate job ahead of us. Our client does not

---

8 | Khazalid/Kharadrid: The mountain fastnesses of the old Khazalid Empire. Most were overrun in the Age of Chaos, and remain ruined to this day.

want a fuss, of any sort. Keep yourselves below the aethergauge. I don't want a lot of notice. Certainly not like last time, right, Umherth? Umherth? Are you listening? That was embarrassing.'

'If you say so, captain,' said Umherth, not at all abashed. Hrunki, his constant companion, sniggered into her helm.

'A low profile, right?' said Drekki, wagging his finger. 'All of you. Low profiles. So low, I don't want to see your heads over the bar. Got that?'

A rain-sodden chorus of 'aye, captain' came back.

'Right then,' said Drekki. He rubbed his hands together. 'Beer time.' He took a step, stopped, and looked up at Gord.

'Actually, you'd better go first, Gord. Just in case.'

'Right you are, captain,' said Gord. He covered three duardin strides in a single, decisive step, both hands out. They banged into the doors like battering rams, flinging them open with a metallic boom and revealing a big entrance hall, full of lockers for skyfarers' kit. From the atrium, inner doors led into the common room. Gord strode right in and pushed those open too.

Warmth, light and laughter streamed out. Someone was playing an aether-gurdy. Badly.

Gord stopped in the middle of the bar.

'Oi!' the ogor bellowed. 'Clear a table! Captain Drekki Flynt's in town!'

The noise faltered. When the hubbub returned, it had a different flavour. Urgent, excited, somewhat annoyed.

Drekki grinned. 'Say what you like about our ogor,' he said, 'he certainly knows how to make an entrance.'

'I thought you said low profiles all round, captain?' said Evtorr sharply. He could nurse a sulk like no one else.

'Hush now,' said Drekki. 'You're spoiling it.'